Praise for

# MURDERERS PREFER BLONDES

"A beautifully realized evocation of time and place; 1950s New York City comes alive for those of us who were there and even those who weren't. Amanda Matetsky has created a very funny and interesting female protagonist, Paige Turner, and put her in the repressed and male-dominated year of 1954, which works like a charm. This is more than a murder mystery; this is great writing by a fresh talent."

—Nelson DeMille

"Prepare to be utterly charmed by the irrepressible Paige Turner, and take an enchanting trip back in time to New York City, circa 1954 . . . A thoroughly fun read."

—Dorothy Cannell

"Amanda Matetsky has created a wonderfully sassy character in the unfortunately named Paige Turner. In her 1950s world where gals are peachy and cigarettes dangle from the lips of every private dick, a busty platinum blonde finds herself at the wrong end of a rope and Paige is on the case of a swell whodunit, sweetheart. Delightfully nostalgic and gripping. Irresistible." —Sarah Strohmeyer, author of *Bubbles In Trouble*

"A great idea well-executed—funny, fast, and suspenseful."

—Max Allan Collins, author of *Road to Perdition*

"*Murderers Prefer Blondes* is a gas; full of vivid characters and so sharp in its depiction of the fifties when you read it you'll feel like you're sipping champagne in the Copacabana." —Betsy Thornton, author of *Ghost Towns*

"Paige Turner is the liveliest, most charming detective to emerge in crime fiction in a long time. She is the product of her time and place—New York in the fifties—with a little Betty Boop and a little Brenda Starr in her makeup, but she is also her own woman, funny, smart, energetic, brave, hard-working, and determined to get to the bottom of the mystery. She is irresistible, a force of nature."

—Ann Waldron, author of *The Princeton Murders*

"Matetsky adeptly captures the atmosphere of the 1950s, and her characters—especially Paige and her friend Abby—are a delight. This journey back to a time that now seems innocent is refreshing."

—*Romantic Times*

"A fun new mystery series . . . a real page-turner . . . a delightful historical amateur sleuth tale."

—*BookBrowser*

"A fast-paced, smart debut with a feisty heroine that entertains and keeps readers eagerly turning Paiges."

—*The Mystery Reader*

# Murder Is a Girl's Best Friend

Amanda Matetsky

BERKLEY PRIME CRIME, NEW YORK

MURDER IS A GIRL'S BEST FRIEND

A Berkley Prime Crime Book / published by arrangement with the author

PRINTING HISTORY
Berkley Prime Crime mass-market edition / July 2004


Cover design by Rita Frangie.
Cover illustrations by Kim Johnson.


For information address: The Berkley Publishing Group,
a division of Penguin Group (USA) Inc.,
375 Hudson Street, New York, New York 10014.

ISBN: 0-425-19716-6

Berkley Prime Crime Books are published by The Berkley Publishing Group,
a division of Penguin Group (USA) Inc.,
375 Hudson Street, New York, New York 10014.
The name BERKLEY PRIME CRIME and
the BERKLEY PRIME CRIME design
are trademarks belonging to Penguin Group (USA) Inc.

PRINTED IN THE UNITED STATES OF AMERICA

10 9 8 7 6 5 4 3 2 1

For Molly,
because a sister is a girl's best friend

# ACKNOWLEDGMENTS

I have the best group of cheerleaders in the world, and I heartily thank them all: Harry Matetsky*, Molly Murrah, Liza, Tim, Tara and Kate Clancy, Ira Matetsky, Matthew Greitzer, Rae and Joel Frank, Sylvia Cohen, Mary Lou and Dick Clancy, Ann Waldron, Nelson DeMille, Dianne Francis, Art Scott, Betsy Thornton, Santa and Tom De Haven, Nikki and Bert Miller, Herta Puleo, Marte Cameron, Cameron Joy, Sandra Thompson and Chris Sherman, Donna and Michael Steinhorn, Gayle Rawlings and Debbie Marshall, Regina Grassia, Joan Unice, Judy Capriglione, Martha Cevasco, Betty Fitzsimmons, Nancy Francese, Jane Gudapati, Carleen Kierce, April Margolin, Margaret Ray, Doris Schweitzer, Carol Smith, Roberta Waugh and her saintly sidekick, Joseph.

I send heaps of gratitude and good wishes to my dear friends at Literacy Volunteers of America-Nassau County, Inc., and my fellow mystery writers and readers at Sisters in Crime-Central Jersey. And to my wonderful co-agents, Annelise Robey and Meg Ruley of the Jane Rotrosen Agency, and my superlative editor at Penguin Group, Martha Bushko, I shout THANK YOU at the top of my lungs.

*A special nod and a wink to my husband, Harry, for writing the "far out" poems of Jimmy Birmingham. Allen Ginsberg would be green with envy.

"Men grow cold when girls grow old,
And we all lose our charms in the end.
But square-cut, or pear-shaped,
These rocks don't lose *their* shape—
Diamonds are a girl's best friend."

—as sung by Marilyn Monroe in
*Gentlemen Prefer Blondes*

# Prologue

IT ISN'T EASY BEING ME. MY NAME IS Paige Turner, which is laughable enough all by itself, but when you couple the silly name with the fact that I'm a *writer,* my entire identity takes on an aura of absurdity. To put it more succinctly, I'm a living joke. People start giggling the minute they meet me. And then, when they learn that I'm a mystery novelist and a staff writer for *Daring Detective* magazine, the giggles turn into great big snorts and belly laughs. It's so embarrassing and annoying I'm thinking of leaving my job to become a switchboard operator, or a stenographer, or a teacher, or a nurse—like every single other (okay, every other single) woman working in Manhattan.

There I go, lying again (I've been doing a lot of that lately). I'm not really thinking about leaving my job. I've always wanted to be a crime and mystery writer—ever since I was a skinny midwestern teenager, eating potato chips in bed and reading Raymond Chandler's *Farewell, My Lovely* for the first time—and now that I finally *am* one, at the grand old age of twenty-eight, I'm not about to quit. I'd change my name before I'd change my job.

But I'm not going to do that, either. I was deeply in love

with my late husband Bob Turner, and even though he's been gone for three years now (Bob was killed in Korea in late 1951), and even though we lived together as man and wife for only one short, glorious, rapturous month, I will keep my married name until the day I die—or get hitched again, whichever comes first. And the way things have been going for me in the last few months, I'm sure to be pushing up pansies long before my new boyfriend, NYPD Homicide Detective Sergeant Dan Street, ever dreams of popping the question.

You probably think I'm kidding, but I'm not. Dan's so mad at me right now he'd rather kill me than marry me. Plus, I keep getting myself into so damn much trouble—serious, scary, life-threatening trouble—it'll be a flat-out miracle if some overexcited homicidal maniac doesn't beat him to the punch.

Eight months ago, when I started working on my first story for *Daring Detective*—investigating and writing about the rape and murder of a pretty blonde waitress/mother/call girl named Babs Comstock—I learned just how dangerous my line of work can be: *extremely* dangerous, if you must know. I came *this* close to meeting the same awful fate as the pitiful young victim I was writing about. And by the time I finished investigating *this* story—my sixth for the magazine, and the one I'm preparing to tell you now—I was a mangled and bloody mess.

I'm not complaining, though. At least I'm still alive, which is more than I can say for some other people who made the mistake—or simply had the misfortune—of playing a part in this lurid and tragic tale. And even though I'm sitting here in my aqua chenille bathrobe at my yellow Formica kitchen table in my grubby little Greenwich Village apartment on a forced eight-week convalescent leave from work—my shattered leg in a plaster cast and my wounded shoulder strapped tight in five layers of gauze and adhesive tape—I can still inhale, and exhale, and think, and talk, and move all of my fingers.

Which means I can still type—as I'm doing right now—

and put all of my dreadful experiences down on paper. Which means I can now try, once again (with the help of my trusty baby blue Royal portable and about a thousand packs of L&M filter tips), to live up to my corny name and turn my most recent *Daring Detective* story of sex, greed, deception, and murder into the shocking, thrilling, full-length page-turner it was born to be.

My best friend and next door neighbor, Abby Moscowitz, is pushing me into this. She's so bossy it's cruel! My first and only novel—the extended, true-but-slightly-fictionalized account I wrote about the Babs Comstock murder—hasn't even been published yet, and already she's badgering me to write another one. She says I've got to strike while the story's hot. And while the details are still fresh in my brain. Ha! That's another cause for big snorts and belly laughs. Abby refuses to acknowledge it, but my brain is as broken as the bones in my leg and shoulder.

Still, I'm going to be out of work for eight long, lonely, desperately boring weeks. And I can't walk without crutches. And I can't use crutches because it hurts my shoulder too much. So I'm kind of stuck here in my dingy, dwarf-sized, fifty-dollar-a-month duplex with nothing to do but eat, and drink, and sleep, and smoke, and gobble aspirin, and hope that Abby will come over with a pitcher (or two) of martinis, and that Dan will forgive my latest "misconduct" (that's *his* word, not mine!), and stop by for a quick make-up smooch between homicide expeditions.

So I might as well get to work on my second novel, right? It's either that or go crazy. Well, crazi*er,* I guess I should say. And even though it'll be really stressful for me to relive the pain and horror of the past few weeks—and to put all the loathsome and sorrowful details into a hundred-or-so thousand words—it'll be better than just sitting here in my small, dark kitchen, listening to one awful radio soap opera after another, agonizing over what I'm going to have for supper tonight (Campbell's Cream of Tomato soup again?), or what bathrobe I'm going to wear tomorrow (a moronic concern since I only have *one*), or how the heck I'm going to drag my plastered (sic) and bandaged body up the incredibly narrow and precariously steep flight of steps to the bathroom.

Some choice. I can write about murder, or just wish it on myself.

Like I said, it isn't easy being me.

# Chapter 1

WHAT'S BLACK AND WHITE AND RED ALL over? A blood-soaked newspaper—like the Monday, December 20, 1954 edition of *The Daily Mirror* I was reading that fateful morning. The blood wasn't real, of course—not in the sense that I could actually see it, or touch it, or accidentally smear it on the sleeve of my brand new pink angora sweater—but the paper was dripping with it just the same.

Twenty-six people had been killed in a plane crash at Idlewild airport. British troops had opened fire on student demonstrators on the island of Cyprus, slaying an undisclosed number and wounding many more. Chinese Nationalists had dropped forty bombs on two Communist islands off the shore of Formosa—number of casualties unknown. A man in Chicago had taken a rifle from the gun rack in a Sears Roebuck store and shot himself to death in the midst of a crowd of Christmas shoppers (how the gun happened to be loaded wasn't explained), and another berserk gunman had gone on a spree in the Bronx, shooting four people before being brought down in a hail of police bullets. A woman walking her miniature poodle was killed by a hit-and-run driver at the corner of York and 69th Street. The dog was dead, too.

I felt bad about all of these fatalities, including that of the pitiful pooch, but the story that claimed my closest attention was the one about the sixteen-year-old girl who was found stripped and stabbed to death in a roadside motel room in Middletown, Rhode Island. The two sailors who had rented and subsequently fled the room had already been tracked down by police and were being held for questioning. I snatched up my scissors, cut the article out of the paper, and placed it in the labeled and dated manila folder sitting on top of my desk. *This* was the kind of killing *Daring Detective* readers were interested in. Brutal murder, with a nice thick slice of sex on the side.

*What a way to start the day,* I thought, taking a bite of the buttered English I'd bought at the coffee shop in the lobby downstairs. *A muffin and a murder for breakfast.*

The office entry bell jingled and in walked Harvey Crockett, my boss, the corpulent, white-haired, cigar-smoking ex-newspaperman who—in spite of his gloomy, cynical, don't-give-a-damn outlook on life—was still shocked and dismayed to find himself employed as the editor in chief of a lowly (okay, *sleazy*) true crime magazine. "Coffee!" he grunted, giving me his usual one-word greeting. He took off his hat, tapped it against his thigh to remove the snow, and then looped it on an upper branch of the coat tree near the front door.

"Good morning, Mr. Crockett," I said, batting my lashes, grinning like an idiot, doing my best to look properly submissive and worshipful. (If there's one thing I've learned in this odd, out-of-bounds-for-a-woman occupation of mine, it's that you must treat the men you work for like gods. If you don't, they will act like the gods they know themselves to be, and make your life a living hell.) "Did you have a nice weekend?"

"Lousy," he said, removing his wool overcoat, shaking off the snow, and hanging it on the rack. Not bothering to explain himself further, he straightened his too-tight tie, gave me a gruff nod, then propelled his colossal belly past my desk and down the aisle of the large front workroom toward his small private office in the rear. "Coffee!" he repeated over his retreating shoulder. "Bring the newspapers, too."

"Yes, sir," I said, growling to myself and making a cross-eyed face at the ceiling. Would it have killed the man to give me a polite hello and ask about *my* weekend? Apparently *yes*, since Crockett had never once—in all the time I'd worked my fanny off for him—offered me anything more than one long-overdue raise and an occasional surly smile. I still liked the guy, though. He was smart, shrewd, and fairly open-minded—which was a heck of a lot more than I could say for three of the other four men who (along with me, the only woman) made up the rest of the *Daring Detective* staff.

I was standing at the small worktable where (thanks to me, the only woman) the electric coffeemaker and clean cups were always set up, when the entry bell jingled again. My back was to the door, but I didn't have to turn my head to find out which of my male "superiors" had arrived. The loud huffing and puffing noises told me all I needed to know.

"Hiya, Zimmerman!" I called over my shoulder. "How's it going?" Lenny Zimmerman was my only friend at the office—the one member of the staff who didn't make lousy jokes about my name and gender or treat me like a personal servant.

"Fine," Lenny sputtered, still gasping for air.

I knew without looking his face was as red as a radish. Yours would be too if you'd just trudged up nine full flights of stairs to the office, as Lenny did every Monday-through-Friday morning of his life. The rail-thin, dark-haired, bespectacled twenty-three year old art assistant was deathly afraid of elevators.

"Still snowing up a storm outside?" I asked, stirring cream into Crockett's coffee and turning to face my breathless, red-cheeked chum.

"Sure is," he said, giving me a wide, slightly snaggle-toothed grin. He set his lunch sack on the nearest chair (when you work on the ninth floor and you're too scared to use the elevator, you always bring your own sandwich), then hung his slouch hat and overcoat on the tree. "Got three, maybe four inches already. By the time we get off work we'll have to hail dogsleds to get home."

I smiled. There was a time when Lenny wouldn't have been so genial and chatty with me. He would have mumbled a shy answer to my question and scurried off to his desk at the back of the workroom, as breathless and red-faced from embarrassment as from exertion. But that was eight long months ago—before Lenny and I had become true comrades. Before we'd discovered our ardent respect and esteem for each other. Before he had saved my life.

But that's another story. (The Babs Comstock story, to be exact. See, I was trapped on the fifth floor landing of the office stairwell, being molested and strangled by a cold-blooded murderer—the same man who had murdered Babs Comstock—when Lenny just happened to come barging up the stairs on his way to work, in the miraculous nick of time to prevent my sudden death and accidentally *cause* the sudden death of my assailant. It was a freaky, but *very* fortuitous outcome. Ever since then Lenny and I have been as close as brother and sister—two peas in a mutually protective pod.)

"How was your weekend?" Lenny wanted to know. He picked up his lunch sack and headed for his desk at the very back of the front workroom.

"Not bad," I said. "Dan took me to see *The Silver Chalice* at the Paramount. It's in Cinemascope. Stars that popular new actor, Paul Newman. And Pier Angeli."

"Was it any good?"

"Okay, I guess, if you like those sprawling, pompous, bigger-than-life biblical spectacles. Personally, I'd rather see a neat Alfred Hitchcock mystery. Or a slew of Tom and Jerry cartoons."

"Hey!" Mr. Crockett interrupted, sticking his head through the door of his office. "Where the heck's my coffee?"

"Coming right up, sir!" I chirped, pasting another phony smile on my kisser. Why do so many bosses feel they have a *right* to be rude? I gave Lenny a knowing wink, then took Mr. Crockett his morning fix of newsprint and caffeine.

When I got back to my desk at the front of the workroom, Mike and Mario marched in. Mike Davidson was the tall, fair, flattopped assistant editor of the magazine, and Mario Caruso was the short, dark, ducktailed art director. Both were married and in their early thirties. They lived on opposite sides of town from each other, but for some weird reason I'd never been able to figure out, they almost always arrived at the office in tandem. Went out to lunch together every day, too. A regular Heckle and Jeckle.

"Morning, Toots," Mario said, unwinding his plaid muffler and ogling my bosom as usual. "You're looking very pink and fuzzy today. Is that sweater as warm as it looks?"

"Yes," I said, wary of the question, knowing Mario's motive for asking it would be ulterior.

"Then take it off immediately!" he said.

I didn't bite. I just sat there, glowering at Mario and saying nothing, waiting for him to deliver the rest of his typical (i.e., sexually suggestive and incredibly stupid) gibe.

"I need to borrow it for a while," he said, shooting Mike a wicked glance, then leaning down over the top of my desk till his nose was just inches away from mine. "It's colder than a witch's you-know-what outside, and my you-know-whats are freezing!"

Mike burst out laughing, but I didn't crack a smile. "Oh, really?" I said, staring down at the big stack of proof sheets on my desk and shuffling the pages around. "Then you should have worn your flannel bra."

Mike laughed even louder, but Mario turned quiet and put on a long face. He could make 'em, but he couldn't take 'em—and I knew he wouldn't rest until he'd made me pay for the comeback, lame though it was. "What's that you're reading?" he soon asked, wrinkling his bumpy nose and pointing toward the pile of proofs in my hand. "A new Paige-Turner?"

This was another of Mario's typical routines. Whenever he couldn't think up something funny to say, he called attention to my funny name. And my funny career goals.

"These are the proofs for the next issue," I said with a sniff, deciding to ignore the name game and play it straight.

"Take a look at the production schedule. We're up against an urgent deadline. You have to do the cover, and I have to do the backyard paste-up. *Today*."

"Oh," Mario said, at a momentary loss for words. He didn't like it when I talked seriously about work. There was a brief lull in the conversation, and then—frantic to regain control of the situation—Mario turned himself around, lifted the hem of his overcoat up over his rear end, and thrust the seat of his gray flannel slacks in my direction. "Hey, baby! How's about pasting up *my* backyard instead?"

Now, really! I ask you! Was this any way for a full-grown man—a City College graduate, a married Catholic, a successful professional in the field of illustrative and commercial art—to act? And how was I—a well-educated but decidedly dirt-poor twenty-eight-year-old widow trying to make her own way in the perilous male-dominated world of publishing—supposed to respond?

As far as I could see, there were only two courses of action open to me: I could kiss him on both cheeks, or kick him in the pants.

Determined (okay, *desperate*) to keep my job, I chose to kiss instead of kick. "Maybe later, big boy," I said, doing my best imitation of Eve Arden (which meant I probably looked and sounded more like a drunken Thelma Ritter). "I'm too busy to play in your backyard right now."

Mario was satisfied. My demeanor had been sufficiently obsequious and flirtatious. He gave me a slick, triumphant smirk, hooked his hat and coat on the rack, and then swaggered down the aisle toward his desk in the rear, across the way from Lenny's.

Copying all of Mario's movements (including the swagger), Mike followed closely on his cohort's heels, stopping at his own desk in the middle of the room. He sat down in his squeaky swivel chair and lit up a Lucky. "I trust you're not too busy to bring me some coffee, doll," he said, blowing smoke out of his freckled nose and leering at me across the seven or eight feet of space that separated our cheek-to-cheek work areas. "I need a warm-up, too."

*Warm this!* I fumed to myself, keeping my outward appearance under frigid control. Pretending that I was Lauren Bacall's much cooler, more collected sister, I slowly straightened my stocking seams and leisurely combed my fingers through my thick, wavy, shoulder-length brown hair. Then I bit the bullet and got up to get the coffee.

THE PHONE CALL CAME IN AT 11:25 THAT morning.

I had finished the required newspaper clipping and story editing and proofreading, and was just starting to work on meeting the backyard paste-up deadline. Brandon Pomeroy—the editorial director of the magazine and the primary plague of my pitiful professional existence—had made his way into the office a few minutes before, and was sitting straight as a stick at his desk across the aisle from mine, smoking his pipe and fingering his mustache, looking petulant and arrogant as always. He was just biding his time, I knew—counting the minutes till he could go out for his three-martini lunch.

When the phone rang Pomeroy lurched and spun around to face me, making frantic gestures with his pale, aristocratic hands. "I'm not here!" he sputtered. "Tell whoever it is I'm in a meeting."

"*Daring Detective,*" I said, answering the call in my usual upbeat manner.

"Is Paige Turner there?" The voice was tense, troubled and masculine. "Could I speak to Paige Turner, please?"

I didn't know who it was. And from the anguished tone of the caller's voice, I wasn't sure I *wanted* to know. "Who's calling, please?" I asked, keeping my own identity to myself. "And may I ask what this call is in reference to?" Ever since my near encounter with the icebox at the city morgue, I'd become as jittery and self-defensive as a Hollywood screenwriter during the McCarthy hearings.

"My name's Catcher," the voice said. "Terence Catcher."

I still didn't know who it was.

"Is Paige Turner there, please?" he asked again. "I really need to talk to her."

"Then you'll have to tell me what you need to talk to her about." I wasn't taking any chances. The last stranger who'd insisted on having a phone conversation with me had been a sex-crazed killer.

"Look, I don't have time for this. Is she there, or not?" The man's anguish had turned to exasperation. "Tell her I was an Army buddy of her late husband's. We were in Korea together."

My heart stopped beating and hurled itself against the wall of my chest. "Bob?" I croaked. "You were a friend of Bob's?"

"That's right. We were in the same outfit."

I could hardly breathe. I felt dizzy and devastated—the way I always felt whenever my dear departed husband's magnificent smiling face came flashing back into my consciousness.

"Is this Bob's wife I'm speaking to?" Terence Catcher asked. "Are you Paige Turner?"

"Yes," I said, still struggling for air. And equilibrium.

"Thank God!" he said. "I was afraid you wouldn't be working there anymore and I wouldn't be able to find you."

Deep breath. "I'm in the book."

"Yes, I know. I tried you at home, but there was no answer, so I figured you went to work. And I couldn't wait till tonight to talk to you."

"But how did you know where I work?"

"Well, Bob mentioned it once, but I also knew it from the letters."

"What letters?"

"Your letters to Bob."

I stiffened. "How do *you* know what my letters to Bob said?"

"He showed them to me. All of them."

*What?!!!* I felt bewildered and betrayed. Why on earth had Bob let this man read my letters? They were so emotional, so intimate—so *personal*. How could he have shared them with somebody else?

"Look, don't be upset," Terence Catcher said, proving he could read minds as well as other people's mail. "I can explain everything—but not on the phone. I need to see you. Now. When do you get off for lunch? Will you meet me someplace? I'd like to talk to you about Bob, and there's something else I want to discuss with you, too."

I was hooked but still hesitant. What if the "something else" he wanted to discuss with me was something I didn't want to know? "Sounds complicated," I said, "and I only get an hour for lunch. Can't we meet tonight, after I get off from work?"

"I won't be here tonight. I'm going back home to Pittsburgh and my bus leaves at three-thirty."

*Oh, great. Another urgent deadline.* "All right," I said, heart ticking like a time bomb. "I'll meet you at Horn & Hardart's, on the corner of 42nd and Third, in twenty minutes. I'll be the brunette in the red beret."

# Chapter 2

I TOOK OFF MY HIGH-HEELED PUMPS AND zipped on my fur-lined snowboots. As I was putting on my camel's hair coat and my black leather gloves and my red wool beret, Brandon Pomeroy gave me a supercilious sneer and said, "It's a bit early for lunch, Mrs. Turner. Twelve minutes early, to be exact. I hope you have a good reason for going out so soon." The look on his face told me I'd *better* have a good reason.

"I do, sir," I said. (Pomeroy was only six years older than I was, but from my first day on the job he had insisted that I call him "sir." And treat him like a titled duke. And since he was a genuine blood relation of the owner of *Daring Detective*—the outrageously wealthy and powerful publishing magnate Oliver Rice Harrington—I knew it was in my own best interests to comply.) "I have to meet a friend of my late husband's," I told him. "Someone who served with Bob in Korea. He's going to be in town for just a few hours."

Mike, Mario, and Lenny all looked up from their work, suddenly interested in the conversation. Fully aware that we were being watched, Pomeroy leaned back in his chair and shot a meaningful glance at the big round clock on the wall.

Then he lowered his bullet eyes and trained them on another target—my face. "You have my permission to go," he said, glaring at me through the glittering lenses of his expensive horn-rimmed glasses, "but see that you're back by twelve forty-eight. On the dot."

"Yes, sir," I said, smiling like an angel, successfully resisting the urge to give him a mock Heil Hitler salute. I was annoyed by Pomeroy's strict time limit, but not terribly concerned about making (okay, *breaking*) it. I knew he'd never know what time I came back to the office. He wouldn't be back from his own lunch—his regular belly-to-the-bar repast of peanuts, olives, and gin—until at least two or two-thirty.

All eyes watched me leave (okay, *flee*) the office. I hurried down the hall to the elevators, buttoning my coat up tight around my neck, preparing to face the cold. As I stood waiting for an elevator to arrive, two young women strolled through the glass-walled reception area of Orchid Publications (the largest suite of offices on our floor), then pushed their way through the heavy glass doors and joined me in the hall. They were both dressed in the usual Orchid Publications style—form-fitting suits with tight sheath skirts, ruffled pastel blouses, white gloves, seamed silk stockings, stilettos, and they both carried large leather clutch bags. They had on their hats, but not their coats, so I figured they were going down to lunch in the lobby coffee shop.

They began chatting immediately—to each other but not to me.

"I can't decide on a title for that story," one of them said. "I might use 'My Lover Got Me Pregnant on My Best Friend's Kitchen Floor!' How does that sound?"

"Has a nice ring to it," the other one said. "But shouldn't it be a little racier? You could change the word Kitchen to Bedroom."

"But then I'd have to change the whole story, too. And besides, isn't the kitchen racier than the bedroom? I mean, one *expects* people to have sex in the bedroom."

"Yes, I guess so. But I still don't like the word Kitchen in the title. It makes me think of dirty aprons and greasy pots and pans. And I don't like Pregnant, either. That's the *un*sexiest word in the whole English language!"

The first one laughed. "I see what you mean. Maybe I'll just go back to my original title: 'Raped After Dinner by My Best Friend's Husband!' "

"Better," the other one said. "Much better."

The elevator came and we all stepped in.

In case you're wondering, Orchid Publications was the largest publisher of grade B (some would say *trashy*) women's periodicals in the country. They put out a slew of confession magazines (in which department my two elevator mates were obviously employed), and they published tons of movie, gossip, beauty, and horoscope magazines. They also published *Daring Detective,* but this fact had always been kept a deep dark secret—both from the industry in general and the public at large. Orchid's owner (yep!—the one and the same Oliver Rice Harrington) didn't want the company's "clean" feminine image sullied by *DD*'s "dirty" (not to mention *bloody*) concerns.

When the elevator doors popped open, I lunged into the lobby and hurried down the black rubber runner leading across the marble floor to the row of revolving glass doors on the Third Avenue side of the building. I stepped into one of the doors and pushed my way through to the sidewalk. A wall of cold wet air slammed me in the face, and my eyelashes were immediately caked with snowflakes. The sidewalk had recently been shoveled—you could tell by the knee-high banks of snow at the curb—but the fast-falling flakes had already formed a crunchy new white carpet underfoot.

Lowering my head against the oncoming snow, I clasped my collar close around my chin and forged down Third to the automat. The restaurant was just one block away from my office, but with my lungs in shock from the freezing cold, and my heart caught up in my throat the way it was, I felt like I was crossing the tundra.

• • •

HORN & HARDART'S WAS CROWDED AS usual. It wasn't yet noon, but lots of people were already sliding their lunch trays along the waist-high service railings, popping nickels into allotted coin slots, then opening the little chrome and glass doors of the individual food compartments to remove their chosen dishes. The line at the change-maker's register was long, and quickly growing longer. It seemed that everybody in Manhattan—rich or poor, beautiful or ugly, weak or strong—liked to meet and eat at the automat, even during a snowstorm.

I spotted an empty table for two and went to claim it. Taking the seat facing the door, I shrugged out of my coat and tucked it over the back of my chair. I removed my red beret, shook off the snow, and put it back on. Then I raked my eyes around the crowded room, looking for the total stranger who had been a friend of my husband's—the man who could be bringing me a measure of peace and solace, or a load of sorrow and despair. I didn't know what to expect, but I was ready (okay, *resigned*) to meet both the past and the future head-on.

I didn't have to wait long. Within minutes, a medium-tall, well-built man wearing a brown felt fedora and a brown suede bomber jacket, carrying a shoebox tied with twine, pushed his way through the door and began shooting his eyes around the restaurant, from one corner of the dining room to the other, obviously looking for someone. And that someone was obviously me, since the minute he spotted my red beret, he snapped to attention. He lowered his bright blue eyes to my brown ones, then strode over to my table—our table—with the energy of a man on a mission.

"Paige?" he said. "Is that you?" His lean, clean-shaven face was burning with curiosity. And such a fiery intensity I wanted to back away from the heat.

"Terence?" I said. "Terence Catcher?" I didn't stand up from the table. I was afraid if I tried to balance my jittery body on my numb, unsteady feet, they'd slip right out from under me, and I'd find myself flat on my back—or, worse, face down—on the speckled beige linoleum.

"Terry," he said, sitting down and placing the Thom McAn shoebox on the table. He reached his gloved hand across the table and grabbed hold of mine. "Please call me Terry."

"Okay, Terry" I said, removing my fingers from his leathery grip. I peered into the depths of his big blue eyes, searching for some clue to his character, but all I could see was a keen, penetrating intelligence. And pain. A truckload of pain.

Terry returned my stare, then gave me a thin, crooked smile. "You're even more beautiful than Bob said you were."

"Thank you," I said, quickly lowering my gaze to the tabletop. If the blazing temperature of my cheeks was any indication of reality, my face had turned as red as my beret. (I'm what you might call a double blusher. First I blush because I'm embarrassed about something, then I blush again because I'm embarrassed by my own embarrassment.)

"I'm glad to finally meet you," Terry continued, taking off his hat and gloves and putting them down next to the shoebox.

I was shocked when I saw his hair. It was thick and pure white—as white as the snow swirling past the window outside. Yet his slim, handsome face was unlined, and his eyebrows were as black as crow feathers. I guessed him to be about twenty-nine or thirty—around the age Bob would be now if he'd lived.

"I'm glad to meet you, too," I said, though I wasn't yet sure that I was. "Were you very good friends with my husband? He never mentioned your name in any of his letters."

"That's because Bob never used my real name. He called me Whitey. A lot of the guys did."

"Oh, Whitey!" I cried, heart doing a happy flip-flop. "So *that's* who you are! Bob wrote about you all the time! He said you were his closest friend."

"I was. And he was mine. He saved my life. Twice." Terry's face turned serious and sad—very sad. "If only I could have saved his."

I didn't say anything. I was too choked up to speak. And so was Terry, who was now wringing his hands and staring into space like a zombie. I wondered if he might be suffering from shell shock.

We sat in silence for a few seconds, letting our emotions peak and subside, then Terry snapped out of his trance and directed his damp blue gaze at me. "I'll never forgive myself, you know." His tone was dead serious. "When Bob was shot, I was curled up on the floor of the foxhole, shaking and crying like a baby, hiding from the action like the miserable, disgusting coward I am. I didn't even *try* to save him. Hell, I didn't even know he'd been hit until two hours after he died."

Terry's words demolished me. I felt as if I were thrashing around in the dirt, squirming on my belly like a reptile, looking for a deep, dark hole to dive into. *Please don't tell me any more!* I wanted to scream. *Please don't make me think about the bullets ripping through my beloved husband's lungs and heart. Don't make me think about the unthinkable moment when his warm, sweet blood began spilling out of his warm, sweet body onto the blistered, bombed-out North Korean earth . . .*

"I tried to write to you after I got home," Terry went on. "I wanted to tell you how brave and humane and heroic Bob was, how he had saved both my life and my sanity. I wanted to tell you how much he loved you, and missed you, and how proud he was that you were making your own way in the world. I wrote you about twenty different letters, but I never mailed any of them. I tore them to pieces and threw them away."

"But why?" I asked, stifling a strong impulse to howl.

"Because I'm a gutless bastard, that's why. I was so ashamed of myself I felt I didn't have the *right* to communicate with you. If I had looked after Bob the way that he looked after me, he might still be alive." Terry's head dipped low between his wide shoulders, like a melon from a trellised vine. He looked as though he might start crying.

"That's ridiculous!" I sputtered, reaching over to touch the sleeve of his jacket. "You aren't responsible for Bob's death.

Nobody is responsible. There was a war going on. People get killed in a war. You shouldn't be so hard on yourself."

Terry raised his heavy head and looked me in the eye again. "Thanks for the kind words, Paige, but I don't deserve them. I really *am* a coward, you know. How do you think my hair got so white? From fear—total fear. It turned white during my first few weeks of fighting."

"It isn't a sin to be afraid."

"It is when you're in the Army."

There was so much pain in Terry's eyes it hurt me to look at them. I shifted my gaze toward the table to our left, where two middle-aged businessmen in gray flannel suits were dining on meatloaf and mashed, not speaking at all. I was envious of their placid boredom. Knowing there was nothing I could say to heal Terry's deep wartime wounds, or even just make him feel a little better, I fished around in my wretched brain for a gentle way to change the subject.

Changing the subject was easy, but the gentle part was hard. "Why did Bob let you read my letters?" I blurted out, screeching in spite of myself. I sounded like Ma Kettle reminding the lazy ranch hands that the barn was on fire. "The things I said to him were so *private,*" I gasped. "My letters were meant for Bob, and Bob *alone*. It really upsets me that he showed them to you." My cheeks flared up in another hot blush.

"I don't blame you for being angry," Terry said, nervously fidgeting with the salt and pepper shakers. "But you should be mad at *me,* not Bob. He was just trying to help me save myself from myself."

His words were a tad too cryptic for my comfort. "What in the world are you talking about?" I snapped. "And how do my letters enter into it?"

"It only happened once," Terry said, giving me a pleading look. "The bombing had been real bad that morning, so bad that even after it stopped—after the shells stopped whistling and exploding all around us—I couldn't stop shaking. I couldn't speak without stuttering, and I couldn't breathe right either. Bob saw the shape I was in, and he pulled me into the brush, propped me against a tree, and splashed some water in my face. Then he gave me your letters to read. He said they would set me straight for sure, take my mind off what was happening and remind me of what we were fighting for—all the worried, wonderful, devoted people back home."

I was too humiliated to speak. I felt like a petty, self-centered stooge—like Ralph Kramden always does when Alice finally makes him see the error of his thoughtless ways.

"See, I didn't get many letters from home," Terry went on, fanning the flames of my shame. "I didn't have a girlfriend or a wife, my mother was dead, my father was a drunk, and my little sister Judy was just trying to get through high school and take care of our father at the same time. She wrote me a few times, but her letters were pretty dismal. All she talked about was how disgusting Dad was, and how crazy she was about her latest boyfriend, whoever he happened to be—she had a new one every week. So her letters weren't very encouraging.

"But *yours* were," he added, eyes begging me to understand. "They were so loving, and sensitive, and interesting, and hopeful. They actually calmed my fears and made me feel strong . . . for a little while, anyway." Terry started fidgeting with the salt and pepper shakers again." Your letters were Bob's most prized possession, you know. He kept them with him at all times. He knew how special they were, and he only showed them to me because he believed they would bring me some courage and peace of mind. And he was right. So please don't be mad at him. He was just being a good friend. The best friend I ever had."

I melted faster than the snow on my eyelashes. "He was my best friend, too," I said, writhing in the agony and ecstasy of having once been truly loved. Then, unable to endure even one more second of such open (okay, *naked*) emotion, I hastily excused myself and bolted for the ladies' room.

# Chapter 3

I STAYED IN THE BATHROOM FOR ABOUT five minutes. I would have stayed longer, but some woman (a rather tall redhead in a green wool dress, I soon found out) kept knocking on the door and asking if I was all right, did I need any help. I told her I was fine and that I'd be out in just one second. Then I flushed (even though I had no reason to), wiped the tears out of my swollen eyes, powdered my nose, and went back to the table.

"Are you okay, Paige?" Terry asked as soon I took my seat.

"I'm fine," I lied, hoping the sight of my raw, puffy, mascara-smeared eyelids wouldn't make him feel worse than he already did. "I just needed a little breather."

"Then do you mind if I talk to you about something else? Something really important. Something that doesn't have anything to do with Bob?"

"Not at all," I said. Truth be known, I was desperate for a change of topic.

The expression on Terry's face went through a series of dramatic transformations. First he looked bewildered, then horrified, then violently enraged. Then he reared back in his chair, heaved an enormous sigh, lowered his head, and sadly scraped his fingers through his ghostly white hair. "I hate to burden you with my problems like this," he said, groaning, "but I really don't know what else to do. You're the only person I can think of who might be able to help me."

"Me?" I said, in wonder. "Why me?"

"Because I trust you," he said. "And because you're brave and smart, you live in New York City, and you write for a national true crime magazine. I've read all your stories and I know how gutsy, clever, and driven you are. And I know that truth and justice are very important to you."

His flattering words made me giddy. I was used to being ridiculed for these "unfeminine" traits, not praised. "What is it you need?" I said without hesitation. "I'll help in any way I can." The theme song of the *Superman* television series was swelling against the sides my cranium.

"I need somebody to believe me," Terry said, clenching his teeth between words. "I need to be taken seriously, for once. I've tried everything under the damn sun! I went to the police again this morning—for the *third* time—and I begged and pleaded with them to continue the investigation, but they just won't pay any attention to me. They keep insisting I don't have any proof. They say the case is as good as closed." His chin began to tremble.

"Police? Evidence?" I perked up like a puppy with a pork chop. "What case are you talking about?"

Terry's face had turned almost as white as his hair. "My sister's murder case."

"Oh, my Lord!" I croaked, head spinning. "Your sister murdered somebody?"

"God, no!" Terry cried, looking at me as if I'd just sprouted fangs and fur. "Somebody murdered *her!*"

I was shocked into silence (a few moments too late, as usual). My stomach turned over and a new stream of grief spewed down my spine. Choking back another rush of tears, I reached across the table and grabbed Terry's hand. "Oh, Terry, that's so horrible!" I said. "I'm so, so sorry . . ."

"She was just a kid," he moaned, shaking his head in despair. "She hadn't even turned twenty . . ."

"When did it happen?"

"Three weeks ago."

"Where?"

"Here. In New York. Judy moved here about a year and a half ago," he said, "soon after I got back from Korea. Well, *moved* isn't really the right word. She sort of ran away from home."

I was curious to know *why* Judy had run away, but other, more pressing questions were popping out of my mouth. "Where in New York did it happen?" I sputtered. "How was she killed?"

Terry's pale face tightened up like a fist. "She was shot to death in her apartment on West 26th Street. Two .22 caliber bullets to the heart. Her watch and her purse were taken, so the police are convinced she was killed during a random burglary, that her death was in no way premeditated."

Terry's account jostled my memory. I recalled reading about the murder in the papers, cutting out the brief articles for our clip files, and asking Pomeroy if he wanted me or Mike to do a write-up for the magazine. He said no, it was a boring crime—that dispassionate, unplanned homicides were "as interesting as his Aunt Martha's grocery list." For obvious reasons, I chose not to relate Pomeroy's remarks to Terry.

"And you're not convinced it was a chance killing?" I asked Terry. "You don't agree with the police?"

"You bet your sweet ass I don't!—forgive my French. For one thing, there were no signs of breaking and entering. No smashed windows or locks, no jimmy scrapes on the door. And there were no signs of a physical struggle, either. Aside from the bullet wounds, Judy's body didn't have a mark on it. No cuts or scratches, not even a bruise. And, believe you me, Paige, if my little sister had caught somebody trying to rob her apartment, there would have been a *big* struggle—gun, or no gun. She wasn't a coward like me. As young as she was, Judy was tougher than nails—and she loved a good fight."

"You told this to the police?"

"Of course I did! I told them a lot more, too. They just chose not to listen."

"Who did you speak to?" I nervously inquired. "Who was the detective in charge?" Since my homicide detective boyfriend's precinct didn't encompass West 26th, I was certain it wasn't Dan Street, but I held my breath and mentally crossed my fingers anyway.

"Sweeny," Terry said. "Detective Sergeant Hugo Sweeny."

*Whew!* My relief was palpable. I was eager to help Terry if I could, and I was raring to pursue the story of his sister's murder, but if Dan had been working on the case, I would have had to decline. I would have had to bow out completely—or at least *pretend* to. Even with Dan *not* directly involved, I'd have a lot of pretending to do . . .

"What makes you so sure Detective Sweeny is wrong?" I asked, snatching my cigarettes out of my purse and lighting one up. "Maybe the burglar shot Judy the minute she saw him, before she could put up a struggle, or react in any way to what was happening." I offered Terry a smoke, but he didn't seem to notice.

"I could believe that if the shooting had been sloppy," he said, becoming more agitated, "if at least one of the bullets had missed the heart and hit her shoulder, say, or her leg. But both slugs hit dead center, and they were fired at close range. Judy wasn't killed by a burglar," Terry insisted. "Whoever shot her stole her purse and watch just to make it *look* like a burglary!" His face wasn't as white as his hair anymore. Now it was chili-pepper red.

"Was her apartment ransacked?" I asked, keeping my tone as calm and professional as possible.

"The place was a mess," he said. "At least that's what the police told me. They said everything was turned upside down. And I believe them, since the apartment was a wreck when I got here. The police were responsible for some of the disorder themselves, of course—they had rummaged through everything looking for clues—but they weren't the cause of the major destruction. *That* was the murderer's handiwork."

"Was anything else taken?" I asked, still exploring the burglary angle.

"I don't know for sure, but I doubt it. Judy never owned anything worth stealing. She was a salesgirl in the lingerie department at Macy's, and she didn't make much money at all. I don't even know how she could afford to rent her own apartment. She used to room with two other girls down on 19th Street, but she moved out and took her own place a few months ago." Terry pulled a paper napkin out of the table dispenser and dabbed it over his perspiring forehead.

"Anyway," he went on, "it doesn't matter if anything else was stolen or not, because if it was, it was taken just for show. This was no burglary, I'm telling you! Judy was intentionally *murdered!* And her apartment was trashed because the murderer was looking for something specific—something he never was able to find."

Terry was so adamantly convinced of his theory, I found it hard to argue with him. "What do you mean by *something specific?*" I asked, crushing my half-smoked cigarette in the glass ashtray. "Do you know what the murderer was looking for? And how do you know he never found it?"

"Because I found it myself!" Terry declared. He locked his eyes onto mine and pierced me with his pure blue stare.

"Go on," I coaxed. "Tell me everything."

"I've been living in Judy's apartment for the past three weeks," he began, speaking very slowly and intently now. "I had to come into town to identify her body . . . then I stayed on to make her burial arrangements . . . sell off her furniture and stuff . . . pack up her clothes for Goodwill . . . clean all her blood off the carpet . . ." His chin started trembling again. "I had to dispose of the food and pack up the dishes—clear everything out of the apartment for the landlord. That's when I discovered it, when I was sorting through the stuff in the kitchen cabinets."

"Discovered what?" I urged, acting as solemn as Madame Curie, but feeling as sleazy as Hedda Hopper. I probably shouldn't admit this to you (or anybody else, for that matter), but rather than shrinking from the horror of the things Terry was telling me, I was yearning to know all the dirty details. The truth is always lurking in the details. "What was it you found?" I asked again.

Terry sat up straight, lifted his chin, and squared his wide, muscular shoulders. "The buried treasure," he announced in a deep, resounding, pirate-like voice. "I found the buried treasure."

I thought my ears weren't working right. "What did you say?"

"I found it yesterday afternoon," he went on, "wrapped in tissue paper and buried in a box of Quaker oatmeal."

"Oatmeal?" I asked, suddenly wondering if, along with his courage, Terry had lost his marbles in Korea, too.

"I took everything, including the oatmeal, straight to the police first thing this morning," Terry rattled on, "but they still don't believe me. They said this doesn't prove anything. They're so damn sure Judy was killed during a random robbery, nothing's ever going to change their minds!" His face was turning purple now.

"What—exactly—did—you—find?" I pronounced the words calmly and carefully, as though speaking to a hysterical child.

"Here! I'll show you!" he cried, in a voice so clamorous the fat gray-haired woman sitting to our right looked up from her macaroni and cheese and gaped openly at us, her heavily rouged cheeks sagging in surprise. She continued to stare as Terry shoved his hat and gloves aside and slid the Thom McAn shoebox into the center of our small table. He untied the twine, lifted the lid, and pulled out a cylindrical cardboard Quaker oatmeal container.

"Go ahead, open it!" Terry said, pushing the round, red-white-and-blue cereal box toward me. "See for yourself what's inside."

I was so curious I wanted to seize the carton, yank off the top, and dump the contents out on the table. But I didn't want to make a mess. Or a scene. And I didn't want the nosy old girl sitting next to us to see what was in the box. I mean, what if it was something really gruesome—a mutilated ear, or a severed toe, or something horrible like that? (I had just written a story about a recent murder case in which a plucked eyeball had provided the major clue, so I *wasn't* being overly imaginative.)

Carefully pulling the container in close to my chest, I propped my elbows on either side and hunched my shoulders over the top, creating a darker, more private space. Then I sank my head low over the carton and slowly, gingerly, removed the saucer-shaped lid.

The dusty smell of oatmeal was distinct. And there, sitting on top of at least three inches of grain, was a crumpled mass of white tissue paper which, I discovered as soon as I touched it, contained something hard and beady and prickly, something that moved when I poked it with my forefinger. Overcome with curiosity, I stuck all of my fingers into the cardboard cylinder and pried a wide opening in the tissue paper, exposing the contents of the crumpled package.

I was bedazzled. Even in the confined space and murky shadows of my lowered head and hunched shoulders, the mound of diamonds sparkled, sending a thousand tiny but brilliant shafts of light into my astonished, disbelieving eyes.

"Are these real?" I gasped. "Or are they rhinestones?"

"They're real," Terry said. "I had them appraised before I showed them to the police. There's a necklace, a pin, a pair of earrings, and two bracelets. Altogether, they're worth about thirty thousand dollars."

"Wow." I wanted to take the diamonds out of the oatmeal carton and examine them more closely, but I didn't dare. I thought the snoopy old lady sitting next to us might see them and swoon, her heavily rouged face landing smack in the middle of her mac and cheese casserole.

"There's no way on earth Judy could have bought that jewelry herself," Terry said, in a calmer, more serious tone. "So it was either given to her by somebody who's very rich, or it was stolen."

"Could she have stolen it herself?"

"No! Absolutely not. Judy would never steal anything. She was a bit on the wild side, but she was no thief. She *could,* however, have been talked into hiding stolen goods for somebody else—if that somebody was a man, and if she fancied herself to be in love with him. Judy would do anything for the man she loved, even if she'd only just met him, and loved him for just a few hours. That's just the way she was. Every time she fell for a guy—which was way too often, if you ask me—she gave herself to him completely."

"Was she in love at the time of the murder?"

"Not according to Mrs. Londergan, the older woman—a widow—who lives across the hall. She told us—me and Detective Sweeny—that she and Judy had developed a very close relationship, a mother/daughter kind of thing. She said my sister often confided in her, and she claimed Judy definitely wasn't involved with anybody at the time of her death. She was, as Mrs. Londergan put it, "between boyfriends."

"That implies a new boyfriend was on the horizon."

"With my sister, a new boyfriend was *always* on the horizon."

"Did Judy ever have any *rich* boyfriends?"

"I don't know."

"Did Mrs. Londergan know?"

Terry shook his head and shrugged. "I never asked her. Before I found the jewelry I had no reason to ask her, and after I found it I had no time to ask her. I didn't discover the diamonds until late yesterday afternoon, remember, and after that I was so busy getting them appraised, and taking them to the police, and trying to convince Detective Sweeny they proved that Judy was murdered—and then, when he didn't believe me, trying to contact *you*—that I never had a chance to speak to Mrs. Londergan again."

"I'm surprised Sweeny didn't confiscate the diamonds."

"He did."

"What?!!!"

"He said he was going to catalog them and keep them as possible evidence, but I knew by the way he was acting he'd just stick them away in a locker somewhere, never use them to try to solve the case. So when he left his office to get the proper forms to fill out, I grabbed the oatmeal container off his desk, stuffed it back in the shoebox, snuck down the hall, and scrammed."

"Pretty nervy," I said, smiling. "I thought you said you were a coward."

Terry smiled back. "Only when I'm being shot at."

I found his motive noble and his conduct commendable, but I knew the police wouldn't see it that way. "Does Sweeny know where you live?" I asked him.

"Of course. He questioned me extensively the first time we met."

"Then he'll come after you, you know. He probably won't sleep a wink till he gets the diamonds back. He may even arrest you—for theft, or tampering with evidence, or some such charge."

"I'll cross that bridge when I come to it."

I peered down into the oatmeal box and took a long, lingering look at the tangled heap of glittering gems. Then I scrunched the surrounding tissue paper back together, put the top back on the cereal box, tapped it down tight, and slid the closed container across the table to Terry.

"Better put these someplace safe," I said. "Someplace safer than a shoebox."

"No!" he cried, pushing the oatmeal carton back in my direction. "I brought them for you. I want you to keep them."

"Are you nuts?!!!" I gulped, beginning to believe that he really was. "I can't possibly do that! Those diamonds don't belong to you. They're not yours to give away."

"I don't mean that you should keep them forever," Terry quickly interjected. "I just want you to keep them till the case is solved. They're the only real clue we have. You'll need them to catch Judy's murderer."

I'd been afraid he was going to say something like that—something about me chasing down Judy's killer. And I guess I'd known from the moment he told me about the murder that *that* was what he wanted me to do. But I also knew that I was a writer—*not* a detective—and even though I had, by some incredible, unimaginable fluke, managed to flush out the psycho who had murdered Babs Comstock (and who then almost murdered *me!*), that didn't mean I'd ever in a hundred million years be able to uncover (much less *catch!*) the monster who killed Terry's sister. And even if I *did* catch him, what was I supposed to do with him? Pronounce him guilty and lock him up for life in my broom closet?

"Hold it right there!" I said, sticking my hand up like a stop sign. "*You're* the one named Catcher, not me! And maybe you haven't noticed, Mr. Catcher, but I'm a journalist, not a cop. I don't *solve* crimes, I just write stories about them."

"Yes, but you do it so well. And you do it here in Manhattan, so you know how the city's criminal justice system works. And Bob said you're a *very* tenacious investigator. The word he used was 'relentless.' He said that once you start searching for something—a lost key, a lost soul, even a hopelessly lost cause—you never give up. You stick to the bitter end. And that's what I need—someone who believes that my sister was deliberately murdered and who will stop at nothing to prove it."

"Yikes!" I cried, suddenly catching a glimpse of the big chrome-rimmed clock on the wall. "It's two-fifteen! I've got to get back to the office immediately." I shoved my arms into my coat sleeves, grabbed my purse and gloves, and bounced to my feet like a startled kangaroo. "I'm not kidding, Terry. I have to go right now. I could lose my job for staying out so long."

Terry looked at his watch. "Good God! I didn't realize it was so late! I've got to go, too, or I'll miss my bus." He shoved the oatmeal container back into the shoebox and slapped his hat on his head. Then he jumped up from his chair, picked up his gloves and the shoebox, and followed close behind me as I lurched away from the table and hurried through the still-crowded restaurant to the exit.

"But what about my sister?" he begged, bounding ahead to open the door for me. "Will you at least *try* to dig up some new evidence—something that will convince the police to get back to work on the case?"

We stepped out onto the icy sidewalk. The air was so cold it was hard to breathe; the snow so thick it was hard to see. "I'll do my best," I promised, benumbed and blinded by the bright white storm. Then I took Terry's arm and held on for dear life as he escorted me up the block toward my office.

# Chapter 4

**DUCKING OUR HEADS AGAINST THE DRIV**ing snow, Terry and I helped each other stay on our feet as we skidded up the slippery sidewalk and across the slushy street to the tall, sand-colored brick building I worked in. It wasn't until we had pushed our way into the warm, steamy lobby, and I got a whiff of the burnt hamburger smell wafting from the adjoining coffee shop, that I realized we'd never had any lunch.

I was so hungry I wanted to dart into the coffee shop and grab a sandwich to take upstairs, but I didn't dare take the time. If Pomeroy got back to the office before I did, I'd be in big trouble. And if he saw me eating lunch at my desk during working hours—or, as he liked to put it, "working-*class* hours"—he'd blow his top.

"So you're definitely going to help me, right?" Terry said, anxiously tugging me over to a secluded corner of the lobby, beyond the bank of partitioned telephones and directories, behind the huge, tinsel-draped Christmas tree. "You'll find out everything you can about Judy's murder?" His azure eyes were gleaming with expectation.

"Against my better judgment, yes," I said. "But don't

expect any miracles. I'm just a woman who writes about crime. I'm no Sherlock Holmes. And I'm no Miss Marple either!"

"Who?"

"Never mind," I said, heart sinking at the thought of the danger and disappointments that no doubt lay ahead. "It's just that I don't want you to get your hopes up too high. I could fail in the end, you know. To tell the truth, I don't even know where to *start*."

"Here!" Terry said, shoving the Thom McAn shoebox into my hands. "Start with this. Maybe you can trace the diamonds to a certain jeweler, and then find out who bought them, or stole them. And there's some other stuff in this box, too—a couple of photographs, the address of the building where my sister lived, Mrs. Londergan's apartment number and phone number, the names and address of Judy's former roommates."

"Did Judy have a personal calendar or an address book?"

"Yes, but the police took them into evidence before I got here. I never even got a look them. All I can give you is the stuff in this shoebox—things that should be of help."

Suddenly, my nerves went haywire. And a flood of adrenaline shot through my veins. "But what about *you?!!*" I said (okay, *shrieked*). "*You'd* be the most help of all! Why do you have to go back to Pittsburgh today? Why can't you stay here for a while—at least give me a chance to talk to you some more about Judy and learn everything I can about her life, and," I added sadly, "her death. I can't do this all by myself, Terry. I need you. Please don't go!" In case you haven't noticed, I wasn't quite ready to be left to my own devices.

"I've already given you the most important information," Terry insisted. "And we can always talk to each other on the phone. And besides," he added, "you don't *have* to work on this alone. Get the other agents at the magazine to help you. This could be a major story, and it's a *Daring Detective* exclusive! They'll be chomping at the bit to get in on the investigation."

*Other* agents *at the magazine?* Boy, did he have the wrong idea! (Along, I should add, with the rest of the detective magazine–reading public.)

"You don't understand," I told him. "There are no *agents* at *Daring Detective*. Just writers and artists and editors. And there aren't any big investigations going on either. Practically all the stories we publish are nothing but clip jobs. They're written in-house and rehashed from assorted newspaper and magazine articles that are already in print." I wasn't exaggerating, either. To the best of my knowledge, the only exclusive, firsthand story *Daring Detective* had ever published had been the one about the Babs Comstock murder. My story.

"But you've got a police consultant on staff!" Terry argued. "A real homicide detective. What's his name? . . . Street! Detective Dan Street. There's a picture of him and a write-up about his career in every issue. Can't you get him to help you?"

Terry looked so hopeful I didn't have the heart to tell him the truth: that the *DD* police consultant job was just a sham; that Dan Street didn't actually *work* for the magazine, but was merely paid a small retainer for the use of his name and photo just to make the magazine look official; that even if he wanted to (which he most definitely wouldn't!), the parameters of Dan's *real* job—as a highly respected NYPD homicide detective in the Midtown South Precinct—would never allow him to join forces with a fledgling crime journalist (like me) to reopen a murder investigation that had already been shut down by a detective in another district.

And that wasn't all. There was another truth I wasn't in the mood to divulge, a rather awkward and personally disturbing (okay, *embarrassing*) truth: that in spite of the fact that he was my dearly beloved boyfriend, and had been for the past seven months, Dan would rather lock *me* up in jail than see me get entangled in another unsolved murder case.

"Street's a pretty busy man," I said, waffling, finding myself unwilling to destroy *all* of Terry's naïve expectations so early in the game, "and this case isn't in his precinct. But I'll tell him about it, see if he can help me out."

"Good," Terry said, satisfied. He lifted his brown fedora, swiped his gloved hand over his silvery hair, then repositioned the hat lower on his forehead. "Look, I hate to leave you like this. I wish I could stay. But now I really have to go home."

"But what about Detective Sweeny? He'll *find* you if you go home!" Okay, I admit it. I was trying to scare him into staying.

The prospect of being arrested didn't seem to disturb Terry at all. "Maybe he will, or maybe he won't come looking, but I can't worry about that now," he said, eyes narrowing with resolve. "I *have* to go home. I can't stay in Judy's apartment anymore, and I've run out of money. But the main cause is my father. He's having a really hard time over Judy's death, and I've been away for the past three weeks. I simply can't leave him alone over Christmas."

"Oh," I said, unable to challenge Terry's reasoning. Nobody, but nobody, should have to be alone over the holidays. Three years ago—right after Bob was killed—I'd suffered through a solo Christmas, and I wouldn't wish the same on my worst enemy. Not even Brandon Pomeroy.

"Actually, I have to go right *now,*" Terry said, checking his watch, then giving me an apologetic smile. "My bags are in a locker at the station and my bus leaves in one hour. With all this snow, it'll take me at least that long to get across town to the terminal."

"But it's not safe to travel in this weather!" I whined, still trying—in spite of my own urgent need to get back to the office—to delay Terry's departure. "I'll bet the buses aren't even running!"

"That's a chance I'll have to take."

The fat lady was singing loud and clear. "Okay," I said, heaving a huge, deflating sigh, "but promise you'll call me when you get home? There's so much more I need to know."

"Don't worry. I'll call you. I have your home number and your office number in my wallet. And you have mine. It's in the shoebox."

"It's better to call me at home."

"No problem. I'll call you tomorrow night."

"Okay," I said, forcing myself to stand up tall and straight, putting on a big show of self-confidence. I was a towering Eleanor Roosevelt on the outside, but a teetering Mamie Eisenhower within. As curious as I was about the case, as committed as I was to helping my late husband's good friend, as determined as I was to find out everything I could about Judy Catcher's horrible, untimely death, I still couldn't help thinking what an idiot I'd been to let myself get so involved.

Terry leaned over and gave me a quick hug. "Thanks for everything, Paige," he said, pulling back and resting his forearms on my shoulders. "You're the best. Bob was a very lucky man." He stared into my eyes for one brief but meaningful second, then spun himself around, strode across the marble floor, pushed his way through the revolving glass door, and vanished in a frosty flurry.

I was left standing there like a statue, holding a shoebox full of contraband diamonds in my hands, feeling as lost and lonely as Snow White in the forest—before all the birds and bunnies came out of the woods to comfort her. *Where are my birds and bunnies?* I wondered, though I knew from past experience they'd be hiding out like bandits till the heat blew over.

LENNY WAS STANDING UP FRONT, NEAR THE entrance, when I walked (okay, *lunged*) into the office. "Where the hell have you been?" he said, keeping his voice down to a scratchy whisper. "Do you know what time it is? You are so, so lucky Pomeroy's not back. I was afraid you wouldn't make it in time."

"I was afraid of that, too," I said, setting the shoebox down on the nearest table, tearing off my hat and coat, and hooking them both on the tree. I took a peek at Pomeroy's empty chair and grinned. "I guess the gods and goddesses of good fortune haven't totally abandoned me yet."

Lenny looked at the box on the table and muttered, astonished, "You went *shoe* shopping? In the middle of a snowstorm, you went *shoe* shopping? You risked your steady job plus your entire freelance writing career to go shopping for *shoes?*"

His voice had climbed a little too high on the audio meter. Both Mike and Mario looked up from their work and began watching our little drama as if it were a mesmerizing segment of the "I've Got a Secret" game show. A Mark Goodson–Bill Todman Production.

"Hush!" I said, giving Lenny the evil eye. "Of course I didn't go shoe shopping! There's something *else* in this box. I'll tell you about it later." Turning away from Lenny before he could utter another syllable, I picked up the shoebox, whisked it over to my desk, shoved it way in the back of my lower left-hand file drawer, and sat down.

Jaw hanging open like a hatch, Lenny gawked at me for a couple more seconds, then shrugged, stuffed his hands into his pockets, and shuffled back to his own desk in the rear. I knew that he was miffed at me—unnerved by my brusque demeanor—but I also knew that he would forgive me. Ever since the day he'd saved my life, Lenny Zimmerman thought I was the best creation since waxed paper.

I'd barely gotten out of my boots and back into my pumps when Brandon Pomeroy returned. He was quite drunk, as usual, but—unless you were as familiar with his façade of sobriety as I was—you'd never know it. He wasn't staggering or stumbling (or, God forbid, singing), and his spine was as straight as a drum major's baton. He had no trouble at all removing his hat, muffler, and overcoat and hanging them—neatly—on the rack. His gray flannel suit looked freshly pressed; his crisp white shirt was spotless; his maroon silk tie wasn't the least bit crooked.

And when he spoke, he didn't slur a single word.

"Good afternoon, Mrs. Turner," he said as he walked past my desk and sat down at his own. His nose was so high in the air I was surprised it wasn't snowcapped. "I trust you've been having a productive workday. Is the backyard paste-up ready to go to the printer?"

There are times when one *has* to be honest—when the truth, and nothing but the truth, will do. This wasn't one of those times. "I'm almost finished, sir," I said, shuffling some galleys around on my desk, trying to look busy and efficient. "I'll have it ready for the afternoon pickup."

"See that you do," Pomeroy said with a sniff, swiveling around in his chair till his face was to the wall and his back was turned to me. Though he kept his head held high and continued to sit up straight as a fence post, he was, I knew, about to take his afternoon sabbatical (i.e., his alcohol-induced afternoon nap).

"Yes, sir!" I said, making a cross-eyed face at the ceiling and mentally shouting *Arrrgh!* I didn't know what was worse—having to figure out a covert way to do four hours worth of work in two, or having to lick Pomeroy's expensive Italian leather boots in the process.

Okay, I'm lying again. I *did too* know what was worse. It was the bootlicking. Definitely the bootlicking. The work I could handle.

And that's what I proceeded to do. I gathered up my scissors, my Scotch tape, my pica ruler, the backyard galleys, the list and measurements of all the backyard ads, a big stack of three-column layout sheets, and a large folder of black and white cartoons. Then I snuck into the file room, where I spread all the materials out on the center worktable and went furiously to work.

First I measured and placed all the pinup calendar, bodybuilding, hair-thickening, rupture-easing, how-to-be-a-hypnotist ads, carefully marking them up on the layout sheets, then I trimmed the story runover galleys and put them in position—leaving room for the necessary continued lines, of course. After choosing, sizing, and placing several spicy cartoons to fill the leftover space, I finally taped all the trimmed galleys to the layout sheets—without an eighth of an inch to spare—as if they were the key pieces of a large, complicated jigsaw puzzle.

I was very lucky. I only had to cut eight lines of copy to make everything fit exactly. If the mock-up had come out a few lines too short, I would have had to write new copy to fill, and that would have taken longer. As it was, I finished the backyard paste-up in record time, and placed the complete forty-four-page package in the pickup basket a good five minutes before the printer's messenger arrived.

This was *not* the world's most exciting accomplishment, I realize, but at least it kept me from getting fired—and from fretting my fool head off about the diamond-stuffed shoebox buried, like a land mine, in the depths of my desk drawer.

My timely completion of the backyard paste-up wasn't the only miracle that occurred that afternoon. Brandon Pomeroy's drunken coma lasted a full hour longer than usual (he must have had an extra martini), Harvey Crockett was out of the office all day at a meeting with our distributor, and Mike and Mario were laboring so hard to meet their own pressing deadlines that they didn't have the time or the inclination to torment me with coffee demands and crummy jokes.

As a result, I had the time to look for the newspaper clips about Judy Catcher's death that I presumed were still in our files. And since I was in charge of all the filing (that's woman's work, you know!), I knew exactly where to look: in the folder labeled MURDERS—NOV. 1954.

There were numerous homicide reports in the folder, but just three short clips on the Catcher murder. And each gave the same few details: A young woman named Judy Catcher had been shot to death in her West 26th Street apartment on Saturday, November 27th. The shooting was estimated to have occurred between 5:00 and 8:00 P.M., during a random burglary. The victim's purse and watch were stolen and her apartment was ransacked. Anyone with information relating to the crime should notify Detective Hugo Sweeny at the 10th Precinct.

I hoped to have that privilege soon.

Taking the clips out of the file folder and stuffing them in my skirt pocket, I marched back into the front workroom and carefully (okay, *sneakily*) transferred the clips from my pocket to my purse. Not that I really needed them. Aside from the actual date of the murder and the estimated time of death, they didn't tell me anything I didn't already know.

I looked at the clock on the wall and was surprised to discover I still had twenty minutes to waste (I mean *work!*) before closing time. I was able to clip all the crime stories from the afternoon newspapers and file a big stack of fake corpse photos before Pomeroy became fully conscious, and before the hands of the office clock hit 5:30—at which point I changed back into my boots, pulled on my beret, slipped into my coat, snatched the shoebox out of my drawer and tucked it tight under my arm, bid a hasty goodnight to Heckle and Jeckle, blew a quick kiss to Lenny, and made a smooth getaway.

# Chapter 5

THE TRIP HOME WASN'T SO SMOOTH. Though I made the entire journey by subway and didn't have to deal with the snow until I emerged at Sheridan Square, I still had to deal with the ragged, hairy, smelly creature who boarded the crowded train at 14th Street and decided the best way to keep himself warm was to snuggle up real close to me. If the creature had been a dog, instead of a man, I could have handled it—but of course I wasn't that lucky. My stop was next though, and I got off the train in a hurry, leaving the shaggy beast to search for another source of body heat.

It was already dark outside, but the sky and the streets were twinkling, the former with stars, the latter with Christmas lights. Bright shiny bulbs were strung everywhere—across store windows, around lampposts, over the doorways of apartment buildings and the awnings of restaurants—casting their red, green, gold, and blue reflections on every glistening, snow-covered surface. It was still very cold, but the snowfall had slowed considerably. The flakes were floating lightly now, like scattered tufts of goosedown from a slightly torn pillowslip.

It was a beautiful scene, but I was much too distracted to

do more than give it a quick, appreciative glance. I hurried down Seventh Avenue to Bleecker Street, slipping and scrunching with every step, gripping the shoebox under my arm as if it were a football and I were a crazed quarterback scrambling for the goal line. I couldn't wait to get home, hide the diamonds in a safe place, and then go next door to talk to Abby. I needed to talk to Abby.

Abby Moscowitz, I should tell you, was the best friend I'd ever had in all the world. At the time, we'd known each other only one and a half short years, but I felt as though we'd spent our whole lives together; that we were twin sisters and had shared the same womb.

Not that we were *anything* alike.

At least not in the looks department. Abby was tall and buxom and bohemian-looking, with long black hair that hung, when loose, below her waist. Her deep brown eyes were huge and heavily lashed, her nose and cheekbones were proudly prominent, and her wide, smiley lips were as plump as throw cushions. I was tall and thin and normal-looking, with wavy brown hair that fell to my shoulders, and facial features that had, to the best of my knowledge, never caused a traffic jam. I'd been told that I was beautiful on occasion, but I wasn't stupid enough to believe it.

Abby really *was* beautiful, though, and everybody knew it, Abby included.

When it came to likes and dislikes, personal beliefs and ideas, Abby and I agreed on some things, but certainly not all. We both liked jazz, cigarettes, whiskey sours (okay, *any* kind of cocktail), tight sweaters, and Halo shampoo—and we both wished Adlai had been elected president instead of Ike—but whenever the subject of sex came up, we had a parting of the ways: Abby believed in free love and would go to bed with any young man who struck her fancy (and her fancy was *very* easy to strike), while I was determined to sleep alone—as our current social conventions so cruelly commanded—until the day I got married again (or until the night Dan and I became so wildly overcome with drink and desire that I simply couldn't help myself—whichever came first).

Turning left on Bleecker, I forged through the snow and up one and a half blocks to the tiny, three-story brick building I lived in. There were just two apartments in the whole building—Abby's and mine—and both sat atop small street-level storefronts. Abby's little duplex was perched above Angelo's Fruit and Vegetable Market, while mine was mounted on top of Luigi's Fish Store. I guess I don't have to tell you which apartment smelled better.

I took out my keys, opened the door between the two storefronts, and tore up to the top of the dark, narrow stairwell leading to the living quarters. Abby's place was on the left, mine was on the right. Panting as hard and fast as DiMaggio must have done after dashing across home plate (or getting to third base with Marilyn), I stood on the tiny landing between the two apartments, madly jiggling the keys on my overloaded chain, searching for the one that would open the gate to my safe haven.

But before I could find it, Abby's door flew wide open.

"Boom chicky boom!" she said, stepping into the portal and leaning her left shoulder against the jamb. She was wearing her tight black capris and her color-streaked white painter's smock. Her long, pitch-black hair was pulled back from her glowing face and wound into a braid the length and breadth of an elephant's trunk. "It's about time you got home," she said. "I was getting ready to send out a pack of Saint Bernards—with little casks of booze on their collars, of course—to look for you. It is, after all, the cocktail hour." To prove it, she raised the pale pink drink in her right hand to lip level and took a noisy sip. "I'm making pink ladies tonight," she said. "Can you dig it?"

My anxiety melted away and my cold feet turned toasty. This was the kind of effect Abby usually had on me—and most other people, too. She was as warm and welcoming as a potbellied stove. "You heard my prayers," I said, deciding to go straight into Abby's apartment—shoebox and all—and worry about hiding the diamonds later. Why get in a dither about thirty thousand dollars' worth of secret (possibly *stolen*) jewelry, when you can sit yourself down, light up an L&M filter tip, and have a pink lady?

The minute I stepped inside, however, I wanted to turn around and go home. The lights were low, the smoke was thick, and the hi-fi was playing Miles Davis at a deep, vibrating volume. A short, dark, beefy young man—dressed in nothing but a purple loincloth and sitting cross-legged on the living room floor—was thrumming his fingers on a set of bongo drums and giving me the kind of look that said, "If you come in here and wreck this wild thing I've got going with this unbelievably hot, groovy babe, I'll have to kill you."

I didn't feel so welcome anymore.

"Oops!" I yelped, "I'm intruding."

"Oh, don't mind him!" Abby chirped, hopping over to her round oak kitchen table to pour me a drink. "That's just Tony Figaro, from the bakery down the street. He's been posing for me today. I got a new cover assignment from *Lusty Male Adventures*."

In case you haven't already guessed, Abby was an artist. Not your average flower-vase-and-fruit-bowl kind of artist, but the kind who painted bold, dramatic pictures of bold, dramatic people in exotic (okay, *erotic*) scenes and situations. In other words, she was a *commercial* artist. A freelance magazine illustrator, to be exact.

And that's how we happened to meet—the day Abby came up to the *Daring Detective* office to show Mario some samples of her work. She was sitting in the guest chair near my desk, waiting for Mario to see her, and we struck up a conversation. I mentioned that I was looking for a new, cheap place to live, and she told me the "pad" next door to hers was available. I went to see the apartment right after work and rented it that very same evening.

Mario's reaction to Abby had also been immediate. He was so knocked out by her artistic flair (okay, *figure*) that he gave her three full-page illustration assignments on the spot. As Abby was fond of saying, "If the skills don't get 'em, then the sweater will."

Carrying a cocktail in each hand, Abby sauntered over to where I was standing, next to the little red loveseat that separated the kitchen area from the living area (actually the *painting* area, since Abby had always used the living room as her studio). "When the *Lusty Male* art director called me this morning," she said, "and begged me to do a rush illustration of a brawny, bare-chested snake charmer, I immediately thought of Tony. I knew he would look cool in the costume."

(Translation: She wanted to see him without any clothes on. Abby was the only person I knew who could call a purple diaper a *costume,* and still keep a straight face.)

"And he does, doesn't he?" she added. "Look cool, I mean. The bongos are a stand-in for the snake basket. I'll paint a turban on his head eventually, but I didn't see any reason to make him actually *wear* one. Sitting cross-legged on the floor for three hours is enough punishment for one day, wouldn't you say?"

"Uh . . . yes," I said, feeling very uncomfortable. I wasn't used to standing in front of a near-naked man and talking about him as if he weren't there. (And trying, but failing, to keep my eyes off his bulging loincloth.)

"You know, I never even called the model agency this time," Abby blithely continued. "I figured why hire a high-priced professional yo-yo when I can get the world's hippest, sexiest baker to pose for free? Right, Tony?" Smiling from ear to ear, she gave me a knowing wink, then handed me my drink.

"Right!" Tony proudly replied, straightening his spine and expanding his brawny bare chest to the limit. Then, beating his fingers lightly over the bongos, he gazed deep into my eyes and sent me another mental message. This one said, "Whoever you are, please leave now. If you go home and leave us alone, I'm gonna get laid. I know it! I can feel it! Please don't spoil it for me!"

I gazed at Abby for a second or two, wondering if she wanted me to stay or go, trying to gauge if she was feeling amorous or not. But I quickly realized what a silly waste of time *that* was. Abby was *always* feeling amorous. And as much as I wanted to tell her about everything that had happened to me that day, I did *not* want to tell the whole story—or even one itsy bitsy little part of it—to Tony Figaro.

"Cheers!" I said, throwing my head back and downing my frothy pink drink in two gulps. Licking the foam off my lips, I set the empty cocktail glass down on the kitchen table and began backing toward the still-open door. I was glad I hadn't removed my coat. "Gotta go now, kids," I warbled, backing all the way out into the hall. "Brought some work home from the office." I gave the shoebox under my arm a meaningful little pat, waved a brisk bye-bye, then pushed the door closed, leaving Abby alone with Tony to rehearse his new snake-charming techniques.

BURSTING INTO MY OWN APARTMENT, I flipped on the lights, locked the door behind me, and set the shoebox down on my yellow formica kitchen table. I was eager to go through all the stuff in the box—to look at the diamonds again and find a good hiding place for everything—but I was in way too much physical discomfort to even consider it. My feet were cold and wet, my shoulders were drooping from the weight of my heavy coat, my head was spinning from the chug-a-lugged pink lady, and the starving animal in my stomach was growling louder than the MGM lion.

I had to feed it—fast.

Kicking off my soggy boots and tossing my hat and coat on the chair nearest the door, I darted into the kitchen half of my narrow living area and skimmed my stocking feet over the black-and-white-checked linoleum to the refrigerator. I opened the rounded door and peered inside. I was looking for a nice roast chicken, some cornbread stuffing with mushroom gravy, a crispy spinach and bacon salad, and a bottle of white wine. What I found was a wedge of cheddar cheese and a bottle of Dr. Pepper.

I took both items out of the refrigerator and put them on the kitchen table. A box of saltine crackers and a can of Campbell's chicken noodle completed the menu. It was a feast fit for a Bowery bum, but I relished every salty, slurpy mouthful.

And when I had finished eating, I felt like myself again. My usual frantic, screwball self.

Lighting a cigarette and taking a deep drag, I shoved the empty soup bowl to one side. Then I pulled the Thom McAn shoebox into the center of the table, under the beam of yellowish light from the kitchen table lamp, and nervously lifted the lid. The oatmeal box was still there, thank God (or Christ, or Zeus, or Buddha, or Vishnu, or Allah, or Whoever might have been in charge at that particular moment)—and so were the diamonds. I took them out of their tissue paper package and spread them out on the table. There were two bracelets, a pair of earrings, a pin, and a necklace—just as Terry had said.

They were pretty, I guess, in a blinking, twinkly sort of way, but I had never understood why everybody always made such a big fuss about diamonds—or why these useless bits of glassy stone were worth so darn much money. You couldn't eat them, or drink them, or talk to them, or make love with them. They couldn't make you laugh, or keep your feet warm, or teach you a foreign language. All they could do was just sit there and sparkle. And if you turned out the light, they couldn't even do that!

You could *wear* them, of course, but—unlike every other living woman in the entire Western Hemisphere—I had never had the slightest desire to adorn myself with expensive gems. I had a feeling they would be uncomfortable (in many more ways than one), and I knew for a fact they wouldn't go with the rest of my wardrobe. I can honestly say that if *I* had been the one who owned this jewelry—this mass of crystalline carbon sitting here on the table in front of me—I probably never would have worn it at all. I probably would have balled it up in a wad of tissue paper and stashed it away in an oatmeal box.

Madly scooping the diamonds up in both hands, I tucked them back into their tissue nest and squashed the paper package back inside the Quaker carton. *Great hiding place, Judy!* I said to myself, and to my new spiritual protégé. *You were probably murdered because of these diamonds, but at least you kept your killer from finding them and profiting from your death. And by hiding the diamonds so well, you may have provided a traceable clue to your killer's identity. Clever girl.*

Stubbing my cigarette in the ashtray, I put the top back on the cereal box and whisked the closed container across the room to the cabinet above my kitchen sink. Sliding my small stock of Campbell's soups to one side, I made room for the container in the back of the cabinet, next to an unopened jar of peanut butter. As I was putting the carton on the shelf, my stomach growled again, and for a moment I actually considered making myself a bowl of oatmeal. (Can you believe that? I'm such a dope sometimes.) Luckily, I came to my sleuth-based senses before I ate the evidence.

Stomach still gurgling, I scooted back to the kitchen table to look through the other stuff in the shoebox. Everything Terry had said would be there *was* there: Terry's home phone number and address, Judy's address, Mrs. Londergan's apartment number and phone number, the names and address of Judy's former roommates.

The two photographs were there as well, and I snatched them both up for a closer look. The first was a grinning close-up—a wallet-sized headshot of a slightly pudgy blonde, with short bangs and a long ponytail, and a pair of dimples deep as canyons. She was wearing a dark sweater over a white-collared dickey.

I recognized the uniform—it was a high school yearbook photo. Judy Catcher's, I presumed. She looked so young, and so sweet, and so *vulnerable* that I wanted to pat her dimpled cheeks and tell her everything was going to be all right—even though it clearly wasn't.

The other picture was a candid snapshot, a slightly blurry black-and-white image of two people cavorting on the sidewalk in front of a Walgreen's drugstore. One of the people was Judy. She was older and thinner now, wearing a plaid sheath skirt, a black sweater, black nylons, black flats, and her short blonde hair was styled like Marilyn's (Monroe or the former Mrs. DiMaggio, take your pick). One hand was propped on her hip and her head was thrown back in laughter—such outright laughter you could almost hear it.

Judy's other hand was stretched out in front of her, gracefully, like a dancer's, and was resting on the shoulder of the other person in the picture—a tall, thin, dark-haired young man dressed all in black and sporting a neatly trimmed mustache and a Vandyke beard. He was looking directly into the camera, glowering like a comic book villain, and cradling one of those long skinny little weenie dogs—a pointy-faced dachshund—in the crook of his arm.

I gazed at the two photos for an eternity (okay, five or ten minutes), smoking another cigarette and peering deep into those gray paper faces (even the dog's), searching for psychic clues, trying to pull the truth—like a rabbit—out of my perfectly empty hat. But I finally abandoned that balmy endeavor. Who did I think I was, anyway? The Great Houdini? The Great Goof was more like it.

How had I ever let Terry talk me into this mess? What part of my feeble brain had allowed me to think—even for a second—that I could crack another murder case? Was I a mindless, thrill-seeking adventuress or just a mad glutton for punishment? And now that I'd given my *promise*—my truly honest and heartfelt promise to help—how was I going to keep my big fat commitment to Terry a big fat secret from Dan?

Head spinning, and heart reeling with the fear of my own inadequacy, I couldn't bear to think about the murder anymore. I stuffed the names, addresses, phone numbers, and photos back in the shoebox, and put the shoebox on the top shelf of my coat closet. I hung up my coat, propped my snowboots on the floor near the radiator, washed the dishes, and cleaned out the ashtray (I may not be a mental magician, but at least I'm tidy!). Then I heaved a dramatic, self-pitying sigh and directed my stocking feet toward the squeaky narrow staircase leading to my creaky narrow bed.

# Chapter 6

I WAS HALFWAY UP THE STAIRS WHEN THE phone rang. I spun around and scrambled back down to the living room to answer it, hoping it would be Dan.

"Hellohhhhh?" I said, making my voice as soft and sultry as possible in case it *was*.

"Hi there," Dan said, in his deep, delicious baritone. "Did I wake you up? You sound kind of groggy."

So much for sultry. "I wasn't sleeping," I admitted, reverting to my normal voice, "but I *am* tired. I was just on my way up to bed."

"Tough day?"

He should only know. "It was the worst!" I exclaimed, widening my eyes and flapping my lashes, doing my best Lucille Ball—even though Dan couldn't see me. "We had to meet a major deadline at work," I told him, furtively evading all mention of you-know-who and what, "and all the afternoon pickups and deliveries were late because of the snow."

I felt terrible that I had—once again—put myself in the position of having to hide the truth from Dan, but I soothed my feelings of guilt by reminding myself that it was his own darn fault. I mean, if Dan hadn't *forbidden* me to ever get involved in another unsolved murder case (which was a pretty harsh ordinance when you consider my line of work!) then I wouldn't have *had* to be keeping any secrets from him. I could have told him all about my late husband's friend Terry Catcher, and the horrible murder of his little sister Judy, and the diamond jewelry hidden in the oatmeal box. And then Dan might have been able to *help* me instead of making me feel like a felon—and lie like a rug.

Okay, okay! I guess I'm not really being fair here. I mean, I *knew* the main reason Dan ordered me off the Babs Comstock story—and all dangerous murder stories thereafter—was for my own protection. And I knew he felt even *more* protective of me now that we'd become romantically involved. And I loved the fact that he worried about me so much—I really, really did! But that didn't change the fact that I'd wanted to be both a true crime writer and a mystery novelist since I was a freshman (freshgirl?) in high school. And—though Dan's deep concern for me was a continuing source of joyous, heart-soaring delight—it still wasn't enough to make me relinquish the only real career goals I'd ever had. No matter how dangerous (or unwomanly) they happened to be.

And now I had an even more compelling reason to pursue those goals. I had someone who was *depending* on me to exercise my sleuthing skills. How could I possibly turn my back on Terry Catcher? He had been Bob's best friend in Korea, and one of the last people to see my husband alive. Bob had risked his own life to save Terry's. Twice! So wasn't it only natural that I should feel responsible for Terry, too? I couldn't save his sister's life, but I *could* try to find out who had caused her death. And I knew that's what Bob would want me to do.

"I had a rough day, too," Dan said, oblivious to my inner turmoil. "Two prostitutes slashed to ribbons in Bryant Park. No witnesses because of the storm. Luckily, a mailman decided to cut through the park and found the bodies. He notified the station immediately, and we got there pretty quick, but it was snowing so hard that whatever clues there may have been were already buried. No footprints except the mailman's. By that time, even the corpses were covered. And the ambulance had a hell of a time getting down the snowbound street to the scene. I was there all afternoon and evening, digging through the bloody ice, freezing my castanets off."

"That's awful!" I cried, glad the focus of our conversation had shifted from my day to his, and hoping I could keep it that way. "But how do you know the victims were prostitutes?" I asked. "Have the bodies been identified?"

"Yes, that was the easy . . ."

"And what about the weapon? Did you find a knife or anything?"

"Uh, no, we . . ."

"Did you check out the mailman? His story sounds kind of fishy to me. Why would he cut through the park in the middle of a snowstorm?"

"Hold it right there, Paige!" Dan said, in his toughest law enforcement tone. "No more questions. I've told you too much as it is. And don't think for one second you're going to play detective again and write a big story about this case. I'll stop you before you even sharpen your pencil." He sounded so cute I wanted to kiss him on the neck. His lovable but insufferably *stiff* neck.

"The thought never crossed my mind," I said, telling the truth and nothing but the truth (if you don't count the pouty inflection I put in my voice to give Dan the impression—just the slightest hint, I swear!—that he may have hurt my feelings). "I'm innocent of all charges!"

"That's my girl," Dan said, relieved. "You know I hate to be a bear, but it's only for your own good."

"I know . . . I know!" I said, heaving a huge (and totally honest) sigh. Then I quickly changed the subject. "I'm sorry you had to stay out in the cold so long. Have you thawed out yet? Where are you now?"

"Back at Headquarters. Got a lot of paperwork."

"Can't it wait until tomorrow?" I asked, suddenly longing for his company. I wasn't feeling tired anymore. Now I was just feeling lonely. Desperately lonely. (The specter of death often has that effect on me.) "Come on over for a nightcap," I begged, neglecting to mention that all I had in the house to drink was Dr. Pepper.

"I'd love to, Paige, but I really can't. Too much work, and the driving's impossible. I even canceled my regular Monday evening visit with Katy," he said, referring to his much beloved fourteen-year-old daughter—his only child (and the only happy outcome of his very unhappy marriage to the vain, unfaithful wife he divorced some six years ago). "I've got at least an hour's worth of forms to fill out," he grumbled, "and with all this snow, it could take me *two* hours to get downtown to you."

That wasn't what I wanted to hear. "Come on-a my house, my house-a come on," I crooned, trying to sing like Rosemary Clooney, but surely sounding more like Andy Devine. "I'm-a gonna give-a you figs and dates and grapes and cakes . . ."

Dan chuckled, and the way his laughter curled around in his throat made my skin tingle. "Very tempting," he said, "but I've got to write these reports up now, while the facts are still clear in my mind. And I thought you said you were tired . . . on your way up to bed."

"The sound of your voice rejuvenated me," I told him. "And I feel sorry for your cold castanets."

The minute those words were out of my mouth, my face turned hot as a bonfire. I hardly ever made suggestive comments like that (except to Mike and Mario, when I was trying to deflect *their* suggestive comments to *me*). And I *never* spoke that way to Dan. Really! I don't know what came over me. Either I'd lost my head in the whirlwind of the day's startling and emotional events, or I'd picked up a racy (okay, *raunchy*) new manner of self-expression just from hanging out with Abby.

If Dan was shocked by my risqué remark, he didn't let on. If anything, he seemed pleased. Another deep chuckle came rumbling through the receiver, ending in a long, luscious (dare I say lusty?) sigh. "I'll come tomorrow night," he said. "Snow or no snow. Around nine o'clock. Will that be okay?"

"Sure thing, Sergeant," I said, trying to sound cool though my face was still flaming. "Be there or be square."

• • •

AS ON-EDGE AND ANXIOUS AS I WAS, I FELL asleep the minute my bones hit the mattress. It wasn't a deep and restful sleep—I kept thrashing around in the tangled covers, dreaming about guns, and diamonds, and dimples, and dachshunds, and soldiers with snow for hair—but at least I squirmed through the night in a somewhat unconscious state, and when my alarm clock woke me up in the morning I felt somewhat refreshed.

I showered, dressed (black wool skirt, pale yellow sweater set), slapped on some makeup, and hurried downstairs to the coat closet. The Thom McAn shoebox was there, right where I'd put it on the shelf, proving beyond the shadow of a doubt that the upsetting events of the previous day had been real, not an invention of my freaky imagination. I took the shoebox down, yanked off the lid, and dumped Terry's notes and the two photos out on the table. Then I scraped the scattered items into a neat little pile, stuffed the pile into the side pocket of my large black leather clutch bag (next to the newspaper clips about the murder), and zipped it closed.

After putting on all my outerwear—my camel's hair coat, black beret, black gloves, green plaid muffler, and warm, dry, fur-lined, ankle-high snowboots—I stepped over to the cabinet above the kitchen sink and pulled it open. The white-haired man in the Quaker hat was still there, smiling out at me from the shadows, standing tall behind the Campbell's soup cans like a faithful yeoman of the guard. I gave him a sly wink and a grateful curtsy, closed the cabinet door, and left for work.

No traffic was moving on Bleecker. The cars lining the curb were all buried under a foot of snow, and there was an accumulation of at least ten inches in the street. The sidewalks weren't much better. A few bundled-up pedestrians were making their way to the subway (and onward, I assumed, to work), but they were walking very slowly and carefully, in single file, along narrow footpaths that had been worn, like trenches, through the hardening snowbanks.

It was colder than a butcher's freezer, but at least it wasn't snowing anymore. Wrapping my muffler over the lower half of my face so my breath would keep my nose warm, and hugging my clutch bag in close to my chest like a baby, I joined the slow-moving procession toward Sixth Avenue and the West 4th Street entrance to the BMT.

It was freezing cold below ground, too. The handful of people waiting near the track for the uptown train were standing unusually close together—in an almost-but-not-quite huddle—hoping, I realized, to draw some warmth from each other. I wormed my way into the middle of the small crowd and stood there, shivering, watching everybody's breath turn to steam, until the train screeched into the station.

It was one of the older, heavier, clankier trains—the kind that had been around since the late 1920s—with the long, segmented, caterpillar-like cars. When the doors slid open, I scurried into the closest car, hoping the air would be warmer inside. It was—a little. Sitting down in the first forward-facing seat I came to, I carefully arranged my coat underneath my legs to keep my nylons from snagging on the frayed rattan seats.

The train was old, but the overhead advertisements were new. Judy Garland smiled down from one of the posters, proclaiming that Westmore lipstick had been KISS-TESTED, and had PROVED BEST in movie close-ups, while right across the aisle—dressed in a white evening gown and proudly smoking a cigarette—Mrs. Francis Irénéé du Pont II of Wilmington and New York, "one of Society's most charming young matrons," declared she wouldn't go anywhere without her Camels. Dean Martin and Jerry Lewis made hostile faces at each other in an ad for *The Colgate Comedy Hour,* and the owners of a certain brewery were proud to present Miss Adrienne Garrott—a golden-skinned girl with a thick, foamy head of light blonde hair—as Miss Rheingold of 1954 (I wondered if she'd been chosen for her likeness to a glass of beer). There were lots of other ads, too—for products like Ovaltine, Tussy lotion, Duz detergent, Camay soap, Odo-ro-no cream deodorant, and (eerily enough) Thom McAn shoes—and I dutifully scanned them all.

I was beginning to read the ads all over again, for the

fourth and (I hoped) final time, when the train pulled into the Times Square station. As soon as the doors opened, I jumped out onto the platform and dashed through the underground depot to the 42nd Street shuttle. Then I got on *that* train, and stood—lurching and swaying from a leather hand strap near the door (not even *one* of the male passengers got up to offer me his seat!)—until the shuttle reached the Third Avenue stop. My stop.

A short block's trudge through the snow, a quick dash into the lobby coffee shop for my take-out morning muffin, a fast flight up nine floors in the elevator, a brisk stroll down the hall to the third door on the left, and I finally walked into the cold, dark *Daring Detective* office.

As always (i.e., as *required*), I was the first employee to arrive. One of my primary daily duties was to make the place comfortable—turn on all the lights, warm up the radiators, open the blinds, gather up the newspapers, sort the mail and so forth—for my five male "superiors," who wouldn't begin rolling in until thirty minutes later.

The early bird catches the worm, they say, but in my case it just meant I got to make the coffee.

"SO WHAT WAS IN THE SHOEBOX?" LENNY asked me as soon as he stumbled into the office. He was still gasping for breath from his nine-floor climb. His black-rimmed glasses sat crookedly on his large hook nose, giving him the appearance of a cockeyed goose.

"Shhhhhh!" I hissed, holding my index finger up to my lips, jerking my head toward Harvey Crockett's private office, where our ex-newsman boss sat swilling coffee and reading the papers—with his door (and probably his ears) wide open. "I'm secretly working on a new story," I whispered. "I'll tell you all about it later."

Lenny looked like he was going to pop. "Another murder story?" His lips were murmuring, but his eyes were screaming their heads off. He was, I knew, scared that I might be getting involved in something I shouldn't. Something perilous and catastrophic. Something that might—in some seemingly indirect, but still horribly injurious way—involve him. Like the last time.

"Don't worry, Lenny," I quickly replied, trying to soothe him with my soft, steady tone. "I'm not in any danger at all. This is just a simple, straightforward murder case that the police are too lazy to solve. I'm looking into it for a friend of mine, actually a good friend of Bob's."

"Oh, I get it!" Lenny said, in a voice so acidic it could have stripped the enamel off the side of a bus. "You're just skipping through a field of daisies, singing 'Little Things Mean a Lot,' and looking for another cold-blooded killer to play hide and seek with." His normally thin, pale face was puffed up like a pink balloon. "And there's nothing for me to worry about because you're doing this for a good friend, right? Oh, no! Excuse me! I've got that all wrong, you're doing it for a good friend of *Bob's!* Your wonderful, perfect—need I remind you, *dead?*—husband Bob."

Lenny had gone too far, and he knew it. Way too far. His puffy face registered a sudden look of horror and disbelief, then melted into a soggy mass of shame. "I'm sorry, Paige," he muttered, staring down at his feet with the intensity of a man who'd just discovered he was standing barefoot in a briar patch. "Please forgive me. That was an awful thing to say. I didn't mean it the way it sounded."

"I know you didn't mean it, Lenny," I said, quickly brushing my fingers down the side of his cheek and shoulder, then resting them on the damp sleeve of his thin black overcoat. "And I don't blame you for being worried. But, please believe me, there's no reason for you to . . ."

The office entrance bell jingled, and in walked Mike and Mario.

"Hey, what's going on here?" Mario cried, when he saw me standing up close to Lenny with my hand on his arm. "This is an office, not a dance hall! So ditch the tango, Zimmerman, and get to work!" Ever since Lenny had saved my life, Mario had been extremely jealous of his assistant's newborn hero status (and of his newborn friendship with me).

"Maybe he's not dancing," Mike chimed in, snickering. "Maybe he's just turning a Paige!"

They laughed like insane hyenas for a couple of seconds, then began hanging their hats and coats and mufflers on the tree. Embarrassed by their gibes (and still mortified by his own hurtful remarks to me), Lenny pulled away from me and slunk over to his desk, plopping down in his chair with his coat still on. Then, as if prompted by a slapstick comedy director with a sadistic sense of timing, Harvey Crockett stuck his big bulldog head out of his office and hollered, "More coffee!"

My workday was off to a splendid start.

# Chapter 7

POMEROY SAUNTERED INTO THE OFFICE around noon, and I scooted out ten minutes later. It was foolhardy of me to even *think* of traveling all the way across town and back on my short lunch hour, but I was so eager to meet Mrs. Londergan and talk to her about Judy that I simply couldn't wait until the end of the day.

Retracing part of my morning commute, I took the shuttle back to Times Square, then the IRT down to 28th Street. Two blocks south on Seventh, a half a block west on 26th, and I found myself standing on the snowy sidewalk in front of the gray stone tenement building where Judy Catcher had lived. And died. A shiver ran down my spine that had nothing to do with the cold.

Sucking in a blast of frosty air, I made my way up the shoveled but slippery stoop to the building's front door and stepped inside. The tiled entryway was equipped with sixteen metal mailboxes and sixteen buzzers. Each mailbox had a name on it, so I didn't have to rummage through the papers in my purse—the notes Terry had given me—to figure out which bell to ring.

Mrs. Londergan lived in 2C. I pushed the buzzer—hard. No answer. I waited a few seconds and pushed it again.

"Who's there?" came a crackly voice over the intercom. "If you're selling, I'm not buying. And my soul doesn't need saving either."

I had a feeling I was going to like this woman. "You don't know me, Mrs. Londergan," I said, speaking into the intercom. "My name is Paige Turner and I—"

"Oh, sure!" she broke in. "And I'm Jim Dandy. So what's your real name and what's your game?"

"No, really!" I said. "Paige Turner *is* my real name, and I'm a friend of Judy Catcher's brother Terry. I was wondering if I could come in for a moment and talk to you about Judy? I won't take up too much of your time."

There was a long silence and no reply. Then, suddenly, the inner door buzzed open, and I pushed my way into the hall. The lighting was dim, but I could see the numbers on the apartment doors: 1A to my left, 1B to my right. I dashed up the stairs to the second floor and headed straight for the left rear apartment, which I figured would be 2C.

It was. I heard a rustling noise on the other side of the door, so I knew Mrs. Londergan was standing right there, probably peering at me through the peephole. Trying to mask my nosy detective face with a look of pure sweet innocence, I lifted my brows, fluttered my lashes, and lightly knocked on the door.

She opened it at once. Standing tall (very tall!) in the doorway, with one hand on the doorknob and the other one on her hip, she thrust her chiseled chin in my direction and said, "How'd you ever get a stupid name like Paige Turner?"

I giggled—not just because she had so cheekily branded my stupid name with the adjective it deserved, but also because she was the spitting image of John Wayne. I kid you not. An aging John Wayne in a red flowered dress. With a swipe of bright red lipstick and a cap of short wavy blue-gray hair. It would have made you giggle, too.

"It's my married name," I told her. "My parents are wise and kind. They never would have saddled me with such a silly signature."

She smiled. A sly, smirky John Wayne smile. "So you actually took the name of your own accord? Love makes us do the craziest things!" Shaking her head and shrugging her brawny shoulders, she moved her large frame out of the doorway and motioned for me to enter. "Come on in, Paige Turner. I'll make you a cup of tea."

"Thank you," I said, stifling the urge to giggle again. I'd never thought of John Wayne as a tea drinker.

ONE STEP INSIDE THE APARTMENT AND I was in the kitchen. A cozy little kitchen with a green linoleum floor and a ruffled gingham curtain on the only window, which offered a sunless view of the gray stone wall of the building next door. A small table and two chairs sat near the window, and I thought *we'd* be sitting there, too, but my husky hostess led me on through the tiny kitchen, into the next chamber of her small railroad flat—an even tinier sitting room with no window at all.

"Take off your coat and have a seat," she said, directing me to one of the two chintz-covered wing chairs positioned on either side of a low, round coffee (okay, *tea*) table. On the table were several silver-framed family photographs, a silver cigarette box, and a lamp with a fringed shade. The only other furniture in the room was a Philco television—a large wooden floor model with a small round screen.

I handed Mrs. Londergan my coat and she carried it into the next room—her bedroom—and put it on the bed. I could see what she was doing because there was no door, no wall—not even a folding screen—between the bedroom and the sitting room.

"Hold on a second," she said, walking back through the sitting room and into the kitchen again. "I'll put the kettle on."

I was starting to get antsy, afraid the whole tea-for-two ritual would take up so much time I wouldn't get to ask enough questions. Deciding not to wait for her to return to the sitting room to begin my investigation, I called out, "Are all of the apartments in this building the same as yours, Mrs. Londergan? Same layout, same number of rooms?"

"Yep!" she answered, running some water, clanging a pot on the stove. "They're all the same. Skinny little railroads with open-ended rooms. Makes it easier for the cockroaches to get around. The only room that has a door is the bathroom. Gotta be grateful for small favors." She had a deep voice for a woman, and a flat midwestern accent.

"Judy Catcher lived right across the hall from you, right? In 2D?"

"That's right," she said, adding nothing but a long, sad, heavy sigh. She opened and closed the refrigerator, scraped and scrambled through the silverware drawer, then rattled some china around. I thought she was making more noise than was absolutely necessary, but I could have been imagining things. Or maybe this was just the normal kind of racket made by a very large woman living in a very small space.

"Did you hear or see anything the night Judy was shot?" I asked..

"No. I wasn't home. I was down the street at Milly Esterbrook's playing canasta. Our landlord discovered the body and it had already been removed by the time I got home."

"Terry told me that you and Judy were really close—that she was like a daughter to you."

"That's true," she said. "I really loved that girl. Did my best to help her. Her mother died when she was just a baby, so . . . hey, whaddaya want in your tea? Cream? Lemon? Sugar?"

"Nothing at all, thank you," I said, just hoping to speed the process along. I really wanted cream and sugar, but I *didn't* want to make her take the time. My throat was getting sore from talking so loudly. "So what was Judy like?" I probed, trying to get her involved in the conversation instead of the tea preparation. "Was she as tough and feisty as Terry said she was, or was that just an act—a ploy to hide her insecurity?"

For some reason, that question got Mrs. Londergan's undivided attention. Suddenly planting her large body in the doorless doorway from the kitchen to the sitting room, she propped both hands on her hips, craned her sharply sculpted chin toward me, and said, "Okay, Paige Turner. Why are you *really* here? You say you're a friend of Terry Catcher's, but how do I know that's true? You could be a goddamn insurance investigator, for all I know. Why do you want to talk to me about Judy? Why are you asking me all these sneaky questions?"

"I'm sorry, Mrs. Londergan," I quickly replied. "I should have explained myself sooner. I'm a writer, a true crime reporter. I work for *Daring Detective* magazine, and Terry Catcher has asked me to look into the facts surrounding his sister's death. He believes Judy was intentionally murdered, *not* killed during a random burglary."

She softened her wide shoulders and pulled in her chin. "Oh," she said, staring down at the sitting room carpet for a few seconds. Then she returned to the kitchen and knocked some more china around. Finally, after what seemed like an hour but was probably less than a minute, she came back into the sitting room carrying two cups of tea on a small tray. She set the tray down on the table, and sat herself down in the chair across from me.

"You know, I wondered about that myself," she said, aiming her eyes (which were every bit as blue as the Duke's) directly into mine. "I thought, what if there really wasn't any burglary? What if Judy *knew* the person who killed her? I asked the police about this, but they said I was barking up the wrong tree—that I had no reason to question their findings. The detective in charge, a nasty little man named Sweeny, actually told me to stop being a busybody. I don't know about you, but I really hate it when a man patronizes me like that. Makes me want to knock his block off."

I laughed out loud. Not only did I share Mrs. Londergan's sentiments about patronizing men, but I knew that if one of them really deserved to get his block knocked off by a woman, *she* would be the best one for the job.

"Sweeny gave Terry Catcher the brush-off, too," I told her. "Once he latched onto the random burglary premise, he wouldn't let go. Case closed. He wouldn't even *consider* Terry's theory about the murder. That's why Terry asked me to scout around. He's hoping I can dig up enough evidence to convince the cops to get back on the case."

"Poor Mr. Catcher," she said. "Such a nice young man. And so devoted to his sister!"

"Yes," I said, keeping a lid on my emotions, too pressed for time to sink into the sadness of the situation. "You said you tried to *help* Judy," I interjected, hating to change the subject so abruptly, but feeling desperate to speed things up. "What did you mean by that, Mrs. Londergan? What kind of help did Judy need?"

"Call me Elsie," she said. "My friends all call me Elsie, but my given name is Elspeth." (I was surprised it wasn't Marion.) She picked up her tea and slurped it noisily.

"Okay," I replied, groaning to myself, watching a steady stream of sand plummet to the base of an imaginary hourglass. "Elsie it is." I held my teacup aloft, as if in a toast, then took a big swig. After nursing my scorched tongue for a second or two, I urgently repeated the question. "So tell me, Elsie, what kind of help did Judy need?"

"Every kind."

"Can you be more specific?"

"Mothering, understanding, encouragement, advice—she needed it all. She was over here all the time, asking me what should she do about this, and what should she do about that, and which blouse looks best with this skirt, and what should she have for dinner, and why does every man she falls in love with have brown eyes? She was a bundle of self-absorption and instability. Just what you would expect from a girl who had no mother, and whose father was a worthless drunk."

"But Terry said she was strong and tough—that she was a real fighter. That's one of the reasons he doesn't buy Sweeny's conclusion that she was shot by a burglar. Terry thinks that if Judy had found an intruder in her apartment, she would have jumped him and beaten him to a pulp. Or *tried* to, anyway—in which case there would have been at least one or two cuts or bruises on her body. And there was nothing. Not even a scratch."

Elsie frowned. "Yes, Judy *was* very strong. Physically, I mean, not emotionally. Emotionally, she was weak as a kitten. But bodily? Ha! She had more muscles than Marciano! And she wasn't afraid to use them. She had a violent temper too—could be a real hellion sometimes. She kicked our landlord in the shin once, when he tried to pinch her on the bottom, and she ripped a big hank of hair out of her former roommate's scalp because the girl was flirting with her boyfriend."

Finally we were getting somewhere. "Speaking of boyfriends," I said, leaping to take advantage of the lead-in, "was Judy seeing anyone special at the time of the murder?"

"No. Her most recent beau had just ended their relationship, and she hadn't found a new replacement yet. She was gearing up for a serious manhunt, though. Judy couldn't bear to be without a boyfriend for long."

"Who had just broken up with her?"

"A man named Gregory Smith—but if you believe that was his *real* name, you're as big a fool as Judy. He was an older man—much older than she was. Hell, he was probably even older than me! He was married, too, but that didn't bother Judy one bit. She really loved the guy, and as far as she was concerned, he could do no wrong." Elsie's voice was dripping with disapproval.

"I take it you didn't like him very much."

"It wasn't personal. I hate *all* snakes."

"What made you think he was a snake?"

"I didn't think it, I *knew* it. Show me an oversexed old married man who's lured an emotionally unstable nineteen-year-old girl into becoming his love slave, and I'll show you a snake."

"From what I hear, Judy was quite capable of turning *herself* into a love slave. Terry said she would do anything for the man she loved, and that she fell in love at the drop of a hat."

Elsie took another slurp of tea. "Well, that's true, too, but . . ." she placed her teacup back down on the tray and gave me a mournful look, ". . . but Judy deserves your sympathy instead of your scorn. She was so hungry for love she would accept it from almost any source. Gregory Smith, on the other hand," she said, pronouncing the name with a thick slur of contempt, "was merely hungry for sex. And he was willing to deceive his wife—and ruin a young girl's future—just to satisfy his own greedy desires. In my book, he's nothing but a snake. A perverted and poisonous snake."

"Did you tell Judy how you felt?"

"Of course. I was always honest with her. I told her to dump the bastard and move back to her old apartment, with her old roommates."

"But why would she have had to move?"

"Because, cheap and shoddy as it is, she couldn't afford this palace on her own. She only lived here because *he* wanted her to. And because he signed the lease and paid the rent."

*So Judy* did *have a rich boyfriend!* I squealed to myself. A *little* rich, at least. Rich enough to put Judy up in a private playhouse without breaking his own household budget. But was he rich enough to buy her thirty thousand dollars' worth of diamonds. too?

My pulse was pounding with the thrill of the chase. I was Philip Marlowe on the verge of a brilliant breakthrough! I was Sam Spade on the prowl! I was Nick and Nora Charles rolled into one! I was taking so long for lunch I was going to get canned the minute I got back to the office!

"Oh, my God!" I cried, gaping at my watch in disbelief. "I totally lost track of the time! I was supposed to be back at work a half hour ago. I have to leave right now!" I jumped to my feet and lunged into the bedroom for my coat.

"But you didn't drink your tea."

"I know, I know! I'm really sorry, Mrs. Londergan . . . er, Elsie," I said, heading back into the sitting room, buttoning my coat, and putting on my gloves. "I wish I could stay. There's so much I wanted to talk to you about, and I haven't even scratched the surface! Can I come back later this evening, after I get off from work, and talk to you some more?"

She stood up and walked me into the kitchen. "Sorry, Paige Turner," she said, patting her blue-gray permanent waves into place. "I'm playing bingo tonight, and I'm feeling lucky. If I hit the jackpot I could win three dollars! And I really need the extra dough."

Centrifugal force, my foot. Whether it's thirty thousand smackers or only three, it's *moolah* that makes the world go round.

"Then how about tomorrow evening?" I begged. "Around six? I'll buy you a hamburger."

"Throw in a bottle of beer and we're on." She was patting her hair like Betty Furness, but she still looked—and sounded—like John Wayne.

"Bottles are for babies," I said, mimicking a corny cowboy drawl. "We'll roll out the whole darn barrel."

# Chapter 8

SOMETIMES I'M LUCKY, BUT USUALLY I'M not. And this was one of the usual days. When I got back to the office, Brandon Pomeroy was sitting smug as a prison warden at his desk, smoking his pipe, fingering his neatly trimmed mustache, and glaring at me as if I were an inmate who'd just been caught trying to dig through the wall of her cell with a spoon.

"Did anyone ever teach you how to tell time, Mrs. Turner?" His voice was dripping with condescension. "When the big hand is on the twelve, and the little hand is on the one, your lunch hour is officially over."

"Yes, sir, I'm sorry I'm so late, but . . ."

"Just look at the clock, Mrs. Turner, and tell me what you see. Where is the big hand?"

"On the three, sir," I said, with a sickening sigh of surrender. I knew better than to try to explain myself. Even if I'd had a perfectly reasonable and *true* explanation to offer, it would have fallen on deaf (or, rather, *diabolical*) ears.

"And the little hand, Mrs. Turner? Pray tell, where is the little hand?" His beady brown eyes were gleaming with pleasure. Stripping and whipping the slaves was Pomeroy's all-time favorite hobby.

"On the two."

"*Sir,*" he said. "On the two, *sir.*"

"*Sir,*" I repeated, looking at the clock again. "On the two, *sir.*" Time sure does fly when you're having fun.

Pomeroy shot a quick glance over his shoulder to make sure Mike and Mario and Lenny were all paying attention. They were. Turning back to me, he said, "So, Mrs. Turner, if the big hand is on the three, and the little hand is on the two, what time is it?"

"Two-fifteen, sir."

"Very good, Mrs. Turner!" he jeered. "I see you *can* tell time after all!" He took a deep pull on his pipe, then puffed a stream of fruity fumes in my direction. "Which means you knowingly and willfully—and totally without permission, I might add—extended your lunch break a full hour and fifteen minutes past your allotted time. Which means I would be well within my rights to terminate your employment right now—this very *minute*—before you can steal any more of the *company's* time."

All this from a man who typically spent a grand total of three hours and ten minutes a day at his desk, and most of it in a drunken snooze. I wondered what ugly twist of fate had caused him to be awake and sober now.

"But I'm a softhearted man," Pomeroy went on, "and it would pain me to have to dismiss you right before Christmas." (And I believed *that* as much as I believed in Santa Claus.) "So I'm just going to dock ten dollars from your salary this week, and disallow your lunch hour tomorrow. That's more than equitable, wouldn't you agree?" His cocky smirk dared me to protest.

"Fair enough, sir," I said, standing tall as a tree, looking him straight in the eye, refusing to let him—or any of my gawking coworkers—see me squirm. I'd do all my squirming later, when I was alone—when I could moan and wail about how I was going to pay all my bills, and purchase Christmas presents, and take Elsie Londergan out to dinner, in private.

"I'm glad we understand each other," Pomeroy said with a sniff. "Now take off your coat and get to work. Mike's new story needs editing."

What he meant was rewritten. Mike's lousy stories *always* had to be rewritten. By me, of course—which was the *real* reason Pomeroy didn't fire me. Without me (or somebody else with a halfway literate brain), Pomeroy might actually have to do some of the editorial work himself. Which would put a serious crimp in his afternoon napping activities.

"Yes, sir," I said, hanging up my hat and coat, then beginning the short but endlessly humiliating walk to my desk. Halfway there, I stopped dead in my tracks for a second—just long enough to throw an imaginary pie in Pomeroy's smirking face. I made sure the pie was made of soap suds and sawdust, so it couldn't possibly taste good. Even in my most feverish fantasies, I'm a stickler for details.

THE MINUTE I GOT OFF WORK I WENT TO Chockful O' Nuts. I was so hungry I thought I was going to die. A woman can't live without lunch, you know. No lunch yesterday, no lunch today, and no lunch hour tomorrow. The Case of the Missing Lunch! I had to figure out a way to solve this one, or I'd wind up playing the title role in the soon to be released sequel—The Case of the Walking Skeleton.

I sat on a stool at the crowded counter and ordered the same thing I always order when I'm at Chockful—cream cheese on datenut bread and a bowl of chicken noodle soup. Chockful has the best soup in the world. Even better than Campbell's.

When I finished eating I hit the subways again. West on the shuttle, south on the IRT. I was dying to go home and tell Abby about everything that was happening (and have a cocktail or two—okay, *three*), but instead of going all the way down to Christopher Street—the subway stop closest to my apartment—I followed a sudden urgent impulse and got off at 34th Street, the stop for Macy's. Christmas was just four days away, you see, and though I'd already sent a box of gifts home to my family in Kansas City, I still had three presents to buy: one for Abby, one for Lenny, and one for Dan. And while I was there, I figured, I might as well pay a little visit to the lingerie department—Judy Catcher's department.

The sidewalks around Macy's were snowless. So many people had been walking in and out all day, and circling the store to look at the dazzling window displays, that even the cement was worn down. Ordinarily I would have taken the time to join the crowds of oooohing and aaaahing window gazers—to observe and admire the magical exhibits of mechanical angels, puppies, children, elves, and reindeer that Macy's was so famous for—but tonight I had more important things to do: buy gifts for my friends, and try to solve a murder.

I entered the store, crammed myself into the crowded elevator, called my number out to the operator and headed up toward the seventh floor, wondering how many times Judy Catcher had stood in this same tiny wood-paneled box, rising toward the same destination. When the doors popped open, I squeezed my way out and approached the heavily decorated entry to the floor, trying to get my bearings. I looked for a sign saying Lingerie, but there was none. There were just tons of twinkling lights, dancing candy canes, and great high clouds of angel hair with little cherubs sitting around on top of them like babies at a picnic.

Music was coming from somewhere to my right. Choral music. A crisp, perky rendition of "Come All Ye Faithful." I wondered if the song was beckoning me to come to Bethlehem, or to the Lingerie department. Repelled by the grating sound, I turned left and began walking down a wide aisle thick with boughs of holly, sprigs of mistletoe, and herds of people in a hurry. I didn't know where I was going, but I figured I'd run into the brassieres and underpants eventually. All roads lead to Rome. (Or is it Bethlehem?)

Unfortunately, the road was long. I had to fight my way through Women's Robes, Women's Nightgowns, and Women's Hosiery before I reached the underwear zone. And—even more unfortunately—when I got there the real live Christmas carolers were there, too, looking every bit as robotic as the other mechanical holiday displays, singing "It Came Upon a Midnight Clear" in voices so loud and chirpy I wanted to pluck some angel hair off the lowest cloud and stuff it in my ears.

There were three salesladies working the Lingerie department, and I made a beeline for the youngest one—a plump, freckled redhead wearing a fuzzy white scoop-neck sweater and a wide green velvet ribbon tied around her neck in a bow. She was short and cute, and she looked to be about Judy's age.

"Merry Christmas!" she piped as I lurched up to her counter. "May I help you?" She had big green eyes and a surprisingly throaty voice.

"I hope so," I said. "I'm looking for a present for a friend of mine. Her favorite color is red and she loves sexy lingerie almost as much as the men she wears it for."

The girl let out a husky giggle. "I think we have just the thing—a red bra, panties, and garter belt set. It's a special Macy's Christmas item." (Sounded more like Frederick's of Hollywood to me.)

"Perfect," I said. "May I see it?" I knew I couldn't afford such an elaborate gift, but I decided to take a look anyway. And while I was at it, I figured, I could look for a good way to bring Judy Catcher's name into the conversation.

"Sure. Come this way. We have the set on display." The girl led me down to the far end of the counter, then pointed out the three red lace-trimmed items arranged on the middle shelf of the glass-topped showcase.

The minute I saw the outrageously bright and naughty see-through undergarments, I knew Abby would love them. (And get a lot of use out of them, too.) "How much for the whole trio?" I asked.

"You're in luck," she said. "The set just went on sale this morning. It was originally priced at nine dollars and ninety-four cents, but now it's just seven eighty-five."

I gulped. That was a whole lot more than I paid for underwear from the Sears Roebuck catalog. And I felt a little funny even considering buying Abby such an expensive and intimate gift. Still, I knew she would go wild for the lacy red stuff, and I wanted to give her something really nice and uplifting. (That's not a dumb bra joke, I swear! I meant as nice and uplifting as the free cocktails Abby was always giving me.)

"Can I pay by check?" I asked. I knew without looking I didn't have that much cash in my wallet. I never had that much cash in my wallet. I *did* have that much money in my checking account, though—plus a whole four dollars and fifteen cents more.

"Do you have any identification?"

"Yes . . . a Social Security card and a driver's license." (When Bob and I ran away to New York and got married, we both took the New York State driver's test even though we didn't have a car. We wanted to prepare ourselves for our undoubtedly glorious future, when Bob would return from Korea, and get a good job, and we'd buy a little house in Levittown on the GI bill, and then get ourselves a brand spanking new two-toned Ford convertible. So much for planning ahead. Instead of a car without a top, I got a life without a husband.)

"That'll be fine," the salesgirl said, taking a box from the shelf behind the counter and lining it with tissue paper. "Now, what size brassiere does your friend wear?"

"34C," I said, with certainty. I knew the size because Abby bragged about it at every opportunity. She also boasted about her waist and hip measurements (23 inches and 35 inches respectively), which I gave to the salesgirl to help her choose the right size panties and garter belt. Then, as she was selecting the flimsy undergarments, arranging them in the box, and writing up the sales slip, I sneakily launched my investigation.

"A good friend of mine used to work in this department," I said. "Her name was Judy Catcher. Did you know her?"

The girl gasped and stopped what she was doing. She raised her head and gave me a look that teetered between shock and sorrow. "Judy? You were a friend of Judy's?"

"Yes, that's right," I said. "We used to live in the same

neighborhood." I felt bad about lying to this perfectly nice and innocent-looking person, but I was, after all, working on a *murder* story, and I knew from past experience that the fewer people who knew my true identity and occupation, the better off (i.e., *safer*) I would be.

"But you *do* know she's *dead,* don't you?" the girl inquired. Her hoarse voice crackled with deep concern. "It was in the papers and everything."

"Yes, don't worry. I know all about it . . . I'm not going to start crying and cause a scene or anything."

The girl relaxed somewhat, and as she did, her own eyes—her incredibly large and luminous green eyes—welled up with tears. One drop fell out and landed on the tissue paper with a crinkly splat.

There were lots of customers at the lingerie counter now—impatient, irritable shoppers scrambling to make their last-minute purchases before closing time. A surprising number of them were men. They looked embarrassed and uncomfortable, but utterly determined to get what they came for. I hadn't realized that sexy underwear was such a must-have Christmas item. That seemed a little bizarre to me. (Unless, of course, the customers were all acquaintances of Abby's.)

"Are you okay?" I said to the grieving salesgirl. "I'm so sorry I upset you. Do you think we could go someplace private for a minute or two?"

"I can't leave my station. My supervisor would kill me." She took a handkerchief out of her skirt pocket and dabbed her eyes dry. "Come," she said, picking up her sales book and Abby's present and glancing nervously in all directions, "let's go around the corner to the other side of the counter. It won't be so crowded back there."

She was right. The area around the corner—the girdle section—was practically deserted. I guess girdles haven't yet made the stretch from secret stomach-cinchers to public stocking-stuffers.

"We can talk here," the girl said, "but I'll have to pretend that I'm showing you some merchandise in case my supervisor comes around."

"Fine," I said. "Show me anything you want." To enhance my image as a serious shopper, I put my purse down on the counter and took out my checkbook. Then, when the girl bent over to get a stack of girdles out of the stock drawer, I unzipped the side pocket of my purse and took out the picture of Judy—the one that was taken in front of Walgreen's, with the bearded weirdo and the weenie dog. I slipped the photo under my checkbook just as the salesgirl's fluffy red head and despondent freckled face popped up above the counter again.

After she put her armful of girdles down on top of the display case, I reached over and touched her hand. "My name's Phoebe Starr," I told her, resurrecting the trusty pseudonym I'd used throughout the Comstock case. "What's yours?"

"Vicki," she said. "Vicki Lee Bumstead." I smiled but I didn't say a word. Far be it from *me* to point out the whimsy of other people's funny names. Besides, Vicki's name wasn't funny in and of itself like mine. Only her surname was comical, and only because Dagwood (or, more precisely, the cartoonist Chic Young) had made it that way.

"I'm really sorry I made you cry, Vicki," I said. "Were you a friend of Judy's, too?"

"Yes," she said, leaning against the counter and nodding so vigorously I thought she might shake something loose. "Judy was my best friend. The best friend I ever had. We worked here together, five days and two nights a week, for over a year. I miss her so much I can't stand it." She hugged her arms in close to her chest as though protecting herself from the cold. I felt so sorry for the girl I wanted to hug her myself.

"I know exactly how you feel," I exclaimed. (You probably think I was lying, but I wasn't.) "She was gone so suddenly, and so violently, it's . . . well, it's just so hard to accept . . . and impossible to understand." I fought to keep myself from falling into my own deep well of loss and misery.

Vicki pulled herself together, too. "Phoebe Starr . . .

Phoebe Starr . . . Phoebe Starr," she suddenly repeated, cocking her head and narrowing her eyes, looking at me as if seeing me for the very first time. "Were you and Judy very close?" A visible seed of suspicion had taken root in the loamy depths of her mind. "I'm only asking because Judy never mentioned your name to me—not even once. And it's kind of funny that she never told me about you, because she always told me everything."

"Well, to tell you the truth, Judy and I weren't *that* close," I blurted, trying to sidestep Vicki's abrupt scrutiny. "It was my Aunt Elsie she was really close with. They lived right across the hall from each other." For a person who truly hates to lie, I sure am good at it.

"Elsie Londergan is your aunt?" Vicki's eyes were softening now, returning to their normally bulbous and luminous state. "Judy talked about *her* all the time. She loved her so much! She said Elsie was the mother she had always wished for."

"My aunt feels the same way—as though she's lost her only daughter."

"Uh-oh!" Vicki said, suddenly shifting her gaze from my face to a point in the distance behind me. "My crabby supervisor's headed this way. Act like you're looking at the girdles." She slid the stack of foundation garments under my nose and held the top one up for my inspection. "This is one of our bestselling models," she said, raising her throaty voice to a loud, conspicuous frequency. "It features cotton elastic gores, a perforated rubber waist cinch, coiled wire boning, front clasps, back laces, and six adjustable garters."

*What, no thumbscrews?*

"Very nice," I said, pretending interest. "Does it come in black?"

"Yes, I think so. Let me check." Vicki dropped down behind the counter again and began a bogus search through the lowest stock drawers. "Keep an eye on my supervisor," she whispered up to me, "and let me know when she's gone."

I turned around and surveyed the area behind me, trying to

pick out Vicki's boss—which was a pretty easy task since there were only two women walking through the department, and only one of them was coatless. She looked like the Wicked Witch of the West, and she was headed straight for the girdle counter. Before she got there, however, she made a sudden sharp turn and marched off toward the hosiery section, disappearing behind the band of Christmas carolers, who were now strolling down the crowded aisle, singing "Silent Night" at the top of their everloving lungs.

"Pssssst, Vicki. It's safe to come up now."

Vicki rose to her feet and looked around. "She's gone?"

"Long gone," I said, sighing, hoping to ease the girl's anxiety and get on with my investigation. "As I was saying . . ."

"Yes, I heard what you were saying," Vicki whimpered. "Your aunt feels like she's lost her only daughter. How horrible for her! Please tell her how sorry I am." She looked as though she might start crying again.

"But that's not all my aunt feels," I went on, staring deep into Vicki's big green eyes and using my most serious tone. "She feels certain that Judy's murder was premeditated—that she was killed by somebody she knew."

Vicki's eyeballs virtually sprang out of their sockets. "But the paper said she was shot during a . . ."

". . . burglary," I said, finishing her sentence for her. "That's what the police decided—and that's the story they're sticking to. But Aunt Elsie doesn't agree with them at all. She's convinced that Judy's murder was committed intentionally."

"Oh, my God!" Vicki cried. "How could that be? Who would want to kill Judy?"

"I was hoping *you* might have some ideas on that subject. Aunt Elsie and I are trying to dig up some new leads, looking for something—*anything*—to persuade the police to reopen the case."

"But I don't know anything about it!" she screeched. "I can't even believe it's true!"

"Yes, but there's a good chance it *is* true," I said. "And since Judy always told you everything, you probably know more about it than you think. For instance, have you ever seen this picture before?" I slipped the snapshot out from under my checkbook and handed it to Vicki. "Do you know the name of the man in the photo?"

Vicki gaped at the picture for a second or two, then handed it back to me. "Yes, I do!" she proudly announced. "That's Jimmy. Jimmy Burgerham, or Hamburger, or—oh, I can't remember his last name! He was Judy's boyfriend for a while. The dog's name is Otto. He's a miniature dachshund and Jimmy takes him everywhere. He brought Otto up here once, hidden in a shopping bag, just to get a laugh out of Judy. She adored that dog."

"More than she adored Jimmy?"

"No! She was crazy about Jimmy, too . . . Hey, what're you driving at? If you think Jimmy killed Judy, you've got another think coming. He really liked her, and it really tore him up when she stopped seeing him. He told me so himself."

"*She* stopped seeing him?" This didn't sound like the Judy Catcher I had come to know and love.

"Yeah, but it wasn't because she didn't dig him anymore. It was because he had so many other girlfriends besides her. One or two would have been okay, but Jimmy is addicted to women—especially *new* women—and Judy just couldn't stand being crazy jealous all the time. Jimmy never had enough time for her. She broke up with him to keep herself from breaking down."

"Do you have Jimmy's address or phone number? I'd like to talk to him."

"He lives down in the Village somewhere, but I don't know which street. I don't have his phone number either. You could probably find him at the Village Vanguard, though. That really cool jazz place down on Seventh Avenue? Judy said he goes there almost every night and sits at the bar sipping beer, flirting with the chicks, just waiting for the chance to get up on stage and read his poetry."

"He writes poems?"

"Yeah. He's pretty good, too. At least that's what Judy said. I wouldn't know. I read mysteries, not poetry."

A girl after my own heart.

"Aunt Elsie said Judy was involved with another man right before her death," I said. "An older man named Gregory Smith. Do you know anything about him?"

"Oh, sure. He was the greatest love of Judy's life! She said he was her lord and savior. But what he was, really, was her substitute father—she always called him Daddy-o. Or sometimes just plain Daddy. He was . . . oh, no! Here comes my supervisor again! Please put that picture away before she sees it. If she catches on we've been having a personal conversation, she'll demote me to Accessories, and it's pure hell to work down there during the holidays." She folded a flap of tissue paper over Abby's present and put the top on the box. "That'll be seven eighty-five, plus twenty-four cents tax, for a total of eight dollars and nine cents," she said in a booming voice. "Please make the check payable to Macy's." She gave me a big salesgirl smile and handed me a ballpoint pen.

I stuffed the photo back inside my purse and made out the check. "Thank you so much for your help," I bellowed. "My friend is going to love this gift." Then I lowered my voice and murmured, "I need to ask you some more questions, Vicki. What time do you get off work? Can we meet somewhere to talk?"

"Okay," she whispered. "But I don't get off till nine."

I flipped a coin in my brain. Heads, I would stay to meet Vicki. Tails, I'd go home to meet Dan. It came up tails. Like I said, sometimes I'm lucky.

"Sorry, Vicki, I can't wait till then. I have a previous engagement. But maybe you'll give me your phone number, so I can call you later?"

"Uh, yeah, I guess that would be all right," she said, looking kind of confused. "It's Gramercy 4-2244." She wrote the number down on the back of my sales slip. "But make sure you call me before eleven or my mother will have a conniption."

"Before eleven," I said, nodding agreement. I gathered up

all my stuff and put on my gloves. "Thanks again for your help."

Giving Vicki a quick but significant salute, I turned and sprinted for the elevator. The perky carolers had launched into yet another Yuletide favorite, and I wanted to get out of there—fast. Instead of chestnuts roasting on an open fire, I was hot to have Jack Frost (okay, *Dan Street*) take a nip at my nose.

# Chapter 9

DID YOU EVER HAVE THE FEELING THAT your life has a life all its own; that the most momentous occurrences of your pitiful earthly existence actually have very little—if anything—to do with you? Well, that's the way it was for me that night, at thirty minutes after eight, on December 21, 1954, when I lugged my cold and hungry body up the stairs to the landing outside my apartment and started fumbling through my keys, looking for the one that would allow me to open my thoroughly inviting—but securely locked—front door.

All I wanted to do was go inside, check to see that the diamonds were still there, cram a few crackers in my mouth, guzzle a cup of hot cocoa, smoke a cigarette or two, fix my makeup, spritz on some Shalimar, and relax for a minute before Dan arrived. Not so much to ask for, right?

I'd have done better to ask for the moon.

Before I could even fit my key in the lock, Abby's door banged open and she swooped like a vampire into the hall, the wide sleeves of her white painter's smock flapping like the wings of an albino bat. "Where the holy hell have you been?" she shrieked, grabbing hold of my shoulder and pulling me around to face her. "You're so late the Mai Tais are all gone! Now I'll have to fix you a plain old rum and Coke!" Her bright red lips were pouting, her dark brown eyes were blazing, and her long black hair was loose and swirling around her head like a storm cloud.

I was unnerved by her troubled demeanor. "What's the matter, Abby? There's no reason for you to be so upset. It's too cold for Mai Tais anyway. This is hot toddy weather."

"That's not the point!" she screeched, stamping one fuzzy pink slipper-clad foot on the bare wood floor of the landing. "The point is why are you so late? Where the hell have you been? We've both been going *meshugge*. We were *worried* about you!"

"We?" I said. "Who is *we?* Did Dan get here already, or is Tony the baker still here from last night, charming your pants off with his trick snake?"

"Hardeeharhar," Abby said, relaxing her shoulders a bit, but refusing to smile. "You're wrong on both counts. And I wouldn't be making jokes if I were you. There's nothing funny about murder."

Now I was as upset as she was. "What murder are you talking about? And *who* are you talking about? Do you have somebody in your apartment? And, if so, who the hell *is* it?" I was too exhausted (okay, *exasperated*) to keep playing her little guessing game.

"Come see for yourself," she said, turning aside and bowing low, gesturing with one sweeping, outflung arm for me to enter her mysterious domain.

I gave Abby a snotty look, then took a deep breath and stepped inside. I didn't know what to expect, but I can truthfully say (and you should trust me on this), that if I'd walked in to find Vice President Richard Nixon himself lolling on Abby's little red loveseat in a complete state of undress, it wouldn't have surprised me in the least.

It wasn't Richard Nixon, though. It was Terry Catcher, and I was shocked right down to my snowboots.

He wasn't undressed, I'm happy to report, but he *was* lolling (well, *sleeping,* I guess I should say), on his back, on the love seat, with his lower legs hanging over the armrest like two large salamis strung from a delicatessen ceiling. One arm was folded over his chest, and the other was dangling over the edge of the tiny couch, fingertips grazing the floor.

I tiptoed up to the couch and leaned over him. "Terry?" I whispered. "Are you okay? What are you doing here?"

His only response was a snort and a whistle. He was sleeping so soundly even the A-bomb wouldn't have budged him.

"He doesn't look so *worried* to me," I said to Abby, resuming a normal speaking tone and walking back over to where she was standing, not bothering to tiptoe. "If you ask me, he looks *drunk*."

"Well, he is *now!*" she said, still pouting. "But that's just because you were so late getting home. He was worried out of his gourd about you, and he said if anything happened to you it would be *his* fault." Abby flounced into the kitchen area, plopped down at her tiny dining table and lit up a Philip Morris.

I sat down and lit up, too, trying to collect myself. "So what's going on?" I stammered. "How long has he been here? Did he tell you about his sister?"

"Sure did. Told me the whole sickening saga. But what I want to know is why *you* didn't tell me about it," she whined, looking more petulant by the moment. "When did you start keeping secrets from me?"

So *that's* what she was so upset about. "I wasn't keeping anything from you, silly," I insisted. "I was dying to tell you everything! I wanted to talk to you about the murder last night, but you had *company,* if you recall, and it was obvious that the three of you wanted to be alone."

"The *three* of us?" She gawked at me as if my ears were blowing bubbles.

"You, Tony, and the snake," I said (and if you think it was easy for me to sit there so calmly and crack another stupid snake joke when I was literally jumping out of my skin with curiosity and concern about Terry, then you've got—as Vicki Lee Bumstead would say—another think coming).

Finally, Abby laughed and hopped down off her high

horse. "Okay, you're forgiven," she said. "But you'd better clue me in on every single thing that happens from now on, or I'll cut off your cocktail allowance." Abby liked to play detective, too.

"I will," I promised, "but right now *I'm* the one who needs to be clued-in. So put your answer hat on. What on earth is Terry Catcher doing here?!!!" I was trying to keep my voice down to a reasonable pitch, but I'm not so sure I succeeded. "How did he get here? When did he get here? And why is he flopped out in a coma on your love seat? He should have been back home in Pittsburgh by now! His bus left at three-thirty yesterday afternoon!"

"Are you sure about that?" Abby teased, dark eyes twinkling. She loved to play games when she was holding all the cards—which, when she was playing with little old simple-minded me, was pretty much all the time.

"Arrrgh!" I growled. It was all I could do not to scream and start pulling my hair out by the handful. "Please, Abby!" I begged. "Can't you just give it to me straight? I'm having a nervous breakdown here!"

"Oh, all right!" she said, sighing loudly. "Don't get your tushy in a twist. You're such a prissy killjoy!" She took a deep drag on her cigarette, then blew the smoke out in a forceful gush. "Okay, here's the scoop: I went uptown to deliver my new painting to *Lusty Male Adventures* today, and when I got back, around three this afternoon, your friend Terry—who, by the way, I *much* prefer to call Whitey—was standing right next to the door to our building, leaning his back against the wall and looking as lost and tired and scruffy as a stray dog.

"At first I was wary of him," Abby continued, "but then, when I got close enough to see how well-built and handsome he was, I figured he must have come to see *me*—that the agency had probably sent him over. So I walked right up to him and introduced myself, and asked him if he was looking for modeling work. You can imagine my surprise when he said no, he was looking for *you*."

Abby stuck out her chin, gave me an accusatory look, took another puff on her cigarette, then went on with her story.

"When I told him you wouldn't be home till six or six-thirty, he said that was okay, he'd wait. Well, I couldn't see leaving such a gorgeous, intriguing, and obviously lonely man like Whitey standing all by himself out on the street, in the freezing cold and snow, for three whole hours! So I did what any thoughtful, compassionate, red-blooded American girl would do under the circumstances—I invited him up for a drink.

"Which reminds me," Abby quickly interjected, "do you want a rum and Coke?"

"Yes, please," I said, too weak (okay, *wicked*) to resist. "But keep talking while you're pouring. Dan's due here in . . ." I looked at my watch . . . "twenty minutes, and if he sees Terry, and finds out about his sister, and discovers that I'm working on another sensational murder story, he'll have me locked up for life in the Women's House of Detention."

"Well, at least you'll be close by," Abby said, moving over to the kitchen counter to mix our drinks. "The girlie slammer's just a few blocks away on Greenwich Avenue. It won't be too much trouble to visit you."

I would have laughed, or at least smiled, but I was too anxious to be amused. "Go on with your story," I pleaded, puffing furiously on my cigarette. "Terry came upstairs with you, and then what happened?"

"Well, we got to talking, of course, and we got real friendly, and then—after we'd had a few drinks, and after I told him that you and I were so close we were practically sisters—he came clean and gave me the whole lowdown. He told me that he was an Army buddy of Bob's, and that his sister Judy had been murdered, and that *you* had promised to help him find the killer."

"Did he tell you about the diamonds?"

"Of course! He said he gave them to you to help in your search for the killer. What did you do with them, by the way? Hide 'em in your apartment somewhere? Are they pretty? Can I see them?" If she'd had a tail, it would have been wagging out of control.

"Later," I said, in the strictest tone I could muster. I knew if I showed Abby the jewelry, she'd want to try it on. And once she had it on, it would be difficult (probably *impossible*) to get her to take it off. Call me a killjoy if you want to, but the last thing in the world I needed was for my new boyfriend, Dan Street, to catch even one tiny little glimpse of my best girlfriend, Abby Moskowitz, standing decked out like a Christmas tree in a twinkly tangle of illicit diamonds that had just been pirated from the 10th Precinct police station . . . right out from under Detective Hugo Sweeny's nose.

"But why is Terry still here?" I asked, changing the subject as quickly as I could. "Why isn't he in Pittsburgh?"

"He said he'd been trying to get home for Christmas, but his bus was canceled because of the storm, so he had to spend the night at the station." Abby finished her pouring and stirring and brought our drinks over to the table.

"But what about . . . ?"

"Stop interrupting me, Paige! I'm trying to tell it straight, like you told me to do, and I need to concentrate!" She sat down and retrieved the cigarette she'd left burning in the ashtray. "Now then, where was I?" she said, taking her own sweet time, blowing a slow succession of perfect smoke rings. "Oh, yes, now I remember . . . Whitey spent last night at the station . . . and then this morning, when they announced that no buses would be leaving today, either—and when he realized he didn't have a dime left in his pocket to buy a donut, or a cup of coffee, or even a ride on the subway—he picked up his duffel bag and started walking downtown to your apartment, not having anywhere else to go, not knowing anything else to do. The poor man *shlepped* over forty blocks—through the wind and the snow and the ice—to get here. And he got very, very cold. And very, very tired. So now he's sleeping like a baby on my couch, you dig? End of story. Final curtain. Thunderous burst of applause."

"Sleeping like a *baby?*" I said, poking a hole in her tidy but conspicuously incomplete summary. "Since when do babies get drunk?"

"What can I say?" Abby simpered, batting her thick black lashes and curling her lips in a mischievous smile. "The man's a sucker for Mai Tais."

• • •

AS SOON AS I FINISHED *MY* DRINK (OKAY, I'm a sucker for them *all*), I made Abby promise to take care of Terry—i.e., sober him up if possible, give him something to eat, and keep him out of sight until Dan had come and gone. Then she made *me* promise that, as soon as Dan had, indeed, departed, I would hurry back over to her place and reveal every scrap of information I'd picked up about the murder so far (which, admittedly, was next to nothing, but in the interest of securing Abby's complete cooperation, I didn't tell *her* that). Then I gathered up all my stuff, darted across the landing to my own apartment, and let myself in.

The first thing I did was check on the diamonds. (They were fine—sleeping like drunken babies on the oatmeal mattress in their round Quaker bed.) The next thing I did was start dashing around like a beheaded chicken, dropping my purse and parcel on a kitchen chair, shedding my coat, beret, and boots, madly running upstairs to put on fresh makeup and a pair of stiletto pumps, then stumbling back downstairs again to straighten my stocking seams, fluff out my hair, fire up a cigarette, plug in the lights of my tiny Christmas tree, and turn on the radio. Quickly bypassing all the merry holiday music, I tuned in one of the top pop stations.

Patti Page was singing "Steam Heat," and the lyrics expressed my mental temperature to a T. I draped myself languidly (okay, *leadenly*) over the daybed in my living room, pretending with every ounce of strength I had left that I was a damsel in zero distress—a lovestruck lady in waiting with nothing but romance (and certainly no thoughts of *murder*) on my mind.

By the time Dan arrived, I almost believed it myself.

# Chapter 10

HE WAS RIGHT ON TIME. (OKAY, SIX MINutes after nine, but who's counting?) I buzzed him in, opened my front door, and watched him bound up the stairs in three strides—like a man with a burning purpose. I only hoped that purpose was me.

"Well, if it isn't Sergeant Street," I said, leaning seductively against the back of the open door, doing my best Kim Novak. "What a pleasure it is to see you."

Well, it must have been a pleasure for him to see me, too, because the next thing I knew he was standing up close to me, brushing his cold nose across my cheek, and covering my mouth with a kiss so deep and warm it sent a jolt of electricity down to my toes. My cool, blonde Kim Novak act took a swan dive down the stairwell. Instead of a curvy tower of restrained desire, I was a wobbly wet mass of mush. I'm not kidding. My head was swirling, my spine was melting, and my knees were threatening to ooze right out from under me.

Luckily, Dan pulled away and went inside my apartment before I dissolved into a puddle on the landing. "It's good to see you too, Paige," he said, taking off his hat and coat and putting them down on the kitchen chair closest to the door. If he had any idea that he'd just reduced me to a breathless, quivering pulp, he was gentleman enough to keep it to himself.

Always the vigilant detective, Dan walked straight over to the back door of my apartment (the windowed wooden door that led from my kitchen to a metal balcony, and to a flight of metal steps stretching down to the small ground-level courtyard), then he flipped on the outdoor light and peered outside. Satisfied that no murderers or rapists were lurking in the snowdrifts below, he raked his fingers through his dark brown hair and straightened his dark blue tie. Then, cocking his lips in a crooked smile, he turned his tall, gorgeous, broad-shouldered self toward me and said, without the slightest trace of irony, "I've really missed you, kid."

Considering the fact that we'd seen each other just two nights ago, when Dan took me out to dinner and the movies, I was delighted by his candid—and seemingly earnest—comment. So what if he called me kid? He was within his rights. Dan was thirty-seven years old, and I was quite a bit younger (nine years to be exact, but again, who's counting?).

"I missed you, too," I said, stepping (okay, *staggering*) into my apartment and closing the door behind me. It felt good to be able to tell Dan the truth about *something,* because I knew I was going to have to start lying to him soon. If he discovered what I'd been up to during the last two days and nights, he'd go berserk and read me the riot act—and he wouldn't stop ranting till I dropped the story. So I racked my brain for a way to keep him from asking too many questions.

"Can I get you something to drink?" I asked, quickly wrapping myself in the comfortable cloak of the polite and happy hostess. "Coffee, tea, hot chocolate, Dr. Pepper . . . ?" *Jeez! Why didn't I buy a bottle of wine on the way home? Because I couldn't afford it, that's why!*

"Black coffee would be good," he said. "I've got a job to do tonight, and I have to stay sharp."

"What? You're working tonight?" The deceitful part of me was relieved, but the mushy part was crushed with disappointment. "I thought we'd have some time together."

"So did I, Paige, but it's not going to work out that way. A wealthy Broadway producer—a known homosexual—was stabbed to death in a dressing room at the Majestic theater this afternoon, and we don't have any witnesses or even a single good lead. So, since I was coming down to the Village anyway, I told the lieutenant I'd hit the bird circuit, ask a few questions, see what I can find out."

"The bird circuit?"

"The round of homosexual bars, where all the queers—even rich Broadway producers—hang out."

I smiled. "You'd better be extra careful then. With your looks, you'll get more *pro*positions than *ex*positions."

Dan laughed and shook his head. "I don't have to worry about that. If any of the birdies get too friendly, I'll just flash my badge. They'll straighten up and fly right."

"How can you be so sure?" I said, stepping over to the stove to make the coffee. "I think you'd better take me with you as a bodyguard."

"Thanks for the offer," he said, chuckling, pulling an empty chair out from the kitchen table and sitting down, "but I'll go it alone this time. You'd stick out like a sore thumb in a sea of pinkies—and sore thumbs can be the kiss of death in most homicide investigations." He took a pack of Luckies and a book of matches out of his shirt pocket and lit up.

I turned to face him squarely, sulking, with my arms bent at the elbows and my hands propped on my hips. "Sore thumb? Kiss of death? Have you got any other nice names you'd like to call me?" I was just teasing, of course—trying to prolong the silly quality of our conversation. If he made any serious inquiries about my day, I didn't know what I'd say.

"How do you feel about Fifi?" Dan replied, lounging back in his chair, stretching his muscular legs out in front of him, taking a deep drag on his cigarette and looking at me in such a way that I felt weak in the knees again. "For some strange reason, I've just been struck with a powerful urge to call you Fifi." His pitch black eyes were crackling with wit and humor.

I was so attracted to Dan at that moment I wanted to

pounce on his lap and lick his face. His wonderful, sturdy, noble, scraggly face. I almost did it, too! (It seemed like a perfect way to limit the conversation and be honest at the same time.) But, when it came right down to it, I didn't have the nerve. I was afraid Dan would think me too forward. I mean, a *real* lady—or even an ersatz one like me—just doesn't *do* that sort of thing.

"Fine," I said, taking our coffees over to the table and sitting down next to Dan. "You call me Fifi and I'll call you Francis. With a name like that, you'll make a big splash on the bird circuit."

We grinned at each other for several seconds. (We would do that often, Dan and I—just sit there eye-to-eye, smiling like a couple of half-wits. I believed it was because we were both still shocked and elated that we'd found each other, but—since we had never discussed it, had never even attempted to put our true feelings into words—I can only speak for myself on that subject. I mean, I *thought* all that staring and smiling meant Dan really liked me—but, as mothers of googly-eyed, grinning newborns are quick to suggest, it could have just been gas.)

When Doris Day came on the radio and started singing, "Once I had a secret love . . ." Dan and I both turned a bit bashful. The words of the hit song hit a little too close to home (for me, anyway). We stopped gazing into each other's eyes and started drinking our coffee.

"What was the guy's name?" I asked, jumping to take the lead in our dialogue.

"What guy?" Dan said.

"The Broadway producer—the man who was killed today."

"Lloyd Bradbury," he said, "ever hear of him?"

The name struck a distant bell. "Yes, I think so. I've probably seen his name in Dorothy Kilgallen's column—"The Voice of Broadway," in *The Journal American*. Maybe in Winchell's column, too. What shows has he produced?"

Dan gave me a suspicious look over the rim of his coffee cup. "Why do you want to know?"

"No reason," I said, hoping my sly and shifty expression

would imply otherwise. "I'm just curious, that's all." (When you've got something really important to hide, it is, in my experience, a good ploy to pretend you're hiding something *else*.)

"Forget about it, Paige!" Dan sputtered, sitting straighter in his chair and exhaling a jet stream of Lucky fumes. "You're getting nothing more out of me. If you want to write a story about this murder, you'll have to get your information from the morning paper."

Though Dan willingly (sometimes *eagerly*) told me about the new homicide cases he was working on, he was always very careful to relate just the barest of facts, to give me the same thimbleful of information he knew would soon be released to the press. And whenever I showed too much curiosity about one of his cases, he closed up like a clam. He did it partly for my protection, as I explained before, and partly for his own. Dan was dedicated to his job, and he liked to play by the rules, and as a sworn detective of the NYPD homicide squad, he wasn't allowed to reveal any consequential details about any ongoing murder investigations to the public—and especially not to a budding crime journalist (and snoopy Agatha Christie wannabe) like me.

"Well, you don't have to get so snippy about it," I said, suddenly feeling rebuffed (in spite of the fact that I'd intentionally brought the whole thing on myself). "I was just trying to show some interest in your work." I was doing my haughtiest Maureen O'Hara now, which meant I probably looked—and sounded—a lot more like Howdy Doody. I'm not too good at haughty.

Dan gave me a stern and piercing stare, then tilted his head back and drained his coffee cup. "Contrary to what you may have read in *Ladies' Home Journal*," he said, banging his empty cup down on the table, "I don't *need* you to be interested in my work." He crushed his cigarette in the ashtray, and rose to his feet. "What I need is for you to stop being so phony—stop pretending that you're just being polite and sociable when what you're really doing is pumping me for information in case you decide to write a story. It's obnoxious and insulting," he said, grabbing his overcoat off the chair and violently shoving first one arm, then the other, into their sleeves. "Just shows me what a patsy you must think I am." He put on his hat and anchored it at an angry angle. Then he started for the door.

"Wait!" I screeched, jumping out of my chair and dashing over to block his exit. "What are you doing? Are you mad at me? I didn't mean to upset you! Please don't leave this way!" I was behaving like a hysterical child, but I couldn't help myself. All my acting (okay, *lying*) skills had been sucked right down the drain, and the only thing left was the real me. The frantic, raving, pitiful, pleading me. It's a wonder I didn't throw myself to the floor and wrap my arms in a hammerlock hold around his legs.

"I'm going to work now," Dan said, brushing past me to open the door. "We'll discuss this at another time."

The tight knot of panic in my chest loosened to a ragged tangle. At least there'd *be* another time. "I'm really sorry, Dan," I said. "I never meant to—"

"Later, Paige," he said. Then he lunged through the door and scrambled down the stairs.

UNDER NORMAL CIRCUMSTANCES, I WOULD have closed the door and started bawling like a baby, wretched that Dan had mistaken my self-protective playacting as an insult to his character, and ashamed of myself for even attempting to pull the wool over his honest, insightful eyes. But the circumstances were far from normal, and I didn't have time to wallow in remorse and self-pity. I had work to do, too! I had to hurry next door to confer with Terry and Abby about the murder, and I had to make a call to Vicki Lee Bumstead—before eleven—to see if I could dig up any new clues.

Since it was only ten o'clock (and since I was dying for another rum and Coke), I decided to go to Abby's first.

"Is he conscious?" I asked as soon as she opened the door.

"Not by a long shot," she said, motioning me inside. "I did my best to wake him up, get him to drink some coffee, but he never even opened his eyes. For a minute I thought he was dead, but then I realized corpses don't snore."

I walked over to the love seat and looked down at Terry's senseless form. He was still lying on his back, with his legs hanging over the armrest. His lids were closed, his mouth was open, and his bright white hair gleamed against the crimson seat cushion like a cumulus cloud in a blood-red sky. I put my hand on one of his shoulders and gave it a vigorous shake. No response, so I did it again. Still nothing.

"See what I mean?" Abby said. "The man has the reflexes of a rock. You could hose him down with ice water and he still wouldn't move. We just have to let him sleep it off, you dig?"

"I guess you're right," I said. "Do you mind?"

"Mind what?"

"If he stays here overnight."

"Are you kidding?" she said, with a devilish smirk. "I'm hoping he'll stay much longer than that! In case you haven't noticed, your friend Mr. Catcher is a major dreamboat. Totally transcendental! I want him to stick around for a while, do some modeling for me."

I knew what she meant by that. And, believe me, it wasn't just modeling she had in mind. And I had the feeling Abby's departure-delaying tactics would be far more effective than my own—that Terry would be staying in town for a few more days at least, bus or no bus, snow or no snow. I was glad for myself, but sorry for Terry's father. I hoped the poor man could find somebody else to spend Christmas with.

"I need a drink," I said, moving into the kitchen area and sitting down at the table. "Do you have any rum left?"

"No, but I've got some Scotch. Want a whiskey sour?"

"Just Scotch and water, thanks. Lots of rocks."

Smiling from ear to ear, Abby danced over to the refrigerator and took a tray of ice out of the freezer. Next to painting and sex, bartending was her favorite occupation. She gave the lever on the aluminum tray a lusty yank, then loaded two glasses with the loosened cubes.

"So, what have you found out about Whitey's sister's murder?" she probed, pouring the Scotch, adding the water, and happily jumping into the swing of her fourth favorite occupation: poking around in *my* life and spurring me on to hazardous new heights of professional (not to mention *emotional*) intrigue. "Do you know who did it yet?"

I groaned out loud. As much as I loved my friend Abby and depended on her interest and support, I did *not* like being subjected to her often hasty and unreasonable expectations. "No, I *don't* know who did it yet," I said sarcastically, "do you?"

"Well, no, but I've got a few ideas."

That figured.

"Pray tell," I said, lighting a cigarette and exhaling loudly. "But make it snappy, please. I've got an important phone call to make."

"Well, here's the way I see it," Abby said, breathlessly toting our drinks over to the table and flopping down in a flutter. Her stupendously beautiful face was glowing with the thrill of the chase. "Whoever murdered Judy was after the diamonds!"

I don't know about you, but I found this to be a somewhat *less* than brilliant deduction.

"Of course the killer was after the diamonds!" I sputtered, disappointed in her simple theory. "That goes without saying! The question we need to answer is, *who* was after the diamonds? Was it Judy's closest confidante and short-of-cash, bingo-playing next-door neighbor, or the penniless, dog-loving poet she threw over because he had too many other girlfriends, or the well-to-do, married older man who was paying the rent on her apartment and may have bought her all the jewelry in the first place? Was it Judy's greedy, oversexed, violently spurned landlord, or the devious, down-and-out ex-roommate whose hair she ripped out by the roots? Or did Judy have a brand new boyfriend—a man who may, for all we know, have participated in some big diamond heist, and then coerced his malleable new girlfriend to hide his take in her apartment, and then shot her in the heart when she got scared and wanted to turn the loot over to the police?"

(Okay, okay! So I was stretching things a bit now, but I only did it to make a point—a salient and, I believe, *legitimate* point: that *I* was the one who had been doing all the homework here, and if anybody deserved to get a good grade on this test, it was *me*.)

"It was the well-to-do, married older man who bought her the jewelry in the first place," Abby declared, unimpressed, totally ignoring my sarcasm and bid for distinction. "The richer they are, the deeper the killer instinct, you dig? I bet his wife found out about his pretty young plaything, and about all the pretty trinkets he'd bought for her, and I bet she threatened to haul him into divorce court and sue his playful pinstriped pants off—unless he ditched his little dolly and got all the diamonds back."

"That could be true," I said, so eager to talk to somebody about Judy's murder that I stopped competing with Abby and teamed up with her instead, "but I don't think he would have had to *kill* her to get the jewelry back. From everything I've learned about Judy so far, all he would have had to do was *ask* her for it. Judy wasn't looking for diamonds, she was just looking for love."

"Some girls get the two mixed up," Abby said, raking her fingers through her wild black hair and tying it back in a ponytail with her red chiffon neckerchief. "Who *is* this rich guy anyway? Do you know his name?"

"I know his *fake* name," I told her. "It's Gregory Smith."

"How did you get that name, and how do you know it's fake?"

"I went to Judy's apartment building on my lunch hour today, and I had a little chat with her manly-but-motherly next-door neighbor, Elsie Londergan. Elsie told me about Judy's sugar daddy and gave me his alias. I think she just assumed it's a phony name because of the Smith."

"Does Whitey know who this rooster is?"

"I don't think so, but I can't say for sure. I haven't had a chance to ask him yet. He's been a little—how shall I put it?—under the weather." The sarcasm slithered back into my tone with a stubborn will of its own.

Abby still paid it no mind. "Are there a lot of G. Smiths in the phone book?"

"Just a few hundred thousand," I moaned. And that was

just a slight exaggeration. (Really!) I had looked the name up when I'd gotten back to the office after my lunch hour (okay, *two* hours), and the roster seemed as long as HUAC's blasphemous blacklist.

"Well, if it *is* a fake name, how're you going to find out the real one?"

"From Judy's landlord, maybe—or by tracing the diamonds back to their original source and trying to get the name of the buyer . . . Or maybe Vicki Lee Bumstead can help me."

"Who's that?" Abby said with a scornful smile. "Dagwood's sister?"

"No, but she was kind of like *Judy's* sister," I explained. "They worked together at Macy's for over a year. On my way home from work tonight, I stopped at Macy's to speak to Vicki, and she told me that Gregory Smith was Judy's lord and savior—whatever *that* means—and the greatest love of Judy's life."

"Did she know if Smith was his real name?"

"I didn't get a chance to question her about it. She gave me her phone number, though, and said she would talk to me tonight if I called before eleven."

"*Oy, gevalt!*" Abby cried. "Then what're you waiting for?!!!" She glowered at me and threw her hands up in exasperation. "In case you haven't heard, Moses *already* came down from the mountain. And if you take a look out the window, you'll see that Hell has frozen over, too!"

See how pushy she could be?

"It's only ten thirty-five," I muttered, annoyed. "I was going to call as soon as I finished my drink."

"Bottoms up!" she said, encouraging me—by example—to gulp down the rest of my highball. "Time waits for no woman . . . so you'd be a damn fool to wait for *it.*"

# Chapter 11

I WENT BACK TO MY OWN APARTMENT TO make the call. The sales slip with the phone number was in my purse, and besides, I wanted to talk to Vicki in private, *without* Abby sticking her cheek up next to mine and mashing her ear against the receiver, trying to tune in Vicki's words the very moment they came through the wire.

I dialed and the phone rang twice. Then a woman's voice, much higher and shriller than Vicki's, answered, "Hello, who's there?"

"This is Phoebe Starr," I said, "and I'm calling to speak to Vicki . . . Vicki Lee Bumstead. Do I have the right number?"

"Vicki!" the woman screeched, blasting my eardrum to smithereens, then dropping the phone down—hard—on a table, or the floor, or some other solid surface. "You got a call! Hurry up! It's almost your bedtime!"

A few seconds passed, then I heard footsteps racing toward the phone. "Hello?" Vicki said, huffing as though she'd just run down to the deli and back. "Phoebe?"

"Yes!" I said, surprised that she knew it was me (or, rather, the "me" I was *pretending* to be) without her mother telling her.

"Thank God!" she exclaimed, her gravelly voice giving the words she spoke a rich and smoky intensity. "I was praying you would call."

"You were? Why? What's happening?" This sounded serious.

"I was thinking about everything you said—about Judy being killed on purpose by somebody who knew her—and I started wondering if you were right. And that started me wondering who could have done it—who could have actually pulled the trigger—and why that person wanted Judy dead. And you know what I think?"

"What?!" I squawked (and I'm sure the timbre of my voice was every bit as shrill as Vicki's mother's). "What *do* you think?"

"I think somebody killed her to get the diamonds."

Big sigh. So Vicki knew about the diamonds, too . . . "What? What diamonds?" I said, playing dumb, waiting to see how she would explain the jewelry connection to me.

"Oh, come on, Phoebe! *You* know!" she insisted. "The diamond necklace and bracelets and earrings and stuff that Judy's daddy-o gave her. Your aunt *must* have told you about it! I know for a fact that Judy told *her*."

I wondered if Elsie would have mentioned the jewelry to me today if I hadn't had to leave her apartment so suddenly. Then I wondered how many *other* people knew about Judy's valuable rock collection.

"You're right," I said. "Aunt Elsie *did* tell me about the diamonds. I was just surprised that you knew about them, too." God forgive me for being such a barefaced bamboozler.

"I don't know what you were so surprised about. I *told* you that Judy always told me everything!" She was getting impatient with me now. Was it because she thought I was being too slow and secretive, or because it was getting too close to her bedtime?

Deciding for both our sakes to hurry things along, I took a deep breath and posed the all-important question. "Did Judy tell you whether or not Smith was her daddy-o's real name?"

"She didn't *have* to tell me," Vicki said. "I knew it was a fake. Judy knew it, too. She wasn't stupid, you know."

"Did she ever tell you what his real name was?" I took another deep breath and held it, praying for a definitive answer.

"She didn't have to tell me that, either," Vicki declared. "I knew the man long before she did. See, I started working in the lingerie department about six months before Judy, and he was a regular customer of mine. He bought a lot of sexy undergarments from me, and he charged everything to his account, which was credited under the name of Gregory Smythe, not Smith."

*Hallelujah!* It wasn't wrapped in pretty paper with a bow, but it was still a fabulous Christmas gift. Bursting with excitement, I grabbed the telephone directory out of the drawer of the living room table and opened it to the S's.

"So, is that where he and Judy met? At Macy's?" I asked, greedily pumping for more information and madly flipping through the pages of the phone book at the same time.

"Yep! It was Judy's third day on the job, I remember, and Mr. Smythe came up to buy a black lace bra for his girlfriend. At least I *thought* it was for a girlfriend, since most men don't usually buy stuff like that for their wives. Anyway, while I was back in the stockroom looking for the right style and size, Mr. Smythe and Judy got to talking—and flirting, she told me later—and I guess he took a real tumble for her, because by the time I came back with the brassiere he wanted, he'd already asked her to go out on a date with him that very same night."

"Did she accept?" I asked, running my finger down the short column of Smythes, disappointed to find no listing under G. or Gregory.

"Sure did," Vicki said, "and who could blame her? Her boyfriend Jimmy—the one I told you about before, the poet with the dog?—well, he was giving her a real bad time at that point, spending all his nights at the Vanguard and all his mornings with other girls, and Judy was desperate for a little attention and affection."

"Which, I presume, Mr. Smythe was more than happy to provide." My voice was sounding a tad sarcastic again.

Vicki giggled. "He sure was! He took her out that night—and every night after that—for about two weeks. And then—abracadabra!—he gave her a diamond bracelet, and he told her he loved her, and he talked her into becoming his mistress, and he set her up in her very own apartment, and I guess he ditched his other girlfriend, too—the one he had been buying all the slinky underwear for—because he never came back to the lingerie department after that. And I never laid eyes on him again. He was doing all his shopping at Tiffany's instead of Macy's."

Did I detect a note of jealousy in Vicki's husky alto?

"What does Smythe look like?" I asked her. "Aunt Elsie said he's pretty old."

"I would guess he's in his fifties, but I can't say for sure. He's so handsome and debonair, you really can't tell. He's got sparkly blue eyes and thick, wavy gray hair, and he looks and dresses like a movie star. Like Cesar Romero."

"Do you know where he lives, or what he does for a living?"

"No idea. He never talked about his personal life to me *or* Judy. Judy knew he was married, and that he was rich, but he never told her anything else about his work or his family. She didn't even know if he had any kids or not. She never asked him any questions about his private life, either, because she didn't want to bother him or make him uncomfortable. She said she didn't care if he worshipped his wife and had thirty-six children—she loved him anyway."

"Was it *Smythe* Judy loved, or the jewelry he gave her?"

"Judy wasn't like that!" Vicki said, with an audible exclamation point. "She didn't care about the jewelry at all! She never even *wore* any of it. She only accepted the gifts because Mr. Smythe insisted, and because it made him so happy to give them to her. She would do anything to make him happy."

I thought about what Vicki said for a moment and realized that—in spite of the improbability of her statements—I was inclined to believe her. Her perception of Judy jibed perfectly with both Terry's *and* Elsie Londergan's—and three out of three was good enough for me. For the time being, anyway.

"I'd really like to speak with Mr. Gregory Smythe," I told her. "Could you go into your bookkeeping files and get his address and phone number for me?"

There was a long silence. "Gee, I don't know," Vicki finally answered. "I couldn't do it myself, but maybe I could get a friend of mine who works in the the billing office to look him up."

"Please try," I said. "It's very important that I talk to him."

"What for?" she inquired, with a sudden and unmistakable tone of disapproval in her voice. "You don't think *he* killed Judy, do you?"

"I have to investigate all the possibilities."

"But Mr. Smythe is definitely *not* a possibility!" she said with conviction. "He's a real classy gentleman. I mean it, Phoebe! He wouldn't hurt a gnat."

"But would he hurt a *girl?*" I said. "*That's* the thirty thousand dollar question."

"Thirty thou . . . ? What are you talking about?"

"That's how much Judy's diamonds were worth. Thirty-thousand dollars."

"Wow!" Vicki blurted, obviously surprised. "I had no idea that . . ."

"Vicki!" her mother screamed in the background. "It's past eleven! Get off the phone! Now!

"I've gotta go," Vicki sputtered, responding to her mother's orders on the double. "Call me tomorrow?"

"Uh, sure . . . okay," I said, barely getting the last syllable out of my startled mouth before the line went dead.

I LOOKED AT MY WATCH. VICKI'S MOTHER was right; it was fifteen minutes past eleven. But the way I was feeling, it seemed much later. I was so tired, jittery, and confused—and still so upset about Dan—I wanted nothing more than to creep up the stairs to my bedroom and crawl under the covers with my clothes on. I wanted to curl myself up in a tight little ball and pull Bob's old army blanket all the way over my head, I wanted to drop off into oblivion and forget I ever heard the names of Terry and Judy Catcher. Or, for that matter, Gregory Smythe.

But I didn't have time for oblivion. Or even just a couple of winks. A murderer was on the loose, and I was the only person on earth (well, the only *sober* person on earth) who was trying to track him down. And tired and frazzled though I was, I knew for a fact that eleven-fifteen was the right and perfect time for me to set forth on my next clue-hunting expedition. The jazz (and, hopefully, the poetry) would be getting into full swing at the Vanguard right about now.

In an effort to boost my energy level (i.e., keep myself vertical for a couple more hours), I gulped down another cup of black coffee. Then I pushed myself up the stairs to my closet, took off my pale yellow sweater set, pulled on my black knit scoop neck, switched my sheer flesh-colored stockings for black, and put on a clean black sheath skirt. Lumbering into the bathroom to splash some water on my tired face, I then wiped off all my red lipstick, powdered my nose, and put on a pile of heavy black eye makeup. I looked as wan and bloodless as Count Dracula before his midnight snack, but I would blend in beautifully with the somber, sooty-eyed bohemians.

I went back downstairs and put on my coat and my snowboots. Then, grabbing my purse off the table and slapping my black beret on my head, I carefully let myself out of my apartment and inched my way down the stairwell, being as quiet as a baby chipmunk walking on tiptoes in slippers made of silk. I did *not* want Abby to hear me. If she came out into the hall and found out where I was going, she'd want to come with me. And God only knew what kind of trouble *that* would lead to.

Opening the door at the bottom of the stairwell as quietly as I possibly could, I slipped out onto the sidewalk, clicked the door closed behind me, then quickly started walking west on Bleecker, toward Seventh Avenue. It was freezing and the street was practically deserted. I pulled my coat collar up and held it around my face, breathing into it, trying to keep my nose warm. Nearly gagging from my hurried pace and the gamey smell of damp camel's hair, I turned right onto Seventh and pushed northward, ducking my head against the arctic wind and keeping my eyes trained on the sidewalk, cautiously avoiding the most dangerous patches of hardened snow and ice.

There was more traffic on the Avenue—both human *and* automotive—and many more Christmas lights were twinkling, especially in the Sheridan Square area. From West 4th Street on, however, things got a little quieter—and a whole lot darker. Shaking from the cold (okay, my *nerves* were causing some trembling, too!), I walked as fast as I could past West 10th, Charles, Perry, and Waverly Place, until finally—at the ominous stroke of midnight—I found myself standing under the long, red, snow-topped awning stretching from the curb to the entrance of the Village Vanguard.

Striving to be as brave as Brenda Starr (but feeling as spooked as Cosmo Topper), I sucked in a blast of frigid air and blew out a cloud of white steam. Then I pulled the creaky, heavy wood door open and stepped inside.

# Chapter 12

THE FAMOUS WEDGE-SHAPED ROOM WAS crowded—packed to the low-slung rafters with groovy young artistic types, all dressed in black, all drinking and smoking, and all listening intently, with half-closed eyes, to the hip, cool sounds of the Negro jazz quartet performing on the slightly raised stage. A few Negroes were sitting in the audience, too, thrumming their fingers on the tabletops, scatting, bobbing their heads and rolling their shoulders in perfect sync with the music. The Vanguard was one of the few public places in the city where Negroes and Caucasians could mingle in easy harmony—and one of the few public places in the world that was likely to be so crowded on a late, wintry Tuesday night (okay, *Wednesday morning*) like this.

I spied a small, empty table at the very back of the room, hurried over and sat down, hoping nobody would notice me. Even in the Village—the most liberal and progressive neighborhood in Manhattan (and probably the whole country)—it wasn't considered proper for a woman to go out to a nightclub alone. I slipped my coat off my shoulders, folded it over the back of my chair, took off my beret and gloves, and immediately lit up a cigarette. Then I slumped into a boneless slouch, trying to look cool and intellectual, like a beat jazz–lover whose boyfriend had just gone to the bathroom. (It isn't easy to look cool and intellectual when your heart is banging like a kettle drum and your brain is stuck on the subject of murder.)

Some of the people sitting nearby turned to gape at me—rather suspiciously, I thought—then began whispering among themselves. They probably thought I was a doped-up prostitute on the prowl for a jazzed-up john.

Hunching over till my hair made a wavy brown curtain around my face, I squinted my eyes and scanned the room, searching for a dark-haired, bearded young man with a dog. There were at least twelve dark-haired fellows with beards in attendance, but only one of them had a dog. He (the man, not the dog) was standing and leaning against the bar, watching the show and listening to the music, with one elbow propped on the counter and his fringed chin propped on the shelf of his upturned hand. The miniature dachshund was sitting—in as upright a position as a long narrow dog with extremely short legs can achieve—on the barstool next to him.

My spine snapped to attention. It was Jimmy and Otto. I was certain of it. (Brilliant deduction, right? I mean, am I a shrewd detective, or what?)

I was sitting there straight as a broomstick, staring into space, trying to figure out a good way to approach Jimmy and get him to make a full confession, when one of the waiters—a rangy buck with sandy brown hair and a very broad, decidedly *un*cool smile—suddenly appeared at my table.

"Can I get you somethin' from the bar, Ma'am?" he said, sounding just like Chester B. Goode, Matt Dillon's gimpy deputy on the popular radio show *Gunsmoke*. You could tell from the hick accent and the beaming smile he was new in town. Probably a student at NYU.

"Just a cup of coffee, please," I said. I really wanted another Scotch and water, but I couldn't afford it (money-wise *or* mind-wise).

"Somethin' for your date?" he asked, taking for granted I had come with an escort.

"No, he's not here yet, and I don't know what he wants to drink. He was supposed to meet me here at eleven-thirty. I can't imagine what's keeping him."

"Snow must have slowed him down." The open-faced fellow was *definitely* from out of town, I decided. A born and bred New Yorker would have thought I'd been stood up, and said so.

"You're probably right," I replied. "I guess I'd better wait for him a while, if that's okay."

"S'just fine with me!" he said, with a grin so wide it literally wrapped around the sides of his face. "Sit tight. I'll get you some coffee."

He walked away and I sighed with relief, thanking the gods of Greenwich Village for small favors. If this had been an uptown nightspot, I probably would have been asked to leave.

The jazz quartet ended their set and stepped down from the stage, engulfed in a warm wave of finger snapping, handclapping, foot tapping, and low whistles. As the musicians made their way back to their tables and sat down with their friends, a rather large, clean-shaven man walked over to the mike, thanked the quartet for their inspiring performance, and announced they'd be playing two sets a night, at nine and eleven, for the rest of the week. Then he asked if there were any poets in the audience.

One hand went up. Guess who it belonged to.

"Uh-oh!" the man behind the mike exclaimed, peering toward the bar, holding his hand up over his eyes as if shielding them from the sun. "I see Jimmy Birmingham is here tonight—which isn't so unusual since he's here almost every night!" There was a round of cordial laughter and a couple of loud guffaws. "And from the serious look on his philosophical face," the man continued, "I'd say he's got something important he wants to tell us. Right, Jimmy?"

Jimmy shrugged, then gave a quick, almost imperceptible nod.

"So come on up, boy, and bring your pup with you. You're both welcome on my stage anytime." He motioned for Jimmy to come forward, then returned his gaze to the audience. "Let's hear it for the Vanguard's resident poet, Jimmy Birmingham, and his sidekick, Otto—or, as we say around here, the cat with the dog. I'll leave it up to you to decide which is which!"

There was more laughter and another round of polite applause.

Straightening to his full height—which I judged to be about five foot ten—Jimmy turned and picked Otto up from the barstool, tucking the dog's tiny haunches in the bend of his elbow and bracing the rest of his slim, sausage-shaped body along the length of his forearm. Then, carrying his precious pooch in close to his side, as a woman might carry her favorite clutch bag, he sauntered along the bar to the peak of the pie-shaped room and stepped onto the stage.

As Jimmy moved into the amber glow of the single spotlight, I got my first good look at his face. He was unusually handsome, in a stark, intense, Tony Curtis sort of way, and his dark brown Vandyke beard—as well as the dark brown hair on his head—was sleek and neatly trimmed. He wore a black turtleneck over a pair of charcoal pants. As he grabbed one of the musician's stools with his free hand and dragged it over to the mike, I saw that his body was strong and thin, and his coordination precise.

Propping one buttock and thigh on the seat of the tall stool and planting the foot of the same leg on the crossbar, Jimmy placed Otto astride his charcoal shank and gave one long, loving stroke from the top of his pointy-nosed head to the tip of his string bean–size tail. Then, seeing that his pet was comfortable and perfectly balanced, he leaned his agile torso forward, grabbed the mike with both hands and—in a surprisingly deep, burnished baritone—began to recite:

*Here it be,*
*where we are we,*
*together in the degenerate hell of this life.*

*So what?*
*What are we to do about it?*
*Maybe you can't care.*
*Even a snail eats.*
*It's our cause to complain.*
*Surround yourself with your own orchestra*
*because we will always survive the creeps,*
*hear our own music,*
*defeat the streets.*
*Our jumbo world is ours.*
*Inside we will stay,*
*away from our enemies and the luster of injustice.*

A few seconds of silence ensued, then—as Jimmy let go of the microphone, tucked Otto under his arm and breezed off the stage—the crowd broke out in restrained but rapturous applause. Heads were nodding in profound agreement and faces were awash in earnest reverence. Some people rose to their feet and signaled their approval by raising their glasses in a silent toast to Jimmy Birmingham's verbal brilliance.

Was I the only one in the room who felt like laughing till my sides split open?

I was straining my ears, hoping for a concurring giggle, or at least one poorly stifled snicker, when the waiter appeared with my coffee and set it down in front of me. "Here you go, Ma'am," he said, putting a small bowl of sugar cubes and a puny pitcher of cream down next to the coffee mug. Then he turned aside, hoisted his drink-laden tray back up to his shoulder, and began worming his way toward other customers.

As the waiter moved away, clearing my line of vision, I saw that somebody else had suddenly appeared at my table. It was a medium-tall somebody with dark brown hair, a dark brown beard, and an adorable dark brown creature nestled in the curve of his arm. It was the cat with the dog. And the way the cat was leering at me, I realized I was the canary.

• • •

"YOU LOOK LIKE YOU COULD USE SOME company," Jimmy said, sitting down—uninvited—in the chair closest to mine. Cradling his little dog against his chest, he gave me a cocksure smile and said, "Otto saw you sitting here all alone, and he thought you were a real gone chick, and he told me he was itching to meet you right away."

"Maybe he just has fleas," I said without thinking. *Aarrrrgh!* For a true crime writer whose main purpose in life, at that moment, was to find out the truth about a certain crime, I couldn't have come up with a worse (i.e., less enticing and manipulative) reply. Jimmy and Otto had been dropped in my lap like a gift from the gods, and if I knew what was good for me, I wouldn't make a stupid joke out of it. I would gratefully accept the gift, and use it in good health.

"Just teasing, Otto," I quickly added, leaning over to pat the dog's tiny head and fondle his warm, silky ears. "I'm sure you never had a flea in your life." To prove the sincerity of my contrived (and, hopefully, *conciliatory*) words, I began rubbing the underside of Otto's narrow chin and staring, like a lover, into his small, round, worshipful eyes.

Mission accomplished. Otto was in seventh heaven, and so—it would seem—was Jimmy Birmingham.

"He really likes you," Jimmy said, lowering his deep voice to an intimate croon, writhing in his chair like a python, slithering so close to me I could feel his hot breath on my cheek. "And Otto's the best judge of females I've ever known. He picks all the best tomatoes for me."

*Oh, brother! Does this line work on most women? Did it work on Judy?* I wanted to believe that Terry's little sister had seen through Jimmy's come-on in an instant, that she had toyed with his affections as much as he had no doubt toyed with hers, but—hard as I tried—I couldn't bring myself to embrace that theory. Judy had been young and hungry, and all alone in the world. And from everything Elsie Londergan and Vicki Lee Bumstead had told me, I knew she had probably soaked up Otto's—I mean Jimmy's—attentions like a sponge, and begged her desperate little heart out for more.

"So Otto picks your girlfriends *and* your vegetables," I

said, shifting my gaze from Otto's face to Jimmy's. "He's a hound of many talents. Does he write your poetry for you, too?"

(Look, I *know* that was another really stupid response. I should have been flirting with the suspect, flattering him, trying to gain his confidence and coax some information out of him, instead of casting aspersions on his literary skills. But I couldn't help myself. Really! I was so crazed and exhausted—and still struggling so hard to suppress my inner giggle fit over Jimmy's silly poem—that I didn't know what I was doing, or saying, anymore.)

Jimmy was enraged. A fire blazed up in his dark brown eyes and I thought, for a moment, he was going to hit me. But—as I sat there frozen like a dumbstruck deer, trying to decide whether to duck right or duck left—his taut muscles suddenly relaxed and his facial expression underwent a dramatic transformation. And you probably won't believe this (since I couldn't believe it myself), but Jimmy's entire stance toward me flipped, in the space of a single heartbeat, from flaming anger to—of all things!—burning attraction.

"You're a mischievous little minx, aren't you?" he said, putting Otto down on his lap and scooting his chair even closer to mine. "I've got your number now, sweetheart. You're a doll with an attitude, and you like to cause trouble, and I go crazy for women like that." To prove it, he fastened his left hand on my thigh, clamped his right hand around the back of my neck, yanked my face forward, and planted a deep, ferocious kiss on my astonished, gaping mouth.

I would have kicked him in the crotch if Otto hadn't been sitting there. I would have clawed his face to ribbons if it hadn't been protected by his beard. I would have pushed him backward and socked him in the nose if he hadn't been so much stronger than I was. And if I'd had a knife in my hand, I would have (okay, surely *wouldn't* have, but at least *could* have) stabbed him in the stomach.

But I didn't have a knife, or a gun, or any other deadly weapons in my possession. The only instruments of destruction I had at my disposal were my teeth, and I decided—without a second's hesitation—to use them.

"Owwwww!!!!!" Jimmy wailed, shoving me away with one hand and nursing his bleeding lower lip with the other. "You bit me!!! It hurts like hell!!! What did you *do* that for?!!!"

"I did it for Judy Catcher," I said.

I was as shocked by my answer as Jimmy was. Though I had meant to bring up Judy's name and try to get Jimmy to talk about her, I hadn't planned on doing it in such a sudden, brutal, *indiscriminate* way. But now the cat was out of the bag and running down the street like a rabid lion on the loose, and I had no choice but to chase after it.

"Judy was a very good friend of mine," I added, as if that would explain everything.

"So what if she was?!!!" he cried, eyes big as half-dollars. "That doesn't give you the right to *bite* me!" Blood was trickling from the cut on his lip and seeping down into his beard. Otto rose up on his hindquarters and began to paw at Jimmy's chest, whimpering.

"You had no right to kiss me either," I growled.

"Yeah, yeah, yeah! So maybe I shouldn't have done that," Jimmy admitted, gingerly dabbing at his lip with a paper napkin. "But I still don't see what Judy Catcher has to do with the goddamn price of eggs."

"It's simple," I said. "You hurt my good friend, so I felt like hurting you."

Jimmy sat back in his chair and gave me a long, steady, piercing stare. "I don't know what the hell you're talking about. I never hurt Judy." He was getting angry again. "Whatever she told you about me, it wasn't true."

"Judy never said anything bad about you. And now that she's dead she'll never be able to." I paused to let the implication of my words sink in. "But that doesn't change anything, really, because I didn't need any tips from Judy. I figured it all out for myself."

"Figured *what* out?"

"That you were probably the one who killed her."

(No, I wasn't going off half-cocked again. I had decided, during the course of the last few minutes, that I might find out more about Jimmy—and, likewise, his relationship with Judy—if I simply pulled out all the stops and hit him between the eyes with an outright accusation. The man obviously responded to rude and unexpected pronouncements! And besides, it was getting really, really late. And I was really, really tired. I didn't have the time, or the energy—okay, the *sense!*—to conduct a slow and cunning interrogation. Or play any more guessing games.)

"What did you say?" Jimmy snarled, narrowing his eyes and clenching his jaw so tight his Vandyke twitched. He didn't look like Tony Curtis anymore. Now he looked like Bela Lugosi. With a bloody beard.

I took a deep breath, said a quick prayer, and repeated my allegation.

And that's when Jimmy gave me the shock of my life.

Scooping Otto up in his arms again, Jimmy clutched the little dog in close to his heart, dropped his chin to his chest, hunched his shoulders, and began to cry! I'm not talking about your standard case of the weepies, either. I'm talking about great big heaving sobs and blubbers. I'm talking deep, guttural moans of woe. I'm talking yelps, and skreaks, and caterwauls, and the kind of howls caused by a full moon.

And that was just for starters. After three or four interminable seconds of this astonishing clamor, Otto started howling, too.

I didn't know what to do. Every face in the place was turned in my direction, and all eyes were blaming me for causing the disturbance. I had reduced their brilliant and beloved poet to tears! I had brought pain and suffering to their most cherished canine! What kind of woman *was* I? And what the hell was I *doing* here, anyway? Why wasn't I at home in my bed—where I was *supposed* to be—like every other decent God-fearing female who doesn't have a date?

I couldn't stand up to the condemning stares and silent questions. And I couldn't stop Jimmy's crying, either. All my apologies went unheeded, and—though I pleaded with the weeping poet to calm himself and his little dog down—they both kept right on yowling.

As you can imagine, I was dying to know *why* Jimmy was crying his big brown eyes out. Was he stricken with grief—truly lamenting the loss of his former lover and friend—or was he wallowing in remorse and self-hatred, bemoaning his own brutal role in Judy's death? Had he flown into a jealous rage over Judy's affair with Gregory Smythe and killed the only girl he'd ever loved? Or had he knocked Judy off to get his hands on the diamonds—which he had never been able to find (which may have been the *real* cause of all this blatant boohooing)?

These and many other questions were burning a hole in my frontal lobe, but I knew I couldn't get the answers now—not while Jimmy was in the throes of a nervous breakdown. Not while I was so tired and confused I couldn't tell the difference between a mourner and a murderer. I'd have to talk to Mr. Birmingham later—at another time—when he and Otto were in a better mood. When scores of people weren't staring at me in anger, preparing to rush my table and eject me from the premises for causing their adored club mascots such vociferous anguish.

Offering Jimmy and Otto one last apology (which, as far as I could tell, went unheeded by them both), I plunked fifteen cents down on the table (a dime for the untouched coffee, a nickel for the tip), and shoved my arms into the sleeves of my coat. Then I grabbed my purse and gloves, plopped my hat on my head, jumped to my feet, propelled myself to the door, and made a hasty (okay, *hell-bent*) departure.

# Chapter 13

AS SOON AS I HIT THE SIDEWALK I TOOK off running. Well, *skating* was more like it, since the pavement was so slippery and treacherous in places, but whatever you call it, I was moving as fast as I could. I wanted to put some distance between myself and the Village Vanguard before the oh-so-cool and cerebral jazz and poetry lovers formed a bloodthirsty mob and came charging after me.

And I was desperate to get back home—to be warm and safe behind the locked doors of my apartment, one full floor above the dirty snowbanks and icy sidewalks, hidden away from all cold-blooded killers.

I was the only pedestrian on the street, which *really* gave me the creeps. I mean, a New York City–dweller such as myself is practically *never, ever, ever* on a Manhattan avenue all alone. It was so dark—and so *quiet*. Except for the sporadic whoosh of a passing car or taxicab, all I could hear were the echoing sounds of my snowboots scraping the sidewalk, and the rumbling thunder of my own ragged breath.

Right after I crossed Charles Street, however, I started hearing something else. Something that sounded like footsteps (and I don't mean my own). The sounds were coming from pretty far behind me—at least a block away—and every time I stopped to listen, the sounds stopped, too. I kept turning around to see if anybody was there, but nobody was. Nobody that I could *see,* anyway. I tried to ignore the faint but persistent noises and continue my homeward trek with a stout heart, but it was no use. I felt that someone was following me—no, I *knew* that someone was following me—and I flew into a panic only Alfred Hitchcock would understand.

And then something wild—something kind of *supernatural* —happened. A dreadful force invaded my lower limbs, and they became hot as fire, and they began to spin around in my hip sockets like the spokes of fast-turning wheels—like the whirling legs of that crazy bird in the *Road Runner* cartoons. (Well, maybe that's a slight exaggeration, but it's exactly the way I *felt*!) I streaked down Seventh Avenue so fast I must have been invisible. I whipped around the corner onto Bleecker like a racecar without any brakes. I unlocked the door to my building and zoomed up the stairs in a blinding flash. And then I opened my apartment and fell inside, without—miracle of all miracles!—Abby hearing me and making one of her dramatic appearances.

Best of all, I had left the wily coyote who was following me in the dust. (At least I *thought* I had.)

After locking my front door and closing the living room window shades—and checking to see that the diamonds were still nestled in their Quaker bed (they were)—I shed all my outerwear and left it in a pile in the kitchen. Then I dragged my pitiful body up the stairs to *my* bedroom. Every ounce of my superhuman strength had flown. I was a puppet without any strings. All I wanted to do was get out of my clothes, wash the gooky eye makeup off my face, bundle my tired bones in one of Bob's old Army T-shirts, and burrow between the covers.

I might have accomplished this goal, too, if the shade of my bedroom window hadn't been left open. Then I wouldn't have had to walk across the room to close it, and I wouldn't have looked out the window while I was pulling the shade down, and I wouldn't have seen the suspicious figure lurking in the doorway of the laundromat directly across the street. And I certainly wouldn't have leapt to one side of the window like an enormous, demented frog, or flattened myself against the wall like a pancake, or pried a tiny little peephole between the shade and the window frame, and stood peering down through that peephole at the man lurking in the laundromat doorway, until he emerged into the dim glow of a nearby streetlamp and began walking toward Sixth Avenue.

And then I never would have seen that the man had a beard, or that he carried a little dog wrapped in a plaid wool muffler in the crook of his arm. And I wouldn't have come to the frightening realization that—even though I had successfully kept my *name* a secret from him—Jimmy Birmingham now knew exactly where I lived.

So then I might have gotten into bed and gone to sleep like a normal person, instead of pacing around my apartment for the rest of the night, from the kitchen to the living room and back, again and again, drinking a jillion Dr. Peppers out of the bottle and filling every ashtray I owned to the brim with squashed cigarette stubs.

WHEN I CAME OUT OF MY SUGAR- AND smoke-induced stupor it was nine-thirty in the morning, and I was flopped out in a crumpled heap on my living room daybed (a weird but very modern-looking contraption I made myself from an old wooden door, a set of six wooden screw-on legs, and a single-bed mattress tucked into an orange madras bedspread. Poverty is the mother of invention!). I was still dressed in my black skirt, black scoop-neck sweater, and black stockings, and my eyelids were spackled shut with several thick, crumbling layers of black mascara.

When I finally pried them open and took a look at the clock on the table next to the phone, I saw that I was an hour late for work.

Groaning loudly and pulling myself to a seated position, I fell back against the couch cushions (or, rather, the pillows I keep piled against the wall to make the daybed *look* like a couch), wondering what evil stroke of fate had determined that I should have to work like a slave for a living, and still *live* like a slave in the process. Madly searching my addled brain for a good excuse for being late, I finally picked up the phone and dialed the office, hoping against hope that Mr. Crockett was in a forgiving mood.

When Lenny answered, I was so relieved I almost kissed the mouthpiece.

"Zimmerman!" I said, exhaling loudly. "Thank God it's you. I'm so late it isn't funny. I just woke up and I don't know what to do."

"*I'll* tell you what to do," he sputtered, lowering his voice to a near whisper. "Stop working on whatever ghoulish story you've gotten yourself involved in, and start paying attention to your real job. Otherwise, you're gonna lose it." His critical tone reminded me of the way my mother used to sound, when I would come home way past my curfew, or forget to clean up my room.

"Is Mr. Crockett upset? Did he say anything to you?" I wasn't worried about Brandon Pomeroy because I knew he wouldn't be in for another two hours at least.

"Crockett hasn't come in yet. There was some kind of emergency at the typesetter."

"Really?" I cried, stifling a loud *wahoooo!* "I don't believe it! How lucky can a girl get?"

"Not very," Lenny said, dropping his voice even lower, cupping his hand over his mouth and around the receiver (at least that's what it *sounded* like he was doing). "Mike and Mario arrived right on time this morning, and they've been having unholy seizures because the mail isn't sorted and the coffee isn't made. Mario's so furious he said he was going to call Mr. Crockett at the typesetter and tell him you didn't show up."

"What an unspeakable creep he is!" I said, wiping chunks of mascara out of my eyes and nervously lighting up another cigarette. It made me gag, so I put it out right away. "You've got to cover for me, Lenny," I pleaded. "Tell them I was trampled by an elephant or something."

"You mean you're not coming in?"

"No," I said, suddenly deciding to take the whole day off. "It'll be better if I don't show my face at all. That way you can tell them I called in sick, and they'll all just have to accept it. This will be only the *second* sick day I've taken in all the time I've worked for *Daring Detective,* so I think I deserve a little leeway. I've earned it, right?"

Lenny was audibly exasperated. "Pull your fat head out of the sand, Paige!" he scolded. "Pomeroy won't give you any rope, and you know it."

"Maybe that's just as well," I said, trying to smile. "The way things have been going for me lately, I'd probably just hang myself with it."

A SHOWER AND CLEAN CLOTHES LIFTED my spirits a bit. Terry Catcher's mood, on the other hand, was sunk in a hangover of oceanic proportions.

"I should have been killed instead of Judy," he moaned, rubbing his pale, handsome face with both hands, then raking his long, shaky fingers through his thick white hair with a vengeance. "I'm a coward, and a drunk, and no use to anybody on earth." Terry was sitting, slumped over, on Abby's little red couch, in the same spot and position he'd been in several minutes before, when I'd ventured next door to see how he and Abby were doing.

"Listen up, pretty boy," Abby called from the kitchen. She was toasting bagels and stirring Tabasco into the three large Bloody Marys sitting on the counter. "You can forget that 'no use to anybody' crap right now. *I've* got a use for you, you dig? And you're gonna *love* being used by me. I guarantee it."

I laughed and sat down next to Terry on the couch. It felt good to be among friends. "And I'm *really* glad you're still here, Terry," I said, patting his poor, hunched-over back. "Now you can tell me more about Judy and help me figure out the truth about what happened to her. I've made some headway in my investigation, but I still feel as though I've been locked in a windowless basement without a flashlight."

"Well, *I* feel like I'm dying," he croaked, slowly turning his head and looking at me—for the first time since I'd entered the apartment. His bright blue eyes were thoroughly outshone by the bright red rims of his lids. "What *is* a Mai Tai anyway?" he asked. "A mixture of arsenic and chloroform?"

I laughed again. "Abby's known all over the Village for her dynamic cocktails. It's rumored she laces them with gunpowder."

"I can assure you the only explosive I use is booze," Abby said, walking over to the couch with a Bloody Mary in each hand, "and in *this* case it's just a dinky little spritz of vodka." She handed the drinks to us. "Bottoms up, kids! You'll both feel better in no time. And when you're able to walk, come on over to the table for bagels and coffee." She turned and whisked back into the kitchen area.

Terry eyed his drink suspiciously. "Coffee sounds good," he said, forcing himself—with a loud groan—to his feet, then wobbling—glass in hand—toward the kitchen. I took two big gulps of my firewater (Abby uses a *lot* of Tabasco), and followed him to the table.

FINALLY, AFTER THE BLOODY MARYS, bagels, and coffee had been consumed, we got around to discussing the murder. I told Terry and Abby about all my investigative excursions thus far: my little tea party with Elsie Londergan; my talk with Vicki Lee Bumstead at Macy's and my follow-up phone conversation with her, when she told me about Gregory Smythe and said she'd try to get his address and phone number for me; my midnight jaunt to the Village Vanguard, where I'd met the cat with the dog and learned that his name was Jimmy Birmingham. I didn't tell them that Jimmy had followed me home and, therefore, knew where I lived, because I didn't want them to flip out and start worrying about me. (Okay, I also didn't want them to know how incredibly stupid I'd been to allow—all right, *cause*—the whole thing to happen the way it did.)

"I can't believe how much you've accomplished so far," Terry said, lighting a Pall Mall and taking a drag. Some color had returned to his lean, narrow face and his hands weren't shaking anymore. "I'm so grateful to you, Paige. I just wish I could talk to Bob, tell him how swell you've been and how much you're helping me."

My soul shivered. I wished I could talk to Bob, too.

"What's next on the agenda?" Abby asked, urging me onward as usual. Without taking a breath, she cried, "You've got to find Gregory Smythe!" Like Edward R. Murrow, she liked to answer her own questions.

"I know, I know," I said, sighing heavily. "I know what I have to do, but I'm not sure I have the energy to do it."

Abby was unhappy with my lethargic response. "You're not going to just sit around and wait for Dagwood's sister to get Smythe's address, are you? What if her friend in bookkeeping refuses to search the files? Then you'll be up poop creek without a paddle!"

I smiled at her sanitized version of the cautionary cliché. It wasn't often that Abby sanitized *anything*. "No, I'm not going to wait for Vicki. I have an alternate plan. But first," I said, turning to look at Terry, "I was wondering if *you* ever heard of Gregory Smythe. Did Judy ever mention him, or bring him up in any of her letters?"

"No. This is the first I've heard of Smythe *or* Birmingham. Judy never told me about either of them. She used to write me about her boyfriends when I was in Korea, but after I came home and she moved to New York, she didn't write very often. And when she did, all she talked about was her job. She was so proud to be working at Macy's." As Terry spoke of his sister, his voice grew soft and his face turned pale again.

"So what's your alternate plan?" Abby badgered. "How are you going to track down Judy's daddy-o? Are you going to ask Dan to help you?"

My heart flipped over at the mention of Dan's name, but I pretended I hadn't heard it. I didn't want to think about (or have to explain) our recent romantic run-in. "I have a different scheme," I said. "I'm going to pay a visit to Judy's landlord today. According to Elsie Londergan, Gregory Smythe signed the lease on Judy's apartment, so the agency's sure to have his address. If not his home address, then at least his business address. And if I can get the landlord in a chatty mood, maybe he'll have even *more* to reveal about the randy old coot's living arrangements."

"Do you know who the landlord is?" Abby asked.

"No, but *you* do, right?" My words were directed at Terry.

"Sure do!" Terry said, delighted to have some concrete information to offer. "His name is Roscoe Swift and his office is on 27th Street, right around the corner from Judy's apartment. Chelsea Realty. Wait!" he said, jumping up from the table to grab a crumpled newspaper out of the duffle bag sitting on the floor near the couch. "The exact address is printed here, in the classifieds. I saw it yesterday." He folded the newspaper open to a certain page and handed it to me. "See the item circled in ink? It's an ad for Judy's apartment. Swift's already put it up for rent."

I scanned the ad and, with Terry's permission, tore it out of the paper. "Thanks," I said, sticking the scrap of newsprint in the side pocket of my skirt and giving Terry a big grin of approval. "That's all I need to know."

"Maybe not, Paige," Terry said, his proud smile fading to an uneasy frown. "Swift strikes me as a sleazy kind of guy. Slick and tricky. You may not get anything out of him but a fast runaround and a quick pat on the fanny. I'd better go with you."

"No, Terry," I protested. "I don't want him to know that I'm connected to you or Judy in any way."

"Then *I* should be the one to go," Abby broke in, angling her head and arching one black eyebrow to the hilt. "If there's one thing in the world I'm good at, it's dealing with tricky guys like Roscoe. If they gave out an Oscar for Best Manhandler, I'd win it every year."

I had no doubt of *that*, but I was still determined to meet—and interview—Roscoe Swift on my own. And to see Judy's apartment for myself. "Actually, there's something *else* I was hoping the two of you might do today."

"What?!!!" they cried in unison. A girl couldn't ask for two more eager assistants.

"I thought you could take Judy's jewelry—or some of it, anyway—uptown to the Diamond Exchange and show it around to some of the dealers. Maybe one of them will recognize the stones or the settings. Maybe someone there will know where the jewelry came from, or who bought it, or if it was stolen. I would do this myself, but I'm afraid to walk around town all alone with a bag full of diamonds. I'd just be asking for trouble. But if the *two* of you . . ."

"Say no more!" Abby chimed in. "I'm so perfect for this job it's silly! In case it slipped your mind, I'm Jewish! And every Jew on earth has relatives who work at the Diamond Exchange. Three of my cousins work there, and my Uncle Sam and Aunt Dora do, too! If they can't give us the lowdown on the ice themselves, they'll probably know somebody who can."

I gazed at Terry, trying to gauge his reaction to Abby's religious revelation. If he showed any signs of anti-Semitism (as so many white Christian males I knew often did—Brandon Pomeroy and Mario Caruso, to name but two), I'd be so disappointed in him I wouldn't be able to breathe. I wouldn't turn my back on him, or stop looking for his sister's killer, but I'd continue my investigation with drastically diminished zeal—and a *very* heavy heart.

Not to worry. Terry showed no prejudice at all. If anything, he was *excited* about Abby's family connections. "That's great, Abby!" he cried. "Let's get the diamonds and go over there right now!" His cheeks were flushed and his eyes were glowing. And though he didn't look a bit like Mickey Rooney, I still half expected him to add, "And let's get all the kids together and put on a show in the barn!"

Abby looked at me and smiled. Her big brown Judy Garland eyes were glowing, too. As if reading my thoughts, she winked at me and said, "Your wish is our command, Paige. Give us the rocks, and we'll be off to see the wizard."

# Chapter 14

"WOW!" ABBY EXCLAIMED, STARING DOWN at the glittering mound of jewelry I'd just removed from the oatmeal container and placed on my kitchen table. "Nice little stash of sparklers." She poked her index finger into the pile and—with the uncanny precision of a Geiger counter—plucked out the most desirable piece (i.e., the one with the most diamonds). "Now *that's* what I call a necklace," she said, quickly clasping the double string of gems around her throat. "Mind if I try it on?"

I *told* you she was going to do that, remember? Self-restraint was *not* one of Abby's specialties. I only hoped it didn't bother Terry that she was suddenly prancing around my kitchen like the Duchess of Windsor, sporting his poor dead sister's necklace—and now her earrings, too!—with such unbounded glee.

"Do you think you should take all the jewelry with you, or just some of it?" I said to Terry, hoping to divert his attention to more serious matters. "I suppose it's important to have each and every piece checked out . . . but if you happened to get robbed, or anything like that, it would be terrible to lose all the evidence."

"I'm not worried about getting robbed," Terry said. "I'm just worried about getting arrested."

"What?!! What are you talking about?"

"I'm talking about the fact that I stole these diamonds from Detective Hugo Sweeny's office, and he probably thinks I'm trying to sell them now, so he—or one of his bloodhounds—may be sniffing around the Diamond Exchange, looking for me."

"God! I hadn't thought of that!" I said, head spinning. "But what makes you think the police are looking for you here in New York? It's far more likely they're in Pittsburgh, sitting in an unmarked car outside your father's house, waiting for you—and the diamonds—to come home for Christmas."

"You're right about the last part," he said. "Two dicks *are* sitting in a car outside my father's house. But neither one of them is Sweeny. They're two of Pittsburgh's finest, doing a little freelance surveillance work for their fellow flatfoots in New York. I know this because they paid my dad a visit yesterday. They grilled him about where I was, and when I was coming home, and they—or two other jokers like them—have been watching the house ever since."

"So you've spoken to your father."

"Yeah, twice. Yesterday, when I called to tell him I couldn't get home because the buses weren't running, and again this morning, when I called to find out how he was doing and if the cops were still there."

"See? I *told* you they'd be looking for you," I said. "Thank God for the snowstorm! If your bus had left on schedule, you'd be in jail right now—and you wouldn't be getting out until you turned the diamonds over to the police . . ." I had a disturbing afterthought, and added, ". . . which means you would have had to turn *me* over to them, too."

*Oh, lordy, lordy, lordy!* I shrieked to myself, heaving my breast and rolling my eyes like Hattie McDaniel. Why hadn't I foreseen this possible consequence before? Was I a selfless and fearless defender of truth and justice—or just a stupid fool? (Don't answer that!) When I thought how furious Dan would have been to learn about my willing (not to mention *illegal*) participation, I almost wet my pants.

"Hey, what are you two gabbing about?" Abby broke in, finally waking from her diamond-studded daydreams. By this point, *all* of Judy's jewelry—the necklace, the earrings, the pin, and both bracelets—was draped, or screwed, or clipped to Abby's body in the customary places. She looked like a goddamn chandelier. "Am I missing anything?" she asked.

"Just a tiara," I snapped. "But if we ever find Smythe, maybe he'll buy you one."

"*That's* not what I meant!" Abby squawked, giving me a dirty look. "I was talking about your conversation with Whitey, and you know it!"

"Oh, *that!*" I teased, smiling, glad that Abby had returned (sort of) to the realm of reality—and that I hadn't been thrown in jail (yet!) for tampering with evidence. "We were just discussing whether or not it's too dangerous for Terry to go to the Diamond Exchange today. One or more of the detectives involved in Judy's homicide investigation may be casing the joint, looking for him."

"Why would they be doing that?" she wanted to know.

Terry explained the situation to her, and she grasped it quickly. She even came up with a possible solution to the problem.

"You can wear a disguise!" she whooped, getting excited by her own idea. "Something that will hide your white hair and help you meld into the crowd." She wrinkled her brow in thought for a few seconds, and then the light bulb over her head flashed about a thousand watts brighter. "I've got it!" she cried. "The perfect camouflage, you dig? And I think we have everything we need to put the getup together. Hey bobba ree bop! C'mon, Whitey, let's go across the hall. I'll round up the stuff and you can try it on. You wait here, Paige. When we're all finished, we'll come over and you can be the judge of the results."

You could tell from Terry's forlorn expression he wasn't too fond of the disguise idea, but before he could utter a single word of protest, Abby grabbed him by the hand and tugged him back across the hall, into her own apartment. I stood at my open door and watched as she pulled him across the room, then led him up the stairs to the second floor.

I knew where she was taking him. And it wasn't to her bedroom, believe it or not. It was to the tiny *spare* bedroom—the little cubicle she called her Vault of Illusions—the room where she kept all the costumes and props for her paintings. It was just a big closet, really, full of all different kinds of clothes and hats and shoes and wigs, plus a large assortment of oddball items—things like swords and beach blankets and pitchforks and peacock feathers—anything she felt might help her set the scene for one of her colorful magazine illustrations. In order to keep her Vault of Illusions well-stocked, Abby collected castoffs from all her relatives and friends, and made regular appearances at all the local rummage sales.

I wondered what kind of outfit she would rummage up for Terry. And I hoped, for his sake, it would be warmer—not to mention more *concealing*—than a purple loincloth.

AS SOON AS THEY WERE GONE, I TOOK MY baby blue Royal portable down from the coat closet shelf and set it up on the kitchen table. Then I ran upstairs to *my* spare bedroom (the unfurnished nook I planned to turn into an office if I could ever save up enough money to buy a desk) and grabbed a package of typing paper from the small stack of office supplies I kept stashed on the floor in the corner. Then I raced back down the stairs, slapped the package of paper down on the kitchen table, and sat myself down at the typewriter.

I couldn't put it off one minute longer. I had to start making notes for my story (I mean *Judy's* story), and I had to do it *now,* while I had the time. This was probably the last workday I'd be taking off for another whole century at least. More importantly, I knew if I didn't write down all the details soon (i.e., *immediately*), they'd begin disappearing from my flimsy memory like snowflakes landing on the hood of an overheated car. And, as every true crime or mystery writer knows, too many forgotten details can result in a totally forgettable story. Or a clean forgotten crime.

I rolled a sheet of paper into my loyal Royal and began typing like a lunatic, recording every word, fact, clue, conjecture, and impression I could remember, beginning with Terry's initial phone call to me at the office. I paid no attention to spelling, grammar, or punctuation. All I cared about was getting all the data down on paper, where it would be preserved for future reference.

I don't know how long Abby and Terry were gone—or how long I sat there, typing my fingers to the bone. All I know is I had just finished documenting last night's phone call to Vicki, thereby completing my eighteenth page of notes, when Abby came barging back into my apartment.

"Shut your peepers," she said, all aflutter, "and don't open them till I tell you to." She was so excited I thought she might pop.

"Okay," I said, putting my notes aside and covering my eyes with my hands, feeling like a five-year-old.

I heard some whispering and rustling in the vicinity of my front door. Then Abby giggled, and Terry groaned, and Abby bellowed "Open sesame!" in a voice that belonged under the big top.

I uncovered my eyes and took a peek. And then I flat out *shrieked* in amazement. Standing before me—in a long black overcoat, a black fedora, a pair of black pants, a white shirt, and a long brown beard with long brown sidecurls—was a tall, dark, and handsome Hasidic Jew.

For those not familiar with the species, a Hasidic Jew was a man or a woman who belonged to a certain ultra-Orthodox sect of Jewish mystics that was founded in Eastern Europe in the eighteenth century, and was still going strong today—in America, among other places—in 1954. Many of them lived in Brooklyn. Every Hasidic male wore a black overcoat and a black fedora. They all had beards and *payos*—the unshorn ear ringlets which, according to Abby, were the outgrowth of an ancient law forbidding the shaving of the temples.

More to the point (well, to my and Abby's and Terry's point, at any rate), was the fact that hordes of Hasidic Jews were gem traders by profession and, therefore, worked on West Forty-seventh Street in Manhattan, at—you guessed it—the Diamond Exchange. So many Hasidim worked there, in fact, that the street was jokingly called the *Rue de la Payos*. Terry would blend in perfectly—like just another pickle in the pickle barrel.

"It's wonderful!" I cried, standing up to make a closer inspection. "It's the *ideal* disguise! The hat hides his white hair and the *payos* hide his white sideburns." I gave Abby an admiring look. "They look so real. How did you make them?"

"I cut a few tendrils off a curly brown wig and glued them to the inside of the hat." She was radiant with pride.

"I see you colored the hair around the back of his neck, too," I added. "What did you use for that?"

"A toothbrush and a tin of brown shoe polish."

I patted her on the back and gave her an enormous grin. "It's the consummate costume, Abby. Perfect in every way. Edith Head would die of envy!"

"Well, I'm glad *you* like it," Terry growled, squaring his shoulders as if for a fight, "but I think it's god-awful. I feel like a total jerk dressed this way. These frilly things hanging down the sides of my face are annoying and embarrassing, and this ratty old beard smells like a sweaty gym sock."

Abby tossed her head and shot him a haughty glare. "Would you rather spend one afternoon breathing into a smelly beard, or several months suffocating in the smelly slammer?"

"Good point," Terry said, shuffling his feet and relaxing his shoulders. I think he was smiling, too, but it was hard to tell since you couldn't see his mouth for all the hair.

"Well, what are we waiting for?" Abby crowed, reeling toward the door. "It's almost two-thirty! I'll get my coat! Let's get this show on the road!" I'd never seen her so aroused—

except on those all-too-frequent occasions when she was gearing up to make a move on one of her half-dressed male models.

"Hey, hold on a second!" I cried. "Aren't you forgetting something?"

"What?!!" she snorted, with a rather impatient huff.

"The diamonds," I said, with a huff of my own. "Call me crazy, but I think it would be safer if you hid them away in your purse, or under Terry's hat, instead of flaunting them all around town, strung all over your body like a batch of blinking Christmas lights."

"Oh," she said, finally remembering that she still had the jewelry on. She gave me a sheepish look, then reluctantly took it off, piece by glittering piece, putting it back down on the kitchen table. "I didn't like it anyway," she said, with a dramatic flick of her diamond-braceletless wrist. "It made me look too snooty."

We all had a good laugh over that one. Then Abby carefully wrapped the diamonds up in their original tissue paper package and handed them to Terry, who stuck them deep in the pocket of his long black overcoat. "Are you ready, Whitey?" she asked, politely deferring (finally!) to his rightful authority in the situation.

"Yeah, let's go right now," he said, "before I change my mind and rip this moldy carpet off my face."

TWO SECONDS AFTER THEY LEFT, I snatched up the phone and dialed the Midtown South Precinct. Dan's precinct.

Look, I *knew* it wasn't proper for an emotionally undone woman to call the office of the man who'd undone her—unless she happened to be his wife (and even then it was considered overbearing!). But I wasn't exactly the proper type. And I had a very strong suspicion that if I waited until I became Dan's wife to give him a personal call, I'd never speak to him again.

And what harm could one teeny-weeny phone call do?

All I wanted was to hear the sound of his luscious voice and talk to him for a minute or two, ask him to forgive me for the way I had acted last night. (Last night? Was it only last night that he'd flown into a rage and walked out on me? With everything that had happened to me since, it felt more like a month ago.)

The man who answered the phone told me Dan wasn't there. "Street's out on the street," was all he said.

I hung up and smoked a cigarette, giving myself a phony pep talk, working like the devil to keep my soul from sagging to the floor. Dan or no Dan, I couldn't afford to let my energies fall. I had a lot on my plate that day, and there was only one way to deal with it all. Stay hungry.

# Chapter 15

THE CHELSEA REALTY OFFICE WAS ON THE ground floor of a three-story brownstone. The large hand-painted sign in the front window showed the name in bold black letters above a bed of orange-yellow flowers with dark centers. Looked like black-eyed Susans to me. It was odd to see them rising from a windowsill heaped with snow. The company logo appeared again on the entrance door to the office—gold letters with black outlines. Just the name, no posies.

I pushed the buzzer but I didn't hear it ring. Thinking the bell was out of order, I knocked lightly on the door and waited for somebody to let me in. Nothing happened, so I tried the knob. To my great surprise the door clicked open, and I cautiously stepped inside.

At first I thought the place was deserted. There was nobody sitting up front at either of the two old wooden desks that—along with the bank of tall wooden filing cabinets—practically filled the long, narrow room. As I stood there, however, listening to my own jumpy heartbeat and looking around at the pale green walls, dying potted plants, and badly scuffed bare wood floor, I realized I wasn't alone. There was somebody in the back room. A man. I couldn't see him through the half-open door between the two rooms, but I could hear him plainly.

"So what the hell're you tellin' me, Lily? It's not over yet? Haven't you had enough? Jesus H. Christ! I did what you wanted. Give it up already!" His voice was extremely loud, and he sounded *very* angry. Since there was a long silence after he spoke, and no audible reply, I figured he was talking on the phone. To somebody named Lily. (Am I a masterful detective, or what?)

I stood perfectly still in the front office, trying not to make a sound, straining both ears toward the half-open door. If the man in the back room had anything further to say, I wanted to hear every word.

Big mistake. "Screw you!" he shouted at the top of his lungs. "I'm through! Go find yourself another stooge!" There was a loud crash, made—I assumed—by the collision of the receiver with the body of the phone, and then a harsh string of curse words I'd rather not repeat. (Use your wildest imagination, and you still won't come close.)

By this time I was feeling kind of scared. I mean, this guy was going off his rocker in there! There were sounds coming out of that room that brought to mind the breaking of human bones and the gnashing of vicious tiger teeth. Not wanting to meet the madman face-to-face, or madden him further with my surprise appearance, I decided to flee the Chelsea Realty office and come back later, when he was feeling better.

Good plan—bad timing.

I had just opened the front door to leave when the man came storming out of the back room, growling obscenities and flailing his fists against every wall and piece of furniture in reach. He looked like he wanted to kill somebody. And his murderous demeanor became even more pronounced when he saw me.

"What the . . . ?!! Who the hell are you? What the hell are you doing here?" His mean little eyes were blazing and his short, wiry body was poised to attack. And I may have been hallucinating, but I would swear that two big streams of fire were shooting out of his nostrils.

"I'm sorry!" I sputtered, backing away from the heat. "I rang and knocked, but nobody answered, so I came on in. The door was open."

He banged his fist on the closest file cabinet. "I'm gonna fire that stupid girl! She never locks up when she leaves the office!" He looked at his watch and cried, "Goddamn it! It's three-thirty already! I sent the brat to show some office space over an hour ago and she's still not back!" He gave me a closer look and then an overt head-to-toe once-over. "Hey, can you type? You want a job?"

"Uh, no. No, thank you, sir," I said. "I've already got one."

My rejection angered him even more. He shoved his fingers through his coarse brown hair and glared at me, screwing his long skinny pockmarked face into an ugly scowl. "Then what're you here for, sister?" he barked. "Out with it! I haven't got all day!"

Was the man so upset he'd forgotten what kind of business he was in?

"I'm looking for a new apartment," I said, straightening my backbone and pasting a cordial smile on my kisser. I took the ad for Judy's place out of my skirt pocket and handed it to him. "I saw this listing in the newspaper yesterday, and it sounds just right for me. So I was hoping to see the apartment this afternoon. Is it still available?"

He looked down at the ad in his hand, then back up at me. Now he was smiling also—so broadly and intensely I thought his tiny, tobacco-stained teeth would pop out of his gums and blast out of his mouth like buckshot. "Sure, doll," he said, suddenly acting like my best friend. "The pad's available. And it's vacant, too, so I can show it to you right now—soon as you fill out an application." Scooting over to the front desk, he snatched a printed form out of the top left drawer and gave it to me. "Need a pencil?" Before I could answer, he plucked one from the holder on the desk and handed it over.

*What a chameleon!* I thought, marveling at the man's quicksilver mood change. Was he merely busting to make a buck, or was he hustling to unload a bad luck rental where a young woman had recently been murdered? From the way he was smiling and sweating, I figured both motives were applicable.

"Thank you, Mr. . . . ah . . . Mr . . . ?"

"Swift," he said, still grinning, "but you can call me Roscoe. Come sit over here while you fill out the form."

He snaked his arm around my waist and guided me over to the guest chair at the side of the desk.

To avoid any sneaky fanny pats or pinches, I sat down quickly.

"Thank you, Roscoe," I said, gazing up at his lizardlike face and batting my lashes to beat the band. I was trying to look alluring and flirtatious (as Abby always advised me to do), but the effort was making me kind of sick to my stomach, so I probably just looked like a bilious cow with gnats in her eyes.

Deciding to ditch the nauseating coquette routine and get down to business, I turned my attention to the application form and hastily filled it out, giving my name as Phoebe Starr and listing my address as 104 Christopher—which was just a few blocks away from where I really lived. I put down my true phone number, however, in case Roscoe decided to dial it to check me out. Then I gave Abby as a reference, stating that she was my current landlady.

The minute I finished, Roscoe swerved over to the desk, snatched the form out of my hands, and shoved it into the top right-hand drawer. Then he pulled a set of keys out of a different drawer and jingled them in the air. "C'mon, doll," he said with another too-wide grin. "The apartment's right around the corner. And I got a hunch it's the perfect pad for you."

He didn't mention that it had been somewhat less than perfect for the last tenant.

STANDING IN THE HALL OUTSIDE JUDY'S apartment, waiting for Roscoe to fish the keys out of his pocket and open up, I studied the lock, knob, panels, and jamb of the door for evidence of breaking and entering. Terry was right. There were no unusual marks on any of the metal parts, and no telltale nicks or gashes in the wood.

I looked at Elsie Londergan's door for a second, thinking I might learn something by comparing the two entranceways, but quickly lost my train of thought and flew into a major panic. What if Elsie heard us out here in the hall, or saw us through her peephole, and came out to see what was going on? If she let on that she knew me and called me by my real name, my cover would be totally blown! I'd have to confess my real purpose for being here. And then I'd have to deal with Roscoe Swift as my *actual* self, which could significantly lower my chances of digging up any info about Gregory Smythe—not to mention leave me exposed to a possible new source of danger.

(Why, oh, why hadn't I thought of this before? Before I had hoofed it up to Judy's apartment like a demented donkey? Before I had so willingly—okay, mindlessly—placed myself in the position of a sitting duck? If I had any sense at all I'd quit my job at *Daring Detective* and look for work as an oyster shucker. Or maybe a street sweeper. Some kind of job where foresight didn't figure.)

But I was a lucky duck (or donkey) for the moment. Elsie didn't appear. And Swift lived up to his name by opening the door to Judy's apartment swiftly. Then we both stepped inside and he closed the door behind us, flipping on the light.

My heart screeched to a halt. Standing there in Judy's kitchen, holding my breath and blinking against the glare of the bare bulb hanging from the ceiling, I felt as if I had entered a tomb. Or a church. I was both deadened and electrified. And I felt closer to Judy Catcher than I ever had before. A trace of her cheap, spicy perfume still hung—like incense—in the stagnant air. I thought if I closed my eyes real tight, and concentrated real hard, I might be able to hear her humming . . .

But Roscoe quickly broke my spell. "You got to use your imagination," he said, snapping open the kitchen window shade, then flinging wide the door to the bathroom. "The single girl who was living here moved out a few weeks ago, so the place looks empty and dreary right now. Needs some furniture and a homey touch. But just look at this flooring!" he exclaimed, gesturing toward the dingy, cracked linoleum as though it were a layer of marble veined with gold. "It's like a ballroom dance floor! And the carpeting's even better," he said, lurching into the tiny sitting room and twirling once around like Arthur Murray himself. "It's the perfect shade of red. They call it Prussian Passion. It goes with any color."

*Especially the color of blood,* I thought, walking into the room and staring down at the carmine carpet, searching for the section I knew poor Terry had soaked and soaped and scrubbed with his own hands. It was faintly visible in the center of the floor, midway between the sitting room and the bedroom. A dusky oblong stain the size of a bathmat. The very spot where Judy's soul had left her bleeding body.

The location of the stain didn't actually prove anything, I realized, but it *did* indicate that the killer had been admitted to the interior of the apartment before the murder took place. (Okay, okay! I may have been jumping to conclusions. Yes, Judy *could* have been shot in the kitchen when she opened her door to the killer, and then she *might* have stumbled halfway to the bedroom before she fell. But it was far more likely that the two bullets fired straight into her heart would have killed her instantly—i.e., kept her from stumbling anywhere.)

"The apartment's the right size for me," I said, carefully bypassing the barely discernible bloodstain and heading into the bedroom. "And the location couldn't be better. But my major concern is safety." I walked over to the bedroom window, raised the worn shade and looked out at the rusty, partially snow-covered fire escape. "Do you have many break-ins here?"

"Never had a single one!" Roscoe swore, lying through his little brown teeth (the police *had,* after all, declared that Judy was shot during a random *burglary*). "This is the safest building in the whole goddamn city!" he insisted. "The neighborhood's safe, too."

Pretending to test its workability, I unlocked the bedroom window and raised it a couple of inches, checking both the frame and the glass for signs of a forced entry. There were no scratches or scrapes to speak of, and the glass panes were uniformly filthy, suggesting—if not proving—that none of them had been recently replaced. A blast of cold air prompted me to close the window and relock it.

"Next to safety, privacy is the most important thing to me," I said, shivering, turning to look Roscoe right in the eye. "I don't need any new friends or enemies. And I can't stand gossips or busybodies. I'm an unmarried woman with a liberated lifestyle, and I want to live in a building where all the residents keep their noses in their *own* behinds."

Roscoe let out a horsey laugh. I was speaking a language he understood. "Then you've come to the right place, toots," he said, snorting and winking suggestively. "The last renter of this apartment felt exactly the same way you do and was very satisfied with the accommodations."

"You mean the single gal who just moved out?"

"No," he said." Wink, wink. Snort, snort. "I mean the married guy who was paying the rent for the single gal who just moved out."

"Aha," I replied, lifting one eyebrow to a peak—letting Roscoe know, with a salty smile, I had gotten his message. "And how did the neighbors react to this scandalous situation?" I asked. "Did they cause the illicit lovebirds any trouble?"

His scrawny chest puffed out with pride. "I never had one complaint from any of the other tenants."

"That's nice," I said, "but what about the lovebirds themselves? Did any of the residents ever bother *them?* Were they ever hissed at, or spat on, or bombarded with rotten tomatoes?"

Roscoe laughed again. "I don't know where you been livin', sister, but here in Chelsea, we don't do things like that."

"Well, that's good to know," I said, trying to turn on the charm again—i.e., look alluring and bat my lashes. "But you know what would *really* help me make up my mind about this apartment, Roscoe?"

"What?" he said, jutting both his chin and his pelvis in my direction.

"If I could just talk to one of the lovebirds—either the guy or the gal—and ask a few questions, find out what it's like to live here. I'm sure everything you've told me about the apartment and the area is true, but I'd still like to get a firsthand report. Nothing speaks like experience." I paused and gave him a flirty smile. "And I don't mind telling you," I added, flapping my eyelids like a vapid fool, "if I get the good review I expect to get, then you've got yourself a brand new occupant!"

I was hoping he'd clap his hands and jump for joy, and then whip out pen and paper to write down Gregory Smythe's unlisted phone number for me. But he didn't. What he did was stiffen his puny spine, cock his lizardlike head to one side, narrow his steely eyes to the thinnest of slits, and start breathing fire through his nostrils again.

"Forget it, sister," he growled, his swarthy, pockmarked skin turning a puky shade of puce. "You're not getting any goddamn names or numbers from me! My other renters—even the ones who don't live here anymore—happen to like their privacy just as much as you do." He didn't punch me in the face or kick me in the shin or anything like that, but he looked like he wanted to.

"Easy, Roscoe," I soothed, keeping my voice steady and low, striving for a smooth recovery. "I didn't mean to upset you. And I didn't really want anybody's phone number, either. To tell the truth, I was just testing you—trying to find out if you were the kind of landlord who *would* give out information about your tenants. I really couldn't live with that. But I see I shouldn't have worried about you! You passed the test with flying colors!" (Okay, I admit it. If Roscoe and I had been vying for the top chameleon crown, I'd have won it hands down.)

He was mollified but not convinced. He thrust out his jaw, crossed both arms over his chest, and studied me suspiciously. "Look, sister, do you want the damn apartment or not? I got other people comin' to look at it."

"I don't know yet," I demurred. "Can I think about it and call you later?"

"It's a free country," he said, glowering. Then he turned on his heels and stomped toward the door, treading over the scarce remains of Judy's plasma in the process. "But don't think I'm gonna hold it for you," he grumbled over his shoulder. "Somebody else wants it, it's gone."

"I understand," I said, holding back for a moment, taking one last mournful look around the unbearably sad apartment where my dear late husband's best friend's little sister had lived and died, and laughed and cried, and dreamed her girlish dreams, and loved her pitiful little heart out. And as I slowly trailed Roscoe to the door and followed him out into the hall, I realized I was praying.

# Chapter 16

**WHEN ROSCOE AND I REACHED THE STREET** and parted company—thereby ending the threat that Elsie might bump into us and blurt out my real name—I said another silent prayer (of thanks, this time). Then I walked back to Seventh Avenue and headed south, away from the Chelsea Realty office, looking for a coffee shop or a candy store or *any* kind of store where I could slip inside, get warm, and make a phone call. Though I hadn't wanted to see Elsie before, I needed to talk to her now—to find out when and where she wanted to meet for dinner.

The first shop I came to was Henry's Hardware, and I was so cold I went right in. The short, balding man standing behind the waist-high counter in the middle of the store was wearing a red flannel shirt and an enormous I'm-so-glad-to-see-a-customer smile. "Well, hello there!" he said, propping his elbows on the counter and craning his plump round face in my direction. "What can I help you with today? I'm having a big sale on electric fans." He let out a hearty laugh to show that he was joking.

I smiled and walked up to the counter. "I'm not shopping for anything specific," I told him, "but I'd like to look around a bit, if that's okay. And do you have a public phone I can use?"

"I've got a phone, but it's not public."

"I'd be happy to pay for the call."

"Oh, you don't have to do that!" he said, pulling a battered old black telephone up from behind the counter and placing it down right in front of me. "It'll be a frosty day in Hawaii before Henry Thaddeus Hancock makes a nice young lady like you pay for one lousy phone call. It *will* be just *one* call, won't it? A local?"

"That's right," I said, smiling. "Just one local call."

"Then go right ahead, young lady," he said, sliding the phone even closer. "Be my guest. I'll go price some items over in the housewares section so you can have some privacy."

"Thank you, Henry," I said, touched by his kindness and generosity. After my dealings with with Jimmy Birmingham and Roscoe Swift, Henry Thaddeus Hancock seemed like the world's most considerate man. Not wanting to tie up his line any longer than I had to, I snatched Elsie Londergan's number out of the zippered side pocket of my purse and dialed it quickly. She answered on the third ring.

"Hi, Elsie!" I said. "This is Paige Turner, and I . . ."

"Hi, yourself," she interrupted. "I was wondering if you would call. And I'm sure glad you did. I've got a real hankerin' for a hamburger and a beer right about now." (I hadn't noticed it before, but even her vocabulary was similar to John Wayne's.)

"Good," I said, "because I'm in the neighborhood and I'm hungry. Just name the place and tell the time."

"There's a pub on 23rd between Sixth and Seventh called the Green Monkey. I'll meet you there at five-thirty."

"Great. See you then."

I hung up and went looking for Henry. He was in the rear of the store, squatting down next to a cardboard carton full of plastic ice cube trays—the new twist-and-pop kind—removing them one at a time and stamping each with a price of forty-five cents.

"I'm off the phone now, Henry. Thanks so much!"

"Don't mention it, young lady." He gave out a grunt and stood up like a true gentleman, his plump round face pink with exertion. "Glad to be of service to you!"

"I have a few minutes to kill before I meet my friend for dinner," I said. "Mind if I browse around?"

"Please do! I know you'll find something you need. Everybody always does!"

I wasn't intending to buy anything, but I didn't tell him that. He looked so proud and hopeful I didn't have the heart to admit that all I wanted was to soak up some more heat before I hit the frigid streets for the Green Monkey.

Henry walked back to the sales counter, and I took a stroll down the next aisle over, surveying all the rugged, "manly" items in that section—the fishing rods, tackle boxes, hunting knives, boat paddles, lanterns, and inflatable life vests so indispensable to life in the wild on the untamed isle of Manhattan. The adjacent lane featured more of the same: tents, sleeping bags, tool boxes, hand pumps, saws, axes, flashlights, and lunchboxes.

*A lunchbox!* I squealed to myself, struck with a sudden happy inspiration. Stooping to inspect the three different models displayed on a lower shelf, I picked up the nicest one and examined it closely. It was made of steel—black enamel outside, white enamel inside—and it had a rounded top, a sturdy handle, two lock clasps, strong hinges, and a pint vacuum bottle with a screw-on aluminum cup top.

It was perfect! The ideal gift! I couldn't wait to wrap it up and give it to Lenny—who, as I've mentioned before, was so intent on avoiding the office elevators he brought his lunch to work every day in a brown paper sack.

Delighted with my serendipitous and timely find (there were only two shopping days left until Christmas), I merrily hugged the lunchbox to my breast and carried it up to the sales counter.

"May I pay for this by check?" I asked, knowing I didn't have enough cash to buy Lenny's gift as well as Elsie's dinner.

"Of course!" Henry gushed, pink cheeks glowing. "That'll be two dollars and twenty-nine cents."

I made out the check, and Henry put the lunchbox in a shopping bag. "See? I knew you'd find at least one thing you need," he said, handing the bag over to me. "Henry's Hardware has something for everybody!" If he had let out a loud "Ho, ho, ho!" I'd have found it entirely appropriate.

THE GREEN MONKEY WAS FIFTY PERCENT full (or fifty percent empty, depending on your point of view), and most of the mostly male customers were sitting or standing at the long walnut bar, jabbering noisily. I yearned to join the boisterous, laughing crowd and throw down a fast highball or two, but I took a seat in a booth instead. It was the ladylike thing to do. (No nasty remarks, please!)

Before I even had a chance to light up a cigarette, Elsie Londergan breezed in. She hooked her coat on the rack near the door, waved to the bartender, and slid into the booth across the table from me. "Brrrrrr!" she said, removing her green wool gloves but leaving on her green felt hat, which had a sprig of fake holly pinned to the brim. "I'm wearing thick wool stockings, a heavy wool skirt, two slips, and two sweaters, and I'm still freezing! I think I'll have a hot buttered rum instead of a beer, if that's okay with you."

"Sure," I said, nervously adding up the extra cost in my mind. I'd have enough, I figured, if I didn't order a drink. I hoped there'd be a dime left over for the subway.

"So, Paige Turner," Elsie said, craning her chiseled John Wayne chin over the scarred wood tabletop and speaking in a conspiratorial tone. "Have you dug up any dirt? Do you know who killed Judy?"

"No," I said, suddenly feeling very tired and dejected. "I don't have a clue. But I *have* spoken to a few . . ."

I cut my sentence short when the waiter appeared to take our order. Elsie ordered a hot buttered rum and a hamburger with a side of fries. I asked for a hamburger and a glass of water.

As soon as the waiter left, Elsie leaned over the table

again. “Hey, why the water?” she wanted to know. “Are you a teetotaler or something?”

“No,” I said, grimacing at the horrible thought, “I’m just trying to keep a clear head.” I didn’t tell her that my head hadn’t been clear since 1951.

Elsie patted the fringe of blue-gray hair sticking out beneath her hat and smiled sympathetically. Then she turned her attention back to the murder. “So, who did you speak to? Have you learned anything important?”

I gave her a quick summary of everything that had happened since I’d seen her the day before, relating the highlights of my conversations with Vicki Lee Bumstead and Jimmy Birmingham. “Gregory Smith’s real name is Gregory Smythe,” I told her, “and Judy knew it all along. And since she always told you everything, I’m surprised she didn’t tell you *that*.”

“Me, too,” Elsie said, pausing, looking perplexed, obviously giving the matter further thought. Then suddenly her eyes popped wide. “I bet I know what happened!” she sputtered. “I bet Judy *did* give me his real name, but just didn’t *say* it right! She wasn’t very well-educated, you know, and she was always getting her words mixed up. She probably thought ‘Smith’ was the right pronunciation.”

Elsie’s explanation seemed possible—even plausible—to me. “Did she ever give you his personal address or phone number?”

“No, but she probably didn’t have that information herself. Cheating sidewinders like Smythe like to keep that kind of stuff secret.”

“What about Jimmy Birmingham? Did Judy ever mention him?”

“Yeah, he was her boyfriend before Smythe. She said he was a poet or a sculptor, or something arty-farty like that.”

“Did he ever visit her in her apartment? Did you ever see him in your building or around the neighborhood?”

“Can’t say. I never met the man, so I don’t know what he looks like.”

I took the picture of Judy and Jimmy and Otto out of my

purse and handed it to her. She held it up toward the light for a couple of seconds, then slapped it down on the tabletop. "Yes!" she cried, getting excited. "I *did* see this joker around the neighborhood a couple of times! I remember because he was carrying that little dog under his arm. Had it wrapped up in a towel. Do you think he's the one who . . ."

Elsie stopped talking when the waiter reappeared with our food and drinks. And after the waiter left, she was too busy chomping fries and guzzling rum to speak. And when she started chewing on her hamburger with the gusto of a famished fullback, I realized our conversation wouldn't be resumed until she had finished eating. So I took a sip of my water, slathered ketchup on my bun, and tackled my own hamburger—matching Elsie bite for bite.

Our plates were clean in under five minutes. "You want coffee?" Elsie asked, popping the last french fry in her mouth.

The jig was up. I could actually hear my wallet groaning. "Yes, I do, Elsie," I said, sighing, "but I can't have any. And neither can you."

"Huh? Why not?"

"Because I don't feel like washing the dishes."

"You mean you don't have enough money?"

"That's one way to put it."

"Well, why the hell didn't you say so?" she cried. "I can kick in for the java. I got lucky at bingo last night."

"Thanks," I said. "Java would be swell."

The waiter cleared our dishes and brought us two steaming mugs of coffee. Then we both lit up cigarettes and returned to more homicidal concerns.

"Did Smythe give Judy any expensive gifts?" I probed, wanting to find out if Elsie knew about the diamonds. "Any furs or jewels or anything that might have attracted a burglar or a killer?"

"He gave her a bunch of jewelry, but I bet it was just paste."

"Why do you say that?"

"Because Smythe strikes me as a world-class cheapskate, that's why!"

"But he paid Judy's rent . . ."

"Yeah, but that didn't set him back much. Only sixty-five bucks a month. You've seen my apartment! Well, Judy's was just like it—a small dark railroad with no doors and lots of cockroaches. Not exactly the Taj Mahal."

"Yes, I know," I admitted. "I was there this afternoon."

"You were?" Elsie said, taken aback. She braced her broad shoulders against the wooden backrest of the booth and looked at me suspiciously. "And how did that little event come about?" Was it my imagination or was she upset about something?

"I saw an ad for Judy's apartment in the paper so I went to Chelsea Realty and asked to see it, pretending I was looking for a new place to live. I wanted to see the place firsthand. Your landlord took me over."

"Roscoe? Roscoe took you there?" She looked kind of panicky now.

"Yes . . . Is there something wrong with that? I just wanted to get a feel for the crime scene."

"Did you tell him who you are?"

"Well, no. I put down a phony name and address on the application."

She turned quiet for a few seconds, mulling over what I'd just said. Then she took one last drag on her cigarette and crushed it in the ashtray. "I wish you hadn't done that, Paige. You should have spoken to me first."

"But why? What's the problem?" I was feeling kind of panicky now myself.

"After you left my place yesterday," Elsie began, frowning as she spoke, "I couldn't stop thinking about what you said: that Judy was probably murdered—on purpose—by somebody she knew. And I was going nuts wondering if that was true. So, instead of just sitting there like a stump, staring into space and trying to figure out who the killer could be, I decided to get up off my buttocks and do a little detective work on my own."

*Bubble, bubble, here comes trouble . . .*

"So I went down to the realty office and had a little talk

with Roscoe," Elsie continued. "I asked him why he went to Judy's apartment the night she was killed and what time he found the body."

"And what did he say?" I interjected, panting like a high-strung poodle. I had been wanting to know the answers to those very same questions. *Hey, maybe it won't be so bad having John Wayne as a deputy after all!*

"He said he went to Judy's place around eight-thirty to check her radiators. She had complained she wasn't getting enough heat. When she didn't answer the door, he opened it himself—it wasn't locked—and went inside. He found her dead body lying in a pool of blood in the sitting room. The blood was still warm."

"He *touched* it?"

"Yeah, I guess so." She closed her eyes and shuddered. "That little weasel gives me the creeps!"

"Ditto," I said, putting out my cigarette and lighting another. "Did you ask him anything else?"

"I asked him for Gregory Smith's real name."

"Did he give it to you?"

"No. He told me to go jump in a lake. He said he already told the police everything, that I should butt out and leave the detective work up to them."

I hated to admit it (even just to myself!), but Roscoe Swift was beginning to sound a heck of a lot like Dan Street. "So, was that the end of your conversation?" I asked her.

"Not exactly," she said, slumping her shoulders and casting her eyes down at the tabletop.

*Ugh!* . . . "You mean there was more?"

"I realize now I shouldn't have said anything," Elsie muttered, "but at the time it seemed like the right thing to do."

A squirt of adrenaline shot up my spine. "*What* seemed like the right thing to do?" I was trying to keep my voice calm and steady, but I probably sounded like Ralph Kramden in the throes of a roaring hissy fit. "What did you *say?*"

Elsie raised her eyes and gave me an apologetic look. "I told Roscoe about you."

I couldn't speak. A cat had its claws in my tongue.

Elsie nervously cleared her throat and went on. "I thought Roscoe would be more communicative if I told him what was really going on, made him feel like an insider in the investigation," she explained. "So I told him everything I knew about you. That your name was Paige Turner and you were a friend of Judy's brother Terry. That you worked for *Daring Detective* magazine and were trying to help Terry prove that his sister had been intentionally murdered, *not* killed by chance during a burglary. That you were a very nice person who really cared about Judy Catcher and was determined to find out the truth about her death."

"And how did Roscoe react?" I stammered, freeing my tongue and flapping it frantically. "Was he surprised by what you said? Did he show any concern? Did he give you any more information?"

"No," Elsie said, embarrassed. "All he showed was anger, and all he said was, 'Get lost, Elsie, you're bugging me.' " She paused and gave me a sad little smile. "I'm really sorry, Paige," she added. "I was trying to help you, not hurt you."

She seemed distressed so I hastened to reassure her. "Don't worry about it, Elsie," I said. "You may not have hurt me at all. Maybe Roscoe never put two and two together. Maybe he never realized that Paige Turner and Phoebe Starr were the same person."

"Phoebe Starr?" She popped me a questioning look.

"My alter ego," I explained, "the name I put on the rental application." I stubbed out my cigarette and took a few sips of coffee, brooding over the possible ramifications of this unexpected development. And after several more seconds of silence, I sucked up my optimism and proclaimed, "Even if Roscoe *does* figure out the Phoebe/Paige connection, what does it matter now? I don't intend to see him again or ask him any more questions, so it really doesn't make any difference. He never would have given me any significant information anyway."

I was trying to convince myself as well as Elsie that Roscoe's knowledge of my real name and occupation posed no threat to me or my investigation. And, for Elsie's part, I succeeded. Convincing myself, however, turned out to be a hopeless objective. Because no matter how hard I tried to banish a certain unpleasant thought from my muddled, maniacal mind, it kept coming back to haunt me: *If Roscoe Swift had anything whatsoever to do with Judy's murder—or even just knows somebody who did—then I'm up poop creek without a paddle.*

# Chapter 17

HAVE YOU EVER WISHED THAT YOU COULD just pack up your life and leap out of your body and become somebody else entirely? Well, that's the way I felt that cold, dark, disturbing winter evening. All the way home on the subway (Elsie insisted on splitting the check with me, so I had plenty left over) I kept thinking about how great it would be if I could just go to sleep, or fall into a brief coma or something, and wake up as Esther Williams. Then I could swim all my days away, in a graceful aquatic ballet, doing the backstroke in a vast pool of sparkling turquoise water, wearing a dazzling silver bathing suit and pointing one strong, tanned, shapely leg straight up toward the sun.

Okay, so that was a pretty dopey fantasy, but it sure beat the other vision that kept fighting to take over my mind, the one where I was drowning in a murky sea of doubt and suspicion, arms and legs thrashing, with my head being held under by a nameless, faceless killer who was never, ever, ever going to let me come up for air.

Luckily, Abby saved me from both engulfing illusions. As soon as I let myself into our building and began the climb to my apartment, she appeared at the top of the stairs, holding what looked like a whiskey sour—complete with orange slice and bright red cherry—in her left hand. "Hurry up!" she called, dangling the drink toward me like a carrot. "Whitey and I have been waiting for you, and we've got news!"

I was up the stairs in a millisecond.

"What is it?" I spluttered, taking the drink in my gloved hand and lunging into her apartment. "Did you find out something about the diamonds?" Cocktails and clues—they'll get me every time.

"Yeah," Terry said, "but we're not sure what it all means." He was sitting at the kitchen table smoking a Pall Mall and slurping his own whiskey sour. He didn't look like a Hasidic Jew anymore. Now he looked like his normal clean-shaven white-haired self, except for the brown shoe-polished fringe around his ears and neck.

I plopped down at the table—coat, purse, lunchbox and all—and took a big swig of my drink. "So what happened? What did you learn?"

A wry smirk tugged at his lips. "Well, one thing we learned is that a couple of detectives *have* been sniffing around the exchange, looking for me. They were there again this afternoon, in fact, going from booth to booth, asking the dealers a lot of questions, then telling them to be on the lookout for a young man with white hair who recently stole some diamond jewelry and may now be trying to sell it."

"Oh, brother!" I croaked, thwacking the tabletop with my still-gloved hand. "Sweeny and his boys are working much harder to recover the diamonds than they ever did to find Judy's killer. That really burns me up!"

"You and me both," Abby chimed in, joining us at the table. "But you know what really fries *my* tush?" she added, talking to me but focusing her gaze and full attention on Terry. "They wouldn't even *know* about the diamonds if Whitey hadn't found them and taken them to the station!" Flames of indignation (and, if you ask me, *infatuation*) were blazing in her beautiful brown eyes.

"And if you hadn't designed such a great disguise for me," Terry said to her, "I would have been arrested today." He was staring at Abby with a look of sheer awe and gratitude on his face. And what was that glow I saw spreading across his cheeks? Was that a *blush?* I studied it more closely and decided it was. No doubt about it. Terry was smitten. He had finally flipped for Abby. I had known it would happen eventually and, frankly, I was surprised it had taken so long. Abby's potent charms—like her powerful cocktails—usually took effect immediately.

"But what about the diamonds?" I said, hating to spoil the magnetism of the moment, but dying to know if there were any new keys to the crime. "Did any of the dealers recognize the jewelry or know where it came from?"

"Every single piece came from Tiffany's!" Abby piped, happily jumping from one source of rapture to another. "Aunt Dora identified the settings immediately. She said each item came from the same line—a rare and much sought-after Tiffany design that originated in the early thirties. And because of this, Judy's jewelry is worth even more than thirty thousand. Aunt Dora says the true value is in the vicinity of thirty-six to thirty-eight grand!" She was thrilled to the point of hyperventilation.

I mulled over Abby's news for a moment, then fired off a few burning questions: "Did your aunt or any of your other relatives ever see these particular pieces before? Do they have any idea who the original owner could be? Have they ever heard of Gregory Smythe?"

"No to all of the above."

"Do they know if the diamonds were ever stolen? By somebody other than Terry, I mean."

"They haven't heard anything about that," Abby said. "And that's the point, you dig? My cousin Mitchell says if a collection of beautiful vintage jewelry like this *had* been reported stolen, then every dealer in the exchange would know about it—either through the police or industry gossip. So, since nobody there has heard even a whisper about any such heist, you can pretty much bet it never happened."

"Or was never reported," I amended.

"But that's a crazy idea!" Abby cried. "Who in their right

mind wouldn't report a robbery that big? You're talking thirty-eight thousand dollars worth of diamonds! Nobody's going to take that kind of hit sitting down. And what about the insurance? You can't collect the insurance if you don't report the theft."

"Yes, but . . . oh, I don't know . . ." Abby's words made perfect sense to me, but I still had my doubts—vague misgivings I couldn't explain.

And Terry had some doubts of his own. "You can't report a theft if you're dead," he said, growing sad, obviously brooding about what had happened to his sister.

I put my hand over his and gave it a sympathetic squeeze. "That's certainly true, Terry," I said, "and it's entirely possible there could be *other* deaths connected to these diamonds. But we have no way to check that out right now, so we can't waste our time speculating. We have to focus on the only two facts we know—that the jewelry came from Tiffany's and was given to Judy by Gregory Smythe—and then follow the trail from there."

"Did you get Smythe's address or phone number yet?" Abby asked

"No," I admitted, downing the rest of my drink. "Roscoe wouldn't blab." I gave Abby and Terry a full account of my latest excursions—to the Chelsea Realty office and Judy's apartment and the Green Monkey—sadly acknowledging my total failure to unearth any new leads, and ending my dismal tale with the alarming revelation that Elsie had told Roscoe my real name. "She told him where I work, too!" I said (okay, *shrieked*). "And all he needs is a phone book to find out where I live!" To say that I was beside myself is putting it rather mildly. I was beneath myself and above myself as well.

"What the hell was that woman thinking?!" Abby cried, eyes blazing again.

"The problem is that she *wasn't* thinking," I said.

Abby gave me a sidelong look and snarled, "I wouldn't be so sure about that!"

Her vehement demeanor brought me up short. "What do you mean?"

"I mean who *is* this old dame anyway? And how do you know she really *was* like a mother to Judy? All you have is *her* own word for it! For all we know, she could be in cahoots with Roscoe Swift. Or even teamed up with Gregory Smythe! She could be a crazy cat burglar . . . or a deranged killer. Or both rolled into one!"

Abby's wild conjectures almost made me laugh out loud. Almost, but not quite. Because as amused as I was trying to visualize a beastly murderer with Toni-waved blue hair, or a large ungainly cat burglar with a sprig of holly pinned to her hat, I didn't find it so funny when a more common image sprang suddenly to mind. An image I'd seen many times before. A wide-screen technicolor close-up of John Wayne firing a gun.

But the Duke was always the good guy, right?

"Oh, I don't think Elsie had anything to do with it, Abby!" I protested. "In the first place, Vicki Lee Bumstead confirmed that Judy and Elsie were very close. She said Judy told her that Elsie was the mother she'd always wished for. And in the second place, Elsie doesn't seem to have any idea how much Judy's diamonds were worth. She thinks they were made of paste."

"Yeah, yeah, that's what she *says,* but do you always believe everything anybody tells you?" Abby's right eyebrow was hoisted so high you could've parked a Chevy under it.

"Well, no, but . . ."

"I agree with Paige," Terry broke in, giving Abby a penetrating look. "I only had one conversation with Elsie," he said, "and even then we weren't alone. Sweeny was there, too." He pronounced the not-so-diligent detective's name with a drawl of disgust. "But Elsie struck me as a solid citizen," he said with passionate intent . . . "a woman of very strong character—and a true friend to my sister."

Well, that was all Abby needed to hear. One word from her smoldering new flame, and she was ready to capitulate—arched eyebrow and all. "Then consider the subject dropped," she said, leaning toward him in sultry obedience. "Any true friend of your sister's is a true friend of mine."

(Translation: "I'm yours. Do what you will with me.")

It was time for me to leave.

"Okay, kids, I'm splitting," I said, grabbing my purse and the shopping bag and standing up from my chair. "I've got to go call Vicki, see if she got the dope on Smythe." I was glad I was still wearing my hat and coat and gloves. The less to pick up and carry, the better. (When you're the third wheel in an amorous encounter on the verge of its first encountering, it is—in my opinion—a good idea to wheel out of the vicinity as quickly and efficiently as possible.)

My speedy retreat was uncontested. A grateful glance from Terry, a happy wink from Abby, and I was gone.

AS I WAS LETTING MYSELF INTO MY OWN apartment, I remembered the diamonds. I had left them next door. I thought of going back to get them—so I could return them to the clever concealment of their oatmeal box hideaway—but I quickly decided against it. I figured they'd be much safer at Abby's place now—now that *my* place was as incognito as the Chrysler Building.

As soon as I had set down my shopping bag and shucked off all my outerwear, including my snowboots, I sat down on the couch/door/daybed, tucked my cold feet up under my bottom, and dialed Vicki. She answered the phone herself.

"Hi, Vicki," I said. "This is Phoebe. Phoebe Starr." I would have told her my real name (since everybody *else* knew it), but I didn't want to take the time to explain all my complicated reasons for having first used a fake one.

"Oh, hi, Phoebe," she said. "I'm glad you called. I got that information you wanted." Her rough, husky voice was music to my ears.

"Really?" I yelped, too stunned to let myself believe it. "You've got Gregory Smythe's address and phone number?"

"Not his *home* address or phone," she said apologetically. "Just his place of business. All of his Macy's purchases were charged directly to his office."

"Oh, that's okay, Vicki! Any address and phone number

will do. All I need is some way to get in touch with him. Hold on a sec! Let me get something to write with." I dropped the phone down on the daybed and dashed to the kitchen table for a piece of typing paper and a pen. Then I bounded back to the living room, yanked the phone back up to my mouth, and cried, "Shoot!"

"He works at a place called Farnsworth Fiduciary," Vicki reported. "The address is 647 Fifth Avenue, Suite 600, and the phone number is Oregon 6-8000. That's all my friend could find in the files."

"Well, that's more than enough, Vicki!" I said, scribbling the info down and working to keep myself from squealing. "Please thank your friend for me."

"I will," she said, turning silent for a moment. "But I'm still not sure I should have gotten this information for you," she went on. "I mean, how are you going to use it? You're not going to give Mr. Smythe any grief, are you? He's one of the sweetest men I've ever met, and if anything bad happens to him because of me, I'll never forgive myself." She sounded truly concerned.

"I'll be very careful, Vicki," I said. "And if it turns out Gregory Smythe had nothing to do with Judy's murder, then he'll get no trouble from me."

"Can I have your word on that?"

"Of course." My hand wasn't on the Bible when I made this vow, but I felt sworn to it just the same. "And will you promise to call me if you think of anything else—anything at all—that might have some bearing on the murder?"

"Okay," she said, sounding as hoarse as a high school cheerleader after the big game.

I gave Vicki my phone number and thanked her profusely, pledging to keep her informed of my progress in the case and to take her out to lunch just as soon as the holidays were over. Then I wished her a merry Christmas and hung up.

Half a heartbeat later I picked up the phone and dialed Dan's office again.

It was 9:30 P.M.—prime crime time in the Midtown South Precinct—so I wasn't at all surprised when they told me Dan wasn't there. What I *was,* however, was devastated. I thought if I didn't talk to Dan soon I would shrivel up in a ball and die. Can you believe that? I had seen the man just twenty-four hours ago—and he wasn't even being *nice* to me at the time!—and here I was about to start bawling like a deserted wife (or, more precisely, like a colicky infant who had dropped her pacifier).

*Help! Somebody save me!*

I jumped to my feet and started pacing around the living room, taking lots of deep breaths, doing my best to take control of my preposterous emotions. And I might have achieved this worthy goal if I hadn't already been in a full-blown dither about Jimmy Birmingham and Roscoe Swift and Gregory Smythe. And if Abby hadn't knocked me for a loop with her doubts about Elsie Londergan.

And if my buzzer hadn't buzzed.

Leaping straight up in the air (and straight out of my skin), I actually went blank for a moment. I couldn't remember who I was, or where I was, or why my legs were shaking. Then my buzzer rang again, which brought me back to myself, which brought me back to wondering which of the aforementioned possible murderers was at my door. I darted across to the living room window, pulled a big gap in the side of the shade, and peered down at the large, broad-shouldered figure standing one floor below, right in front of the building's entrance.

One glimpse of the man's face (which was entirely visible since his head was tilted back and he was looking straight up through the window at me) melted away all my fears and misgivings. It was Dan. And he was—miracle of all miracles—smiling.

I bounded ballet-style across the floor, buzzed him in, and stood waiting in my open doorway for him to climb the stairs to my apartment. I didn't have to wait long. He took the stairs two at a time and reached the landing in a flash. Then he scooped me up in his arms, crushed me to his chest, and smothered my gasping mouth with the hardest, roughest, deepest, hottest kiss I'd ever experienced in my whole wide wishful life.

"I'm sorry, Paige," he mumbled, after he'd sucked his way across my cheek and planted his panting mouth right next to my ear. "I shouldn't have walked out on you the way I did last night. I felt bad about it all day." His humid breath whooshed into my ear and streamed all the way down to my toes.

"I'm the one who's sorry," I moaned. "I never should have . . ." I guess Dan wasn't interested in hearing the rest of my apology because he gave me another big fat kiss right then, making it impossible for me to speak. And this effective silencing maneuver had—as you've probably already guessed—a profound effect on me.

When we finally came up for air, Dan stepped back and clasped his hands to my shoulders, holding me firmly at arm's length. "I hate to kiss and run," he said with a sexy smirk, "but I've got to go. We're closing in on the Bradbury killer tonight."

"Phwat? Phwoo?" My lips were free but they still weren't functional.

"The Broadway producer who was stabbed at the Majestic," Dan said, somehow understanding my questions. "We know who the murderer is and we're on the way to arrest him now. My partner on this case is waiting for me in the car, so I've got to get a move on." He dropped his hands from my shoulders, anchored his hat at a new angle, and turned toward the stairs. "I'll call you tomorrow, babe." He was down the steps and out the door before I could babble another word.

I SPENT THE REST OF THE EVENING FLOATing on a cloud. (The cherubs lolling on the fluffs of angel hair at Macy's had nothing, and I do mean *nothing,* on me!) I sat at the typewriter for an hour or so, bringing all my notes on the murder up to date, without having a single anxiety fit. I wrote down every clue to the killing I could think of, never worrying—even for a second—about the danger the killer might pose to me. I drank one Dr. Pepper and smoked three L&M filter tips without once jumping up to peek through the shade to see if Jimmy Birmingham was hanging out at the laundromat. I was so cool I was downright cucumberal.

(It's amazing what one little kiss—okay, two great big juicy ones—can do.)

When I finished my story notes I turned on the radio. Eddie Fisher was singing "Oh! My Papa." Well, I was in far too sensual a mood to listen to *that,* so I kept turning the dial, searching for a better song, finally settling on "Make Yourself Comfortable" by Sarah Vaughan. Then I took my Santa Claus paper and red satin ribbon out of the coat closet and wrapped up Lenny's lunchbox. After placing the wrapped package back in the shopping bag and setting it near the door (so I wouldn't forget to take it with me to work in the morning), I turned off the radio and the downstairs lights and floated up to bed.

# Chapter 18

I GOT UP FORTY-FIVE MINUTES EARLIER than usual the next morning, figuring I'd need extra time at the office to deal with the mess from the day before. I knew what the results of my one-day absence would be: a Coffeemaster full of burnt coffee grounds, a slew of dirty cups, a pile of unsorted mail, stacks of unfiled photos and unrecorded invoices, and several unopened deliveries from the typesetter and the printer, which would yield reams of unproofread proofs and heaps of photostats that should have—but no doubt *wouldn't* have—been logged in and distributed to the art department.

And to top it all off, I knew I'd have to spend a good part of my lunch hour (assuming Pomeroy allowed me to have one) buying cookies and eggnog (and a bottle of bourbon, I hoped) for the office Christmas party, which had been scheduled for that same afternoon. And somehow—while juggling all the cup-cleaning and the coffee-brewing and the proofreading and the paperwork and the party preparations—I would have to find a way (preferably a *safe* way) to hook up with Gregory Smythe.

Trying to perk myself up for the difficult day ahead, I took an extra hot shower, applied an extra dab of red lipstick, and put on one of my favorite outfits—a deep green flare skirt and a white angora twinset with tiny pearl buttons. To add a festive touch, I tied a red chiffon scarf around my neck. Then—making a goofy Marilyn Monroe–style smoochy face at myself in the foggy bathroom mirror—I scrambled down the stairs, put on all my winterwear, grabbed my purse and the bag with Lenny's Christmas present in it, and hurried to the subway.

The platform was unusually overcrowded, even for the rush hour. It seemed that everybody in the Village had decided to travel uptown at the exact same moment. Wanting to make certain that I was able to board the very next northbound train, I squeezed into the crowd at the southernmost end of the station and worked my way up to the front line—to the extreme edge of the cement ledge overlooking the tracks. It was so cold the other commuters didn't mind my heated intrusion. We all stood as closely and docilely together as cows in a too-small corral—breathing steam into the frigid air, stamping our feet to improve circulation, and straining our restless ears for the chug, clatter, and clank of the next string of stock cars.

After just a few minutes I heard a loud whistle. Leaning slightly forward, I craned my neck to the left, peering southward, hoping the approaching choo-choo would be coming from that direction. It was. Due to a wide curve in the tunnel, I couldn't actually *see* the train, but the glare of the engine's headlight foretold its imminent arrival. Stepping back from the ledge a bit, I straightened my shoulders and prepared myself for the big push forward—when the train would pull into the station and screech to a stop, and all the prospective passengers would try to crush through the open doors at once.

But the big push came *before* the train arrived, and I was the only one who moved forward. Way too *far* forward. So horribly and hideously far forward that my feet flew off the platform and I sailed out over the tracks like a clown shot from a cannon. Then I plummeted six feet down to the train bed, landing on my hands and knees in a layer of jagged gravel, both shins thwacking—like slender tree limbs—against a steel-hard metal rail.

The pain was so great and the shock so severe that I almost passed out. I surely would have, too, if the train whistle hadn't shrieked again, and if the glare of the madly onrushing headlight hadn't grown much brighter, filling me with terror and making any kind of blackout—however beckoning—next to impossible. The train was coming around the bend at the speed of sound. I had to move!

I vaulted to my feet, leapt back over to the crowded platform, lifted my arms, and grabbed hold of the ledge. Then I jumped as hard and high as I possibly could, desperately trying to swing my weight up onto my arms and haul the rest of my body back up to the floor of the boarding deck.

I couldn't make it. The cliff was too high. And the train was bearing down fast. The people right above me began screaming and crying and scrambling to get out of the way. I guess they didn't want to get splattered. For lack of a better idea (or any idea at all), I flattened the front of my body against the side of the platform, held my arms up over my head (I thought they'd be safer up there), squeezed my eyes shut, and sent a frantic mental telegram to Bob, telling him to meet me at the pearly gate, I'd be there in a minute.

But my train trip to heaven was canceled abruptly. By a large muscle-bound Negro wearing a tan wool jacket, a black porkpie hat, and the world's sweetest smile—details I didn't discover until several harrowing moments later, when I finally found the courage to open my eyes.

Since I didn't actually see what happened, I can't describe it firsthand. All I can tell you is what one of the breathless eyewitnesses told me (while I was still lying on my back in a near stupor on the platform floor): that the huge, strapping Negro kneeling over me in such sweet-faced concern had risked his own life to save mine. That he had leaned out over the edge of the boarding deck (thereby placing his own head and shoulders in the direct path of the incoming train) and grabbed both of my wrists in his big meaty paws. Then he had pulled me—like a sack of potatoes—up and over the ledge of the platform, onto the dirty, cold cement floor of the loading area. A split second later, the train had streaked in . . . and come to a dead stop for a moment or two . . . and then streaked out again, loaded to the gills with new passengers—most of whom hadn't (like the engineer himself, apparently) even caught a glimpse of what had just happened to me.

"You mean I'm still alive?" I asked, not sure that I believed it. It seemed far more likely that I had come face to face with Saint Peter, who just happened to be a smiling Negro wearing a porkpie hat.

After being assured that I was, indeed, still a resident of Earth, I pulled myself up to a sitting position on the floor and began thanking (and rethanking and *re*rethanking!) the man who had lifted and dragged me to safety. I choked and sputtered and spilled out my heartfelt gratitude. I kissed his enormous hands and patted his sweet cheeks and showered him with a thousand blessings. And then I looked around for my purse. I wanted to give my rescuer a cash reward, and though I knew all I had with me was some loose change, I wanted to write down his name and address so I could send him a substantial gift later. (From the holes in his thin tan jacket, I could tell he needed it.)

I didn't see my purse or shopping bag anywhere, and I didn't have the slightest idea what had happened to them, so I asked one of the concerned eyewitnesses (several of whom had stuck around to make sure I was all right) to see if he could find them. The first place he looked was down on the tracks, but neither of the bags was there, so he walked up and down the length of the platform, looking under benches and around the trash bins.

He never found the shopping bag, but he *did* find my purse, right near the spot where I had fallen, wedged under the bottom rim of a large, standing, sand-filled ashtray. I figured I had dropped it when I fell; that it had been inadvertently kicked under the ashtray by one or more of the frantic onlookers. I took my notepad out of my purse (all diligent detectives carry one, you know!) and wrote down my savior's name and address: Elijah Peeps, 248 East 139th Street. Then

I thanked the brave, shy (and, luckily, very *strong*) man yet again and told him he'd be hearing from me soon.

They helped me to my feet and asked me if they should call a doctor. I told them no, I was okay—which wasn't exactly the truth. Though my palms were fine (they had been protected by my gloves), my knees were scathed and bloodied and embedded with bits of gravel, and both of my gashed shins were beginning to swell and hurt like hell. Still, I could tell that no bones were broken. And the last thing in the world I needed was to waste the whole morning having my wounds cleaned up in a doctor's office when I could do that perfectly well myself, in the ladies' room at my own office, using the first aid kit I kept well-stocked and on hand in the supply closet. My nylons were ripped to shreds, but I had a spare pair in my desk.

They asked me if they should call the subway authorities, or a lawyer, or the police. Did I want to report the incident, or file some kind of claim? I told them no; that nobody was to blame but me; that the accident was entirely my own fault since I had been standing too close to the platform's edge.

I was lying, of course. I knew I had been pushed. I also knew that the monster who'd pushed me had—for some utterly unfathomable reason—stolen Lenny's lunchbox.

AS SHAKEN AND BRUISED AND BLOODIED AS I was, I insisted on boarding the next uptown train, which pulled into the station a few minutes later. (If you fall off a horse, blah, blah, blah . . .) Elijah Peeps and my other new friends and protectors got in the same car with me. We all had to get to work (except for Elijah, who was on his way *home* from work), and we were glad to go together. I was the gladdest of all, to be sure. The comforting presence of my band of kindly caretakers kept me from having a nervous breakdown when the train lurched forward—or passing out when the shrill whistle blew.

Two members of our group got off the train before I did—one at 14th Street, the other at 23rd. Two others got off with me at Times Square. As soon as we had squeezed our way out of the crowded car, I turned and peered back through the train window, fastening my eyes on Elijah Peeps's bashful brown face.

I smiled and waved at him; he smiled and waved back. I folded my hands in a prayerful gesture in front of my heart for a second, then blew him a soulful kiss. He gave me another shy smile and then bowed his head in embarrassment (certain unwritten racial restrictions prohibited him from blowing *me* a kiss). I waved again and so did he. And several highly emotional eons later—long after the train had whisked away, spiriting my incomparable hero totally out of sight—I was still waving.

# Chapter 19

THE SECOND PART OF MY MORNING WENT a bit more smoothly than the first. (All evidence to the contrary, I am not *completely* incapable of understatement.) I got to work on time (it's astonishing how brief a full-blown brush with death can be!), so I was able to clean up my knees and shins, as well as all the coffee cups, before Harvey Crockett stomped in.

"Glad you could make it," he scoffed, hanging his hat and coat on the tree. He didn't ask how I was feeling or anything, which was just as well, since—not knowing what ailment Lenny had used for my sickday excuse—I wouldn't have known how to respond. "Coffee ready?" he asked.

I could hardly believe my ears. It was a polite (for Crockett) inquiry instead of a gruff demand.

"Yes, sir," I said, wondering what had caused this odd outbreak of civility.

"Then bring me some, please," he said, stomping away toward his private office.

*Please?* Did the man actually utter the word *please?* Either Crockett had suddenly been struck with the holiday spirit, or he had really, really missed me (his morning coffee, that is).

After I'd taken the boss his newspapers and caffeine and returned to my desk, Lenny stumbled in. He hooked his hat and coat on the rack and—lunch sack in hand—hurried right over to me, still red-faced and out of breath from his nine-flight climb.

"All right, out with it, Paige!" he said between loud intakes of oxygen. "You can't keep me in the dark forever. I want to know what you're up to, and I want to know right *now*."

"Good morning to you, too," I said, pretending to be insulted by his discourteous greeting.

"Yeah, okay, good morning. Now tell me what's going on. Where were you yesterday? I called your apartment at least three times. You've gotten yourself in deep trouble again, right? I can tell by your shifty eyes."

"Don't be ridiculous!" I said, stalling, still pretending to be miffed. "I never had a shifty eye in my life!" It wasn't that I didn't want Lenny to know about Judy's murder and my efforts to find out who killed her. It was just that it was all so complicated and would take me so darn long to explain. And then, afterward—after I'd rehashed all the ugly details till I was blue in the face—I'd still have to listen to all of Lenny's dreadful death warnings, not to mention his dire predictions that I was going to lose my job. Ugh. I simply didn't have the time (or the stomach) to deal with Lenny's anxieties. I could barely handle my own. "Look, Lenny, you really can't . . ."

I was interrupted (okay, *saved*) by the office entry bell. And for once in my life, I was really glad to see Mike and Mario.

"Hello, boys!" I said, flirting, doing my best Jayne Mansfield (which meant I probably looked and sounded just like Francis the Talking Mule). "How's tricks?" I was trying to engage them in a bout of spicy banter, so that Lenny would get embarrassed and sulk away and stop badgering me.

A glint of suspicion flashed in Mario's eye. He knew I was faking, not really making a pass. But for once in *his* life, he didn't try to one-up me. He hung his hat and coat on the rack and turned toward his desk in the rear without making a single nasty crack about my name or sex. All he said (in a *very* sarcastic tone) was, "Nice of you to join us today, Paige. There's a great deal of work to be done. And you can bring me some coffee now, if you're not too busy."

Mike didn't make any jokes either. He merely aped Mario's moves at the coat rack, then sat down at his desk and lit up a Lucky. "I'll have some coffee, too, please," he mumbled.

*What was that word? Did I just hear another* please? *What the hell's* wrong *with everybody today?*

I gave Lenny a questioning look, but he just raised his eyebrows and shrugged, signaling that he didn't understand our coworkers' weird behavior either. Then—knowing full well I'd never say a word about my new story investigation while Mike and Mario were in the same room—Lenny shot me a fierce *you-damn-well-better-tell-me-everything-soon* look and marched off down the aisle toward his desk in the back corner, slapping his sandwich bag impatiently against his thigh.

BY THE TIME THE LUNCH HOUR ROLLED around, I had all the office work under control. And since Pomeroy hadn't come in yet, I was free to leave at the stroke of noon. I grabbed all my stuff—plus the shopping list for the Christmas party and the petty cash Crockett had given me to pay for everything—and made a mad dash for the elevators, praying I wouldn't run into Pomeroy on my way out.

When I reached the lobby, I actually hid behind the big Christmas tree for a minute, peering through the glass wall and revolving glass doors of the entryway, until I was certain the coast was clear—that Pomeroy wasn't approaching or about to enter the building. Then I wrapped my muffler around my face, pushed through the circling door, and scrambled back to the subway.

Even if you haven't believed a word I've written up to now, you should believe this: I really *hated* going down into the subway again. After what had happened to me that morning, the gloomy sights, metallic smells, and hideous skreaking sounds reverberating in that cold cement dungeon made me sick to my stomach. But I had to get across town *fast*—so the 42nd Street shuttle was the only way to go.

As you might imagine, I stood way, way, *way* back from the edge of the platform while I was waiting for the train. And when I changed trains at Times Square, taking the BMT up to 57th Street, I kept looking over my shoulder to make sure no murderers were behind me (which was a big fat waste of energy since I still didn't have a clue who killed Judy—or even a teeny-weeny little inkling who had tried to kill me).

Exiting the subway, I heaved a big whoosh of relief, and then sucked up my stamina again for the next stage of my lunch hour operation—the foray to Gregory Smythe's office.

I walked east on 57th from Sixth to Fifth, then—passing right by Tiffany's, of all places!—headed south toward 54th, hoping against hope that Smythe wouldn't have gone out to lunch yet. The sidewalks of this ultra elegant stretch of Fifth Avenue were completely free of snow and ice (God forbid a *rich* person should slip and fall down!), but so crowded with lunchgoers and partygoers and Christmas shoppers that the going was still pretty slow. Smythe's office was just three blocks away, though, so it didn't take me too long to get there.

The building was large and imposing, with a façade of glistening pinkish sandstone blocks, and a pair of heavy glass doors that led to a sleek yellow marble corridor. One side of the corridor was lined with potted trees and marble busts of the twelve Caesars, the other with elevators of gleaming aluminum. Despite the fact that many people were in the hallway, walking down the passage to the exit or milling about waiting for an elevator, the overall atmosphere was hushed and quiet. *Very* quiet.

I pushed the UP button on the closest elevator and stood waiting with a small group of men and women who were so perfectly primed and polished they looked as if they were on their way to have lunch with Ike and Mamie at the White House. Every hair was in place, every cheek was in bloom, every fingernail was manicured, every trouser leg was sharply creased, and every stocking seam was as straight as the edge of a ruler. The silent air was thick with the mingling aromas of aftershave and Chanel.

I felt conspicuously out of place—like a barn swallow in an aviary of exotic birds. My coat was camel's hair, not mink. My neck was adorned with red chiffon instead of pearls. My purse was leather, not lizard, and my snowboots were designed for a working, walking woman—not a lady of leisure and limousines. Most conspicuous of all was the fact that I was unescorted—i.e., by myself, all alone—*not* draped on the expensively tailored arm of a well-fed man wearing burnished wingtips and an onyx pinkie ring. (And, considering the fact that I live on top of a fish store, I don't even want to *think* about what kind of fragrance *I* might have been casting into that rarefied air.)

One of the well-tended women was staring at me—looking me over from beret to snowboots with a grimace of shock and horror on her face. Luckily, my green flare skirt was extra long—long enough to cover my mangled and swollen knees and shins. Otherwise, she might have fainted.

When the elevator doors swooshed open, I swept inside and swished to the back, telling the handsome young operator in his spiffy maroon uniform (complete with brass buttons and gold braid epaulets) to let me off on six. I wasn't sure that was the right floor, but where else would suite 600 be?

Good guess. As soon as I stepped off the elevator, I saw the entrance to Farnsworth Fiduciary. I couldn't have missed it if I'd tried. The enormous hand-carved wooden door was positioned directly across from the elevator, and the name of the company was spelled out in large, raised, gold metal letters. Looked like *real* gold to me. I walked across the wide marble hall and went inside.

The dignified young woman sitting at the receptionist's desk—a colossal wooden structure situated at least thirty feet from the entrance—looked up when I walked in. She smiled and nodded, but she didn't say anything to me until I had made my way across the vast lawn of ankle-deep moss green carpeting and arrived in front of the desk. Then she smoothed her champagne-blonde chignon, raised her ice blue eyes, widened her scarlet smile, and said, in a voice so soft it fairly whispered, "Welcome to Farnsworth Fiduciary. How may we help you today?"

She was beautiful and perfect. A dead ringer for Grace Kelly.

"I'm here to see Gregory Smythe," I announced, in the strongest, steadiest voice I could muster. I was trying to *look* strong and steady, too, which wasn't at all easy since—standing there in front of that beautiful blonde bird of paradise—I felt reduced to the meekest depths of barn swallowdom.

"Do you have an appointment?" she asked.

"No," I said, squaring my shoulders, straightening my spine to its fullest extent. "But please tell him Paige Turner is here. I think he'll want to see me." Given the possibility that Roscoe Swift, or Elsie Londergan (or anybody *else*, for that matter) had told Smythe about me, I figured my most judicious and effectual approach would be to use my real name.

"Paige Turner?" the receptionist repeated. Her perfectly plucked eyebrows were raised in amusement and disbelief. I could tell from the way her lips were twitching she was struggling not to laugh.

"Yes, that's right," I said with a cocky toss of my head. I was determined to stay strong, to stand tall and proud in spite of my silly name. And I might have accomplished this goal, too, if, when I tossed my head, my beret hadn't flown off and flopped to the floor like a misflipped flapjack.

Well, that did it. Grace Kelly totally lost her cool. She started laughing like a horse. And, though I've never actually heard a horse laugh, I'd be willing to bet the sounds produced by such an equine outburst would mimic exactly the loud snorts and whinnies then emanating from the nose and mouth of Farnsworth Fiduciary's refined receptionist.

Face burning with embarrassment, I picked up my errant beret and repositioned it on my head. And then, when I turned back to look at the receptionist's contorted face, I started laughing, too. What else was there to do? Besides, I found the whole scene really funny, like a skit straight out of *Your Show of Shows*—with me in the Imogene Coca role. And Grace Kelly's horsey laugh was a scream.

When we finally settled down, the ice had been thoroughly broken. Our pretensions had crumbled, and our shared crack-up had made us pals. "I'll see if Mr. Smythe is in," she said, giving me a collaborative wink and picking up the phone. She punched a button on one side of the phone and, taking a quick glance at the gold-plated clock on her desk, said to the person who answered, "Hello, Margaret. Please tell Mr. Smythe that his twelve-thirty appointment is here." After a short pause, she said, "Yes, that's right. Her name is Paige Turner and Mr. Smythe is expecting her." She pronounced my name carefully, with a perfectly straight face.

Hanging up the phone, she let out a little giggle, then returned (reluctantly, I thought) to her well-mannered receptionist's routine, and her whispery receptionist's voice. "Please take off your coat and have a seat, Miss Turner," she said, gesturing toward the brass coat rack and long green leather couch at the far side of the room. "Mr. Smythe's secretary will be out in a moment to show you to his office."

I gave her a very polite and refined (okay, gushing and effusive) thank-you and waded through the carpet to the waiting area.

THERE'S NO PLAINER WAY TO SAY IT: GREGory Smythe was a fool. A very tall, handsome, distinguished-looking, silver-haired fool, to be sure, but a fool nonetheless. I knew it the minute he stood up and welcomed me into his office by grabbing hold of my hand—and caressing it and fondling it and patting it passionately!—and then raising it to his mustached lips for a prickly kiss.

"So good of you to come, Miss Turner," he said, rolling his

big, hazel puppy-dog eyes in ecstasy. "And right on time, too!" The man was obviously accustomed to covering up forgotten appointments.

"It's *Mrs.* Turner," I blurted, and not a moment too soon. I could tell from his daft, voracious expression he was about to start nibbling on my fingers.

"Oh," he said, deflated, lowering my hand and letting it go with a look of sheer bereavement on his face. He seemed so sad I actually felt sorry for him. (Who was being the fool *now?*) Luckily for both of us, Smythe's recovery was speedy.

"Please have a seat, Mrs. Turner," he said, slinking his arm around my back and giving my shoulder a stealthy squeeze. He guided me over to the leather chair at the side of his marble-topped desk and gently helped me into it. Then he sat down in his own chair. "Tell me, what can I do for you, my dear?" he asked, splaying his elbows on the desk and leaning so far forward I thought he might be attempting to touch the tip of his nose to mine.

This was the hard part: trying to figure out a surefire yet *safe* way to get him to talk about the murder. I was convinced that Smythe didn't know who I was, that he'd never even heard my name before. And he didn't show the slightest sign of suspicion—either of me or my reasons for being there. All he showed was a taste for silk ties and platinum cufflinks. And a tendency to forget all about a business appointment (whether he actually had one or not). And a fawning, drooling, hands-on devotion to members of the female sex (whether they were married or not).

Taking all of these things into account, I sat up straighter in my chair, pushed a long wave of hair down over one eye, and—giving Smythe a bold come-hither smile—crossed one leg over the other. I would have raised my skirt up over my knees if they hadn't, at that unfortunate point in time, resembled two lumps of raw hamburger.

"I'm here on a highly personal financial matter, Mr. Smythe," I said. "Can I trust you to keep it confidential?" From the name of the company, I figured Farnsworth Fiduciary had something—if not everything—to do with personal financial matters.

"Of course you can trust me, Mrs. Turner," he said, staring at me as a little boy with a sweet tooth stares at a piece of fudge. "Farnsworth Fiduciary is, after all, a *trust,* and I am its primary *trustee.*" Beaming with pride (the foolish variety), he fingered his silver-streaked mustache and straightened his royal blue tie.

"Then I'll tell you why I'm here." I fluttered my lashes and took a deep, breast-enhancing breath of air. "My favorite aunt," I said, pronouncing the word in the upper crust way (so that it rhymed with gaunt), "died recently and left me a fortune in diamond jewelry—several Tiffany-designed pieces from the late thirties which have been appraised, collectively, at thirty-five to forty thousand dollars." As I said these words, I kept my eyes fastened on his face, watching for a telltale reaction.

"Yes . . . go on," he said, reacting, as far as I could tell, to nothing but the way my white angora sweater hugged the contours of my bosom.

Realizing that my naughty charade was merely slowing my investigation (and that my lunch hour minutes were ticking away far too fast), I decided I'd better change my act. Exit Zsa Zsa Gabor, enter Shirley Temple.

"So could you please advise me on how to handle my inheritance, Mr. Smythe?" I raised my voice to a childish octave, and widened my eyes in girlish innocence. "I just don't understand how these financial things work. Should I keep my aunt's beautiful jewelry or sell it? There's a necklace, a pair of earrings, a brooch, and two bracelets. What should I do about taxes and insurance?"

Smythe *still* showed no interest in the diamonds. I couldn't believe it! Here I was, claiming to have come into possession of a collection of vintage jewelry that matched exactly the jewelry he gave Judy Catcher—extremely valuable diamonds that, as far as he might know, had been *stolen* from his girlfriend's apartment the night she was *murdered*—and he didn't bat an eye. Either he was a stone-faced, cold-hearted thief and killer, or an exceptionally good actor covering up for somebody else, or he was even more of a fool than I'd originally thought.

"I'd like to answer all your questions for you, Mrs. Turner," he said, "and help you in any way I can. But I'm very pressed for time right now." He brushed his hand over his wavy silver coif and glanced at his solid gold watch. "I have a very important luncheon engagement in ten minutes, and the lady doesn't like to be kept waiting."

*Lunch* dates he remembered.

"May I come back to see you later this afternoon? Or tomorrow?" I cajoled, leaning as close to him as I dared and giving him my hand to pat. "I won't be able to sleep a wink until I've decided what to do with my aunt's diamonds. And you're so smart and wise and handsome, I know you're the very best man to help me." I was doing Zsa Zsa again. It seemed the only way to get his attention.

But I got more than I bargained for. Just touching my skin sent Smythe into a state of total bliss. He stroked my hand repeatedly and pressed my palm to his quivering lips. He pushed the sleeve of my sweater up higher on my forearm and kissed the underside of my wrist. "Yes, yes, I must see you again soon," he gasped, eyes rolling in rapture as he began kissing (and licking!) his way up my arm. "But I won't be back this afternoon . . . and the office is closed tomorrow . . . so you must come to the penthouse tomorrow night," he moaned, hot breath blasting into the crook of my elbow. "We're having a party."

"Penthouse? Party?" I hadn't been expecting this. I sat back in my chair and removed my moist arm from Smythe's hungry grasp.

He looked like a dog who'd just lost his bone. "It's our annual Christmas Eve party," he whimpered, adding, unnecessarily, "we have one every year. A lot of Farnsworth clients will be there, so my wife won't even notice if I invite one more. It'll be very crowded, and Augusta will be so busy taking care of our guests, I'm sure you and I will be able to grab a few minutes alone in my study." This thought perked him up considerably, and he lunged for my arm again.

To evade further limb licking, I jumped up from my chair and quickly pulled down my sweater sleeve. "Thank you so much for the invitation, Mr. Smythe. My husband and I will be happy to attend. And I will look forward to seeing you there," I gave him a wink and a little wave, and then walked briskly toward the door (I didn't dare shake his hand!). When I reached the door, I turned and shot him a farewell smile. "Where did you say the party is being held?"

"At the penthouse," he said, straightening his tie and smoothing his steamy mustache. "My home on Park Avenue. You can get the address from my secretary on your way out."

# Chapter 20

I HAD HOPED TO EXPLORE TIFFANY'S ON my way back to the subway, but I didn't have time. I didn't have time for lunch either. I had to rush back across town to the bakery for cake and cookies, to the dime store for paper plates and napkins and plastic forks, to the grocery for eggnog and soda, and to the liquor store for a bottle of bourbon (half of which I planned to consume, single-handedly, before the party even began). Then I had to cart all the stuff up to the office.

Brandon Pomeroy was sitting at his desk when I staggered in, so loaded down with heavy packages my arms were breaking. He didn't lift a finger to help (big surprise!). He just sat there like a sheik, sucking on the stem of his Dunhill pipe, and staring at me through the glinting lenses of his high-priced horn-rims.

"Good afternoon, Mrs. Turner," he said, in a voice so cold I decided to keep my coat on. "It is now two-fifteen P.M., and your lunch hour ended at one P.M. Either your watch has stopped working, or *you* have."

"Sorry to be so late, sir, but I had to go to four different stores to get everything for our Christmas party this afternoon, and they were all very crowded. Especially the *liquor* store," I added, figuring the realization that one of the packages in my arms contained a bottle of booze would soothe his angry soul.

I'm a genius. Pomeroy actually got up out of his chair, walked over to me, and took two of the packages into his own arms. Then he carried them over to the table where the coffeemaker was set up and began to unpack them! It wasn't that he was being gentlemanly, of course. He was just looking for the hooch. Still, it was nice to have a little help for a change. And the fact that he had stopped crabbing about my too-long lunch hour was a welcome boon.

I unpacked the other two bags, took off my hat and coat, and made everything nice for the party. (Well, *tried* to, anyway. When the only Christmas decorations you have to work with are a stack of red and green paper plates and a batch of Rudolph the Red-Nosed Reindeer cocktail napkins, your creative goals are limited.)

At the stroke of three, Harvey Crockett emerged, groundhog-like, from his office to announce that our workday had ended and our Christmas vacation had officially begun. He made a very short (but not the least bit sweet) speech about how it had been a pretty good year, and we all had done a pretty good job putting out a not-too-bad magazine. Then he pushed his fingers through his thick white hair, wished us a happy holiday, and huffed his way around the office, passing out the Christmas envelopes.

My envelope contained my normal weekly paycheck for seventy dollars—*without* the ten-dollar deduction Pomeroy had promised—and a bonus check for fifty bucks. It was a bit short of the million I felt I deserved, and probably only half as much as my male coworkers received, but I was *very* happy to get it. (When your bank account is sitting on empty, and all you have in your purse is a dribble of dimes and nickels, a fifty-dollar windfall makes you feel rich as Rockefeller—John or Nelson, take your pick.) Trouble was, the banks had already closed for the day—and they would remain closed the following day, Christmas Eve—so I wouldn't be able to deposit or cash either one of the checks until Monday. If I lived that long.

After we'd thanked Mr. Crockett and put our envelopes away, we all gathered around the goody table, helping ourselves to cake, cookies, and eggnog—except for Pomeroy, who shunned all the sweets and filled his coffee cup to the brim with straight bourbon. I might have done the same, but I was so hungry I ate a huge piece of cake and four cookies. And I mixed my whiskey with eggnog to make it more filling.

It was a sad little affair. No happy toasts or handshakes. No friendly hugs or backslaps or gaily wrapped gifts. Mike and Mario were being as quiet and boring (i.e., well-behaved) as they always were in Mr. Crockett's presence, and Pomeroy just stood off to the side by himself, focusing his full attention on his drink. Lenny was too shy to talk to anybody, and Crockett didn't have anything to say either. I tried to jazz things up by asking what everybody was doing for Christmas, but that sparked as much merriment as the sight of a corpse in an open casket.

I was dying to break out of there—to hop the subway back to Tiffany's, take a look around the famous store, talk to an employee or two about certain diamond settings and designs, and then ride the rails straight home to have drinks (and hopefully some dinner) with Abby and Terry. Maybe Dan would have time to drop by. But I knew I couldn't leave until everybody else had gone and I had cleaned up after the party.

So I was thrilled when, after just a few more minutes of strained non-conversation, Mr. Crockett sidled over to the coat tree, put on his hat and coat, tucked a couple of the afternoon newspapers under his arm, bid us goodnight, and scuttled away like a giant sand crab. And I was ecstatic when Pomeroy downed the dregs of his drink, mumbled an almost inaudible "Merry Christmas," and followed in Crockett's wake.

Hoping Mike and Mario and Lenny would hit the trail, too, I began the cleanup, making a big show of the fact that—in my humble (okay, *servile*) opinion—the festivities had come to an end. I tossed all the dirty paper plates and plastic forks in the wastebasket and packed the leftover cake and cookies up in one of the shopping bags. I screwed the top on the half-empty bottle of bourbon and put that in the bag, too. Then I lugged the Coffeemaster down the hall to the ladies' room, washed it out, refilled it with water for Monday morning, and carried it back to the office. As I was gathering up all the dirty coffee cups for another trip to the washroom, Mike and Mario were putting on their hats and coats.

"Hey, look what I found!" Mario cried, pulling something out of his coat pocket and holding it up high in the air.

"What is that?" Mike asked, gazing up, looking befuddled.

"Can't say for certain," Mario said, snickering, marching over to me and holding the object up over my head, "but it sure looks like mistletoe to me!" With that, he grasped the back of my neck, yanked my head forward, and—craning his wide clammy face over the assemblage of dirty coffee cups I was trying to balance in my arms—slapped a sloppy wet kiss on my startled mouth.

*Ugh!* First Jimmy Birmingham, then Gregory Smythe, and now Mario Caruso. I was getting really sick of all these surprise smooch attacks (except for Dan's, of course). And when Mario pulled his lips away and sputtered, "Hey, Mike! Wanna jump on the same Paige? Better take your Turner while the mistletoe's still hot!" . . . well, let's just say I dropped a few crumbs of my composure. Oh yeah, I dropped all the coffee cups, too.

Mike and Mario didn't stick around too long after that. Giggling and guffawing like the juveniles they truly were, they slipped out the door and scurried down the hall before I'd even stooped down to start picking up the cups (or, as was the case with the two that had broken, the pieces). Red-faced with rage over our coworkers' childish behavior (and embarrassment over his own feelings of impotence), Lenny shuffled over to where I was stooping and—muttering curses under his breath—got down on his knees to help me.

"They're cretins," he said. "They should be kept in a cage."

"Yeah," I said, adding nothing. I was too pressed for time

to start griping about Mike and Mario. Tiffany's would surely be closing soon.

"I'm glad they're gone, though," Lenny went on, picking up bits of the broken cups and pitching them into the nearest trash can. "Now you can tell me about the story you're working on."

Desperate to avoid a long explanation and discussion about the Judy Catcher murder (and my own life-threatening involvement in the case), I spit out a quick "Hold on a sec!" and snatched up the unbroken coffee cups. Then I whisked them off to the ladies' room to wash them, thereby avoiding Lenny's looming inquiries. And the very minute I brought the clean cups back into the office and set them down next to the Coffeemaster, I launched a discourse on a totally different (and, I hoped, totally *diverting*) topic.

"I bought you a Christmas present yesterday," I said, giving Lenny a big, toothy, Dinah Shore smile.

"Really?" he said, eyes wide with surprise. "Why'd you do that?"

"Because I *wanted* to, silly."

"But I didn't get *you* anything."

"I know. I didn't expect you to."

"So, then, why'd you get something for me?"

"Correct me if I'm wrong, but I think I already answered that question."

He was blushing even redder now. He pushed his glasses higher on his nose and blotted his perspiring upper lip on his shirt sleeve.

"It's the perfect gift, too," I added. "Something I *know* you'll really like." I took my coat off the rack and put it on. "Too bad I can't give it to you."

"Huh? Why can't you give it to me?"

"Because I don't have it anymore." I donned my gloves and beret and tucked my purse under my arm. "I was in such a tizzy to get to work on time this morning, I left it on the subway."

Lenny laughed and wiped his sleeve across his forehead. "Maybe somebody will take it to the Lost and Found. What *was* it, anyway?"

"I'll never tell!" I said, picking up the bag containing the cake, cookies, and bourbon and propping it on my hip. "I'm going to get you another one just like it—just as soon as I cash my Christmas bonus."

"That's really nice of you, Paige," Lenny stammered, staring down at his feet, "but you don't have to do that! You work so hard for your money, I don't want you spending one more penny of it on me!" His face was as red as a Santa suit.

It was time for me to make my move. While Lenny was standing there, blushing, too self-conscious to make eye contact, I stepped up close to him and sprang a surprise smooch attack of my own, landing a loud and loving smack on his ever-so-rosy cheek. "Happy Hanukkah!" I yelped, and before he could curb his embarrassment enough to reply, I zipped through the door and ran down the hall, shopping bag clutched to my chest like . . . well, like a shopping bag. (I saw no reason to leave the leftover cake and cookies for the office mice. And though it would have been a kind gesture to give the surplus bourbon to the building's booze-loving custodian, I was convinced I needed it much more than he did.)

Look, I know it wasn't very nice of me to run out on Lenny the way I did, absconding like a thief with his equanimity and presence of mind (as well as the bag full of goodies). But I was running for my life, you know. I was fixed on finding a killer who now seemed to be fixed on killing me, and the race was on.

EVERY SURFACE IN TIFFANY'S WAS SPARKling. The green marbled walls were gleaming, the long glass showcases were shining, the salesmen's faces were glowing, and the diamonds were so dazzling that the eyes of every customer danced with darts of light reflected from their keen, glistening facets. The showroom's high ceiling was strung with thousands of twinkling white lights and fragrant boughs of pine, producing the euphoric sensation that you were standing beneath a towering tree, looking up through its branches at the stars. No music was playing, but if there had been, it would have been the Hallelujah Chorus.

The aisles between the illuminated glass showcases were so crowded you could barely walk, but I bravely snaked my way along, snatching an occasional glimpse of a bright, black-velvet-backed display. A batch of diamond chokers here, a slew of emerald earrings there, a stretch of sapphire bracelets just ahead. One showcase was devoted entirely to pearls, another to solid gold cigarette cases. I kept walking until I came to the silver section, and then I kept on walking till I reached the lowliest showcase on the aisle—where the more plebeian items were displayed. Items peasants like me might actually be able to afford.

Working my way over to *that* counter, I peered down through the glass-topped case at the various silver sundries perched on the upper shelf. Some of the things were nice enough—elegant *and* utilitarian. The silver cigarette lighters were pretty nifty, for example. Likewise, the pen and pencil sets. The silver baby spoons were kind of sweet, and the key rings were okay, I guess. But some of the other stuff I saw was downright ridiculous. I mean, who needs a silver telephone dialer? Molded in the shape of a finger, no less! And if you show me a woman whose life won't be complete until she has a silver eyebrow tweezer, I'll show you a blooming idiot. And the sterling silver toothpicks? I can't even bear to mention them.

The silver cigarette lighters, however (and as I said before), were pretty nifty.

"How much do these cost?" I asked the salesman, pointing out the most modest (and to my mind, sleekest) line of lighters.

"They're all in the twenty to twenty-five dollar range," he told me.

"Really?" I said, getting excited. I could buy one of these lighters for Dan, I figured, and still have twenty-five dollars of my bonus left over to send to Elijah Peeps. Twenty-five dollars for the new *love* of my life, and twenty-five dollars for the man who had *saved* my life. There was something poetic about that emotional equation.

"I want *that* one," I said, indicating the simplest lighter of all, the one that was shaped just like a classic Zippo, with a satin finish so smooth it was eloquent. "Can I have it engraved? Does that cost extra?" I was so happy to have found Dan's Christmas present, I had forgotten that I didn't have the cash to pay for it.

"You may have it engraved at no extra cost—but not before Christmas," the long-faced middle-aged salesman replied. "The store closes in twenty minutes and won't reopen until Monday, the day after Christmas. You may, however, bring the lighter and your receipt back to the store later, if you wish—after the twenty-fifth—and we'll do the engraving for you then."

"You've got a deal," I said, "providing I can pay by check."

"If you have proper identification, Tiffany's will be happy to accept your check."

*They wouldn't be so happy if they knew I have less than two dollars in my account.*

"Great!" I said, whipping out my driver's license, social security card, and checkbook. Since all the banks were closed until Monday, I wasn't worried that my check would bounce. I knew I'd be covering it first thing Monday morning, when I deposited my bonus. "How much should I make this out for?" I asked.

The sad-faced salesman consulted the hidden price tag and added on the tax. "That'll be $23.48," he said, punctuating his statement with a condescending sniff.

I made out the check and handed it over to him. He slipped the lighter into a little blue velvet pouch, then into a Tiffany's gift box, then into a Tiffany's shopping bag, which he then handed over to me.

"Thank you," I said, smiling. Then I leaned over the counter and added, in a conspiratorial tone, "And now I have a very important, very confidential matter to discuss with the manager. Is he on the floor now? Will you point him out to me please?"

"This is not the best time, Miss . . . Mr. Woodbury *is* here, but he's sure to be overseeing the closing of the store for the holiday weekend. He'll be much too busy to talk to you now."

"Too busy to talk about forty thousand dollars worth of diamonds?"

"That's him right over there," the salesman said, nodding toward the tall, portly, red-haired man standing off to the side of the showroom—away from the now-thinning crowd. He looked to be about forty and he was wearing a sedate but stylish dark gray suit. A white linen handkerchief peeped to a perfect peak from his breast pocket.

I sauntered over to him—shoulders back, head held high, Tiffany bag positioned in *front* of the other shopping bag I was carrying. I was trying to look rich and respectable. (Stop laughing!) "Mr. Woodbury," I said, "may I speak with you for a minute?"

He looked down at his watch, and then raised his watery blue eyes to look at me. "Yes, but just for *one* minute. It's almost closing time." His hair was the color of carrots.

"Can we go to your office or someplace private?"

"Sorry, but I have to keep an eye on things out here." As if to prove his words, he stared right past me, watching the last of the last-minute shoppers complete their purchases and begin leaving the store.

It was clear that Mr. Woodbury would invite me to leave soon, too. "I just want to ask you about the diamond jewelry I recently inherited from my dear departed aunt," I blurted, speaking as fast as I could and trying to capture his interest. "There are several beautiful pieces and they were all created by Tiffany in the early thirties. There's a necklace, a pair of earrings, a pin, and two bracelets. And I was hoping you could tell me what they're worth."

I had his full attention now. His watery blue eyes were gawking at my face and they had grown as big as coat buttons. "What a coincidence!" he declared. "You're the second person today who's asked me about jewelry from the early thirties. And if I didn't know better, I'd think you were both talking about the very same collection."

Now *I* was the one who was gawking.

"What?! Who?!" I spluttered, so dumbfounded I couldn't form a complete sentence. My mind was reeling with questions for Mr. Woodbury, but I couldn't get them out of my mouth. *Who was it who spoke to you? Was it over the phone or here in the store? Do you have the person's name? Was it a man or a woman? What did the person look like? Do you think he or she could be a murderer?*

But even without me asking the questions, Mr. Woodbury gave me the answers. "The attractive young lady who came to see me this afternoon was also inquiring about the value of an inheritance," he said, clearing his throat, straightening his tie, and gazing dreamily up at the ceiling. "And she was very curious about the history of her newly acquired diamonds, so we went upstairs to the Tiffany archives to research the early thirties designs together." A lustful smile spread wide across his pale, plump lips, and his eyes glazed over with what looked like a *very* pleasant memory. He was so entranced he didn't even notice that the closing bell had sounded and that the store was now devoid of customers.

Except for me, that is. But I didn't have to stick around one moment longer. Mr. Woodbury's lustful smile told me everything I needed to know, including the name of the young woman who had visited him that afternoon. It had to be Abby.

# Chapter 21

"HEY, BOBBA REE BOP!" ABBY EXCLAIMED, taking the half-full bottle of bourbon out of the bag and placing it on her kitchen counter. "Who wants a bourbon smash?" Her long black hair was loose and streaming down her back like a waterfall of India ink.

"I'll have one," Terry said, watching Abby's fluid movements with a look of sheer enchantment on his face. It was the first time since I'd met him that I'd seen him show any real sign of happiness.

"I'll have *two,*" I said, feeling decidedly *un*happy. If you've ever been pushed in front of a train, you'll understand why. (You'll also understand why I went straight to Abby's apartment, instead of my own, when I got home. Misery loves company, whether the company's as miserable as you are or not.)

"You don't sound so hot," Abby said to me. She took a tray of ice out of the freezer and cranked apart the cubes. "You don't look so hot, either. What's been going on?"

"Oh, I had a pretty rough day," I said, sighing heavily. I reached for the open pack of Pall Malls sitting on the kitchen table and lit one up. "But I don't want to talk about that right now. I'll tell you all about it later—after I've had a drink . . . and after you've told me about your top secret trip to Tiffany's."

"How do you know about that?!" Abby cried. Both she and Terry were gaping at me in shock. If their jaws had dropped any lower, they'd have broken right off their hinges.

"Yeah!" Terry said. "How did you find out? We wanted to surprise you."

Basking in the pleasure of my sudden one-upmanship, I took a deep drag on my cigarette and exhaled slowly. "No one can surprise the Shadow!" I intoned, referring to the hero of *The Shadow* radio show and trying to mimic his wicked laugh. "The Shadow knows!"

"Knock it off," Abby said, unamused. "Just tell us what happened. You went to Tiffany's yourself, right?"

"Right."

"And you spoke to Jeremy—I mean, Mr. Woodbury."

"Right. *Jeremy* and I are as close as this." I held up two crossed fingers as a visual aid. If Abby noticed the sarcastic tone of my expression (verbal *or* digital) she paid it no mind.

"And he *told* you I was there?" She brought our drinks over to the table and sat down in a huff. "That really frosts me! I thought the manager of a swank place like Tiffany's would be much more discreet than that."

"He didn't tell me your name. He just mentioned that somebody else had been in earlier—somebody who was also interested in jewelry from the early thirties—and that he'd helped her do some research in the archives."

"So how did you know it was me?"

"Just a lucky guess," I said, deciding to forego the diversion of describing Mr. Woodbury's rapturous trance and randy smile. I was afraid Terry would get jealous and stop being so happy. "So what did you find out?" I asked Abby. "Did your, uh, research in the archives turn up any new clues?"

"Just wait'll you hear this!" Terry broke in, excited as a foxhound near the end of a chase. "Abby really hit the jackpot. She discovered that the diamonds were originally purchased in 1933 by one of Tiffany's steady customers—a wealthy socialite named Mrs. Augusta Farnsworth Smythe. She even got the woman's address!" He was bowled over by Abby's brilliant skills of detection.

And frankly, my dear, so was I. "Oh, Abby, that's atomic! How did you ever get Woodbury to give you that information?"

"I didn't," she said, with a mischievous smirk. "I took a peek inside the file when he wasn't looking."

"What file?"

"The file Jeremy took out of the archives when he was trying to help me determine the origin of the vintage diamond jewelry left to me by my dear departed Aunt Hester."

I smiled. Dear departed aunts were all the rage this year.

"You wouldn't believe how thorough and well-organized Tiffany's records are!" Abby went on. "All the invoices in that file were arranged in perfect alphabetical order. And since my real purpose was to get the dope on Gregory Smythe, all I had to do was turn to the S section. There was nothing under Gregory but, thinking Mrs. Augusta Farnsworth Smythe might be Gregory's wife or mother, I memorized the address on *her* invoice. Trouble is, the statement was dated December 1933—twenty-one years ago—so she probably doesn't live there anymore. If she's still alive at all."

"What's the address?" I asked.

"957 Park Avenue."

"Yep! That's the place!" I threw my head back and took a big swig of my drink.

"What place?!" Terry croaked. "What are you saying?"

"I'm saying that's the same address Smythe's secretary gave me. That's where Gregory lives with his wife, Augusta, and that's where the party is being held tomorrow night."

If their eyes had popped any wider, they'd have turned inside out. "What party?!" they cried in unison.

*The Shadow strikes again!* It felt so good to relax and fool around, I wanted to toy with Abby and Terry a little while longer, pull the cards slowly—one by excruciating one—from my stealthy sweater sleeve. But that would have been an unconscionable waste of precious time (mine *and* theirs). And, if you want to know the truth, I was way too skittish (okay, *scared*) to keep on playing games. Because no matter how hard I tried, I couldn't stop one sickening thought from streaking round and round my one-track mind: *If it wasn't for Elijah Peeps, I'd be soup now.*

Anxious to fill them in and get their feedback (okay, *sympathy*), I gave Abby and Terry a quick recap of recent occurrences: how Vicki Lee Bumstead had given me Smythe's business address; how I'd gone to see him at his office, and quietly suffered his slobbering advances, and then been invited to his and his wife's annual Christmas party; how I'd rushed across town to Tiffany's and cornered Mr. Woodbury just as the store was closing. And then finally, after these current events had been described and discussed at length, I took a deep breath, did a little backpedaling, and fretfully revealed the more troubling (okay, *terrifying*) episodes of my recent past.

First, I told them how Jimmy Birmingham had followed me home from the Village Vanguard early yesterday morning, and then had lurked in the doorway of the laundromat across the street till he knew which apartment I lived in—and which window led to my bedroom. Then—doing my best not to break down and start crying like a baby—I told them how I'd almost been obliterated early *this* morning in the subway.

"*Oy gevalt!*" Abby cried, when I pulled up my skirt and showed her my lacerated knees and shins. "That looks really bad!"

"Could be worse," I said, trying not to think about how *much* worse.

One look at my wounds, and Terry flew into a fury. "That does it!" he roared, banging his fist on the tabletop. He didn't look so happy anymore. Now he looked as if his head were going to explode. "I'm calling this whole thing off now, Paige! Stop searching for my sister's murderer immediately! Goddamn it all to hell! I should never have gotten you involved in this. How could I have been so selfish? How could I do this to my best friend's widow? If anything happened to you, I'd never forgive myself!" He bolted out of his chair and started stomping around the kitchen like a deranged Cossack.

I didn't know what to say or do to calm him down. But Abby did. "Come on now, baby," she cooed, slowly rising from her chair and then planting her gorgeous self in his path. She was using the voice of a mother, but the body language of a harem girl. "Don't get your sweet keester in a kink. Paige is just fine, you dig? A few shin bumps and knee scratches never hurt anybody. She'll be fit as a philharmonic fiddle in no time."

Blocked from continuing his stomping rampage, Terry slumped toward Abby and gave her a look of pure anguish. "How can you say that? She was almost *killed*."

This was my cue. "But I *wasn't!*" I said, in what I hoped was a composed and stalwart tone. "And that's the main thing, Terry. *Almost* doesn't count."

"Oh, yes it does!" he insisted, aiming his anguished eyes at me. "Whoever tried to kill you is sure to try it again. What if they *almost* fail?"

He had me there. And instead of feeling stalwart, I suddenly felt as weak as the runt in a litter of kittens.

Seeing that my determination was melting away, that I was on the verge of a moral collapse, Abby threw up her hands and hollered, "Stop it! Both of you! Stop sniveling and face the facts. It's too late for Paige to pull out now. The murderer knows who she is and where she lives—probably even where she works—and there's not a goddamn thing we can do about that." She walked back to the table, sat down, and gave me a piercing stare. "Oh, you could change your name and quit your job and move to South America," she said, "but is that what you want to do?"

"No!" I declared, surprised by my own vehemence. Some stalwartness must have snuck back into my spine when I wasn't looking.

"Good," Abby said, "because even that wouldn't guarantee your safety. The killer still wants the diamonds, don't forget, and I have a feeling he'd follow you to the ends of the earth to get them."

Finally, the light bulb lit. "That's it!" I cried, electrified. "That's why Lenny's lunchbox was stolen!"

My friends were gaping at me again. "What the hell're you talking about now?" Terry grumbled. His endurance was wearing a little thin. He returned to his chair at the table and tossed down the rest of his drink.

I explained who Lenny was, and why I had bought him a lunchpail for Christmas, and how I'd been carrying the wrapped gift to work that morning in a shopping bag. "Why didn't I think of it before?" I stammered. "The devil who pushed me onto the subway tracks must have thought the diamonds were stashed in the jewelry box–sized package in my shopping bag!"

"Now you're talkin'!" Abby crowed. "That would explain everything. I couldn't figure it before, but now I can."

"What do you mean?" Terry asked, exasperated. "What the hell couldn't you figure?" He was looking a lot like Ricky does when he's unwittingly caught up in one of Lucy and Ethel's outrageous schemes.

"I couldn't understand why the murderer would try to kill Paige *now,*" Abby said to Terry, "*before* he'd gotten his hands on the diamonds. See, as far as any of our prime suspects could possibly know, you and Paige are the only two people who might have knowledge of the jewelry's actual whereabouts. And since nobody has any idea where *you* are, Whitey, Paige is the murderer's only hope of finding the diamonds right now. So why would he try to kill her before he knew where the trinkets were? That would be plain crazy—unless, that is, he had reason to believe that the diamonds were concealed in the gift-wrapped container buried in the shopping bag he so greedily snatched from Paige's unwary hand just seconds before he pushed her in front of a train."

Grinning like a cream-fed Cheshire, Abby leaned back in her chair and lit up a cigarette. "Whew!" she said, exhaling loudly. "That was a mouthful."

"But it makes perfect sense!" I said, excited by Abby's new slant on the situation. "And the fact that the diamonds were *not* in Lenny's lunchbox," I added, heaving an inner swoosh of relief, "is a kind of protection for me. Could be I'm not in so much danger anymore."

"Right!" Abby agreed.

"Wrong!" Terry argued, giving me an intensely paternal, admonishing look. "The killer will still be following you around, Paige, looking for a way to trap you and make you tell him where the diamonds are. And *then* he'll kill you."

Parade canceled due to rain.

"Well, at least I'll have some advance notice," I said, looking for a rainbow, however small. "That should boost my odds of survival." I couldn't believe I was sitting there at Abby's round oak dining table, calmly discussing my own death as if it were the next course on the menu.

"Oh, don't be such a *shlemiel!*" Abby heckled. "Why settle for a puny, almost nonexistent advantage when you can beat the odds altogether? Whitey and I will help you. If we pool our resources we can bust this case wide open!" She reminded me of Ethel Merman belting out the title song of her new movie, *There's No Business Like Show Business.* "And when you think about it," Abby added, curving her blood red lips in a sweetly sardonic smile, "there's really only one teensy little thing we have to do."

"What's that?" I asked, though I knew too darn well what her answer was going to be.

"Catch the killer before he catches you."

ABBY MADE ANOTHER BATCH OF BOURBON smashes and Terry ran across the street to get a pizza pie, which we devoured the minute he got back—while it was still hot enough to burn our tongues off. And as soon as we finished the pizza, we consumed the leftover cake and cookies I'd brought from the office. Then, sucking on cigarettes and slurping our smashes, we put our three heads together and got down to business.

We needed a plan of attack, we decided, so we reviewed what we knew about Judy's life up to the murder, the details of the murder itself, and everything we'd found out since. We made a list of the people we still hadn't talked to, and the ones we felt we should talk to again. We made some very calm and careful decisions about when and where and how the new round of interviews should be conducted, and then we fought like cats and dogs over who should interrogate whom.

Abby and I thought Terry should stay out of sight, not let his whereabouts be known to anybody—the police *or* the murderer. We figured that would force the killer to focus all his attention on me—which would not only keep me on my toes, but would allow us to anticipate (maybe even *control*) his impending actions more easily.

Well, Terry had a flying fit when he heard *that* idea. There was "no way on earth" he was going to "hide out" in Abby's apartment—like a "gutless soldier cowering in a foxhole"—while I risked life and limb to find the "bastard" who had killed his sister. If anything, he wanted to make *himself* the target—reveal himself to the murderer (and even to the police, if need be), in the hope that "all the goddamn future catastrophes in this case" would happen to him instead of me.

I appreciated Terry's solicitude. Actually, I was quite moved he was being so protective. But I still didn't like the idea of him prancing around out in the open, calling attention to himself, maybe getting himself arrested by the tenacious (when he wanted to be!) Detective Hugo Sweeny. If Terry got thrown in jail, it would screw up our entire investigation. Not only would he be useless to us behind bars, but then we'd have to turn the diamonds over to the police—thereby losing our prime lure, not to mention my only form of life insurance.

And then Dan would find out about the case. And learn the details of my secret but total involvement. And then all hell would break loose. And I feared Dan's final retributions as much as I did the murderer's. (Okay, okay! So that's a slight exaggeration. I'd rather have lost my lover than my life . . . I guess.)

After lots of arguing and analyzing and compromising (and another round of drinks), we finally agreed on a plan for the following day: Terry would make a surprise appearance at his sister's old apartment on East 19th Street and question her former roommates—especially the one who had lost a handful of hair due to flirting with Judy's then boyfriend, who may or may not have been Jimmy Birmingham; Abby would go with me to pay a call on the same Mr. Birmingham, at the East 8th Street address we found listed next to his name in the phone book. I had originally intended to drop in on Jimmy and Otto by myself, but Terry and Abby quickly nixed that idea. They thought it would be too dangerous—and after closer consideration, so did I.

As for the Smythe's Christmas Eve party, we decided we'd all three go together. I would pass myself off as a new Farnsworth Fiduciary client, Terry would pose as my husband, and Abby would play the part of an out-of-town cousin who was staying with us for the holidays. I wasn't worried about bringing an additional guest since Smythe had said his wife would never notice an extra face in the crowd. And I knew beyond the shadow of a doubt that when girl-happy Gregory got a good look at Abby, she'd be welcomed with open arms (and puckered lips).

I was glad my friends would be going to the party with me. I figured I'd feel a lot safer with a "husband" by my side. And I knew Abby would be the perfect decoy to keep *Mr.* Smythe occupied (and thoroughly distracted) while I focused my investigative attentions on *Mrs.* Smythe. Augusta, after all, had been the one who originally purchased the diamonds, so they had rightfully belonged to *her*. Did that mean Gregory had *stolen* the jewelry from his wife to give to his girlfriend? Did Augusta know that her precious antique diamonds had been removed from the family vault and deposited in the Chelsea apartment of her husband's new mistress—a nineteen-year-old blonde lingerie salesgirl named Judy Catcher?

I hoped to get the answers to these and a few other questions at the party. And now that Terry and Abby would be there to help me, I thought I had a chance. It felt really great to be part of a bona fide team instead of having to wing it so much on my own. But, team or no team, I was still a third wheel. And Abby and Terry were making eyes at each other again! So—as soon as we decided on a new hiding place for the diamonds (wrapped in tinfoil and buried deep in a canister of sugar in Abby's overstocked pantry)—I knew it was time for me to vamoose.

I gathered up my coat, beret, gloves, and the Tiffany bag with Dan's present in it, and said goodnight. Then I stepped across the landing to my own apartment. I wasn't at all eager to be alone, but I *was* looking forward to a warm knee-and-shin-soaking bath, fresh applications of Mercurochrome and Unguentine, a change into something more comfortable, and a phone call—or, preferably—a surprise visit from Dan.

I was in for a surprise, all right, but it wouldn't be delivered by Dan.

# Chapter 22

EVEN BEFORE I TURNED ON THE LIGHT I knew something was wrong. I could *feel* it. And what I felt was *cold*. The temperature in my apartment had dropped to about thirty degrees. I knew it couldn't be a problem with the steam since Abby's place had been perfectly warm, and our Siamese twin radiator systems always functioned—or didn't—in tandem. Heart slamming against the walls of my chest and beating loudly on my eardrums, I dropped all the stuff in my arms to the floor, sucked in a blast of frigid air, and flipped on the light.

At first glance, everything looked normal. Each piece of furniture was in its proper place; my typewriter was sitting right where I'd left it on the kitchen table; my rented floor-model Sylvania was standing upright near the couch/door/daybed; all my books and record albums were neatly arranged on the living room shelves. At second glance, however, my eyes found the chilling source of the trouble. The back door to my apartment—the door that led from my kitchen to the balcony, and to the metal stairway leading down to the small rear courtyard—was standing wide open. One of the panes in the door—the one closest to the lock and the knob—was missing, and the linoleum just inside the door was littered with shattered glass.

Someone had broken into my apartment! Terrified that the intruder might still be there, hiding in the coat closet or lying in wait for me upstairs, I stood frozen in the middle of my kitchen, holding my breath, trying not to make a sound, straining my ears to the breaking point, listening for unusual creaks and squeaks—or somebody *else's* breathing. So much adrenaline was rushing through my veins I felt volcanic.

After several moments of stone cold quiet, I couldn't take it anymore. I threw open the coat closet and peered inside. Nothing. Zilch. Nobody. I darted over to the back door, flipped on the outside light, stuck my head through the door, and raked my eyes down the steps and around the snow-clogged courtyard. Nobody there either. There was a ragged path of deep footprints in the snow, though, giving further proof that somebody *had* been there. And since half of those footprints were pointed *down* the steps and *away* from my apartment, I figured the intruder had already made his retreat—across the courtyard and out through the rear gate.

But I had to make sure, right? So I grabbed the first weapon of self protection I could lay my hands on—the bottle of bleach I kept under the kitchen sink—and dashed upstairs. (I know, I know! I should have grabbed a *knife,* for God's sake. Every kitchen has one. Better yet, I should have run next door and gotten Abby and Terry to come help me. But I wasn't thinking very clearly at the time, and the only plan my poor brain could come up with was to flush the intruder out into the open and throw bleach in his face. It wouldn't kill him, but it might *blind* him, and maybe that would be all the protection I'd need.)

But there was nobody upstairs either. Not a single murderer in sight. Not in either of the clothes closets, or under the bed, or hiding behind the shower curtain. Finally certain that I was alone, I went back downstairs, set the Clorox on the counter, and closed and relocked both my back and front doors. I picked up the stuff I'd dropped on the floor when I first entered the apartment, and put it all down on a kitchen chair. Then, emptying and flattening a small Duz detergent box, I covered the broken pane with the double-thick cardboard container, securing it to the door frame and sealing it on all sides with numerous strips of masking tape. Then I began sweeping up the broken glass. I was moving around in slow motion, like a retarded robot, hardly aware of what I was doing.

Until the phone rang.

Jumping so high I almost conked my head on the ceiling, I dropped the dustpan and the broom on the floor and lunged into the living room, praying to all the deities in all the heavenly kingdoms of all the world's religions that the caller would be Dan. I just wanted to hear Dan's voice. I really *needed* to hear Dan's voice.

"Hello?" I croaked, holding the receiver so tight and so close it almost fused with my ear. "Hello, Dan? Is that you?"

There was no reply. I could hear breathing, though, so I knew somebody was there.

"Hello? Who is this please?"

Still no response. There was more harsh breathing, a few snuffling noises, and then some sounds I couldn't identify.

I stayed quiet for a few seconds, listening intently to the noises on the other end, trying to decipher their causes. At first I thought the caller was chewing on something—a piece of gum or maybe a sandwich—and then I heard something that sounded like licking.

"Who's there?" I asked again, skin crawling, head spinning with sinister possibilities. Was it Roscoe Swift, breathing fire and gnashing his little brown teeth? Jimmy Birmingham and his snuffling, face-licking (perhaps bone-gnawing) dog, Otto? Elsie Londergan slurping tea? Or was it Gregory Smythe, giving his wet lips and wandering tongue a warm-up, letting me know—without words—that he was looking forward to our next tasty tête-à-tête?

None of my questions were answered. Even the chewing and licking sounds stopped. All I heard was a raspy intake of air, a faint, menacing chuckle, a sharp click, and then silence—dead silence. Whoever it was had hung up.

I slammed down the receiver and stomped around the living room a couple of times, cursing my fool head off. Then, still ranting, I marched back into the kitchen to finish cleaning up the broken glass. I wasn't scared anymore. Now I was just mad. Fighting mad. Having failed to kill me, and failing to find the diamonds in either the lunchbox or my apartment, the murderer had obviously decided to terrorize me—try to frighten me into dropping my defenses and revealing the location of the jewelry. And I just wasn't in the mood for that! I was tired and exhausted. My apartment was freezing cold. My legs hurt. I had had a *really* bad day.

I had just tossed the broken glass in the trash and was heading upstairs for a hot bath when the telephone rang again. Steeling myself for another run-in with the killer, I stomped back into the living room and yanked the receiver up to my mouth.

"Listen, you unmitigated creep," I growled, "you might as well ditch the stupid silent treatment right now. You think you're scaring me, but you're not. And I've got a lot better things to do with my time than sit around waiting for you to say 'boo.' "

"Hey!" Dan sputtered. "What's eating you? Maybe I should have called earlier, but I was in the middle of an interrogation, and I didn't think I should stop a homicidal butcher from admitting to three murders just so I could give my crabby girlfriend a buzz."

Oops.

How the heck was I going to explain this one? I couldn't tell Dan that I had thought I was talking so somebody else. He'd want to know *who,* and how could I answer that? I certainly couldn't tell him the truth. And I couldn't think of any good lies to tell him either. "Oh, uh . . . I, um . . . I'm sorry, baby," I stammered, squirming around in my deceitful skin, madly searching for a logical explanation, finally deciding my only way out was to use the oldest, most reliable and effective excuse known to woman: FEMALE TROUBLE. "I'm just not myself today, Dan," I said. "It's . . . well, it's that time of the month, if you know what I mean."

"Oh, I know what you mean, all right," he said, "but that won't earn you a pardon. I've never been called an 'unmitigated creep' before, and I don't think I like it." He sounded really annoyed. "And what's this 'you think you're scaring me, but you're not' business? When have I ever tried to scare you?"

"You haven't!" I cried. "I don't know why I said that! I just feel so depressed and on edge today. I was dying to talk to you, and when you took so long to call, I thought you were still angry at me for the way I acted the other night—that you were punishing me."

"Even if that were true," he seethed, "—even if I *were* punishing you, which I most definitely *wasn't*—would that be reason enough to call me an unmitigated creep?"

"I didn't mean it, Dan. I really didn't!"

"But you *said* it."

"I know! I'm sorry! I hate myself!"

"I can't believe you called me that."

"Well, you called me *crabby,*" I whined.

Dan was quiet for a few seconds and then, all of a sudden, he broke out laughing. And it was *real* laughter, not the sarcastic, mocking kind. "Yes, I called you crabby," he said between chortles, "but you deserved it. Actually, you deserved much worse, but I'm too nice a guy to use *that* word."

"And I'm eternally grateful for your gallant self-censorship," I said, grinning, elated that our argument seemed to be over and that Dan had accepted my false confession. "I may be a bitch, but at least I'm beholden."

Dan laughed again, and the way his deep voice rolled around in his throat turned my cold skin warm as toast. "Can you come see me tonight?" I asked him. "I'd like to make my apologies in person."

"Can't do it, baby," he said, with a loud sigh of regret. "Too much paperwork. And it's getting pretty late."

As much as I wanted Dan to come over, I was relieved when he declined. Though I could easily have hidden my wounded knees and shins under a pair of winter slacks, I knew I wouldn't be able to hide the Duz detergent box patchwork on my busted back door. Dan would insist on knowing how and why the pane of glass had come to be broken, and—as skillful a liar as I had discovered myself to be—I felt I'd already exceeded my cock-and-bull story limit for the day.

"I can't make it tomorrow, either," Dan added. "I'm on duty all day, and I promised my daughter I'd spend Christmas Eve with her. And since Veronica is going out on a date to a big party, it'll be a very late night." (Veronica! Is that the perfect name for a noxious, narcissistic ex-wife, or what?)

I felt another spurt of relief. I had a big Christmas Eve party to go to myself, if you recall, and I was glad I wouldn't have to create another complicated fable to cover up *that* event.

"Will I see you on Saturday?" I asked, crossing my fingers, praying that his answer would be yes. I'd already decided to shelve all my murderer-hunting activities for that day—Christmas day—and I was longing to spend some fib-free time with my fine, upstanding boyfriend.

"You can count on it," he said. "I don't have to go in to work at all. I'll spend Christmas morning with Katy, and the rest of the day with you. How's that?"

"It's great," I said. "I can't wait to see you. I need somebody to make me merry."

"Hey, that's what unmitigated creeps are for."

BEFORE GOING UPSTAIRS FOR MY BATH, I took a tour of my living room and kitchen, checking all the shelves and the drawers and the cabinets, rifling through books and papers and soup cans, trying to trace the intruder's movements around my apartment. Though everything looked normal on the surface, closer inspection proved otherwise.

All the small items in the drawer of the living room table had been displaced, shoved to one side in a sloppy jumble. Everything in the kitchen cabinets had been pushed from one place to another (including the oatmeal box!), and all the gadgets in the utensil drawers looked as if they'd been kicked around by a pack of feral toddlers. The hangers in the coat closet were askew—likewise my coats and jackets. And the now-empty Thom McAn shoebox that had once contained every scrap of evidence Terry had given me about his sister's murder—the names, addresses, photos, *and* the diamonds—was lying upside down on the closet floor.

None of this derangement surprised me too much; it seemed par for the breaking and entering (and diamond-hunting) course. What did surprise me, however, was the fact that all twenty-three pages of my story notes were still sitting in a neat pile next to my typewriter, weighted down by a glass ashtray, exactly the way I'd left them.

As far as I could tell, the notes hadn't been touched—or even *looked* at—which was a darn lucky thing for me, since if the killer had taken the trouble to read any of the pages, he would have seen that they were full of clues about the murder, and he certainly would have destroyed them. (Which would have had quite a destructive effect on me!) All I could figure was that the unmitigated creep had been so focused on looking for the diamonds he literally couldn't see anything else.

Realizing the intruder could return at any point, and that he might not be so shortsighted the next time, I scooped up my story notes and folded them in half. Then I rolled them up into a squat little cylinder, stuffed them down into the oatmeal left in Judy Catcher's Quaker box, and put the closed box back on the top shelf of the cabinet over the kitchen sink. If it worked for Judy's jewels, it could work for mine.

Suddenly feeling as weak and aimless as a sedated baby, I turned off the downstairs lights and dragged my tired, cold self upstairs. Lacking energy for even the simplest efforts, I skipped the hot bath and crawled into bed with my clothes on (minus the skirt and snowboots). Hugging my wounded knees up close to my chest and pulling the blanket up over my head, I fell asleep in an instant.

I didn't have one single dream. I know that for a fact. How could my troubled subconscious concoct any capricious dreams when it was trapped in a continuous nightmare?

# Chapter 23

MAYBE IT WAS THE BRIGHT STREAK OF winter sun shooting through the edge of my bedroom window shade. Or maybe it was the sickening smell of mackerel wafting up from the fish store downstairs (Luigi's refrigerators had probably gone on the blink again). Most likely it was the fact that somebody was banging on my front door with a baseball bat. (At least that's what it sounded like.) But whatever the cause, I woke up with a jolt and leapt out of bed like a startled grasshopper. Then I hurdled into the hall and dashed down the stairs in my stocking feet to see who was at the door.

(Yes, I was still wearing my stockings. My garter belt, too. And my bra and my slip and my sweater set and the red chiffon scarf around my neck.)

"Paige!" Bang bang. "Paige! Are you there?" Bang bang. "Open up!"

It was Abby and she sounded hysterical.

I unlocked the door and pulled it wide open. "What's the matter?" I cried. "Are you okay? Did something happen to Terry? Or the diamonds?" The way she was banging and shouting, I figured all hell had broken loose.

"No way, Doris Day!" she said, sauntering into my apartment with a satisfied smile on her composed and made-up face. "Nothing's wrong. I just wanted to wake you up. It's late, and if we don't get our tushies on track, we'll fall behind in our schedule."

I wanted to strangle her. Any more wake-up calls like that, and I'd die of a heart attack before the killer ever got near me again.

"But hey bobba ree bop!" Abby chirped, studying my appearance with surprise. "I see I shouldn't have worried. You're almost dressed already! All you need are shoes and a skirt. You'd better spend some time on your face, though, and do something about your hair. It looks like a chicken roost."

That did it. "Some detective *you* are," I growled. "If you had been paying attention, you'd know these are the same clothes I was wearing yesterday. And if you took more than a cursory look at my face and hair, you'd realize that—up until just a few moments ago—both of these cranial appendages were buried in my pillow."

"Well, it's good I woke you up then," she said with a sniff. "The later we get there, the less chance we have of finding the Ham at home."

"Ham? What ham?"

"*Birming*ham, you nitwit. As in Jimmy. As in the poet with the dog. As in Judy's fickle ex-boyfriend. As in the possible murderer who's been stalking you."

"Oh, yeah," I mumbled. The crime-busting plans we had made for the day came crawling back into my consciousness. "What time is it?"

"Almost eleven."

"Jeez! It really *is* late. Where's Terry?"

"He left already. Went to see Judy's old roommates. Up on 19th Street. Do you remember *that* part of the plan at least?"

"Yes, of course I do," I said, ignoring her raised eyebrow and sarcastic tone. "So, uh . . . well . . . I guess I'd better get a move on. Take a shower and get dressed."

"Slick scheme, Sherlock," she said, smiling, backing out of my apartment and turning into her own. "Come over as soon as you're finished. There's still some coffee in the pot."

I went back upstairs and took off all my clothes—except for the stockings, which were stuck to my knees and shins as if glued with epoxy. I had to take a shower with my nylons *on* before I could (carefully!) peel them *off*. Then I slathered my wounds with various tinctures and ointments and bandaged them with gauze. Hiding the bandages under a pair of navy blue wool slacks, I put on a baby blue sweater and a white dickey, and zipped on my snowboots. A bit of lipstick, mascara, and rouge, followed by a fierce hair brushing, and I was ready—actually raring—to go.

Hurrying down the stairs, however, I caught sight of my flimsily patched, taped-up back door and almost lost my nerve. What the hell did I think I was doing? Who the hell did I think I was? Joe Friday? Mike Hammer? Sky King? Ozzie Nelson was more like it! I was begging for trouble, and I knew I was going to get even more of it. The killer had broken into my apartment once and now there was nothing but a Duz detergent box to stop him from doing it again.

*He could have let himself in last night while I was sleeping,* I screamed to myself, *and smothered me with a pillow! Or strangled me with my own neckerchief! He could come back today while I'm out and destroy everything that I own! He could set fire to my books! He could smash up my typewriter! He could . . . he could . . . he could . . .* the possibilities were endless.

But my capacity for self-torture wasn't. I finally gave myself a mental slap in the face, hoisted myself up by the bootstraps (okay, *snow*bootstraps), and swaggered down the rest of the steps to the kitchen. I scrunched up the Tiffany bag with Dan's present in it and stuck it down between the cleaning products in the cabinet under the sink, setting the bottle of bleach in front, within easy reach. Then I grabbed my purse and gloves and coat off the kitchen chair and skedaddled over to Abby's.

• • •

THE SUN WAS STRONG, BUT THE COLD WAS much stronger. None of the snow was melting. The sidewalks were dry in places, icy in others, and the air was as clear and sharp and brittle as glass. Making our way toward Jimmy Birmingham's address on East 8th Street, Abby and I kept our noses buried in our mufflers, walked as fast as we could, and did very little talking for fear our teeth would freeze. Entering Washington Square Park from the south, we cut through the very center of the paved arena, heading straight for the triumphal Washington Arch—the gateway to lower Fifth Avenue.

If it had been summertime, the huge fountain in the middle of the park would have been flowing, and the raised circumference of the fountain basin would have been lined with poets and singers and musicians giving free performances for anybody who would stop and listen. The cement tables on the outskirts of the fountain area would've been crowded with old Italian men playing chess, and the double-barred iron railing near the trees—the stretch of fence everybody referred to as the "meat rack"—would've been strung with promiscuous young men looking for partners with whom to play other, more physical, kinds of games.

But it was the middle of winter, and—except for a handful of pedestrians and a few hardy souls sitting bundled up on benches, holding their pale faces up to the sun—the park was empty. Abby and I hurried along the shoveled path, past the round, snow-filled sink of the fountain, and onward through the arch, exiting the park and heading due north toward 8th Street. To our right stood No. 1 Fifth Avenue, the high-rise apartment building where the poet Sara Teasdale committed suicide in 1933, and about a mile and a half ahead, at 34th Street, rose the Empire State Building, its lofty spire piercing the clear blue sky like a humongous hypodermic needle.

Hanging a right on 8th and walking two blocks east, we finally reached the Birmingham residence, a four-story, tan brick structure housing a street-level chop suey restaurant. (If I smelled like fish, Jimmy probably smelled like fried rice.)

There were no buzzers near the building's entrance, and no lock on the door either, so Abby and I simply went inside and trudged, in single file, up the dark, narrow staircase to the second floor.

There was just one apartment on that floor, and the name on the door said Potter, so we continued our climb to the next level and the next apartment. And there it was—written in letters so tiny they *almost* all fit in the window of the small brass nameplate—BIRMINGHA.

"Should we ring or knock?" I whispered to Abby, glad not to have to make such a momentous decision on my own.

"Ring," she said, pressing the bell. She took off her hat, pulled her long braid over one shoulder, and started warming up her lash-batting muscles.

Nobody came to the door.

"And then ring again," she added, jabbing the bell about three more times.

Still nobody.

"Then knock," she said, rapping her knuckles hard against the wood.

Nothing happened.

"And if that doesn't work, knock harder," she said, pounding the side of her fist like a sledgehammer on the door. "Hey, Birmingham!" she shouted at the top of her lungs. "Get your lazy ass over here and open the door!"

Mission accomplished. There were some plodding and groaning noises on the other side of the portal, then a couple of clicks and scrapes, then a wide opening appeared between the door and the doorjamb. And standing smack in the middle of that opening was Jimmy Birmingham, yawning loudly and wearing nothing but a high school ring, a silver ID bracelet, and a dirty brown blanket wrapped around his narrow hips. Otto was standing at Jimmy's feet, whimpering and whirling his skinny little tail in circles.

"Hi, Jimmy," Abby said, pushing the door even wider and stepping inside. "Did we wake you up?" Her bright red lips were smiling and her thick black lashes were flapping like the wings of a raven on takeoff. It was quite a show.

"Yeah," he said, holding the blanket up around his waist with one hand and scratching his beard with the other. "Didn't get to bed till a couple'a hours ago." He cleared his throat, rubbed his eyes, and took another—closer—look at Abby. "Hey, gorgeous, do I know you?" he asked, raising his heavy lids and cocking his lips in a sleepy smirk.

"You do now," she said, brushing past him and moving deeper into the apartment.

"Allow me to introduce you," I said, stepping into the doorway and standing in front of Jimmy. "This is Judy Catcher's cousin, Muffy Gurch." (If I live to be a hundred, I'll never know where *that* name came from!) "She just came into town from Pittsburgh. Muffy's still really broken up about Judy's murder, and she thought she might find some comfort in the company of her cousin's closest friends."

Looking at me for the first time, Jimmy took a step backward and winced. "Yeah, okay, fine—but what the hell're *you* doing here?" He touched his fingers to the scabbed-over lesion on his lip. "You wanna sink your teeth in me again?"

"Oh, no!" I cried, telling the absolute truth (for a brief second, anyway). "I thought I could use some comfort, too. And I wanted to apologize for what happened the other night—and for the nasty things I said."

"Yeah, well . . ." He looked skeptical, to say the least.

"I'm really sorry, Jimmy," I pleaded. "I'm so sick about what happened to Judy, I don't know what I'm doing or saying anymore."

"Are you serious?" he asked, scratching his beard again.

"Dead serious."

"No more biting or crazy accusations?"

"Not even a nibble."

"Well then," he said, moving aside and pulling the door all the way open, "I guess you can come in, too."

Jimmy seemed to have forgiven me, but Otto definitely hadn't. As I walked into the apartment, the teeny-weeny dog let out a great big weenie growl. And then—nails clicking madly against the bare wood floor—he started jumping all over the place and yapping his pointy-nosed little head off. I was the only one in danger of being bitten now.

"Cool it, Otto!" Jimmy commanded, and the little dog immediately quieted down. Jimmy picked him up in his free hand (the other one was still holding the blanket around his waist) and cradled him in the crook of his arm. "That's a good boy," Jimmy gurgled, lowering his cheek for Otto to lick. (Was that the same sound I'd heard on the phone with the anonymous caller last night?)

"My cousin used to write me letters about you, Jimmy," Abby said, taking off her coat, inflating her ample chest, giving him an eyeful of her fuzzy, well filled-out red sweater. She threw her coat on the foot of his rumpled bed (it was a studio apartment—no bedroom) and draped her thick braid over the opposite shoulder, allowing it to slither, like a python, over one breast. "Judy told me how handsome you were, and that you were a brilliant poet. I can see for myself that the first part was true," she said, twirling the end of her braid around her index finger and giving him a slow, slinky smile, "but how can I be sure about the second part?"

Jimmy was a goner. Signed, sealed, and delivered. Abby had him by the short hairs (and I'm not talking about his beard). "I can read you some of my poems," he said, writhing, strutting, blushing, inflating his own (bare) chest to the bursting point. "Or you could come to the Vanguard tonight and watch me perform. It'll be real gone, babe. Far out. I'll be reciting my new Christmas opus."

*Opus?!* I hooted to myself. I had to fight to keep from laughing out loud. *A real gone, far out Christmas opus?!* Now, *that* I had to hear.

"I have an idea," I broke in, stepping up close to Jimmy, trying to get his full attention (no easy feat with Abby in the same room). "Why don't you go take a quick shower to wake yourself up, and then get dressed, and then come out and read us your new poem. We'd both really like to hear it, wouldn't we, Muffy?"

"Boom chicky boom!" she said. "That would be sooooo groovy."

Jimmy grinned at Abby and nodded. "Okay!" he said, getting even more excited. He put Otto back down on the floor and charged around the room—from the closet to the dresser and back to the closet again—gathering up various items of clothing and putting them in a pile, doing his best not to step on his trailing blanket. Then, scooping the pile of clothes up under his free arm, he scrambled toward the bathroom at the far end of the studio.

"I'll be right back!" he croaked, stepping up to the closed bathroom door and trying to open it with the same hand that was clutching the blanket—an impossible maneuver which left him flushed and frustrated. Finally, he dropped the blanket to the floor, opened the door, and ducked into the bathroom—giving us a real gone, far out glimpse of his pink, poetic backside.

# Chapter 24

THE VERY SECOND JIMMY CLOSED HIMSELF up in the bathroom, Abby and I got to work. She started going through the drawers of his dresser, while I tackled the closet. Otto kept dashing back and forth between us, whimpering at Abby and growling at me.

Glad that Jimmy had a miniature dachshund and not a Great Dane, I rifled through the boxes on the upper shelf of the closet, finding nothing but a flattened football, a stack of pinup magazines, a 1949 bowling trophy, and a Dodgers baseball cap. I searched the pockets of Jimmy's coat, pants, and jackets and came up empty—except for a snotty handkerchief and a slew of movie ticket stubs from the Waverly Theater. There were a couple of shoeboxes on the floor of the closet which held nothing but shoes. Neither box was from Thom McAn.

"Did you find anything?" I whispered to Abby, closing the closet door and turning to see how she was making out.

"I found a few holsters," she said, dangling a handful of jockstraps in the air, "but nothing that even remotely resembles a gun."

"Then check out the kitchen shelves and drawers," I said.

"I'll do the bookshelf and look under the bed. Besides the gun, keep your eyes peeled for a black lunchbox."

"Aye, aye, captain!" she whispered, turning toward the area near the bathroom door, where the small kitchen appliances and cabinets were lined against the wall like cartons in a stockroom.

I zipped over to the side of the bed and dropped down to my hands and knees. Lifting up the edge of another brown blanket, I put my face down next to the floor and peered into the darkness underneath. Nothing but dust, a well-chewed steak bone, and a bunch of dead cockroaches. Otto darted under the bed and crouched down over the bone, staring out at me, snarling, protecting his treasure with unabashed zeal. I backed away from the bed, lowered the blanket, and crawled a few feet over to examine the small, low, dusty bookshelf—which also revealed nothing, except that Jimmy liked to read dime store novels with titles like *Hot Rod* and *Pickup Alley.* He also had a copy of *The Catcher in the Rye*—but then, so did everybody.

"Any luck?" Abby asked, moving back into the middle of the room. "There's hardly anything in the kitchen. He doesn't even have any food."

I stood up and walked over to her. "I couldn't find anything either. And there's no place left to search but the bathroom. I'll look around in there after Jimmy comes out."

No sooner had these words left my mouth than Jimmy exited the bathroom and joined us in the studio. He looked very handsome in his black turtleneck, black pants, and sexy, cocksure smile. His thick, dark, Tony Curtis hair was still wet from the shower.

"Hi, girls," he said, raising both eyebrows and stroking his sleek Vandyke. "Did you miss me?" He was talking to both of us, but he only had eyes for Abby. At the sound of Jimmy's voice, Otto scurried out from under the bed, scampered to his master's side, and dropped his dust-covered steak bone at his feet.

"May I use the bathroom?" I asked immediately, anxious to complete my search of the premises. I also had to pee.

"Sure, doll," Jimmy said, still looking only at Abby. "Knock yourself out."

Tearing myself away from the happy trio (nobody—not even Abby!—was sorry to see me go), I slipped into the bathroom and locked the door. Turning on the sink faucet full blast (I hoped the sound of running water would mask any other sounds I might happen to make), I opened the medicine cabinet and peeked inside. Just the usual stuff: a bottle of aspirin, a razor, a shaving mug with a brush (which had seen very little use), and one of those weird-looking nosehair clippers. No small handgun or box of .22 caliber bullets. No lunchbox either, but I didn't expect there to be, since it could never have fit on one of those shallow glass shelves.

Except for the bathtub, which was wet and empty, there was only one hiding place in the room big enough to conceal a lunchpail—the dirty clothes basket. Yanking the lid off the small white hamper, I plunged both arms into the stash of soiled underwear, feeling around the sides of the hamper, and all the way down to the bottom, for something hard. Nothing doing. No gun, no lunchbox—no cigar. Jimmy had either hidden the murder weapon and the lunchbox in another location entirely, or disposed of them altogether, or he was no murderer at all.

Wondering which of these three possibilities was true, I peed, flushed, washed my hands, and left the bathroom. To my utter surprise, Otto ran over to meet me, wagging his little tail in ecstasy, gazing up at me with the sweetest expression I'd ever seen on any creature's face. I picked the little dog up in my arms, gave him my cheek to lick, and then looked over at Abby and Jimmy, trying to determine the cause of this welcome canine windfall.

It wasn't too hard to figure out. Jimmy was so entranced with Abby—and Abby was working so hard to *keep* Jimmy entranced—that Otto had no one left to turn to but me. I gave the pup a soft little squeeze, fondled his warm, floppy ears, walked over and sat down on the side of the bed, settling the little dog snuggly on my lap. It felt so good to have a new friend. One who wouldn't stalk me, or push me onto the subway tracks, or break into my apartment, or be looking for new ways to kill me.

"Hey!" I said, loud enough to bust up the near-coital experience taking place between Abby and Jimmy, "I'm back now, and I'm in need of brilliant poetry! My soul is starving! Bring on the Christmas opus!" Though I was dying to ask Jimmy a few leading questions about Judy Catcher, I felt I could use a little diversion first.

And Jimmy was eager to provide. "Okay!" he cried, placing his hands on Abby's shoulders and guiding her—backwards—to a seated position next to me on the bed. "Prepare to be transported to the truth!" he said, puffing out his cheeks and chest in pride. Abby and I gave each other a stealthy little smile, then focused all our fawning attention on Jimmy.

Jimmy walked back across the width of the room, picked a notebook up from the small table against the wall, spun around to face us, and struck a dramatic pose—feet planted firmly apart, one arm behind his back, the other dangling down his side with the notebook in his hand. The wall behind him was decorated with three (yes, *three!*) bullfighting posters. (I'll never understand why everybody—but everybody!—in the Village has huge bullfighting posters hanging in their apartments. Is it a craving for violent public spectacle, a mythical fear of mighty animals, a passionate lust for blood, or just a faddish devotion to the bullfighterly novels and stories of Ernest Hemingway?)

Looking straight at Abby, Jimmy gave her a slow, suggestive wink, then raised the notebook to reading level, and—in a deep, pompous, pontifical tone—began transporting us to the truth:

*Snowflakes soundless pure commingling*
*Falling to the rotted dizzy ground*
*Seasoned with spirits of meaningless holiday cheer*
*Noisy mindless sleighbells pound*
*Yearly eternal cerebral Christmas blues*

*For all another round of bloody boozy fizz*
*Drink up you fools and wish yourself a merry tight*
*In the skunk bright moonlight goodnight*

Something horrible had happened to me. I was starting to kind of *like* Jimmy Birmingham's goofy poetry. It still made me want to laugh, though, so—in an effort to stop any giggle fits before they began—I clenched my teeth and didn't say a word.

Which worked out just fine, since Abby was being more than effusive enough for both of us. "Ohhhh, Jimmy!" she panted, jumping to her feet and darting over to give him a wild embrace. "That was the living end! So cool and honest and true! I never heard such wonderful words in my life! You're the new Robert Lowell! You're better than Dylan Thomas! I'm swooning with the way out passion of your soaring vision!"

*Oh, brother!* I groaned to myself. *If she lays it on any thicker, he'll be buried alive.* Deciding to cut in on the spinning dancers before they swirled right out of control, I rose to my feet and—cradling Otto like a baby in my arms—walked up close to the tangled twosome. "Loved your Christmas opus, Jimmy," I said. "Really did. But aren't we forgetting something here? Like the real reason we came to see you today?" I gave Abby a secret poke in the ribs with my elbow. "Muffy is so upset about her cousin Judy's death that she just *has* to talk to you about it. She's hoping you can shed some light on the murder, help her learn to live with the pain."

"That's right," Abby said, finally remembering that she had come to look for a cold-blooded killer, not a new model—or a new lover. She backed away from Jimmy's grasping arms and flipped her smile into a frown. "I'm so devastated over what happened to Judy," she said, whimpering in much the same way Otto had earlier, "I can't ever get to sleep at night. I just lie in bed thinking about the horrible way she died, wondering why anybody would want to shoot my sweet, beautiful cousin, and praying with all my heart that the killer will soon be found." She stopped talking for a moment and gave Jimmy a pleading gaze. "Do you miss her as much as I do, baby?"

*Baby?! She's calling him baby? What went on while I was in the bathroom?*

"Sure I do," he said. "I miss her a lot. She was my one and only girlfriend for three whole months."

*Hip, hip, hooray! Let's hear it for the Ham! Greater love hath no man than to stay faithful for three, count 'em, three* whole *months!*

"So what happened, Jimmy?" I asked. "Why did you break up with her?"

"*I* wasn't the one who cut loose," he insisted. "*She* broke up with *me.* I was really torn up about it for a while." His eyes were getting teary. (From true pain, deep guilt, or pure "poetic" sensitivity? I couldn't tell.) I hoped he wouldn't start bawling like he had at the Vanguard.

"But my cousin was so in *love* with you!" Abby broke in. "Every letter she sent me was all about you! Why would *she* call it quits?"

"Well," he said, looking down at the dusty floor and shuffling his feet, "I guess I didn't treat her too good. I didn't mean to hurt her. I really didn't. But I just couldn't walk the line. I'm a wild and crazy poet, dig it? I'm a natural-born, hot-blooded man. One chick's just not enough for me."

"So why were you so torn up when she broke it off?" I asked.

"Because I loved her. She moved me. I wrote good poems when she was with me. Otto loved her, too." Looking around for his little dog, and finding him nestled in my arms, Jimmy stepped over to me and scooped Otto up in his own arms. "I really hated it when Judy moved in with that old rich guy," he muttered, hugging Otto tight to his chest, beginning to pace the room in circles like a caged panther.

"You mean Gregory Smythe?" I asked.

"I don't know. She never told me the cube's name. She knew I didn't want to hear about him. It made me too mad."

*Mad enough to kill her?* I wondered. "Did you keep seeing

Judy after she moved to Chelsea? Did you visit her at her new apartment?"

"Are you kidding? I wouldn't go inside that pad for all the bread in the bank. I wouldn't set foot in the whole fucking neighborhood. It made me sick to think about her living there with that perverted old fart. I saw Judy sometimes—at the Vanguard, or the Kettle of Fish, or some other Village hangout—but I never went anywhere near that lousy damn apartment."

*That's not what Elsie Londergan says,* I thought, remembering that she'd seen Jimmy in the neighborhood a couple of times. "You mean you never went to Chelsea while Judy was living there? Not even once?"

"Not on your life!" he declared. "I never even . . . no, wait a second . . . I just remembered something . . ." He stopped his angry pacing and turned to face us. "I *did* go there one time. But I didn't go up to Judy's apartment. I just went to the Chelsea Realty office to tell Judy's fucking landlord to leave her the hell alone."

"What?!" Abby and I cried in unison.

"You went to see Roscoe Swift?" I sputtered.

"Yeah, Swift. That was the creep's name."

"Why did you tell him to leave Judy alone?" Abby urged. "Was he bothering her somehow?"

"Sure was. All the time. He kept showing up at her apartment, late at night, without even calling first, claiming there was some problem with the heat, or that her sink was leaking into the apartment underneath, or that somebody had complained she was playing the radio too loud. And once he was inside the apartment, he'd make a pass at her. He'd tell her she was really sexy, and then he'd try to cop a feel or give her a kiss. Once he even pinched her on the ass. He always came late so he could catch her in her nightgown."

"But he knew a man was paying her rent," I said, "so he knew she had a lover. How could he be so sure she'd be alone?"

"I can answer that one," Abby said. "Swift knew that Smythe was *married,* right? I mean, that's the way these arrangements usually work. So it was a pretty safe bet that if he went to Judy's place real late, her dear old daddy-o would have already gone home to his dear old wife."

Suddenly feeling exhausted, I sat down on the side of the bed again. So many complicated questions—so many confounding answers. I looked up at Jimmy and said, "So Judy told you that Swift was making advances and asked you to take care of it?"

Jimmy started pacing in circles again. "She told me Swift was bugging her, but she didn't ask me to do anything about it. Going to see the little creep was my own idea. I marched into his office and told him if he ever touched Judy again I'd break his legs and cut his filthy rod off. Scared him pretty good. He didn't bother her so much after that."

"Did Judy tell Smythe that Swift was annoying her?" I asked.

"I don't know," Jimmy grunted. "Like I said, she never mentioned Smythe—or whatever the hell the old fart's name was—to me."

My brain was spinning with the new information. And the new details were getting all tangled up with the old ones. And I didn't know what to believe, or what not to believe, or what to believe just a little bit. Finally realizing I couldn't possibly come up with any sound conjectures on the spot—that I needed some time to think things over, try to fit the pieces of the puzzle together—I decided to just fire off a few more questions while Jimmy was in a talkative mood.

"Do you have any idea who killed Judy?" I asked, training my eyes on Jimmy's face, watching for telltale expressions. "Do you think it could have been Swift?"

"I don't know who did it," he said, frowning. "The newspapers said it was a random burglar, but it could have been Swift, I guess. He's a nasty little fucker. But does that make him a murderer? I don't know, doll. I really don't know." Looking as sad and tired and frustrated as I felt, Jimmy came and sat down next to me on the bed. Otto stretched his skinny body over Jimmy's bent arm, nuzzled his nose into the cup of my hand, and licked my palm and fingers.

"Did you know that Smythe gave Judy some diamond jewelry?" I asked.

"Nope," he said, fingering his beard again. "But she wouldn't have told me even if he did. And I never saw her wearing any ice, either. Judy wasn't the diamond-flashing type."

I stored his response in my mental file cabinet and moved on. "Why did you follow me home from the Vanguard the other night?"

Jimmy widened his eyes and furrowed his brow. "You knew about that?"

"I saw you lurking in the laundromat doorway."

He looked embarrassed for a moment, but quickly regained his composure. "It was only because you said you were a good friend of Judy's," he declared, "and I wanted to see you again. You never told me your name, so the only way I could keep track of you was to find out where you lived."

Since he already knew where my apartment was (and may, in fact, have already *broken into* it), I didn't see any reason to keep my identity a secret from him any longer. "My name is Paige Turner," I said, ripping a piece of paper out of the little notebook in my purse, which I had tossed on the bed when I began my search of *his* apartment. "And here's my phone number." I wrote the info down on the slip of paper and handed it to him. "Will you call me if you think of anything—anything at all—that might help the police find Judy's murderer?"

"Sure thing, doll." He started to fold the paper up and stick it in his pocket, but thought better of it. "Can I borrow your pen?" he asked. Then, still holding Otto in his arms, he stood up, walked over to Abby, and handed the pen and the slip of paper to her. "Here you go, Miss Muffet," he said with a goatish grin. "Better put your number down here, too. If I ever get to Pittsburgh, I'll give you a ring."

"Okay, baby!" Abby cooed, flapping her lashes so fast I thought they'd stir up a dust storm. She wrote what I assumed was a fake number down on the piece of paper and handed it back to him. "I'd ask for *your* number, too," she said, "but the phone book already gave it to me. Mind if I use it the next time I'm in town?"

"I'll be waiting for your call," he said, still grinning.

I had a feeling he wouldn't have to wait long.

# Chapter 25

"MUFFY GURCH?!" ABBY SCREECHED AS soon as we hit the street. "How could you saddle me with a stupid ugly name like that?! I was mortified!"

"Sorry," I said, smiling. "It was the first moniker that came to mind. It just popped into my head like a weasel."

"Well, it better pop right out again! I hate that name! Especially the Muffy part." She wheeled around and started walking (okay, *stomping*) toward home. This being Christmas Eve day, all the stores were closed, and the sidewalks were practically deserted, so she was moving pretty fast.

"I don't understand what you're so upset about," I hollered, running to catch up with her and tramping alongside. "It was just a temporary alias, you know. Nobody but Jimmy Birmingham will ever think of you as Muffy Gurch again . . . Or even Miss Muffet," I added, unable to resist the temptation to tease. (When your *real* name is Paige Turner, you've got a license to make fun of other silly appellations, even when you've made them up yourself.)

"But I don't *want* Jimmy to think of me with that name," she whined. "I *like* him! He may not be the world's best poet, but he's damn good-looking. And he's got a cute tushy. And he's sexy as all get-out. And," she added, almost as an afterthought, "I don't think he's a murderer, either."

"But shouldn't you be *sure* of that before you hop in the sack with him?" I asked, trying, but failing, to keep the sarcasm out of my tone.

Abby came to a dead stop on the sidewalk, in front of a store window full of ladies' hats. "I resent that question!" she huffed. "Do you really think I'm so oversexed I'd go to bed with a possible killer?"

"Well, no, but . . ."

"Then why did you say it?"

"I don't know, I just . . ."

"Something *else* must be bothering you," Abby seethed, "something you don't feel comfortable talking about. So what is it? You might as well say it and get it off your chest."

"I really don't know what you . . ."

"C'mon, out with it Paige! What's going on in that *meshugge* twisty brain of yours?"

"Well . . . er . . . um . . . it's really none of my business," I stammered, staring at one of the hats in the window behind her. (In case you're interested, it was a large pink and white cartwheel hat with a black net veil and a black satin streamer down the back. Pretty awful.) "But I can't help wondering how you can be all wrapped up in Terry Catcher one minute, then wrapped around Jimmy Birmingham the next. I mean, Terry's obviously crazy about you. And he's such a great, really wonderful guy. Don't you feel any loyalty to him at all?"

"Oh, Paige, you're such a simpleton!" she said, linking her arm through mine and towing me on down the sidewalk. "You just don't get it, do you? I'm as loyal to Whitey as he *wants* me to be—which means I won't sleep with anybody else while I'm sleeping with him, and his concerns will be my concerns as long as he's here in New York, living with me. But he's not going to be here very much longer, Paige. We've discussed it at length. As soon as his sister's murder is solved, he's going back to Pittsburgh to take care of his father, and to start a new life in the city he knows and loves. And I'm going to stay right here in the city *I* know and love.

"So all Whitey and I have is the here and now," she went on, walking and talking, her hot breath vaporizing in the arctic air. "And we plan to enjoy it as much as we can. And since we both know we'll have no long-term future together, we're each free to make contingency plans. And that's all Jimmy Birmingham is, you dig? A contingency plan with an adorable ass."

I laughed out loud. "You mean it wasn't his soaring poetry that won you over?"

"Not a chance," she said, chuckling. "I always keep my feet firmly planted on the rotted dizzy ground."

TERRY WAS SITTING AT ABBY'S KITCHEN table—smoking a cigarette and reading a newspaper—when we got home. His white hair was glowing in the bright kitchen light. His blue eyes started glowing, too, when we walked in. (The gleam was mostly for Abby, of course, but I could tell one sweet, shiny shaft of it belonged to me.)

"Hello, baby," Abby said, darting over to give him a tight hug around his neck. I wanted to hug him, too, but there wasn't enough room. I settled for sitting across the table from him and lighting up one of his ciggies.

"How'd you make out today, Terry?" I asked. "Find out anything interesting?"

"Not really," he said, blushing from the warmth of Abby's embrace. "One of the two girls Judy used to live with wasn't there. She went out to Long Island to spend Christmas with her family. And the one who *was* there—Angela Prickens—hadn't seen or spoken to Judy since she moved out, and didn't know anything about her subsequent life . . . Or her death," he added sadly. "She had heard that Judy was murdered, but she didn't seem to care very much."

"That's odd," I said. "Why wouldn't she care? Was she the one Judy had the hair-pulling fight with?"

"Yes, and she's still upset about it."

"Upset enough to kill?"

"No!" Terry insisted. "She's just a young girl with her head in the clouds. All she thinks about is boys and romance and finding a good husband. She's a lot like Judy was."

"Did she know about the diamonds?"

"She says she didn't, and I believe her."

Abby took off her coat and sat down next to Terry. "Did you find out the name of the guy Judy and Angela were fighting over? Was it Birmingham?"

"The one and only." Terry leaned back in his chair and took another puff on his Pall Mall. "Did you go to see him today as planned? Was he at home?"

"Yes, we did," Abby said, smiling, "and, yes, he was."

Terry gave her a teasing look. "Angela says he's a real dreamboat—her word, not mine—and that every chick who sees him falls for him. Do you agree with that assessment?"

"Well, let me put it this way," Abby said, giving him a teasing look in return. "He may be dreamboat material, but my ship's already come in." Adding weight (okay, *heat*) to her words, Abby snaked her hand across Terry's shoulder and began stroking her fingertips up and down the side of his neck.

Aaaargh! It was time for me to leave again!

I really didn't want to go. There were so many things that Abby and Terry and I needed to talk about. So many theories and clues to mull over. I hadn't even told them that my apartment had been broken into! (I'd started to tell Abby earlier, but she'd been so focused on the time—and the need to get over to Jimmy's place in a big fat hurry—that I'd finally decided to break the news later, when we were all three together, so I wouldn't have to tell the story twice.)

And that was just the half of it. We still had tons of preparations to make for the party we were going to attend that night. We had to draw up a synchronized plan of attack—decide which of us should do what, and talk to whom, when—and then we had to go through Abby's Vault of Illusions, looking for elegant, upper-crusty clothes to wear to the fancy uptown shindig.

Okay, I admit it. Those weren't the only reasons I didn't

want to leave Abby's right then. Truth was, I was scared to go back to my place alone.

But being an unwanted guest would cause me even more discomfort, I felt, so I bid my amorous friends a quick "catch you later," and hopped across the hall to my own habitat. Either because of my stupid name or in spite of it, there's one thing I'm pretty darn good at: knowing when to turn the page.

EVERYTHING WAS JUST AS I'D LEFT IT—specifically the flattened Duz detergent box, which was still taped over the broken door pane in the exact same position as before. I inspected it carefully, checking for rips in the tape or dents in the cardboard, finally deciding that the makeshift patch had in no way been disturbed. There'd been no drop in the indoor temperature, either, so—even though I still didn't feel the slightest bit secure—I was, at least, warm.

I looked at the clock. It was only three-thirty. Hours to kill till party time. I had a bowl of Campbell's tomato soup and ate about a thousand Nabisco saltines. I typed up three more pages of story notes and stuffed them into Judy's oatmeal box. I turned on the radio and fiddled around with the dial, hoping to find some good jazz or blues, finally giving up and settling for Frank Sinatra. I tried to read a few pages of the new novel I'd recently borrowed from the library—*Lucky Jim* by Kingsley Amis—but soon gave up on that, too. I prayed for Dan to call, but of course he didn't.

Luckily, all the time I spent dashing around like a loon, from the front window to the back door of my apartment—peering out onto Bleecker Street or down into the rear courtyard looking for stalkers or murderers—kept me pretty busy. Likewise the nine cigarettes I smoked down to the nub.

When Abby knocked on my door at six-fifteen and told me to come next door for cocktails and a confab, I almost fainted with joy. Now I knew how Otto had felt when Jimmy gathered him back into his arms.

Wagging my tail and panting for company, I bounded into Abby's living room–cum–art studio and sat down next to

Terry on the little red couch. My whiskey sour was waiting for me on the coffee table. Terry's was half gone. Perched on the big wooden easel in the corner was Abby's new painting, a wild western bar scene with a lean and sexy cowboy standing—legs apart, hips cocked, both six-guns drawn—in the foreground. A busty blonde floozy sat on a barstool behind him. The cowboy didn't have white hair, but he sure did look a lot like Terry.

"Did you pose for that?" I asked him.

"Yeah," he said, face reddening.

"How ever did you find the time?" I teased, thinking—but not saying—*since Abby's been keeping you so busy in the bedroom.*

"It wasn't easy," he said, giving me a sheepish (and, I thought, weary) grin.

"What are you two yakking about?" Abby asked, toting her own drink into the studio and sitting down, cross-legged, on the canvas drop cloth that covered the floor.

"Nothing much," I answered, dying to get our homicide investigation back on track. "We were just waiting for you. We need to fill each other in on everything we learned today, and then map out a plan of action for tonight."

"Right," Terry said, obviously eager to get down to business, too.

"I'll go first," I said, taking a big gulp of my drink, lighting a cigarette, and proceeding to tell them about the break-in.

They both went crazy. (I'm talking *all* the way out of their minds!) They took turns screaming and shouting their heads off about all the horrible things that could have happened to me, and then they both gave me hell for not coming to get them the very second I discovered that my window had been smashed and the back door left wide-open. They were furious, really *furious* at me for spending the whole night in my apartment alone, with nothing but a piece of cardboard, a few strips of tape, and a bottle of bleach to protect me. They were mad at me for spending the afternoon alone there, too.

And throughout their long, vociferous diatribe about my incautious behavior they called me some very unflattering names: reckless fool, blithering moron, donkey with no brain, irresponsible daredevil, thoughtless nitwit—to list but a few. Not once did either one of them suggest that I had been strong or self-sufficient or brave—or deserving of their praise instead of their scorn.

And I never gave voice to the thought that kept circling through my allegedly absent donkey brain: that if they hadn't been so fixated on each other, they might have been more available to help me.

Some team we three were turning out to be!

Still, I was glad that they were going to the party with me tonight. So, as soon as they finished their tirade over the break-in—and after we'd exhausted our thoughts about the other new developments in the case—I brought up the subject of the impending Christmas Eve festivities. "What are we going to wear?" I asked, knowing this was the question most likely to grab Abby's full attention. "The Smythe's are *very* rich, and all of their guests will probably be rich, too, so we have to at least *try* to look elegant and wealthy as well."

"Oh, I have that all figured out already," Abby said, eyes glittering with purposeful intent. She stood up from the floor and started pacing back and forth—like a maniacal movie director—in front of the couch. "Whitey can wear my Uncle Morty's tuxedo. He gave it to me right before he died—which was a lucky thing for us, because otherwise he might have been buried in it. It's a very old tuxedo, but it's classic and it's clean. And it looks to be just the right size.

"I'll be wearing my sexy black satin strapless with the white organza skirt," she went on, still pacing. "And I have a pair of long, black, over-the-elbow gloves that'll add a classy touch. And for you, Paige," she said, stopping in her tracks and giving me a big red smile, "I have the perfect dress. It has a tight-fitting dark green velvet bodice, with a deep scoop neck and three-quarter length sleeves, and the full skirt is made of dark green taffeta. There's a lighter green sash and bow at the waist. I bought the dress at a secondhand store over on Orchard Street, but it's in pretty good shape."

Uh oh. "*Pretty* good shape? What does *that* mean?"

"Well, there's a button missing in the back, and there's an ever so slight brownish stain on the sash. Looks like gravy to me. There *was* a big rip in the side seam, but I sewed that up so you'd hardly even notice."

"Jeez, I don't know, Abby," I whined, letting out a fretful groan. "This dress sounds a long way from perfect to me. I mean, how wealthy and classy can a girl look if she's missing a button and sporting a gravy stain?

"Oh, don't worry about that!" Abby snorted, with a meaningful wink and a smirk the size of Texas. "Nobody will notice your dress when you're wearing a dazzling, stupendously expensive array of antique diamonds around your neck."

I HAD TO ADMIT IT WAS A GOOD IDEA. OH, I protested at first—saying it was far too risky; that the necklace could be lost, or stolen; that it might be ripped right off my neck at the party. But the more I thought about it, the more it seemed like a shrewd thing to do. Both Gregory and Augusta Smythe were sure to recognize the necklace. And they would have to *react* in some way. And I would be sure to learn *something* from their reactions. What that something would be remained to be seen, but I was as eager as a fervent voyeur to get a glimpse of it. (I hoped they wouldn't accuse me of being a thief and call the police! Was the Smythe penthouse in Dan's precinct? I wasn't sure.)

Terry was against me wearing the necklace at first, too—not because he was afraid it might be lost or stolen, but because he was worried about me. He thought the mere sight of the diamonds might incite the murderer (if, indeed, the murderer happened to *be* at the party) to do something rash (i.e., kill me or something like that). But once Abby and I reminded him that he would be with me the whole time—standing close by my side as my husband, primed and poised to protect me—he withdrew his objections and threw himself into the spirit of the operation.

It was almost party time, so we went upstairs to get ready. I wanted to go home to get dressed, where I could primp in private, but Abby and Terry wouldn't let me. They thought it was too dangerous. *Oh, great!* I grumbled to myself. *Now when I* want *to be alone, I can't.* They eventually let me go next door to remove my shin and knee bandages and put on a garter belt, stockings, and my dressy black suede pumps, but Terry insisted on going with me and standing watch at the kitchen door.

Back in Abby's apartment, we finished dressing and checked out each other's appearance. Terry looked fantastic in Uncle Morty's classic black tux. It fit him almost perfectly. The pants were just a tad too short, but with his glorious white hair and sparkling blue eyes it was a cinch nobody would be looking at his feet. Abby looked even more fantastic. She had swept her hair up in a sleek French twist and then coiled the long ends around the top of her head in a smooth ebony crown. Her face was beautiful, her black and white dress was beautiful, her long black gloves and her milky white shoulders were beautiful. She looked like Ava Gardner on a really good night.

I, on the other hand, looked like Milton Berle in a hand-me-down prom frock. The dress fit me okay, but it was ugly. And heavy. I felt like I was wearing a bathmat with a skirt attached. And there was nothing "slight" about the gravy stain on the hideous pea-green sash. It was as big as my palm and in a very prominent place. I took one look at myself in the full-length mirror on the back of Abby's coat closet door and shuddered in horror.

"This is awful!" I cried, glaring at Abby. "I don't believe this is the best thing you could come up with for me to wear. You're just getting even with me for Muffy Gurch!"

Abby laughed. "That's crazy talk," she said. "This is the only fancy dress I have that's sure to hide your unsightly legs."

"My legs aren't half as unsightly as this dress!" I exclaimed. "Quick! Get me the scissors!"

Shooting me a questioning look, Abby took the shears out of the sewing kit sitting on the coffee table and handed them to me. "What are you going to do?"

In the interest of cutting time (okay, cutting short Abby's possible objections), I decided to show instead of tell. I slipped the open scissor blades down over the waistband of the sash and snipped clean through it. Then, grabbing the ugly thing by its big fat ugly bow, I yanked the whole darned gravy-stained sash free of the dress's belt loops and tossed it on the couch. I cut off all the belt loops, too.

"Oh, that's so much better!" Abby cried, not the least bit upset by my violent attack on her dress. "Why didn't *I* think of that? You look really groovy now. All that's needed is the necklace."

She opened her pantry and took out the canister of sugar. Then she opened the canister and took out the tin foil–wrapped package of diamonds. Prying the edges of the tin foil apart and plucking Judy's necklace from the jumble of Tiffany jewelry inside, she walked over to me and fastened the two-tiered string of oh-so-valuable gems around my oh-so-humble neck.

Transformed, I wasn't. I didn't like wearing the diamonds any more than I liked being harnessed with the gravy-smeared sash. I may have been the only woman in the Western world (besides Judy) who would ever have felt this way, but I found the necklace to be garish and unseemly. I thought it made me look tacky and—strange to say—cheap.

Abby couldn't have disagreed more. "Ooooooh!" she squealed, practically passing out from the thrill of the glistening vision. "I'm *kvelling* all over the place! You look regal! Like a fabulous fairy-tale queen!"

"Yeah, well . . ." I didn't tell her that I felt like a royal ass. *Do people really kill each other over this useless sparkly stuff?*

"You look beautiful, Paige," Terry said, moving close to me, cupping my chin in his big warm hand. "I wish Bob could see you now. He would be so proud."

I was grateful for the compliment, even though I knew it wasn't true. (Bob would never have been *proud* of me for wearing diamonds. As a man of very simple tastes, he'd been most impressed when I was wearing nothing.)

"Thanks, Terry," I said, blushing. I could feel the pinkness wash across my face—and the sadness wash across my heart. Looking to change the subject before the mirage of Bob's loving smile caused me to wash the floor in tears, I mumbled, "So is everybody ready? It must be time to go."

Abby looked at the clock on her kitchen wall and gave a start. "We're running late, kids!" she cried. "Let's goose it."

# Chapter 26

HEY, DID YOU EVER SEE THE MOVIE *THE Thing*? It came out about three years ago. Actually, the whole title was *The Thing from Another World,* but everybody just called it *The Thing*. It was about a being from outer space, the pilot of a downed spaceship, who is found frozen in ice at the North Pole, and then thawed out—much to the horror and dismay of the isolated band of scientists and military personnel whose blood, it turns out, the hungry spaceman (actually he's a hungry space*plant!*) must feed on.

I mention this movie, *not* as a science fiction film buff who wants to bend your ear about the scientific—or, in this case, truly *un*scientific—details of a certain film, but as the pilot of a downed spaceship who wants to relate, as accurately as possible, her observations and impressions of the alien world in which she suddenly—at 9:06 P.M. on Christmas Eve, 1954—found herself defrosted.

The Smythe penthouse occupied the entire top floor of the elegantly appointed twelve-story building. We stepped off the elevator, walked across a small beige marble foyer, and entered the apartment through two colossal, wide-open, hand-carved wood doors. A butler greeted us at the door and two maids helped us off with our coats, whisking them away to an unknown location down the gold-veined marble hall to the left. Not knowing what we were supposed to do next, we stood like sticks in the enormous entrance hall, gaping at the six-foot-high floral arrangements positioned around the marble walls, and gazing up at the colossal crystal chandelier, which hung down from the center of the cavernous ceiling like a cluster of shimmering stalactites. The large round gilded table in the middle of the entrance hall was topped with a beautiful gold Christmas tree. Its only ornaments were hundreds, maybe thousands, of perfect red rosebuds.

We had definitely landed (okay, *crashed*) on a foreign planet. Due to the fragrant roses, and the tinkling crystal, and the celestial music wafting in from another room, I figured it was Venus.

"Well, what are we standing here for?" Abby croaked, breaking us out of our collective spaced-out trance. "Let's go find the booze."

"Down the hall to your right," the butler announced, in a deep, echoing, butler-like voice.

Terry and I followed Abby through the entrance hall into another hall, turned right, and then headed down *that* hall in the direction of the music. Eventually we came to the large arched doorway to the living room—the passageway to the party. Gregory Smythe was standing just inside the doorway talking to a lovely older woman in a navy satin gown, but ogling a much younger woman in red chiffon who was standing nearby.

"Mr. Smythe!" I said, walking right up to him and holding out my hand. "How nice to see you again."

He grabbed my hand and started fondling it, even though he clearly didn't remember who I was. "Oh, hello, Miss . . . uh . . . Miss . . ."

"It's *Mrs.* Turner," I said quickly. "We met in your office yesterday, when I came to see you about a recent inheritance."

"Oh, yes, Mrs. Turner!" he exclaimed, bowing to kiss my hand. After he gave it one smooch, I snatched it away and hid it behind my back.

As soon as he was upright again, I stuck my neck out (literally) and said, "We still have some unfinished business to discuss, Mr. Smythe. Do you think we might have a brief private talk later?"

"By all means, Mrs. Turner!" he said, grinning lasciviously and giving me an overt wink. Smythe was the kind of fool whose feelings were always flashing on his face. I fingered the diamonds around my neck and watched for his reaction, but he gave no sign of even *noticing* the necklace, let alone recognizing it.

The refined silver-haired woman standing next to him, however, looked as if she'd just been hit between the eyes with a two-by-four.

"And you must be *Mrs.* Smythe," I said, stepping toward her to give her a closer look. "It's so nice to meet you! And may I present my husband, Terry Turner, and my cousin, Bathsheba Lark." (Don't look at me. That's the name Abby *wanted* to use!)

While the four of them were shaking hands and making small talk, I kept my eyes trained on Augusta Smythe. She was a tall, thin woman in her late fifties (I guessed) with a dainty smile, a perfect manicure, and a heavily hairsprayed hairdo. Her floor-length navy blue satin gown was sleeveless, but she kept her thin arms covered with a long, wide, matching navy blue satin shawl. Instead of diamonds she was wearing pearls. Though she seemed quite composed standing there, welcoming Terry and Abby—I mean Bathsheba—to her party, I could see that she'd been shaken by the sight of my (okay, *her*) necklace.

"You have a beautiful home, Mrs. Smythe," I said, taking my first look around the luxurious, crowded room we'd just entered. It was the size of a football field, but the many paintings on the pale yellow walls, the huge Oriental carpets on the polished teak floor, and the colorful multitude of chatting, smoking, laughing guests gave it a warm, intimate glow. "Can I persuade you to give me a quick tour later, after the rest of your company has arrived?" (Translation: *Can I get you off in a corner somewhere and ask you a bunch of rude questions?*)

"Of course, dear," she said, staring at the necklace again. "I'll be happy to show you around in a little while. But first you must go inside and have some hors d'oeuvres and champagne." She gestured toward midfield.

I waited for Terry and Abby to finish their handshakes and small talk, then led them deep into the party crowd. I figured it was the best place for us to huddle without attracting undue attention (or suspicion). Surrounded by well-groomed men in tuxedos and transcendent women trimmed in fur, feathers, and jewels, we each grabbed a glass of champagne from a wandering waiter's tray and stood drinking together in a tight little circle. The jazz ensemble in the far corner of the room was playing an absurdly perky version of "O Holy Night."

"Wow!" Abby said, keeping her voice down to a loud whisper. "This is atomic! We just passed right by a Cézanne. And there's a van Gogh on that wall over there! I think it's from his Arles period."

I didn't have time for an art lesson. "How did you make out with Smythe?" I asked her, anxious to make the most of our Christmas Eve vigil.

"Fine. I'm meeting him in his private study in twenty minutes. He wants to show me his piggies."

"His what?!" Terry sputtered.

"His piggy banks," Abby said, taking a swig of champagne, then giggling through her nose. "The man collects piggy banks. Isn't that a scream?"

"It's a howl," Terry said, looking disgusted. "But I don't think you should be alone with this screwball. It isn't safe. What if he's the killer?"

"Well, that's what we're trying to find out, Whitey! And I'll learn a lot more if I can spend some time alone with him. We discussed all this before. Don't get cold feet on me now!"

"Okay, okay!" he grumbled. "But I'm going to be standing right outside the whole time, listening for trouble. If Smythe bothers you in any way, just give a shout. I'll bust in and break the swine's neck. And his piggy banks, too."

"Thanks, baby," Abby said, fluttering her lashes and

brushing her fingertips down his cheek. "It's so good to have a brave boyfriend."

Had Terry ever confessed to Abby that he'd been a coward in combat? If so, it was a cinch she didn't swallow it. She looked as though she wanted to swallow *him* up instead.

"Break it up, kids," I said. "I've got news."

"What is it?" Abby yelped, snapping her head in my direction. "What happened?"

"Augusta noticed the necklace," I told them. "She kept staring at it the whole time I was talking to her, and she looked like she was going to explode." I threw my head back and sucked my champagne glass dry.

As I straightened my spine and started looking around for a place to set the empty glass, I saw her. A strawberry blonde in a slinky pink dress with a tiny upturned nose and big hazel eyes that were gazing straight at me—or, rather, my neck.

"Of course Augusta noticed the necklace!" Abby blurted. "It belonged to her for twenty years! She'd have to be blind as a bat, or totally demented, not to recognize it."

"Shhhh! Keep your voice down!" I whispered. "And don't look now, but there's a young woman standing a few feet behind you who seems to have noticed the necklace, too. I wonder who she is. She keeps staring at me and . . . Oops! Here she comes! Be quiet! Don't say anything!" I nervously raised my glass back up to my lips and took a sip of nothing.

The young woman waltzed right over to us and wriggled into our little circle. "Hello," she purred, patting a strawberry blonde wave over one eye and puffing on her cigarette (or, rather, the long slim ivory holder in which her burning weed was rooted). "I don't believe we've met. And I thought I knew everybody at this dreary old party! I'm Lillian Smythe, the wayward daughter of the house. And who, may I ask, are you?" Her words were aimed at all three of us, but her eyes were aimed at the necklace.

"I'm Paige Turner," I said, offering my hand for a languid shake. I hated to give her my real name, but I didn't have any choice. I'd given it to her father the day before, and there was some small chance he might remember it. "And this is my husband, Terry," I added, quickly transferring her hand from mine to his, hoping the flurry of activity coupled with Terry's startling good looks would keep her from paying attention.

No such luck.

"Paige Turner?!" she whooped. "You *can't* be serious! That's an utter riot!" She was talking and laughing so loud people were turning to look at us. Her laughter wasn't real, though. It was the fake and showy kind—the kind that's based on taut nerves instead of true amusement. "So, tell me, Paige Turner," she said, stopping her laughter on a dime and tucking the tip of her ivory cigarette holder into the corner of her livid pink smirk. "How does a girl get a wacko name like yours? Were you born with it, or did you make it up yourself?"

"I married it," I said, as if it were any business of hers. Miss Lillian Smythe was starting to bug me big-time.

Abby didn't like her much either. "My name's Bathsheba Lark," she told her, conspicuously *not* extending her hand. "Are you going to laugh your silly head off about that, too?"

Jolted by Abby's impertinence, Lillian turned and gave her a snotty look. Then she took a step back, sucked on the end of her cigarette holder, and gave her a very slow and *studied* look. "Bathsheba?" she said, wrinkling her tiny upturned nose as if she were standing downwind from a fetid sewage facility. "Isn't that a *Jewish* name?"

At that moment I fully understood how a fairly well-adjusted, nonviolent person like myself might be moved to commit murder. *Kaboom!* I bellowed to myself, blasting Miss Lillian Smythe off the face of the earth with my imaginary A-bomb.

Terry wasn't content with a fantasy killing. He preferred the verbal variety. "You're a stupid, narrow-minded cow, Miss Smythe," he said in a most polite and gentlemanly manner. "You're not fit to shine Bathsheba's shoes." With that, he stepped into the middle of our little circle, turned his back on Lillian, put one arm around Abby's waist and the other around mine, and escorted us toward the opposite side of the room, where the full-sized built-in bar was located.

"God!" I said to Abby, after Terry had parked us a few feet from the bar and gone to get our drinks. "What a ferocious little snot she is! But Terry really gave it to her, didn't he? I'm so glad he did."

"He's my hero," she said, lips trembling. "You'd think I'd be used to the anti-Semitic crap by now, but I'm not. I guess I'll never get used to it." She took a cigarette out of her purse and lit up. "Still, it wasn't very smart of Whitey to mouth off at her the way he did."

"Smart? No. Cool? Yes!"

"But now she won't talk to you anymore . . . You won't be able to ask her any sneaky questions, or find out what she knows about the diamonds."

"Oh, she'll be talking to me, all right!" I said. "She's *dying* to know how I got this necklace. She'll be coming to ask me about it. I predict she'll be crawling all over me, apologizing her bigoted little head off and acting like my best friend, as soon as you and Terry take off for Smythe's study."

Abby laughed. "You're probably right. And speaking of Smythe's study," she said, looking at the watch she was carrying in her purse, "I'm supposed to be there right now. Where's Whitey?"

"You rang?" Terry said, suddenly appearing at our side with the brandy Alexanders we had asked for.

"Oh, there you are!" Abby sputtered, smashing her cigarette in a nearby ashtray. She took a big slug of her drink, linked her arm through Terry's, and began to tow him in the direction of the hallway. "C'mon, baby, let's go!" she urged. "Mustn't keep the big shot piggy banker waiting!"

# Chapter 27

PART OF MY PREDICTION CAME TRUE. LILlian Smythe came marching through the crowd and over to me before I'd taken the third sip of my brandy Alexander. She wasn't the least bit apologetic, though. And she was acting a whole lot more like my real worst enemy than my fake best friend.

"You've got a lot of nerve coming to this party tonight," she said, blasting the words out of her mouth like shrapnel. "Get out! You're not welcome here." People were turning to look at us again.

"What do you mean?!" I said, in shock, working to hold onto my composure. "I was *invited,* you know. Your father *asked* me to come."

"Oh, I'm sure he did! That's just the kind of thoughtless, selfish, brainless thing he would do. But he had no *right* to invite you here. And you had no right to come.

I was confused. Was she mad about the necklace, or just angry that I had come to the party? "I don't understand," I said. "Your father's the host. Why can't he invite anybody he wants?"

"He can," she said. "Anybody but *you.*" Her hazel eyes were burning with hatred.

"But I'm a *client* of his," I persisted, determined to get to the bottom of this mystery. "Why can't he invite me?"

She was near the end of her rope. Her contorted face was turning blue and she was having trouble breathing. One more word from me, and I thought she might crumble. So, in the interest of science (i.e., just to see what would happen), I delivered *several* more words. "I have as much right to be here as anybody else," I said, squaring my shoulders and stretching my spine to its ultimate height. In my long, heavy, sashless green dress, I felt (and, no doubt, *looked*) as turgid and plantlike as The Thing.

She didn't crumble. She didn't even wobble. "You filthy whore!" she screeched. "How dare you come into our home, wearing that necklace and prancing around like the goddamn Queen of England! Have you no shame? You aren't the first tramp my father's had an affair with, or pilfered my mother's jewels for, and you won't be the last. You *are* the oldest, though," she added, with a perverse gleam in her eye. "Daddy usually buys himself much newer toys."

So *that* was it. She thought her father had stolen her mother's necklace and given it to me in return for sexual favors. And she thought I was now rubbing both the affair *and* the necklace in her mother's face! Under those circumstances, I didn't blame Lillian for being mad at me. And if she hadn't been such a prejudiced, nasty, snotnosed shrew, I would have felt quite sorry for her. And very, *very* sorry that I'd worn the diamonds to the party.

As it was, though, I just felt tired. Tired and disgusted with the whole blam case. Was I ever going to unravel any clear-cut clues? Would I ever stop running in circles and dashing into blind alleys? Would I ever, ever, ever find out who killed Judy Catcher?

And what should I do right now? Should I tell Lillian the truth and give the necklace back to Augusta? Or should I stick to my guns and stay saddled on the lie I rode in on?

It didn't take me long to decide. I had to keep lying. It was all too possible that Lillian had had something to do with the murder. She must have been just as mad at Judy then as she was at me right now. And she must have been busting to get her mother's diamonds back. Maybe she had found out where Judy lived and tried to kill two birds with one stone.

"I don't know what you're talking about," I said, standing even taller than I had before (which wasn't easy, since all I wanted to do was curl up in a ball on the closest Chippendale sofa and go to sleep). "I never even *met* your father until yesterday, and this necklace was *not* pilfered. It was willed to me by my dear Aunt Rosemary, who just happened to be one of the sweetest, most generous angels who ever walked the earth. I only wear these diamonds to honor her memory." (Okay, okay! So I was laying it on a little thick—but desperate times call for double helpings.)

Lillian narrowed her eyes and swept a clump of salmon-pink hair off her face. "You're lying through your teeth, Paige Turner. I know who you really are. And if you don't round up your nasty little friends and get out of here right now, I'm going to call the cops and have you thrown out!"

I had no reason to doubt what she was saying. And I had no desire to spend the rest of the night explaining things to (okay, hiding things from) the police. I guzzled down the rest of my brandy Alexander and started looking for my nasty little friends.

HEADING FOR THE DOORWAY THROUGH WHICH Abby and Terry had disappeared, I bypassed a long, narrow dining table topped with the most beautiful and tempting array of food I'd ever seen in my life. Caviar, smoked salmon, chilled oysters, baked clams, sliced beef with horseradish sauce, shrimp cocktail, lobster thermidor, asparagus vinaigrette, deviled eggs, stuffed tomatoes and mushrooms—oh, god, was I hungry! I didn't stop to eat anything, though, for fear Lillian would cause another scene—or call the cops to do it for her.

Exiting the living room, I turned left and started walking down the mile-long Oriental carpet that stretched—unbroken—

from one end of the long, wide hall to the other. A dozen or so people were milling about in the hall, smoking cigarettes, looking for the restrooms, admiring the paintings on the wall. Straining my eyes down to the far end of the corridor, I finally spotted Terry. He was leaning against the wall, his left shoulder planted three inches from a closed door, with both hands in his pockets and one ear cocked, like a small radio receiver, toward the hinged spine of the door.

I was just about to wave to him and hurry down to the end of the hall where he was standing, when I saw Augusta Smythe coming out of a different door and gliding, swanlike, up the corridor toward me. Now realizing that the sight of me and my necklace would probably cause the poor woman a good deal of pain, and wanting to save us both from such an ordeal, I quickly turned my back on her approaching figure and veered over to gaze at one of the pictures on the wall.

"It's a Seurat," she said, gliding up behind me, the skirt of her long satin dress swooshing against the carpet. "A portrait of Madeline Knoblock, the artist's mistress. Do you like it?"

Oh, great! There were at least six other paintings on that particular expanse of wall, and I had to stop and stare at the *mistress?* You really can't take me anywhere.

"It's okay," I said, not wanting to show any enthusiasm for that particular work, "but I much prefer the van Gogh in the living room." I sucked in my breath and slowly turned to face Augusta. "It's from his Arles period, isn't it?" I asked, suddenly grateful for Abby's brief course in art appreciation.

"Yes, it is," she said, offering me a thin, dry smile. "You have a very good eye, my dear. Gregory and I consider the van Gogh to be the prime piece in our extensive art collection." She was staring at the necklace again. Had she considered it to be the prime piece in her jewelry collection?

"I see you're looking at my diamonds," I murmured, wishing to heaven I had never set eyes on them myself. "They're beautiful, aren't they?"

"Yes, they are, dear. They're exquisite. Have you had them long?"

"Not very long at all. I didn't acquire them until last month. They were left to me by my dear Aunt Rosemary, may she rest in peace. (This *could* have been true, you know! The necklace was part of a Tiffany-designed *line,* after all, so it definitely *wasn't* one of a kind.) "Actually, these diamonds are the main reason I'm here tonight," I went on. "I was hoping your husband could appraise the necklace for me and offer some advice on how I should handle this and the rest of my inheritance, what I need to do about taxes and insurance and so forth."

She raised her eyebrows and gave me a questioning look. "Gregory?" she said. "You want Gregory to give you financial advice?" I couldn't tell what she was doubting the most—my motive for being there or her husband's financial judgment.

"Yes, I really do need his help," I said. "I heard that Farnsworth Fiduciary was *the* place to go for economic guidance, so I went to your husband's office yesterday and spoke to him for a few minutes about my situation. He said he would be glad to advise me, but he couldn't do it right then because the office was closing early. So he very kindly invited me to your party tonight, saying he'd try to find a few minutes to devote to my concerns."

Was it my imagination, or was Augusta giggling? "I'm sorry, dear," she said, trying, but failing, to wipe a sardonic smile off her pale, powdery face. "I don't mean to laugh at your inheritance concerns. It's just that . . . well, how can I put this? Gregory is *not* the expert financial planner you seem to think he is. He barely knows the difference between a dollar and a dime. *I'm* the one who owns and controls Farnsworth Fiduciary—as I have for fifteen years, ever since my father died. My husband is just a guest there. I gave Gregory his own office just so he would have an address to put on his business card—and a place to take his afternoon nap."

So *that's* the way it was. The Smythe millions were really the Farnsworth millions. I can't say I was surprised. It was hard to imagine the foolish, forgetful Smythe running a successful financial enterprise. It was quite easy, on the other hand, to conceive of him renting cheap apartments for a string of impressionable young girlfriends, then nipping gems from the family vault—or from his wife's jewelry box—to keep them impressed.

And it was easy to see how a smart, wealthy businesswoman–cum–art collector–cum–socialite like Augusta Farnsworth Smythe might choose to overlook her husband's petty thefts and affairs rather than bring shame to her father's name and to her own family. It was even easy to see how being the ultra-privileged (and no-doubt ultra-*neglected*) daughter of such a spurious pair could have driven Lillian Smythe to become so nasty and aggressive.

The question was, just how nasty was she capable of being? Nasty enough to fire two .22 caliber bullets into Judy Catcher's young, unsuspecting heart?

Hoping to gather more clues to Lillian's character (and hoping that Augusta would continue to be so revealing!), I probed a bit deeper into the Smythe family profile. "I met your lovely daughter Lillian a few minutes ago," I told her. "Do you have other children?"

"No, just the one."

"Does Lillian work for Farnsworth Fiduciary, too?" I asked. "She seems to have a sharp, decisive head on her shoulders."

"Lily?" Augusta said, raising her eyebrows again. "No, Lily doesn't work at all. Unless you call being cross and causing trouble work." Her face grew even paler and she glanced off to the side, letting her sad gray eyes go out of focus. "She's sharp and decisive as you say, but about all the wrong things."

I wasn't sure what she meant by this, but I felt I'd just heard something important. Something Augusta had said—or maybe it was just the *way* she'd said it—had set off a flickering signal in my brain. But what the heck was that signal trying to tell me? I didn't know! It kept flickering and flickering, but I couldn't get the message. It was driving me insane. I wanted to dart off by myself somewhere—to some quiet, secret corner—where I could close my eyes, let my thoughts settle, and then try to sort them out.

The bathroom. When in doubt, go to the bathroom.

"Please excuse me, Mrs. Smythe," I said, "but I need to powder my nose." (What I meant was *take a powder*, but I couldn't very well say *that!*) "Would you mind pointing me to the little girl's room?"

"Not at all, dear," she said, looking relieved. She was glad to be getting rid of me. "It's right across the hall, second door down."

"Thank you."

As I was hurrying down the corridor toward the designated doorway, I saw Abby emerge from Smythe's study and rejoin Terry in the hall. They embraced and kissed each other (completely forgetting, I suppose, that Terry was supposed to be *my* husband), then began strolling, arm in arm, up the Oriental carpet in my direction.

The flickering signal flickered out. I couldn't even remember what had set it off in the first place. All I could think about was hooking up with Abby and Terry and getting us all out of that apartment before Lillian lost her cool and called the police.

Rushing to meet my fellow aliens halfway, and telling them we had to split, I urged them onward to the penthouse entrance hall, where we retrieved our coats and took the elevator down to Earth. A mad, freezing-cold dash to the subway, then we hopped inside our trusty underground spaceship and zoomed back to the Village—a more familiar and forgiving planet.

"GREGORY SMYTHE IS *NOT* THE MURderer," Abby insisted. "I'd stake my life on it." Still dressed in her sexy black and white strapless, she was standing in her stocking feet at her kitchen counter, stirring up a pitcher of martinis.

"What makes you so sure?" Terry asked, taking off his

bow tie and loosening his collar. "He looks like a real degenerate to me."

"He *is* a degenerate," she said, "but he's not a killer." She set the martini pitcher down on the kitchen table, then brought over three glasses. "He has no conscience and he has no soul . . . but he has no brain, either! The man simply isn't *smart* enough to plan and carry out a murder, you dig? He has the IQ of a chimp."

I agreed with her on that score. "Were you able to get him to talk about what happened? Did you pick up any new clues, or learn anything about his relationship with Judy?"

"No, no, and no," she said, sitting down and pouring our drinks. "All I learned is that he's a slobbering, gooey-eyed old Romeo who isn't happy unless he has some part—any part!—of the female anatomy to suck on. Look! He gave my *elbow* a hickey!"

Terry laughed. "Did the earth move?"

Abby snickered and gave him a playful slap on his shoulder.

*Uh oh!* I cautioned myself. *If I don't steer this conversation in a more serious direction, they'll be hitting the sheets in no time!* "Daddy Smythe may not be the murderer," I interjected, using my most serious and solemn tone, "but his darling daughter could be."

"What?!" Abby cried, tearing her attention away from Terry and plastering it on me. "Did you talk to her again? What did you find out? What did the little Nazi slut have to say?"

I filled them in on everything that had happened after they left the living room. I gave them a dramatic description of Lillian's violent outburst, and a detailed account of my hallway chat with Augusta. I told them how Lillian had jumped to the conclusion that I was her father's new mistress and ordered me to leave. I related my surprise that Augusta, the picture of upper crust propriety, had so willingly revealed—to me, a perfect stranger!—her total disdain for both her husband and her daughter. And then I told them that Augusta, not Gregory, controlled the family fortune, and that Lillian was the couple's only heir. I mean heiress.

"That cinches it!" Abby cried, slapping her hand down on the tabletop so hard our martinis shook. "Lillian did it! Lillian Smythe killed your sister!" She was staring into Terry's eyes with a look of sheer certainty on her face.

"What makes you so sure?" Terry asked, befuddled (and, I thought, a bit bemused). "You have any proof?"

"She's the only *heir,* Sherlock!" Abby stressed. "What more proof do you need?"

Terry wasn't convinced. "So what? Lots of people are heirs and heiresses," he said, "that doesn't make them murderers."

Spoken like a true pragmatist (i.e., reasonable guy). "He's right, Abby," I said. "We can't come to any conclusions yet. We don't have enough facts."

"What about the fact that Lillian Smythe's a raving Fascist?" Abby snapped, angrily yanking the bobby pins out of her hair and shaking it loose down her back.

"That proves she's an awful person," I said, "but it doesn't prove she's a killer."

"Okay then, so what about the ice?" she croaked. "You can't deny it played a big role in Judy's death. And you can't deny the fact that Lillian—more than any of our other suspects—has a true, vested interest in the diamonds. They are, after all, going to be *hers* someday—if her dear old daddy-o doesn't give 'em all away first."

"That's true," I said, "and it all adds up to a pretty strong motive. But it doesn't confirm that Lillian pulled the trigger."

"Diamonds are a girl's best friend," Abby insisted, taking a big gulp of her martini.

"But if we're ever going to get Sweeny to reopen the case," Terry added, smiling, "we've got to have much harder evidence than that."

"So what the hell do we have to do?" Abby sputtered. "Find a pistol with her prints on it?" She threw her head back and tossed down the rest of her drink.

"That's about it," I said, with a heavy sigh. "Unless we can find an eyewitness. Or get her to confess." (And the chances of anything like that happening were—I knew—very, very slim. Or fat, take your pick.)

I didn't say anything to Abby and Terry, but I felt, at that moment, so sick and tired of our seemingly endless (and endlessly frustrating!) investigation that I just wanted to call the whole thing off. I wanted to give the diamonds back to Sweeny or Augusta, rip up all my story notes, take a scalding hot bath, and crawl into bed for a century or two. I had a sinking feeling we would *never* find Judy's killer; that all our efforts and adversities—including my close shave on the subway tracks and the break-in at my apartment—had been for nothing; that the smartest thing Abby and Terry and I could do right now would be to terminate our fruitless, bungling search for the truth and get on with our pitiful little lives.

I didn't know at the time, of course, how pitifully short our pitiful little lives were likely to be.

# Chapter 28

I WANTED TO GO HOME AND SPEND THE night in my own bed, but my fretful friends wouldn't let me. They accompanied me next door for a few minutes—just long enough for me to see if my apartment was still taped shut (it was), and to grab my flannel nightgown, robe, and toothbrush. Then they ushered me right back to Abby's, where I was expected to sleep like a baby on the lumpy little red couch in her studio.

Abby fixed me up with a pillow, a blanket, a glass of milk, and a plate of cookies. Then she and Terry hurried upstairs to their bouncy, blissful double bed, giggling like teenagers. They were beyond tipsy, and so was I. We had definitely had—as Dean Martin is so fond of saying—tee many martoonis.

As soon as the door to the upstairs bedroom slammed shut, I stumbled over to Abby's kitchen phone and dialed Dan's apartment. As inebriated as I was, I had no trouble remembering the number. Though I rarely allowed myself to use it, it was engraved in my heart like a Tiffany monogram.

There was no answer.

Hoping I had misdialed, I hung up, then tried again.

Still no answer. Dan was probably still over at his ex-wife's place, watching over his innocent, sound-asleep young daughter, while the girl's partygoing mother drank and danced herself stupid in the grasping arms of sundry lecherous men. (If you think that sounds too catty, please blame it on the martoonis. Mine, not hers.)

Staggering back over to the couch, I sat down and devoured the cookies. I was so hungry I'd have eaten the box they came in. I drank all the milk, too, even though I was afraid it would curdle when it hit the sea of alcohol in my stomach. Leaving the empty glass and cookie plate sitting on the coffee table (if Santa came down the chimney looking for goodies, he'd be out of luck), I took off the diamond necklace and returned it to the security of Abby's sugar canister. Then I changed into my nightgown, curled up on the little red love seat (it was a cinch I couldn't stretch out!), and went to sleep (okay, fell into a coma).

I was unconscious for a while—about three hours, I think—and then a most astonishing thing happened. I woke up suddenly—in a dazzling flash—with a single word (or, rather, *name*) bouncing against the walls of my skull: *Lily . . . Lily . . . Lily.* Augusta Smythe had called her daughter Lily.

Certain that this was the same flickering signal that had been driving me crazy at the party—and also certain that I had heard the name Lily *before* the party, but very recently, during the course of my five-day investigation into Judy's murder—I sat up stick straight on the couch and racked my brain to remember the details. *Lily . . . Lily . . . Lily.* Where and when had I heard that name? Whose voice, besides Augusta's, had spoken it?

Closing my eyes and putting my hands over my ears, I began replaying my mental recording of the last five days, starting at day one, listening to the echoes of my initial conversations with Terry and Elsie Londergan and Vicki Lee Bumstead and Jimmy Birmingham and Roscoe Swift and . . . *Hold it!* I cried to myself. *Play that part over again!*

And so I did, from the beginning—from the very moment I first entered the Chelsea Realty office. And many of the details came back to me. Before I ever saw Roscoe Swift's face, I remembered, I heard him yelling at someone over the phone. He was furious, and banging furniture around, and screaming his lungs out at someone named . . : Lily.

But what had Roscoe been so angry about? And what exactly had he said to the woman named Lily? I couldn't, for the life of me, recall. And every time I tried to repeat that part of the soundtrack, the record got stuck. It was driving me nuts. I couldn't stand it another second. I *had* to know what Roscoe had said, and I had to know right now! Luckily, there was one way I might be able to find out.

I snatched the key to my apartment out of my purse, leapt across the hall, and let myself in. After turning on the light and checking my back door again (the Duz detergent patch still hadn't been disturbed), I made a beeline for the cabinet over my kitchen sink, shoved the soup cans out of the way, and pulled out Judy's trusty oatmeal box. Yanking my story notes out of the Quaker container and blowing off all the oatmeal dust, I pressed the twenty-six pages flat on the kitchen counter, and madly searched for the section I was burning to see—the Roscoe Swift section. Had I been careful and thorough enough to write down Roscoe's words to Lily?

Yes! There they were, plain as day, on page fourteen. They probably weren't the *exact* words Swift had used, but I figured they were pretty close: "Jesus H. Christ!" he had shouted (in a voice loud enough to wake the dead). "Haven't you had enough? I did what you wanted, Lily. Give it up already! I'm through! Go find yourself another stooge!"

So somebody named Lily had been making unwelcome demands on Roscoe Swift, and he was *really* upset about it. The question was, were Roscoe Swift's Lily and Augusta Smythe's Lily one and the same? I had a very strong feeling they were. But feelings—no matter how strong they are—don't qualify as evidence. I needed to *prove* that there was a connection between Lillian Smythe and Roscoe Swift. But how the heck was I going to do that?

It was 4:30 in the morning. *Christmas* morning. Everybody in Manhattan was sleeping but me (me and untold numbers of overexcited, insomniac children who were sneaking downstairs to see what Santa had left them under the tree). Abby and Terry were sleeping soundly. Dan was surely snoring up a storm. And here I was—so wide awake and stimulated I could barely breathe—tottering around my apartment like a demented ostrich, desperately trying to think of a way to contact Roscoe Swift and get him to talk about his association with Lillian Smythe.

I looked Swift up in the phone book, but he wasn't there. Either he didn't live in the city, or he had an unlisted number, or he was entered under a different name, or he didn't have a home telephone at all. Not knowing what else to do—and so crazed I just had to do *something*—I looked up the number for Chelsea Realty and wrote it down. And then—even though I knew it was really, really early in the morning, on Christmas Day, of all days; and even though I knew I had a better chance (at that particular hour, on that particular holiday) of reaching *God* than getting through to Roscoe Swift—I picked up the phone and dialed the Chelsea Realty office.

Nobody answered. But that was no surprise. What was surprising was the *reason* nobody answered—which was because the phone never rang in the first place. And *that* was because the line was busy.

You heard me right. The line was *busy!* Somebody was actually *there,* in the Chelsea Realty office, at 4:30 (by now, 4:45) in the morning, on Christmas Day, talking on the telephone! I was in shock. I couldn't believe it. It couldn't be true. I slammed the phone down, then picked it up and dialed the same number again. And I got the same busy signal again. Who was on the phone? Was it Roscoe? And if so, who was he talking to?

Knowing I'd probably never learn the answers to these questions, but determined to at least *try,* I ran upstairs and threw on some clothes. Then I scrambled back down the stairs and dialed the number again. It was still busy. If I hurried, *really* hurried, I might be able to get to the Chelsea Realty office in time to see (and hopefully speak to) whoever was there.

Moving at breakneck speed, I pulled on my coat and my snowboots, and darted next door for my purse, checking to see if I had enough money for the subway. (I did—a half dollar and two dimes). Then I lunged down the stairwell and burst out onto the street—smack into the frigid, pitch black, pre-dawn air—feeling like Brenda Starr on a heroic fact-finding mission, but surely looking like a half-drunk harridan who'd lost her everloving mind.

LOOK, I *KNEW* IT WASN'T A SENSIBLE THING for me to do. Whoever had been using the phone in the realty office when I got the busy signals would probably be long gone by the time I got there—*if* I ever got there (the subways were running on early-morning holiday schedule, which meant the next train might not arrive until sometime next year). But that was a chance I was willing—make that *compelled*—to take. Once I had made the connection between Roscoe Swift and Lillian Smythe, I simply couldn't sit still. Or wait for the rest of the world to wake up. I had to take action.

By some unimaginable stroke of luck, a train pulled into the Sheridan Square station just minutes after I did. I jumped on and grabbed hold of the strap closest to the door, too hopped-up to sit down. I held on tight as the train lurched out of the station and hurtled its way uptown. There was only one other person in the car with me—a skinny old man in a coonskin cap who sat next to a window, smoking a cigarette, and staring out at the black blur of the vanishing tunnel walls as if enjoying the view.

When I emerged from the subway depths at 28th Street, it was still dark as night. But I had no trouble seeing. Thanks to the shining street lamps and the radiant holiday displays (many of the store windows were decorated with glowing Christmas lights), I made my way down Seventh Avenue with ease. When I turned onto 27th Street, however, the world grew a whole lot dimmer. The lampposts were few and far between, and none of the office or apartment windows facing out onto the dark, deserted street were lit from within.

The front window of the Chelsea Realty office was completely obscure. I walked up close to it and, standing on my tiptoes so I could see over the large, flower-strewn sign covering the entire lower half of the window, I pressed my nose to the glass, cupped my hands around my eyes, and peered inside.

Not a single lamp was lit in the long, narrow front room, but I could see a tall, thin sliver of light emanating from one side of the almost-closed door at the far end of the room—the door leading to Roscoe's private office.

My heart started beating like a conga drum. There was a light on in the back room! Somebody might be there! Maybe it was Roscoe! I was panting so hard and so fast I felt lightheaded.

(I know what you're thinking. You're thinking I'm *always* lightheaded. And considering the various sticky situations I'd so blithely put myself into since my search for Judy's killer began, you may be right. But let me just say this about that: The situation I'd put myself into *this* time suddenly felt a whole lot stickier than the others—and my head felt a whole heck of a lot lighter than usual. So there!)

Forcing myself to move quickly, before my cold feet got any colder, I stepped over to the Chelsea Realty entrance and tried the knob. To my great surprise, the door clicked open, just as it had the first time I'd come. Had Roscoe's assistant forgotten to lock it again? Or had Roscoe himself neglected to lock it when he let himself in? Taking care not to make the slightest sound, I slithered into the dark front office . . . and then I just stood there—like a tree—for a few minutes, listening for noises from the back room.

At first I didn't hear anything. Just the echoing whoosh of my own breath and the loud, walloping beats of my own heart. I was straining so hard I thought my eardrums might pop. The profound silence told me one thing for sure: Nobody was talking on the phone anymore. It was so quiet I wondered if anybody was even *there* anymore.

I stared at the thin strip of light at the edge of the door for a while, watching for silent shadows, sudden movements, any breaks in the beam. When nothing disturbed the steady shaft, I came to believe that the person had either gone or was being very still. Unimaginably still. Dying to know which of these possibilities was actually true, I slowly—very slowly!—began to sneak toward the lighted crack in the door, holding my breath and creeping along the creaky wood floorboards like a cartoon mouse.

When I was about six feet away from the door I heard something. It was a very faint sound, but at least it was audible. Stopping dead in my tracks, I sucked in a quick breath of air, aimed one ear toward the crack in the door, and focused all my energy on listening.

There. I could still hear it. It was a kind of hum. Not the musical kind of hum people use when they're singing to themselves. More like the kind of hum a bee makes. Like a droning, whining buzz. Like a busy signal.

My heart sank down to my snowboots. What a complete and utter jerk I was! I had gone dashing out of my apartment on a freezing cold Christmas morning—and rushed down the deserted, night-black streets, and suffered a gloomy subway trip uptown, and snuck around all by myself in a dark, creepy real estate office—just because some other utter jerk had been in such a hurry to start his Christmas vacation that he had fled the office in a breezy daze, leaving a light on, the door unlocked, and the phone off the hook.

Well, it *could* have happened that way! And I'm not ashamed to say that my first reaction was to accept that comfortable, hastily formed scenario. After further consideration, however (and after the hairs on the back of my neck refused to stop bristling), I had to admit that my initial conclusion was preposterous—that something far more evil and insidious was probably afoot.

Determined to find out what that something was, I lunged two steps forward and flung open the door.

# Chapter 29

I WAS BLINDED BY THE BRIGHT OFFICE light. But, unfortunately, the blindness was only temporary. As my vision returned, a truly hideous sight flew up and hit me right between the eyes.

Roscoe Swift was lying on his back in the middle of the floor. His beady little eyes were startled and wide-open, staring up at the flat, white ceiling in dead dismay. There was a dime-sized hole in the center of his chest, and a huge circular bloodstain on his sleeveless undershirt. There was another bloody hole in his scrawny neck, just to the left of his prominent Adam's apple. His pockmarked face was a ghastly shade of gray. Mouth gaping in a rictus of pain and alarm, he seemed to be growling, or howling—baring his little brown teeth in outrage.

I didn't bother checking his pulse or holding a mirror to his nose to see if he was breathing. He was so dead it was definitive. And I didn't want to touch anything—disturb any of the evidence. So I just stood there for a few minutes, gasping and crying, fighting the urge to throw up, doing my best not to scream or faint. And then—once I had myself under control (sort of)—I stood there for a few more minutes, taking careful mental notes on the crime scene.

Roscoe was wearing only a white undershirt, white boxer shorts, and a pair of black socks, which were held in place on his thin, bony shins by a pair of elastic garters. The rest of his clothes—his suit, tie, shirt, and belt—were draped over a chair near the desk. His watch, wallet, and keys were sitting on top of the desk. Tucked into the far corner of the room was a small, narrow cot—complete with dingy white sheets, a single pillow, and a drab green Army blanket. The bed looked lonely, messy, and slept-in. Lying on top of the rumpled blanket was an open copy of *Confidential* magazine.

*So that's the story,* I remarked to myself. *Roscoe was living here in his office. That's why he's not listed in the phone book.*

I scanned my eyes around the rest of the small, windowless room, looking for clues as to what had happened, hoping to discover something that would identify Roscoe's murderer (and maybe Judy's murderer, too). But there wasn't that much to see. No weapon. No signs of a struggle. Except for his personal effects and a big brown coffee-stained blotter, the top of Roscoe's desk was bare. There were no ledgers, papers, or files in sight. No photos. No address book.

There *was* a phone, though, and—as you may have already surmised—the receiver was off the hook, dangling from its cord down the side of the desk like a gigantic legless black spider. The busy signal was still going strong, filling the air with its annoying bee-like buzz.

I wanted to stop the horrible sound. I wanted to walk into the room, step wide around Roscoe's bloody corpse, shoot over to the desk and hang up the phone. Then I wanted to sit down at the desk, go through all the drawers, locate Roscoe's telephone and address book, and find a listing for Lillian Smythe. And then—armed with hardcore proof of the Roscoe Swift/Lillian Smythe connection, proof that would force Detective Sweeny to revisit the Judy Catcher case—I wanted to pick up the phone again and call the police.

But I didn't dare attempt to do any of those things. What if

Lillian's prints were on the receiver and I destroyed them by touching the phone? What if her prints were on the desk drawers, too? And what if Roscoe didn't have Lillian listed in his address book? What if he didn't even *have* an address book? My hands were tied. I couldn't take the risk of destroying evidence while looking for it.

Deciding I should get out of there (fast) and call the police (anonymously) from another location, I stepped out of the room, returned the door to its original near-closed position, and made a hasty exit—leaving everything at Chelsea Realty just the way I'd found it. Then I dashed back out to Seventh Avenue and started walking (okay, *sprinting*) downtown, thinking I'd find at least one open candy store or coffee shop with a public phone.

No such luck. Every store I passed—including Henry's Hardware, where I'd bought Lenny's lunchbox—was closed up tight. I hurried all the way down to 24th Street before realizing the only open facility with a public phone I was likely to find would be a subway station. So I took off running, as fast as I could, toward the IRT entrance at 23rd Street.

But halfway there, I had another realization. All I had in my purse was one fifty-cent piece and a dime! And the subway change booths wouldn't be open yet (if they opened at all on Christmas Day)! And if I used the dime to telephone the police, I wouldn't be able to catch a train home (half dollars don't fit in the turnstile slots)! I considered going straight home and calling the police from my apartment, but I really hated that idea. I felt the police should be notified immediately—and who knew how long I'd have to wait for a train? And what if the cops were able to trace the call back to me?

*Aaaargh!*

I was on the verge of a nervous breakdown when a brilliant (okay, *beefheaded*) solution suddenly occurred to me. *John Wayne!* I cried to myself. *The Duke will save the day!*

I turned on my heels and hit the trail back up to 26th Street, where I made a sharp left and galloped for Elsie Londergan's apartment.

• • •

SHE ANSWERED RIGHT AFTER I BUZZED. "Who's there?" she snapped, voice spooky over the crackling intercom.

"Elsie, Elsie! It's me, Paige Turner! Please let me in! It's an emergency!"

She didn't say anything more. She just buzzed the door open and I lunged inside. I was up the stairs in a flash. Elsie was standing tall in her open doorway, fully dressed in a green pleated skirt and a dark red cable stitch sweater. She even had on her lipstick. *What is she doing up so early?* I wondered. *Rushing out to a Christmas morning Mass? Tearing off to a sunrise canasta game?*

Elsie took one look at me and croaked, "What's the matter with you?! You look like you just saw the devil!" She pulled me inside and locked the door behind us.

"Oh, Elsie!" I cried, shuddering, still huffing from my wild race up the stairs. "I did just see the devil! And he's dead!"

"Well, that's good news for all of us," she said, smiling, humoring me, giving her permanent waves a girlish pat. "So what's the big emergency? What got you out of bed at this ungodly hour? Come sit down and tell me all about it." She led me into the sitting room and motioned for me to take a chair.

"I can't sit down, Elsie," I said, still gasping for air, pacing in circles around the tiny room. "I have to call the police to report a murder. It's your landlord! Roscoe Swift! He's been shot!"

Her smile crumpled and her blue eyes widened in shock. "Roscoe? Shot? Are you sure? I can't believe it!" She lowered herself into one of the two chintz-covered wing chairs that took up half the room and snatched a cigarette from the silver box on the table between them. Striking a match with unexpected force, she lit up and exhaled loudly. "How do you know about this?" she asked. "Did you see the body?"

"Yes! I did! Roscoe's lying dead on the floor of his office, with one bullet hole in his chest and one in his neck. It's horrible! Can I use your phone? I've got to notify the police."

"Of course," she said. "It's on the night table in the bedroom. The number for the police station is there, too, on the pad right next to the telephone. I've been keeping it handy ever since Judy was killed."

*How convenient.*

I charged into the bedroom, sat down on the edge of the made-up bed, snatched up the receiver, and dialed the number on the pad. It rang about forty times. I was beginning to think the whole department had taken the day (or the night, or whatever) off, when a gruff voice finally answered.

"I'm calling to report a murder," I said, in the steadiest, most masterful tone I could muster. (I was trying to imitate Perry Mason, but in my addled and breathless condition I probably sounded more like Daffy Duck.) "Please take this information down, sir. A man named Roscoe Swift has been shot to death on West 27th Street. The body can be found in the back room of the Chelsea Realty office." I gave him the exact address, told him the office was unlocked, and begged him to send somebody in a hurry.

"Did you get all that down?" I asked. "Should I repeat the information?"

"I got everything, sister," the gruff voice said. "Everything but *your* name and location. Who are you and where are you? How do you know the victim is dead? Did you discover the body? Are you calling from the scene?"

"Yes. I discovered the body, and I'm certain the victim is dead. I left the scene exactly as I found it. Please send a team out right away." I hung up before he could ask for my name again.

I hated having to handle things in this cowardly, dishonest way. I wanted to get Detective Sweeny on the line, give him my true identity (as well as a big piece of my mind), and then tell him about everything that had happened since Terry Catcher first came to me and asked me to help him find his sister's murderer. But I couldn't do it. It was way too chancy. What if Sweeny refused to follow up on any of my leads, or acknowledge a connection between Roscoe's and Judy's homicides? What if he ignored all the data I'd gathered and continued to insist that Judy was shot during a random burglary? What if he demanded that the diamonds be returned to the police, and then threw Terry in jail for tampering with evidence? What if Sweeny told me—as he had told Elsie when she dared to question his facile conclusions about Judy's murder—to stop being a busybody?

Then I'd have to kill *him,* and that wouldn't do anybody any good.

Heaving a loud sigh of resignation, I stood up from Elsie's bed and turned back toward the sitting room, head lowered in fatigue and dismay. I was in such a zombie daze that, even though I was standing right next to Elsie's bedroom wastebasket, and staring straight down at the wastebasket's colorful, crumpled contents, I didn't really see what I was seeing.

It took a few seconds for the ripped, partially wadded-up scraps of paper to come into focus. And a few more moments passed before the bold, familiar image printed on those scraps of paper began to register in my fuzzy brain: the curly white beard, the plump pink cheeks, the twinkling blue eyes, the bright red suit and cap, the big round belly like a bowl full of jelly. It was *my* Santa Claus—the very same one that was pictured, repeatedly, on my Christmas wrapping paper.

The very same paper I had used to wrap up Lenny's lunchbox.

A string of firecrackers went off in my brain. *Elsie?* Pop! *Could it have been Elsie?* Pop! *Did Elsie steal the lunchbox and push me down onto the subway tracks?* Pop! *Did Elsie break into my apartment?* Pop! *Did Elsie kill Judy? And Roscoe, too?* Pop! Pop! Pop! My head was so full of explosive questions I thought it would blast right off my neck.

"So what happened?" Elsie said, suddenly appearing in the doorless archway between the bedroom and the sitting room. "Was that Sweeny you were talking to? What did the dumbbell dick have to say?"

"It wasn't Sweeny," I mumbled, frantically trying to pull myself together. "It was somebody else. I told him about the homicide and they're sending a team out right away." So much adrenaline was shooting down my spine I was having trouble standing.

"Hey, you look horrible, Paige!" Elsie said. "Are you all right? You better come sit down. I'll make you a cup of tea." She put her arm around my shoulders and tried to guide me into the sitting room.

"No!" I cried, recoiling from her touch. "I can't stay! I've got to get home!" Translation: *I don't drink tea with murderers.*

"But you should rest a while first. You've had a big shock. You look as pale as a ghost."

*Oh, yeah? Well, that's better than actually* being *a ghost—which might become my fate if I stay here any longer . . .*

"Just one cup of tea," she insisted. "That'll fix you up."

"Thanks, Elsie," I said, through clenched teeth, "but I really have to go home now and put my turkey in the oven. It's Christmas Day!"

*Put my turkey in the oven?* I screeched to myself. *What a nitwit thing to say! I couldn't have come up with a sillier excuse if my life depended on it! (Which*—I thought at the time—*could very well be the case!)*

If Elsie noticed my frantic flight into absurdity, she didn't let on. She had taken off on a frantic flight of her own. "But you haven't told me what's going on!" she shrieked, jutting her chiseled John Wayne chin in my direction. "What the hell made you go to the realty office so early this morning? Did you know something was going to happen? Do you know who killed Roscoe?" She narrowed her big blue eyes into slits so thin they were knifelike.

"I don't know who killed him for sure," I blurted, "but I have a hunch it was Lillian Smythe." I gave Elsie this tidbit just to throw her off the track. If she caught on that I was beginning to suspect *her* (Elsie, that is), my goose could be cooked long before my turkey.

Elsie pulled in her chin and wrinkled her brow in confusion. "Huh?" she said, looking like Elmer Fudd after yet another baffling skirmish with Bugs Bunny. "Lillian who?"

"I can't explain it all right now!" I sputtered, forging my way back through the sitting room and the kitchen with Elsie hot on my heels. "It's a long, complicated story, and I don't have time!" I opened the door and stepped out into the hall. "But don't worry, Elsie, I'll phone you later and tell you all about it." Forcing my lips to form a big bogus smile, I waved bye-bye and made a mad dash for the stairway. "Merry Christmas!" I called out as I began my descent.

If Elsie wished me a happy holiday in return, I didn't hear it. She must have been whispering.

# Chapter 30

ON THE WAY HOME IN THE SUBWAY I MADE a firm decision. I would tell Dan everything about the Judy Catcher homicide today, as soon as he arrived at my apartment. I would tell him how Terry and Abby and I had launched a murder investigation of our own, and I would give him the lowdown on everything that had happened before and since. Dan would be really angry with me, and it would ruin our first Christmas together—maybe even make it our *last* Christmas together—but I couldn't keep up the charade any longer. Somebody had tried to kill me, and somebody had succeeded in killing Roscoe, and the time had come to bring the police in on the case.

(Okay, okay! You're absolutely right! I should have told Dan long ago—*before* I was almost obliterated by the uptown express, and before poor Roscoe was eliminated. And, looking back, I'm really, really sorry I didn't. But hindsight is always clearer than foresight—especially *my* foresight—and since Sweeny had already dropped the case, I truly thought Terry and Abby and I were doing the right thing. But that's a lousy excuse, I know—even lousier than my stupid turkey-in-the-oven routine. Because any way you look at it, I was a selfish fool and a raving idiot to let my pursuit of the story—and my burning desire to keep it secret from Dan—get in the way of a full-fledged professional search for the killer.)

Filled with contrition and new determination, I got off the train at Sheridan Square, made a beeline down to Bleecker, and hurried home.

It was starting to get light outside, but no lights were on in Abby's apartment, so I knew the lovebirds weren't up and chirping yet. As soon as I let myself into the building, though, and climbed the stairs to the landing between our apartments, I started banging on Abby's door instead of unlocking mine. I didn't care if they were awake yet or not. I needed a team conference, and I needed it *now*.

It took forever, but I kept right on banging and shouting, until Abby finally made her way downstairs and yanked the door open. "What?!" she screeched. "What the hell's going on?!" Her eyes were puffy with sleep, her tangled hair was tumbling over both shoulders, and all she was wearing was Uncle Morty's tuxedo shirt, which barely covered her bare bottom—a fact I didn't notice until she spun away from me and padded barefoot to the kitchen counter. "What are you yelling about? What the hell time is it?" She pulled the top off the coffee pot, slammed it down on the counter, and started filling the pot with water.

"Six-fifteen," I said, looking at the clock on her kitchen wall.

"In the fucking morning?!"

"Yep," I said, "but it feels like noon to me. I've been up for hours."

Abby whipped her head around and gave me a doubtful look. Then, as she took in the fact that I was, indeed, up, and fully dressed—even wearing my coat, beret, and snow-boots—her look turned to sheer surprise. "You went *out?* In the middle of the night? You weren't supposed to leave this apartment! Did anything happen? Where have you been?" She was screeching again.

"I've been uptown," I said, "and a *lot* has happened. But I really can't bear to explain the whole thing twice. So do me a favor, will you? Go upstairs, wake up Terry, and then bring him down here for a council. And put some clothes on while you're up there! I'll finish making the coffee."

I must have been acting much more authoritative than usual, because Abby didn't give me any of her usual back talk. She just set the coffee pot down on the counter, pulled her wild hair back off her shoulders, scooted over to the foot of the stairs, and hauled her bare bottom to the top.

"SO THAT'S THE WHOLE STORY," I SAID, winding up my detailed summary of the early morning's untimely events. Abby and Terry were each on their third cup of coffee, I had just finished my first. "I feel certain there was a strong connection between Roscoe Swift and Lillian Smythe," I added, "but I'm not sure what it was. Maybe it had something to do with Judy's murder and the diamonds, or maybe it didn't. Whatever the case, they must have had a very emotional and volatile relationship for him to yell at her the way he did."

"Yeah, and that's why she killed him!" Abby hissed, gesturing wildly with her hands. "I've got the whole deal figured out! First Lillian convinced Roscoe to kill Judy and get her mother's diamonds back for her. She probably promised him one of the bracelets for his trouble. But when Roscoe couldn't find the jewelry—either in Judy's apartment, or in Lenny's lunchbox, or in *your* apartment, Paige—he demanded that Lillian pay him anyway. And so the little Nazi slut killed *him*—to keep him from hounding her, and to make sure he would never, ever, ever be able to tell anybody what really happened!"

Terry looked at Abby and let out a dramatic groan. "You know what I think, Ab? I think jumping to conclusions has become your favorite sport."

"So what?" Abby snapped. "Somebody's got to jump at *something* around here! Where's your goddamn *chutzpah,* Whitey? The way you and Paige keep pussyfooting around, saying that we don't have enough hard evidence, we're never going to come to any conclusions at all!"

Oh, dear. Were they working up to having their first lovers' spat? I certainly hoped not. I didn't have time for this!

"Well, I *have* jumped to a conclusion now," I exclaimed, dropping my fist like a gavel on the tabletop. "And I'm sorry to disagree with you, Abby, but I really don't think Lillian is the killer. I'm beginning to think it's Elsie."

"For cripesakes, why?!" Abby blustered. "Just because of that stupid wrapping paper?"

"Well, yes, but . . ."

"That *dreck* doesn't prove diddly!" she broke in, hands flapping in the air like agitated birds. "That Santa Claus paper's all over town! Woolworth's sells it by the mile. Elsie was probably using it to wrap her own presents . . . or maybe she got a gift that was wrapped in the same gaudy stuff!"

*Gaudy? Did Abby just call my Christmas paper gaudy? Guess I'd better find something else to wrap her gaudy lingerie in.*

"Abby's right," Terry said, giving me a patronizing look. "The gift-wrapping in Elsie's wastebasket is *not* conclusive. It could have been there by pure coincidence."

"And besides," Abby interjected, "Elsie didn't have near as clear a motive as Lillian!" She was still intent on casting the prejudiced Miss Smythe in the role of the killer. "Lillian hated Judy for sleeping with her father, and she wanted to get her mother's jewelry back. What could Elsie's motive have been?"

I couldn't believe she was asking that question. "I feel safe in declaring," I said with a sniff, "that the motive for Judy's murder was the diamonds—no matter *who* the murderer turns out to be. Maybe Elsie wanted to *become* rich as much as Lillian wanted to *stay* rich."

"Oh, well, okay!" Abby said, throwing her hands up in exasperation. "But then how does Roscoe Swift enter the picture? You can't possibly believe that Elsie killed him, too!"

"Well, yes, I do," I said.

"You're walking on the weird side now," Terry said, raising one of his thick black eyebrows and shaking his head in doubt.

"What's weird is the fact that Elsie was fully dressed when I got to her apartment," I insisted. "And her bed was made up too. And it was five-thirty in the morning! I would swear she'd been up for hours—or at least long enough to slip around the corner and kill Roscoe."

Abby let out a heavy sigh. "But why would she want to do that?"

"There could be a million reasons!" I sputtered, growing tired of explaining the obvious. "Maybe Roscoe knew that she killed Judy and was blackmailing her. Or maybe Elsie just suspected that he knew. Or maybe they had been in cahoots from the very beginning and were starting to distrust each other."

"Or maybe Judy and Roscoe were killed by two different people," Terry said, getting caught up in the guessing game.

"I kicked that idea around, too," I said, "but finally dismissed it. I believe Judy and Roscoe were killed by the same person . . . or at least by the same gun."

"What makes you say that?" Terry asked.

"The shootings seem to follow a pattern," I said. "Both Judy and Roscoe were shot at close range, and they both were shot twice. Judy, we know, was killed with a .22 handgun, and—though I'm no firearms expert—I'd say Roscoe was, too. Both of the holes in his body were kind of small, and that's a fact about .22 caliber bullets—right, Terry? They're smaller than the others?"

"Right," Terry said, nodding.

"Yeah, that's what I thought," I said. "The guys at work call a .22 a 'girlie gun.' And *that's* what leads me to believe both murders were committed by the same murderer—the size of the bullets and the number of bullets fired. Once the police complete their ballistics analysis, of course, they'll know for sure."

"*Providing,*" Abby said, with a very skeptical look on her face, "they ever compare the bullets that killed Roscoe with the bullets that killed Judy. And from where I sit, that looks like a distinct impossibility."

"Don't worry," I declared, letting my fist drop (okay, *pound*) on the tabletop again. "I'm going to make *sure* those bullets are compared."

Abby perked up and gave me a big wide smile. "*Now* you're talking! It's time to take action! So what's the plan, Fran?"

"Dan's coming over this afternoon to spend Christmas with me, and I'm going to tell him everything. The whole truth and nothing but. And once Dan knows how Sweeny bungled the investigation, you can bet he'll do something about it!"

"Dan? Dan who?" Terry wanted to know.

"Homicide Detective Dan Street," I told him. "*Daring Detective*'s esteemed police consultant, and my esteemed new boyfriend."

Terry looked puzzled. "You mean . . ."

"That's right," I quickly broke in. "I have a new boyfriend. I still love Bob—and I always will—but now I'm in love with Dan Street, too." I paused, watching to see how Terry would react to this information. Would he perceive my new romance as a betrayal of Bob?

A myriad of emotions flitted across Terry's face—surprise, embarrassment, tension, distress. But not a hint of anger or disapproval. Mostly he just looked confused. "So you never told Detective Street about Judy's murder like you said you would?"

"Uh, no. I'm ashamed to admit I didn't. I knew he would never butt into another detective's case, and I also knew, from previous experience, that he would forbid *me* to get involved."

Terry's penetrating gaze turned doubtful. "So what makes you think he'll butt into the case now?"

"So much has happened, he'll *have* to intervene," I said. "First I was pushed onto the subway tracks, then my apartment was broken into, and now Judy's landlord has been murdered. Dan's no fool. He'll see immediately that these events are connected and that Judy's murder case has to be reopened. And he won't be the least bit protective of Sweeny anymore. He'll cause a huge interdepartmental stink at headquarters if he has to.

"Believe me. I know him," I added, overcome with deep admiration for Dan and an even deeper dread of losing him. "He's a man with a stout, dependable heart. He despises liars and pretenders and people who act without conscience. He may throw *me* over for good after this," I said, "but he'll never abandon Judy."

Terry gave me a knowing smile. "He sounds a lot like Bob. I'll be very happy to meet him."

"Don't count on it," I said, "because he ain't gonna be so happy to meet you."

AFTER DOWNING A BAGEL WITH CREAM cheese and another cup of coffee, I announced that I was going home. I wanted to take a shower, get dressed, straighten up my apartment, update my story notes, plug in the lights on my little tree, wrap my presents, and have some quiet time alone before Dan arrived. I needed to organize my thoughts and recharge my batteries, prepare myself for the confessional ordeal ahead.

Abby and Terry weren't too thrilled with the idea. They thought I should use Abby's shower and wait for Dan in Abby's apartment. They finally gave in, though, after I begged and pleaded till my face turned blue, and after they accompanied me next door to check out my entire apartment and strap another thick layer of masking tape over the cardboard patch on my back door.

"I don't like this at all, Paige," Terry said. "It would be so easy for somebody to bust through this flimsy Duz box. Why didn't you have the glass replaced?"

"I couldn't! All the glaziers were closed for the holidays. And what difference would it make anyway? It's just as easy to bust through glass as it is cardboard. Whoever broke in the first time had no trouble at all!"

"Paige is right," Abby said, taking my side for once. "And, today being Christmas, this is probably the safest time for her to be here on her own. I say we go next door and let her have some time to herself—and some time alone with Dan—as long as she promises to hook back up with us as soon as she can, and to spend the night at my place again."

"I promise! I promise!" I said, so eager for them to leave I would have sworn to swallow a live bullfrog. "I'll call you back over here as soon as I've broken the news to Dan and absorbed his initial rage. Trust me," I said to Terry, "you don't want to meet him until his righteous anger is spent—or at least partially subdued." (I didn't mention that this felicitous transformation was unlikely to occur during any of our lifetimes.)

"Oh, all right!" Terry grumbled, stomping to the door and heading out into the hall. "But if you see or hear anything fishy, you better come get us right away."

"She will, she will!" Abby urged, moving in close behind him, pushing him along. "Catch ya later, Paige," she said, turning to give me a quick wink before disappearing inside her apartment.

Not wanting to waste a second of my precious solitude, I slammed and locked my door, dashed upstairs, and tore off all my clothes. Then I luxuriated in the shower for a good ten minutes—letting the hot steamy water splash down on my head and pour over my body—until my brain turned soft, and my muscles relaxed, and the wounds on my shins looked rosy and clean. After drying myself off, I sprayed on so much perfume and slapped on so much bath powder the air in the bathroom became unbreathable.

Coughing, sneezing, and gasping for oxygen, I staggered into the bedroom and put on my silkiest, sexiest underthings—black bra, panties, garter belt, slip, and a brand new pair of sheer, seamed stockings. I thought smelling sweet and feeling slinky might help me diffuse Dan's anger somehow. Or maybe the perfume and silk would cloud his senses—turn his fury into a different kind of passion. (Ha! What a laughable notion that turned out to be! More about that later.)

Not wanting to put on my high heels yet, but also not wanting to get any runs in my stockings, I slipped my feet into my warm, furry horse slippers. (They were both supposed to look like Roy Rogers's horse Trigger, but they actually looked like two fat, yellowish, narrow-faced groundhogs with oversized eyes and odd, pointy ears.) Then I trotted back into the bathroom to put on my makeup.

After *that* interminable primping process, I set my wet hair—in the enormous mesh rollers that were supposed to turn my natural curls into long, soft, billowing waves of velvet (another laughable notion!)—and pulled on the huge, puffy vinyl cap of my hairdryer. Plugging the long air hose into the dryer cap, and then plugging the wire for the whole contraption into the wall socket near my bed, I turned the dryer on full blast. And then I sat there like a dope, on the edge of my bed for a full fifteen minutes, while the hood over my curlers swelled with a deafening surge of air so hot my ears turned crispy.

It was at that point, I'm sure—while I was sitting senseless on my bed, clad in my sexiest underwear, with both feet encased in misshapen palomino horseshoes and my head and ears enclosed in a roaring hot air balloon—that the murderer entered my apartment.

# Chapter 31

WHEN I COULDN'T TAKE THE NOISE AND the heat anymore, I turned off the dryer and unhooked the air hose from the hood. Leaving the hot vinyl cap on my head so my still-damp hair would continue to dry, I scooted into the bathroom to retouch the spots where my makeup had melted.

That's when I heard it—a noise from downstairs that sounded like a book dropping to the floor.

What was that? Was somebody there? Had Abby come over to borrow my copy of *Pride and Prejudice* again? Had Dan arrived early, let himself in with a police department passkey, and decided to make a secret study of my current taste in detective fiction? I tiptoed into the hall and stood at the top of the stairs, holding my breath so tight I felt faint, and listening with all my might for other suspicious sounds.

The silence was so thick it was sliceable. All I could hear was the soft, low hum of my refrigerator. No pages were rustling; no floorboards were creaking; no knuckles were cracking; no sighs were escaping through unsealed lips. *'Twas the last day of Christmas and all through the house, not a creature was stirring, not even a louse.* Finally coming to the conclusion that I had imagined the original noise, I started breathing again. Then I began making my way downstairs to take a quick look around.

Halfway there, I came to a dead stop. The kitchen door had suddenly come into view, and I was paralyzed by what I saw. The flattened Duz detergent box wasn't covering the shattered door pane anymore. It was dented and twisted and dangling down from the edge of the perfectly square hole by several tangled strips of masking tape. The linoleum by the door looked wet and splotchy, as though somebody had walked through a giant snowdrift before entering and tracked plenty of slush inside.

Frozen in fear, I stood stiff as a stick in the middle of the staircase, madly searching my brain for a swift, safe plan of action. Should I run back upstairs, climb the little wrought-iron ladder bolted to the wall by my bathroom, and try to escape out onto the roof of the building? No! I'd never be able to get the heavy, snow-laden overhead trap door open in time. The intruder would catch up with me before I could even pop my noggin through the hatch! Should I dash down the rest of the stairs, throw open the kitchen door, flee out onto the icy landing and over to Abby's back door—or down into the courtyard—screaming my head off for help? God, no! That seemed a surefire way to get my screaming head shot off.

The only scheme that made any sense to me at all was to go all the way downstairs and talk to the intruder (okay, by this time I was pretty sure it was the *murderer*). Since he or she was still desperate to get hold of the diamonds—and still had no idea where I'd hidden them—I figured I wouldn't get killed immediately. If I played my cards right, and said all the right things, I might be able to confuse the killer and delay my death indefinitely. Maybe I could stall everything for an hour or so, until Dan was due to arrive. Or maybe I could work my way over to the cabinet under the kitchen sink, and get my hands on my trusty bleach bottle . . .

Having no idea how I might accomplish any of these goals, but determined to make a hearty attempt, I sucked up all my courage (which, at that point, would have barely filled an eyedropper) and walked down the rest of the stairs. As soon as my horse slippers hit the kitchen floor, I reared back on my heels and spun around a full ninety degrees to face the monster who had killed Judy Catcher.

"WELL, DON'T YOU LOOK CUTE," ELSIE LONdergan said, voice oozing with sarcasm. She was standing tall, very tall, in the middle of the room—right where the kitchen linoleum ended and the wood floor of the living room began—with one hand stuffed into the pocket of her coat and the other stuck straight out in front of her. *That* hand (as you may have already guessed) was holding a gun. A very small gun, to be sure, but it looked big as a bazooka to me.

"What the hell have you got on your head?" Elsie asked, aiming the pistol at my plastic-capped cranium. "A fucking turban?" Her chiseled John Wayne features were twisted in a grisly scowl.

"It's the hood of my hair dryer," I said, trying to breathe evenly and keep my knees from knocking. Both efforts were unsuccessful.

"And your feet?" she said, targeting my toes. "What the hell have you got on your feet?"

"My horse slippers," I stammered. "I got them in the children's department at Klein's. They're supposed to look like Trigger." I regretted the use of *that* word, hoping Elsie wouldn't be tempted to pull it.

"And what's with the sexy underwear?" she said with a nasty smirk. "Got a hot date?"

"My boyfriend's coming over." I considered telling her that my boyfriend was a homicide detective, and that he'd be there any minute, but I was afraid that would spook her, make her anxious to kill me and get the hell out of there—with or without the diamonds. I decided to save that information for later use, when things got really hairy, as I was sure they would.

"When's he coming?"

"In about an hour."

"Good. Then you'll have plenty of time to show me where the diamonds are."

"Yes, I will," I declared, encouraging her wholehearted belief in that scenario. Then, hoping to divert her attention to other subjects, I added, "And you'll have plenty of time to tell me how a mature and motherly widow like yourself could find it in her heart to kill an innocent young girl like Judy Catcher."

Bingo. I hit the emotional jackpot on my very first spin.

"I'm no widow!" Elsie shrieked, her contorted face turning three shades of purple. "I'd give anything if my lying, cheating rat of a husband was dead, but he isn't! He's living the high life somewhere in Hawaii with his 22-year-old whore of a girlfriend. They ran off together six years ago when he was fifty-two and she was only sixteen!" Elsie's fierce blue eyes were darting all over the place, but her gun was pointed straight at me. "If that filthy, thieving snake was here right now, I'd plug him so full of holes he'd do nothing for the rest of his short, painful little life but bleed."

Ugh. A rather disgusting—not to mention distressing—image. "Thieving?" I said quickly, trying to keep her talking instead of shooting. (I just love to reminisce, don't you?) "Why did you call him a *thieving* snake? Did he steal anything from you?"

"He stole every goddamn cent of our life savings. All my jewelry, too."

"How horrible!" I sputtered, doing my best to sound sympathetic. "I don't blame you for wanting to kill him! . . . But," I added, working to keep up my end of the conversation, "I still don't understand why you wanted to kill Judy."

Elsie lowered the gun to waist-level, propping her elbow on her hip and squeezing her upper arm tight against her ribs. "Because she was a goddamn homewrecker, that's why!" Her shrill voice was vibrating like a wire stretched to the limit. "She was young—so young—and stupid as a stump. I couldn't stand the way she was always bouncing around, acting so blameless and bubbly, asking my advice about every goddamn thing under the sun, and raving over her two-timing, slobbery old boyfriend like he was Clark Gable or Kirk Douglas. Made me sick to my stomach!"

I was surprised by her show of repugnance. "I thought you loved Judy like a daughter."

"April fool!" Elsie cried, mouth grinning, eyes twinkling. She looked so crazy I was chilled to the bone.

"This is December," I said, hoping my nonchalant response would disarm her, take some of the fire out of her fury.

Big boo boo.

"Shut up!" she screamed, jerking her arm up and aiming the gun at my face.

I raised both my hands and didn't say a word. The time had come to take Elsie Londergan seriously. Very, very seriously.

"You're a real smart aleck, you know that?" she said, eyes blazing. "I wanted to kill you that first day you showed up at my place and started sticking your nosy beak in my business! But I had to wait because of the diamonds. I figured Judy's brother had found the jewelry when he was staying in her apartment and packing up all her stuff. And then—since he'd asked *you* to help him find his sister's killer—I figured you were hiding the fucking diamonds for him, or at least knew where *he* had hidden them."

"You're a very smart lady," I said, trying to pacify her with praise. "Three giant steps ahead of me! But there's still one thing that puzzles me. Whatever made you think that I had stashed the jewelry in the lunchbox?"

Elsie laughed. It was a wild, mean, hyena laugh. "I saw you through the window of the hardware store when I was on my way to meet you at the Green Monkey. You were buying the goddamn lunch pail and you had such a gloating, self-satisfied smirk on your face, all I could think was that you were buying it to use as a secret jewelry box. It was the perfect size, and a perfect hiding place, and what the hell *else* could you need the stupid thing for? Silly me," she said, giggling. "Sure jumped to the wrong conclusion that time! Guess I'm a woman with a one-track mind."

Hating to think where her one-track mind might lead her next, I took a deep breath and ventured on. Elsie was in a talkative mood, thank God, and I had to make the most of it. "You took a big risk pushing me in front of that train, you know. If I had been killed, you would have lost your chance to find the diamonds forever."

"That wasn't me!" Elsie screeched. "I would never have done a half-witted thing like that! Roscoe was the biggest blockhead on earth!"

"You mean Roscoe was the one who pushed me?" I was surprised, but not completely shocked.

"Yes indeedy!" she crowed, beginning to take pleasure in the telling of the tale. "I told Roscoe about the lunchbox, see? And then I gave him your address and told him to go downtown and watch you leave for work the next morning. After you'd gone, he was supposed to break into your apartment and look for the lunchbox and the diamonds. But when you came prancing out of your building with a goddamn shopping bag in your hand, he freaked out and abandoned the original plan. He felt he had to follow you into the subway to see what was in the bag. And when he snuck up behind you in the crowd and looked down into the bag and saw the lunchbox-shaped package . . . well, he just lost his moronic little mind

"He was certain the diamonds were in the package, see?" Elsie jabbered on. "And he didn't know where you were taking them. So he thought he better grab them while he could. But he knew the minute he snatched your shopping bag you would start screaming and calling for help, maybe even chase him through the station yourself. So he had to do what he had to do. He had to wait till he heard the train coming, and then he had to grab the bag and push you down on the tracks at the same instant. That way nobody—not even you—would know what was happening, and he'd be able to make a clean getaway."

*So* that's *the way it was,* I groaned to myself. *Just a case of being in the wrong place at the wrong time with the wrong bag . . . er, box.* "Did Roscoe hang around to watch me get creamed?" I asked. I could imagine the little beast hovering there in the rush hour crowd, craning his skinny neck to watch me crawling on the tracks, baring his little brown teeth in eager anticipation of the bloody, bone-shattering spectacle to come.

"Sure did," Elsie said, with a sickening grin. "And I don't mind telling you he was really disappointed when that big Negro pulled you up to safety. If you'd been killed, Roscoe said he would have snuck off to a dark corner of the station, opened the lunchbox, and seen that the diamonds weren't inside. Then he would have run back to your apartment, busted in through the back door, and turned the place upside down till he found them. But with you still alive, he couldn't do that. He had to get out of there fast—before you saw him. So he just stepped on the train—the same one that almost turned you into hamburger—and came straight to my place. We opened the package together."

*What a heartwarming scene,* I muttered to myself. *Right up Norman Rockwell's alley. A perfect Christmas cover for* The Saturday Evening Post.

"So, that *was* the same wrapping paper I saw in your wastebasket!" I said, excited, so caught up in the lurid details of Elsie's narration I was forgetting the lurid climax that loomed ahead.

"Yeah," Elsie admitted, also engrossed. Her arm was now hanging at her side, gun pointed toward the floor. "When you ran out of my place this morning like a crazy bat out of hell, I knew you'd seen something, or thought of something, that had suddenly made you suspect me. I didn't know what it was, though, until later, when I went into the bedroom to throw away a snotty Kleenex. And there they were, four or five wrinkled-up, red-cheeked Santa Claus faces, grinning up at me in glee, making me feel like a goddamn idiot for not emptying the trash more often."

Elsie was starting to get agitated, so I changed the subject again. I made a sharp U-turn and bounded back to the beginning of the story, panting and wagging my tail for answers. (Curiosity killed the cat, they say, so I was doing my best to act like a dog.) "Were you and Roscoe in cahoots from the start?" I asked, begging for another bone. "Did you plan Judy's death together?"

"Don't make me laugh!" Elsie snapped. "I would never have *willingly* joined forces with that greedy little weasel. How stupid do you think I am? I killed Judy all by myself! I didn't want to share the diamonds with anybody!"

"So what happened? How did Roscoe get involved?"

"That was the worst damn luck of all," she said, suddenly looking very tired. She must have been *feeling* tired, too, because she sat down on a kitchen chair and rested her outstretched right arm—the one that was holding the gun—on the table. "About ten minutes after I shot Judy, Roscoe came up to her apartment and started knocking on the door, calling out to her to open up for the landlord. I was still there, down on my knees in her bedroom, looking for the diamonds in her bottom dresser drawer. I didn't answer the door, of course. I just knelt there next to the dresser, not making a sound, hoping he'd give up and go away.

"My first thought was that somebody in the building had heard the gun go off, and called Roscoe to report the noise. But then I figured if somebody *had* heard the shots, they would have called the cops instead of Roscoe. And then I realized that even if they *did* call Roscoe, he wouldn't be fool enough to dash upstairs all by himself and start knocking on the door of an apartment where he thought a gun had just been fired."

"So why *was* he there?" I asked. "What did he come for?"

"Oh, he probably just stopped by to make a pass at Judy," she said with a sneer. "He was always doing that—showing up at her place when he knew Smythe wouldn't be there, making suggestive remarks, trying to sneak a feel. What a creep he was! Judy said he made her skin crawl."

"So what happened next?" I urged, so eager for information I forgot I was supposed to be taking it slow. (Hey, am I a born mystery writer, or what?) "Did he go away, or did you let him in?"

"He let *himself* in!" she wailed. "He opened the door with his own goddamn key! I couldn't believe my eyes. He just waltzed inside like he owned the place."

"Well, he did, didn't he?"

"What?"

"Own the place," I said. "He *was* the landlord, you know."

"Oh, who the hell cares? He had no business walking in on me like that, catching me in the act and scaring my fucking pants off, ruining all my plans for the future. If I'd had the gun in my hand, I'd've killed him on the spot! I wouldn't have had to wait until this morning!"

I looked at the gun in her hand and shivered. Was the muzzle still warm? Were there two bullets left in the chamber just for me? "So where was it?" I asked, in a voice so tiny I could barely hear it myself.

"Where was *what?*" Elsie screeched. There was nothing tiny about *her* tone.

"The gun," I said, in a near whisper, hoping against hope that the softness of my speech would induce a softness in her mind (i.e., make her forget that we were talking about a certain firearm—the same one she was grasping at that very moment).

"It was on top of the TV in the sitting room," she said. "I'd set it down there as soon as I was sure Judy was dead, right before I began searching for the diamonds. It wasn't there long, though!" Elsie added, getting agitated again. "When Roscoe came in, the first thing he saw was Judy lying dead in a pool of blood on the floor. The next thing he saw was me kneeling by Judy's dresser, going through the drawers. And the thing he saw after that was the gun lying on top of the TV set.

"And that gun was in Roscoe's hand in a flash!" Elsie sputtered on. "He didn't waste a single second worrying about Judy, or kicking up any kind of fuss, or even asking any questions about what happened. He just grabbed the pistol up off the TV and pointed it at me! Then—acting cool as a cucumber popsicle—he asked me what I was looking for. I didn't have any choice but to tell him about the diamonds."

"So he decided to make himself a partner."

"Give that girl a cigar!" Elsie crowed, tossing her head so hard her hat was knocked off kilter. She laid the gun down on the table and raised both hands to straighten it. I was preparing to leap across the kitchen and pounce on the released revolver, but Elsie snatched it up in her hand again before I could pry the hoofs of my horse slippers off the floor.

Hiding my thwarted intentions behind a sheepish smile, I fired off another question. "So what did you do then? Tear the place up looking for the rocks?"

"Tore it up good," Elsie admitted. "But as you damn well know, we couldn't find the goods. We looked everywhere, too—behind the radiators, in the freezer, under a loose floorboard, even down inside the toilet tank—but we never found a single fucking piece. Not even an earring. Finally, Roscoe said I should go play canasta at Milly Esterbrook's like I do every Saturday night. He said he'd wait for an hour or so, then call the police and tell them he just discovered the body. That way, with the place being such a mess and all, they'd think Judy was killed during a burglary."

"Nice of Roscoe to provide you with an alibi," I said. "He could have turned you over to the cops and come off like a hero."

"Yeah, he covered my ass all right," Elsie said. "I'll give him that much. But don't think for one second he did it to be nice. He figured the diamonds were bound to turn up soon—either the police would dig them up, or somebody in Judy's family would find them—and since I lived right across the hall, I was in the best position to keep an eye on the scene, keep him posted on the proceedings. So he didn't want anything bad to happen to me until *after* the diamonds were discovered. See?"

"I get the picture," I said, wishing with all my soul that I was gazing at a different landscape.

"So where the hell *were* they?" Elsie rasped. "Shoved deep in the stuffing of Judy's mattress? Jammed behind a false wall in her closet?"

"They were buried in a box of oatmeal."

"Oatmeal?!" she cried, clearly shocked by the utter domesticity of the simple hiding place.

"Here, I'll show you," I said, moving slowly toward the kitchen counter, motioning for her to stand up and join me there. (Don't ask me why I did that. I didn't—and still don't—have a clue.)

Elsie rose from her chair and walked toward me, keeping the gun aimed at the center of my chest. Her eyes were burning and her face was smeared with a rapacious smile.

I opened the cabinet over the sink, took out the Quaker container, and placed it on the counter. "This box came from Judy's apartment," I said, trying to infuse my voice with Edward R. Murrow–style drama and mystery, but surely sounding more like Speedy in the Alka-Seltzer commercials. "This is where the diamonds were. Terry Catcher found them when he was dumping all the food in her kitchen." I opened the box, extracted my story notes and tossed them on the counter, then—with an exaggerated theatrical flourish—slowly poured the remaining dry cereal into the sink. (Don't ask me why I did that, either. I guess I was just trying to keep her intrigued and pass the time.)

Elsie gave my little demonstration her full attention, but lost interest the second the last grain of oatmeal hit the porcelain. "Yeah, so that's where the diamonds *were,*" she said, grinding her words through clenched teeth. "Now you can stop all your yakking and stalling and show me where the hell they *are.*" As she issued these orders, she poked the barrel of the gun hard into middle of my chest, right above the black lace edging on the bosom of my black silk slip.

"Keep your pants on!" I cried, raising both hands in the air again. "I was getting to that!"

"Then get to it *now!*" Her jaw was set and the veins in her temples were throbbing. Her talkative mood was officially over.

"Okay, okay!" I said, backing a few inches away from the gun and wondering what the devil I was going to do next. (To say that I was panicked is like calling a massive stroke distracting.) Knowing Dan wouldn't arrive for a good half hour, and unable to think of a safe way of summoning Terry and Abby to my aid (I didn't want them to get killed, too!), I finally came to the conclusion that my best hope of survival was the Clorox.

"The diamonds are right down here," I said, giving Elsie a meaningful nod and slowly lowering myself into a squat by the cabinet under the sink. Heart pounding so hard I thought it would knock me over, I opened the door of the cabinet and took hold of the bottle of bleach. As I pulled the bottle forward, praying I'd find a way to open it, splash the bleach in Elsie's face, and grab hold of the gun, my eyes caught sight of the scrunched-up shopping bag I'd hidden there the day before. The bag with Dan's Christmas present in it. The *Tiffany's* shopping bag.

Presto. There was a sudden change in plans.

"*Here* they are!" I said, letting go of the bottle and grabbing hold of the bag. I pulled the bag out of the cabinet, smoothed out all the wrinkles, and held it up for Elsie to see. I thought the sight of the famous Tiffany logo would thrill her, dazzle her, confuse her, make her think the diamonds were in the bag. And I was right! Elsie's eyes lit up like beacons and her face split open in the brightest and greediest of all possible smiles. I had led her to believe—with all her evil, avaricious, murderous little heart—that the treasure was finally hers.

Which was the stupidest thing I could have done, of course. Because Elsie quickly concluded she didn't need me anymore. And to prove it, she took a wide stance, aimed her gun at me with both hands, let out another hideous hyena laugh, and blasted me to kingdom come.

# Chapter 32

WELL, NOT *ALL* THE WAY TO KINGDOM come, thank God. Since Elsie was standing so tall above me, and I was still squatting on the floor when she squeezed the trigger, the bullet didn't have a clear, precise trajectory. It tore into my shoulder instead of my heart (or some other vital organ), and—though it knocked me flat on my back, and made me writhe on the floor in spastic convulsions and scream out in excruciating, unthinkable agony—it didn't make me dead.

Elsie ignored this fact for the moment, stooping down in a mad frenzy to seize the bag I'd dropped at her feet. The bag she thought was full of diamond jewelry. The bag that held nothing but a Tiffany's gift box and a silver cigarette lighter. She opened the sack and literally stuffed her face inside it—resembling, for a moment, a horse wearing a feed bag. Then she lowered the bag, pulled out the gift box, yanked it open, and—seeing that the diamonds were nowhere to be found—threw the bag, box, and the cigarette lighter in my face. (It hurt when the lighter conked me on the forehead and the gift box grazed the corner of my eye, but I was in so much pain already, I barely noticed.)

"You lying bitch!" Elsie screamed at the top of her lungs. "Where the hell are they? What did you do with them?"

I didn't answer. I was too busy squirming and whimpering and bleeding. And praying. Let's not forget praying.

"You might as well give up now, you know," Elsie said, suddenly reining in her violent emotions and speaking in a low, controlled, truly terrifying tone. She leaned down close and gave me a sadistic grin. "The longer you hold out, the more it's going to hurt. I promise you that. There are five bullets left in this gun—one for each limb, and one for the grand finale. The sooner you tell me where the diamonds are, the fewer times I'll have to shoot you, and the sooner I can put you out of your misery for good. That's a damn fair deal. Right, partner?"

She wasn't bluffing. I could tell from the glint in her eye (and the way she was holding the gun to my nose) that she was not only ready—but eager—to proceed with the torturous treasure hunt.

And I don't mind telling you I was scared. Scareder than I'd ever been in my whole sad, sweet, tragic, magic, short, full, too-soon-to-be-over life. I was so scared I couldn't think or speak. All I could do was blubber.

"Still not talking, eh?" Elsie heckled, raising herself to full height. The fake sprig of holly pinned to her hat was as off-kilter as her smile. "What are you, a goddamn masochist or something? Well, that's okay with me, kid, 'cause I'm getting a real kick out of this." She moved a couple of steps back and took careful aim. "Last chance," she said, with a sickening giggle. "No talking, no walking."

When I didn't answer, she shot me in the leg.

I'M NOT TOO CLEAR ON WHAT HAPPENED next. I think I blacked out for a minute or two. And when my consciousness returned, my only wish was that it hadn't. The shocking, blazing, bone-searing pain in my mangled left thigh was unendurable. And the hideous stench of burning flesh (my flesh!), coupled with the metallic smell of warm blood (my blood!), almost made me throw up. Head spinning and stomach turning, it took every ounce of strength I had just to keep breathing (and howling).

"How was *that,* Paige Turner?" Elsie croaked, leering down at me with a look of pure elation on her face. "Kinda uncomfortable, right? Bet you're ready to turn the page now."

And I was, I was! I was ready to do or say anything that would keep her from firing another bullet into my wretched mess of a body. "Okay, I'll tell!" I cried, lifting my unwounded arm up in the air, palm flat like a stop sign. "Please don't shoot me again!"

Elsie grinned and took aim at my other leg. "I'll stop shooting when you start talking."

The words leapt out of my mouth like locusts. "The diamonds aren't here," I sputtered, not knowing what I was going to say, but not caring, either. "Terry Catcher has them. He's had them all along. They're wrapped up in one of his undershirts and stuffed down in the corner of his duffel bag." Using my good arm, I tried to push myself up to a sitting position on the floor. But it was hopeless. I didn't have the strength. My energy was seeping out of my body with my blood. I fell back to the floor with a thud.

"So where the hell is *he?!*" Elsie demanded.

"Who?" I muttered. (And, believe it or not, I wasn't stalling now. My head was so crazed and groggy I think I'd actually lost track of what we were talking about!)

"*You* know who!" Elsie screamed, eyes bulging. "You better tell me where Terry Catcher is, and you better tell me *right now!* Or you can kiss your other leg goodbye!"

Unable to think of (let alone *utter*) an expedient answer, I sucked up my breath, squeezed my eyes tight, and begged God to let the next blast kill me.

KABOOM! There was a sudden, shocking, deafening explosion—but it wasn't the sound of a gun going off. It was the sound of my back door being kicked open, and smashing against the wall so hard that all the remaining panes of glass shattered and fell out in shards and splinters on the floor. I couldn't see what was happening from my prostrate position, but I *heard* it—and sensed the broken glass falling all around me, and felt a great gust of freezing cold air sweep over my skin.

And *then* I heard the gun go off.

Steeling myself against a wallop of fresh pain, I was surprised when I didn't feel any. (Any *new* pain, that is. The wounds in my left shoulder and left leg still hurt like hell!) My eyes flew open and immediately focused on my right leg. It was smooth and unbloody. It was whole. There wasn't even a run in my stocking! My right arm was also intact. And these happy realizations gave rize to a sudden resurgence of energy—which allowed me to push my torso up to a near upright position, which meant I could finally see what was going on.

And that was when I almost died for real.

Terry Catcher—my dear late husband's dear old friend, and *my* dearest *new* friend—was crouched low in the middle of my kitchen, staggering in a sea of splintered glass, with his snowy white hair gleaming, and the snowy white sleeve of his crisp cotton shirt turning red as red could be. He had been shot! And I could tell from the way Elsie was standing, and raising both arms to eye-level, and taking aim through the sight of her ugly little gun, that he was about to be shot again.

"Look out!" I screamed, as loud as I could, hoping my cry would alert him to duck for cover. But I could have saved my breath. Because before those words were even halfway out of my mouth, Terry had sprung through the air like a Flying Wallenda, tackled Elsie below the waist, and brought her down—with a thunderous slam—in a heavy, lumpen sprawl on the linoleum. There was a fierce, vociferous struggle (you wouldn't believe the filthy curses that came tumbling out of Elsie's mouth!)—and then the gun went off again.

Shocked by the blast, Terry and Elsie were frozen still for a moment. But as soon as they realized neither one of them had been shot, they continued their ferocious wrestling match—flailing, thrashing, and rolling around on the floor—until Terry scrambled on top, sat astride Elsie's heaving trunk, pinned her arms down with both knees, and socked her hard (really hard!) in the face with his fist. Twice.

Elsie grunted and groaned and loosened her grip on the gun. Terry snatched the gun from her hand, grasped it in his own, and pointed the hideous, hateful, heinous, horrid thing at her. (Sorry about the excessive alliteration, folks, but I couldn't help myself. A girl's gotta have some fun *somehow!* And besides, the string of h-words listed above seemed the thriftiest way to express my true feelings about firearms.)

"Paige! Paige! Are you okay?" Terry cried out, keeping his gaze and the gun fixed on Elsie. He was still sitting on top of her, fastening her flat on her back to the floor.

"I've been better," I said. "But what about you? Your arm's gushing!"

"It's nothing but a flesh wound. Where's Abby?" he yelped, whipping his head from side to side, frantically searching his limited field of vision. "Is she all right? Has she been hit?"

"Oh, my God!" I shrieked. "Is Abby here, too?" I hadn't heard her. I couldn't see her. Was she behind me? Why didn't she say something?

"I told her to stay out," Terry cried, "but she wouldn't listen. She came through the door right after I did!"

I went into a total panic. Had the last bullet fired struck Abby? Using my good arm and leg for leverage, I madly scooched my disabled self around, until the area behind me was viewable, and the cold wind blowing through the wide-open door was blowing smack into my face.

And then I almost died again.

Abby was lying in a heap—a very *still* heap—on the floor to one side of the door, right at the bottom of the stairs. I couldn't see her face; it was turned away from me, toward the wall. There was no evidence of blood on her clothes or the floor, so I couldn't tell whether or not she'd been shot. Or whether or not she was dead.

"She's back here, Terry," I wailed. "On the floor at the foot of the stairs. I don't see any blood or anything, but she's definitely not moving. I can't get over there. You've got to help her!"

Terry bounded to his feet, screaming at Elsie, "Get up! Get

up off the floor and sit in this chair where I can see you. Quick—or I'll shoot your head off!"

Without a word, Elsie stood up, straightened her skirt, and sat down. I couldn't believe she was being so quiet. Why wasn't she shouting? Why wasn't she cursing? One look at her gaping, lopsided face and I had my answer. Her chiseled John Wayne jaw was broken.

Keeping the gun pointed at Elsie, Terry backed away toward the open kitchen door, each footstep crunching on broken glass. When he reached the spot where Abby was lying, and saw that she was totally unconscious, he let out a heartrending moan and sank to his knees by her side. "Baby! Oh, baby!" he cried, setting the gun down on the floor and scooping Abby up in his arms, pulling her in close to his chest, stroking her face and her hair. He'd forgotten all about Elsie. All that mattered to him right now was Abby. "Wake up, baby," he begged, choking and sobbing between words. "Please, please wake up . . ."

Do I have to tell you how crazy scared I was at this moment? Must I say that the thought of losing Abby—my most beloved friend in all the world—filled me with unfathomable, unbearable dread? Need I mention that the sight of the gun sitting unattended on the floor (i.e., *not* pointed at Elsie) was driving me insane with fear?

I knew I had to get to the gun before Elsie did—or Terry, Abby, and I would *all* be dead. But I also knew I'd never make it. I couldn't walk, or even crawl. Using my good arm and leg like rudders, I'd have to *slide* my wounded body across the splintered-glass-strewn floor, protected only by thin layers of silk (i.e., my stockings and my slip). I didn't stand a chance in hell. Elsie was going to grab the gun. Sure as shootin'.

Shows you what a fool I am. Elsie never even *tried* to reclaim the damn thing. She just vaulted off her chair, lunged over to the front door, threw it wide open, and—holding her hand tight around her broken jaw like a girdle—disappeared down the stairs to the street.

• • •

THE NEXT FEW MINUTES WERE THE longest of my life (if you don't count the minutes—okay, months!—following my receipt of a certain U.S. Army telegram). I believed Abby was dead or dying. I figured Elsie was on her way to Idlewild to catch the next flight to Timbuktu. I thought Judy's murder would go forever unavenged (Roscoe's, too, but I didn't care so much about *that*), and I had a sinking (okay, *sunken*) feeling that I'd never walk again. I didn't think Terry would ever recover, either.

So you can imagine my breathless, joyful, heart-soaring delight when Abby started squirming . . . and groaning . . . and then suddenly opened her eyes! And you must know how happy I was when she pushed herself up to a sitting position, shook her hair down her back, looked over at Terry, and said, "Hey, what the hell happened?"

"Oh, Abby!" Terry sobbed, so overcome with relief I thought he'd start bawling again. "Are you okay? Have you been hurt?"

"My head's killing me." She touched the egg-sized lump on her forehead. "Oh, now I remember!" she said, giving Terry a poke in the ribs. "When we busted into Paige's apartment, you turned around and shoved me down to the floor. I think my head hit the wall when I fell. What did you *do* that for?"

"Elsie had a gun and she was aiming it at us. I had to push you out of the way."

"Elsie?!" she shrieked. "I *knew* it! I *told* you that old bat was involved! Where is she? Locked in the closet? And where is Paige? Is she okay?" Abby shot her eyes around the apartment, looking for Elsie and me. "Oh, my God!" she cried, when she saw me lying on the bloody floor. "Paige has been shot!" She pushed herself to her hands and knees and crawled toward me—fast!—across the glass-littered linoleum.

Terry jumped up and lunged into the living room to the phone. "I'll call for an ambulance!"

When Abby reached my side and saw the shape I was in, she broke down in tears. "Oh, Paige! This is so horrible!" she howled, slobbering all over herself. "And it's all my fault! I never should have let you stay here alone!"

"Don't worry," I said, allowing my head to fall back on the floor. "I'm going to be fine. I'm not losing any more blood, and I'm still conscious. The doctors will fix me up in no time." I didn't believe a word I was saying. The pain was profound, and I was growing weaker by the second. Staring up at Abby's frantic face, I realized my vision was getting blurry.

So when Abby's face vanished and two tall, shadowy figures suddenly appeared above me, I couldn't see who it was right away. It took me several seconds of squinting and straining and forcing my eyes to focus before I realized that one of the apparitions was Dan, and that the other one—get this!—was Elsie. Her broken jaw was hanging open and her wrists were in handcuffs.

"What the devil?" I sputtered, feeling a stab of new energy. I pushed myself up to my good elbow again. "What's going on? How did you . . . ?"

"Don't talk now, Paige," Dan sternly interrupted. "You've got to save your strength. The ambulance will be here soon."

"But I don't understand what's happening!" I whimpered.

"You and me both, babe," Dan grumbled. His blurry face was plastered with a blurry scowl. He dropped into a squat, brushed his fingers down my cheek, and stared into my eyes with fierce concern. "But now's not the time to discuss it. You're too weak. We'll talk later, after the docs get you patched up."

As I lowered my heavy head back down to the floor, a gust of wind blew over my freezing cold body. "Could somebody please close the back door?" I whimpered, teeth chattering, consciousness waning fast.

Then Elsie started singing the National Anthem, and Abby and Terry started dancing "Ring around the Rosy," and Dan wrapped me up in Bob's old Army blanket, and Judy Catcher's face appeared on the ceiling, gazing down at me with the warmest imaginable smile. And then the ceiling started spinning, and Judy's face began to swirl, and I was five years old again, wearing my horse slippers and my plastic turban, riding the merry-go-round so fast and so furiously I thought I'd be dizzy forever.

# Epilogue

HAVE YOU EVER WOKEN UP FROM A CRAZY dream believing that all the wild and scary things you dreamt about had actually taken place? Well, that's what happened to me when I came to that night in the hospital. Except it happened in reverse. I woke up believing that all the wild and scary things that had actually taken place were nothing but a crazy dream.

It took a few minutes for my sense of reality to return—for me to realize that the bed I was lying in was not my own; that my body was all bandaged up for a reason. And when I turned my head to the side and saw Dan sitting in a chair right next to the bed, staring at me intently (and oh-so-seriously) with his searing black eyes, I had all the proof I needed that the ghastly scenes swirling around like smoke in my head had really occurred.

"I don't know whether to kiss you or kick you," Dan said, making his conflicting emotions conspicuously clear. "But since you look like a Martian with that silly thing on your head, I've got to kiss you. A girl in a space suit drives me crazy." With that, he raised himself out of his chair, leaned over the bed railing, cupped my face in his big warm hands, and planted the world's steamiest kiss on my startled but delighted mouth. (And I had thought black silk underwear would turn Dan on! Apparently hair dryer hoods and hospital gowns were more to his liking.)

As soon as he pried his luscious lips away and my heartbeat returned to normal, I sputtered, "Why did they leave me like this? They could have removed the cap and take the curlers out!"

"The docs and nurses had a few more important things to take care of," Dan said. "In the Emergency Room, believe it or not, gunshot wounds take precedence over hairdos."

I didn't want to be reminded of the gun, or the shots, or the wounds. "What time is it?" I asked, quickly changing the uncomfortable topic.

He looked at his watch. "Four-thirty in the morning."

"Oh, shoot!" (As soon as those words were out of my mouth, I wished I'd thought of a better—i.e., less ballistic—way to express my disappointment.)

"What's the matter, babe?" Dan gave me one of his cocky, sexy, melt-your-bones-to-molasses smiles. "Past your bedtime?"

"No, it's past Christmas!" I exclaimed. "And I never got to give you your present, or even wish you a happy holiday!"

Dan chuckled for a second, then turned serious. "Just knowing you're alive makes all my days happy."

*Joy to the world!* I sang to myself. *A girl could get used to this. I should get almost killed more often.*

But these jubilant feelings didn't last long. Because before I knew it, Dan's whole demeanor had changed. One minute he was lovey-dovey and all smiles, and the next he was busting a gasket, ranting and raving like Joe McCarthy himself, telling me off for risking my precious life just so I could play detective in yet another unsolved murder case.

Terry and Abby had told him the whole story, he said, and he didn't care how many times Bob had saved Terry's life in Korea, or how hard Terry had begged me to help him find his little sister's killer, or how much I wanted to write a story about the murder, I should never, ever, ever have gotten involved the way I did. It was an outrageous, unheard-of, unconscionable thing for me to do, and I should have my head examined for even thinking that I could solve another homicide.

(At this particular point in time—while I was lying there immobile on my back and bandaged up like a mummy—I was inclined to agree with him. But I didn't tell him that, of course.)

Dan was really, really angry that I hadn't told him about the case and asked *him* to look into Judy's murder. Why the hell did I keep it a secret from him? Did I actually believe that I was so much smarter than he was? Did I really think I could conduct a better murder investigation than the whole darn NYPD? And how *dare* I put myself in so goddamn much danger?! Did I ever stop to think how horrible it would be for him if I were killed and he had to head up a search for *my* murderer?

I had to admit (to myself and to Dan) that that particular thought hadn't once crossed my mind. And then I had to apologize—profusely—for my lack of consideration. And my lack of trust. And my reckless self-endangerment. And my "idiotically inflated head." (Dan's words, not mine.)

But nothing I said would soothe the savage beast—not even my emotional protestations about the laziness and ineffectualness of Detective Hugo Sweeny, or my sworn testimony that I thought he (Dan) would *never* interfere in another precinct's homicide investigation.

He most certainly *would* have interfered, Dan claimed (more vociferously than I care to remember). Especially since he already knew what a shiftless sonofabitch Sweeny was, and how incompetent he'd been in the past, and how he'd begun closing cases prematurely because his retirement was coming up soon and he wanted to leave the job with a clean slate. And even if he *didn't* know all that stuff about Sweeny, Dan insisted, he would have seen to it that the Catcher case was reopened. With so much glaring evidence in hand, that's what any good cop would do.

Okay, okay! So I was a stupid fool. And everything Dan said to me in the hospital that night (I mean morning) was totally legitimate. I really *should* have told him about Judy's murder. And about the diamonds. And I should have revealed everything at the very beginning—the same day Terry met me at the automat and asked me to help him find the creep who had killed his sister.

But *you* understand why I didn't, don't you? You know how overwhelmed I was by Terry's pain and sorrow, and by his desperate plea for help, and by the fact that he had been so close to my late husband in his final days. And you also know how crazy Dan would have gone if I had even *tried* to discuss the details of the Judy Catcher murder case with him, right? No matter what Dan says, all hell would have broken loose! And he would have banished me from the investigation. He would have forced me to give up my search . . . and give up my story . . . and, well, give up my natural (though most would say *un*natural) career goals.

So what was a girl supposed to do? Be true to her late husband . . . or to her new boyfriend . . . or to herself? Finding that question impossible to answer, I chose to dodge the truth altogether. I heaved a heavy sigh, closed my weary eyes, and fell into a sleep so deep it was deadly.

I WAS IN THE HOSPITAL FOR A WEEK, AND Dan came to visit every day. He was still mad at me, but he was also still pretty crazy about me (I could tell by the way his strong, craggy face turned all mushy when he thought I wasn't looking). And, as much as he didn't want to rehash—or give credence to—my involvement in the Judy Catcher case, he couldn't curb his professional curiosity, or stop himself from picking up the investigation where I'd left off.

It wasn't enough that he'd apprehended the murderer himself; that he'd been sharp and alert enough to chase Elsie down when he saw her burst out of my building and start running away like a thief; that he'd had the sense (and the instinct) to ignore all the rules and handcuff her right there and then, in the middle of Bleecker Street on Christmas Day, and march her—jawbone wagging like a broken gate—back up the stairs to my apartment. And it wasn't enough that Elsie had, just a few days later, in light of all the irrefutable evidence against her, and in the presence of her lawyer and several prison officials, written up and signed a full confession (the prison docs had wired her busted jaw together, but she still couldn't talk).

Nope! That wasn't enough for our man Dan! There were still a few loose ends in the case, and he wouldn't be satisfied until he'd tied them all together. And *I* was the only one who could help him do that. (This fact tickled me pink, but seemed to give Dan a humongous headache.)

Elsie had admitted to killing Roscoe as well as Judy, but her written confession didn't fully explain how Roscoe had become involved. So Dan had to come to me for the answers—which I painstakingly (okay, *proudly*) supplied. I told Dan everything Elsie had said about Roscoe—how he had let himself into Judy's apartment the night of the murder, found Elsie searching for the diamonds, made himself a partner, etcetera, etcetera, and then pushed me in front of a train when he thought I was carting said diamonds around in a lunchbox.

I should have kept that last bit to myself. To say that Dan was upset is like calling an earthquake unsettling. I thought his skull would explode! I guess it should have made me feel good that he was so devastated by my close call in the subway, but the truth is it made me feel awful to cause him such pain. So I changed the subject as fast as I could and told him about Lillian Smythe.

After explaining that Judy's aging sugar daddy was Lillian's *real* daddy, I told Dan about the Christmas Eve party at the Smythe's penthouse, relating the particulars of my chat with Augusta and describing how Lillian had reacted to seeing her mother's antique diamond necklace clasped around *my* neck. Then I told Dan about the phone conversation I'd overheard at the Chelsea Realty office—when Roscoe was yelling his head off at somebody named Lily—and disclosed my belief that Roscoe and Lillian had been in cahoots for some time, scheming to steal back the Smythe family diamonds long *before* Judy was murdered.

And after I related how Roscoe had so often shown up at Judy's apartment unannounced, always giving trumped-up, landlordly reasons why she should let him in, Dan came to accept my idea that Roscoe had in actuality been trying to sniff out the diamonds, and that Lillian had put him up to it. So, in the interest of bringing the Catcher case to a full and complete conclusion, Dan paid a little visit to a certain Park Avenue penthouse, and to the privileged, high-toned residents within.

Beyond admitting that he had "borrowed" a few of his wife's baubles to "loan" to a friend, Gregory Smythe had nothing to add to the body of evidence in the case. According to Dan, he barely remembered a young woman named Judy Catcher, or that she'd been brutally killed. Augusta Smythe, on the other hand, was well-informed about the murder (she'd read all the papers), and well-aware of her "senile" husband's "overly generous relationship" with the "poor dead girl." She had read about the killing of Roscoe Swift as well, but failed to see how the death of that "lowly tenement landlord" could have anything whatsoever to do with her "reputable and prosperous family."

Daughter Lillian, however, was a bit more candid on that subject. Yes, she *had* known Roscoe and he *had* been trying to help her retrieve her mother's diamonds. What the hell was wrong with that? She had tracked "the little worm" down and enlisted his help the same day she found a Chelsea Realty rental receipt in her father's desk at the office. So what of it? The jewelry was rightfully *hers*, you know—or would be as soon as her dear old mother "croaked." So, could you give her one good reason why she should let her "filthy old goat" of a father give her priceless diamond heirlooms away to some "underage bottle-blonde girdle salesgirl at Macy's?"

Dan could think of several good reasons to pronounce Lillian's behavior devious and snaky, but not a single cause to call it illegal. She and Roscoe had *hoped* to steal the diamonds back from Judy, but had never actually attempted to do so. And there's no crime in hoping. If Elsie hadn't killed Judy and tried to grab the diamonds for herself, Roscoe and Lillian might never have made a move on their own. So, Dan had no right to make a move on Lillian. What was he supposed to do? Arrest her for being a prejudiced, greedy, conniving bitch?

Abby was disappointed that Dan couldn't find anything to pin on Lillian. And she was more than a little annoyed to learn that Judy's jewelry would be returned to Augusta Smythe when the case was officially closed. That meant all those "fabulous, glorious, eye-poppin' sparklers" would eventually revert to her archenemy, "Chilly Lily," and how in the world could justice be so unjust?

Terry's feelings were the exact opposite. He was glad the gems would be turned over to their rightful owner, and he was *very* relieved to get them off his hands (and out of Abby's sugar canister). His tampering-with-evidence days were over! He didn't have to hide from Sweeny anymore. Or wear fake *payos* and an artificial beard.

As for me, I just wanted the damn diamonds to disappear off the face of the earth forever. They were a curse, a blight, an execration. If Judy had never been given the so-called jewels, she would still be alive. And so would Roscoe. And Elsie would be playing canasta at Milly Esterbrook's place instead of playing solitaire in the Women's House of Detention. And I would be traipsing all over Manhattan, having Dan's silver cigarette lighter engraved, getting a new lunchbox for Lenny, and buying champagne and noisemakers and funny hats for New Year's Eve, instead of lying flat on my back in a horrid hospital crib, wondering how long it would take my blasted bones to heal. And if I'd still be a good dancer.

THE NEWSPAPERS HAD A FIELD DAY WITH THE story. Sex, diamonds, and murder (*two* of 'em!)—what could be better than that? Most of the articles focused on Elsie Londergan, sporting lurid titles like GRANNY GET YOUR GUN! or THE DIAMONDS OF DEATH or—my personal favorite—MURDER IS A GIRL'S BEST FRIEND. But a few of the papers, unfortunately, also ran stories about me.

Dan had done his best, at my request, to keep the facts of my involvement secret, but the word got out anyway—thanks to Harvey Crockett, my illustrious ex-newspaperman boss, who broke the story to some of his old newspaper pals. He even brought two of those old pals—one reporter and one photographer—along with him when he came to visit me in the hospital.

This was a damn lucky break for *Daring Detective,* Mr. Crockett insisted, and he wasn't about to let my daffy desire to remain anonymous get in the way of a load of free publicity for the magazine. He told me to give the reporter the bare essentials of the story, but to keep all the dirty details to myself, for use in my own sensational, exclusive *Daring Detective* cover story—which would appear in the very next edition, at double the usual print run. Then he told me to sit up and look pretty for the camera. (Luckily, my hair dryer hood and curlers were in the nighttable drawer and not on my head.)

I hated performing like a seal for Mr. Crockett and his cronies, but I hated it even more when Pomeroy and Mike and Mario crept into my room and stood like mourners at a gravesite around the foot of my bed. They came to wish me a speedy recovery, Pomeroy said, looking both ashamed and annoyed that he had to be there at all (this was obviously another command performance), and then Mike and Mario each mumbled something about hoping I'd be back to work soon. (They weren't lying. I could tell from their fidgiting fingers and jittery eyes they were suffering from severe caffeine withdrawal.) Lenny had wanted to come visit me, too, they said, but *somebody* had to stay at the office to answer the phone.

Fortunately, they didn't hang around too long. Just long enough to pose for a few pictures, mutter a few more good wishes, and—miracle of miracles!—bear witness to Mr. Crockett's announcement (sort of to me, but mostly to the press) that he was awarding me a five dollar raise. Then they all said goodbye, shuffled into line, and—walking in a body, like a single twelve-legged centipede—followed Mr. Crockett's lead out of my room and off down the hall.

Needless to say, I was somewhat dismayed when the front page of the morning edition of the *Daily Mirror* featured 1) a really dopey picture of me, 2) a brief article about my participation in the Judy Catcher murder case, and 3) the irksome, embarrassing, and all-too-predicatable headline: PAIGE TURNER'S A REAL PAGE-TURNER!

I WAS RELEASED FROM THE HOSPITAL ON December 31st, which made me really happy since I didn't feel like ringing in the New Year with a bunch of dour night-shift nurses. I wanted to start 1955 off right—in my own apartment, with my own friends, wearing my own nightgown, listening to Guy Lombardo on my own radio, and giving my very own boyfriend a juicy soul kiss at the stroke of midnight.

And all my wishes came true—except the last one. Dan had to work, of course. New Year's Eve was, by tradition, one of Homicide's busiest nights. My daring detective *did* manage to run in for a quick smooch, though, around one-thirty that morning, when he was en route to a new murder scene and Abby and Terry and Lenny and I were just finishing off our third—or was it our fourth?—bottle of champagne. (I don't remember much about that kiss, but I'm sure it was a good one.)

After Dan left, Abby and Terry became antsy to leave, too. They said it was late (true), and they'd had too much to drink (true), and they were very, very tired (false). It was obvious from the frisky way they were eyeing each other they weren't the least bit weary. If you ask me, they were just keen to be alone so Abby could try on the red lace-trimmed bra, panties, and garter belt set I'd gotten her for Christmas, but hadn't been able to give to her till that night. (Actually, it turned out to be a present for *both* of them; I put Terry's name on the gift tag, too. Under the circumstances—i.e., my shortage of money and shopping time, and their red-hot romance—it seemed the ideal thing to do. I knew Terry would get as much pleasure out of the garish getup as Abby.)

And Lenny liked his lunchbox a *lot* (Abby had very kindly trekked up to Henry's Hardware to pick up another one for me). When he opened it, his cheeks turned bright pink, and his forehead got all steamy, and he thanked me so many times I thought his tongue was stuck, like a needle on a broken record. He said it was the best present anybody ever gave him.

And while we're on the subject of Christmas gifts, I might as well tell you I was *ecstatic* over the present Abby and Terry gave *me*—something I had wanted since the age of fourteen, when I first decided I was going become a writer. It was a desk! An adorable, all wood, secondhand desk! And it was already there, *inside* my apartment—sitting next to the window in my little spare bedroom (excuse me, *office*)—when they brought me home from the hospital. Have you ever heard of anything so thoughtful in your life? I was so choked up I couldn't breathe.

And the sterling silver pen and pencil set Dan bought for me at Tiffany's (wouldn't you know it?) had the same profound emotional effect. Not because it was such an intimate or passionate gift—which it wasn't—but because it was so thunderously *meaningful* to me. I mean, what better way could Dan have found to let me know that he endorses—well, at least *accepts*—my writing career? Even a Tiffany engagement ring couldn't have conveyed *that* all-important message! (Quite the opposite, as a matter of fact.)

The first thing I did with my peachy new pen was sit down at my nifty new desk and write out a reward check for twenty-five dollars to Elijah Peeps. My bashful hero. The man who had saved me in the subway. The man I would remember, and be grateful to, for the rest of my everloving life (which, but for him, would already be over).

The next thing I did was write Vicki Lee Bumstead a letter, thanking her for her help in my search for Judy's killer, and telling her I would take her out for lunch—no, dinner!—as soon as I was on my feet again (which, according to my doctors, would be in a couple of months). I considered writing Jimmy Birmingham a note as well, but decided against it, knowing he would want to hear from Abby—not me—and that he would surely be having that pleasure soon. Just as soon as Terry packed up his duffel bag and headed back home to Pittsburgh.

I didn't want Terry to go. I'd gotten used to having him around. And just seeing his handsome face every day made me feel closer to Bob. This'll sound nutsy to you, but a couple of times I felt as though Bob were smiling out at me through Terry's clear blue eyes. I didn't tell Terry about these incidents, for fear he would think I was crazy as a loon, but I *did* tell him how much I admired him and respected him, and how glad I was that my husband had had such a loyal, courageous friend in Korea.

Terry protested, of course, saying once again what a spineless wreck he'd been in battle—how he'd fallen apart at the first hint of gunfire. But I wasn't about to let that obsolete self-assessment stand! What about how gloriously brave he was now? What about the fact that he had pursued his sister's killer with more guts and integrity than the Homicide detective who was in charge of the case? What about the fact that he had—in the face of blazing, close-range gunfire—taken a bullet through the arm *and* saved the lives of his two new best friends? (I meant Abby and me, in case you're wondering.) Didn't that rate for something? Didn't that prove, once and for all, that he, Terry Catcher, wasn't a coward anymore?

I'll never forget the way Terry looked at me after I said those things. His expression was like a sunrise. And when Abby jumped on his lap, and wrapped her legs around his waist, and grabbed hold of his snowy white hair by the fistful . . . well, let's just say he looked triumphant.

Which was sort of the way I felt, too, since Judy's killer was in jail, and I was still alive and kicking. (Okay, so I wasn't really kicking yet, but I knew I would be soon.) Now if I could just get Dan to loosen up and forgive me for playing detective in the Catcher case . . .

Oh, who am I kidding? He'll *never* forgive me for that—or for any other freelance investigations I might be compelled to participate in. He's made his position completely clear: The *writing* part is okay, but I can only write about murder cases when they're over and done with, *not* while they're ongoing.

Which kind of takes the sport out of things, don't you agree?

Don't get me wrong. I totally and unequivocally understand the way Dan feels. And his hard, deep, everlasting concern for my safety thrills me down to the bottom of my soul (okay, *body*). Still, a girl's got to have a little suspense in her life, right? Otherwise, what's the point in turning the page?

## ABOUT THE AUTHOR

**Amanda Matetsky** has been an editor of many magazines in the entertainment field and a volunteer tutor and fund-raiser for Literacy Volunteers of America. Her first novel, *The Perfect Body,* won the NJRW Golden Leaf Award for Best First Book. Amanda lives in Middletown, New Jersey, with her husband, Harry, and their two cats, Homer and Phoebe, in a house full of old movie posters, original comic strip art, and books—lots of books.